DON'T TELL THE RABBI

A Comedy of Religious Proportions

Book I

THREE FRIENDS AND AN OLD LADY

SIGRID FOWLER

True Potential
REACH THE WORLD

DON'T TELL THE RABBI: A COMEDY OF RELIGIOUS PROPORTIONS
Three Friends and an Old Lady—Book I

Sigrid Fowler

Cover and Interior Page design by True Potential, Inc.
Illustrations by Sigrid Fowler

ISBN: 978-1-943852-68-0 (paperback)
ISBN: 978-1-943852-69-7 (ebook)
Library of Congress Control Number: 2017957049

True Potential, Inc.
PO Box 904, Travelers Rest, SC 29690
www.truepotentialmedia.com

Printed in the United States of America.

For RJ with thanks for that assignment and for צפרה,
whose photo gave me שירלי.

Contents

CHAPTER ONE
A Small Crisis

SO, WHAT YOU'VE GOT IS ME, BABY. JUST ME TO TELL YOU what happened in Beulah, SC, the year the rabbi found out. But before I get into all that, I should tell you who you're lookin' at. I'm not very big for a pastor's wife and I have red hair. The church won't let me do anything—it's Baptist—so I mainly get into trouble and try not to. When I say "red," that's a euphemism. My hair looks more like some random October maple—and I don't allow "ginger." That has overtones. I'm the one describin' it so humor me. It's my hair.

Somethin' else you're not allowed to do is tell me there should be a comma before "so." I go by the no comma unless you've got more than five words in the second independent clause. That rule's as firm as South Carolina pink granite.

Enough of the fine points. Well, maybe not quite enough. I better level this bazooka-loaded *caveat* right from the git go. My college boyfriend, a farmer who later died when his beard caught on fire as he was passin' out funnel cakes at the Tyrone county fair and not payin' attention . . . well, this estimable and good lookin' son of central PA once called me a *wunderkind*. What he was sayin' was that I'm Super Woman. Maybe you don't know that word *wunderkind*. Well, you can look it up. I'm not explainin' words—that's another thing you need to know. The third thing is this: I'm not a cornpone. But I'll let you find that out for yourself . . . on your own time.

Right now, we're visitin' an EMS vehicle that's haulin' with some difficulty and tryin' to get Miz Faber to the emergency room before she breaks every window in the vehicle, all the gauges, every shot needle that isn't plastic, all eight of the eardrums present, and the stereo speakers, as well, with her opera-career voice, pore ole thing. She's already broken her arm. Miz Faber's more of a *wunderkind* than me—and yes, the italics are intentional, thank you very much. It's a foreign word, isn't it?

Anyway, here we are in the ambulance. How do I know all this? I know it because I know it. You figure it out, baby. I'll just say one thing: I have a respectable imagination, and I put it to work gettin' into heads and seein' what's to see. This too: one day Joe Paul needed a listenin' ear. He's some kind of cousin and mine were available. Speakin' of ears, he thought he'd be deaf for life, pore ole baby.

The fourth thing is this: I enjoy makin' you think I'm a cornpone.

The ambulance pulls out—lights, no siren. Inside, an unhappy Miz Faber chokes down her sobs and tries that stubborn young man one more time.

"It's not right to kidnap people!"

No luck. He can't hear atall, she tells herself. He's deaf! Deaf . . . and I'm a prisoner! Somebody's tied me down. These young people! Pay no attention, none atall. He's deaf as . . . as a pirate. One eye and that patch. Must be one ear too. That's it, a deaf pirate . . . big mustache and a pirate ship.

"This is a pirate ship!"

Joe Paul's lookin' up, studyin' the old lady. She's glarin' at the ceiling. Launchin' into a line from Gilbert and Sullivan, she searches her memory about pirate ships. Not much there, but singin' helps. No need to open up yet.

She's turnin' her head, lookin' around. Where's the audience and cast? The pirates? That low ceilin's all she can see. Shouldn't be a low ceilin'. Maybe on pirate ships . . . .

Ditherin' pain. She shuts her eyes. I should pity him if he can't hear, she's thinkin', tryin' to take her mind off.

Can't concentrate. Col. Mitchell could deal with a pirate. I'll say, "I forgive you for the roses, Col. Mitchell. You just take out your sword and deal with 'em!" Definitely pirates around here, right—uh, right here . . . here, wherever this is.

The medic's watchin' as her questions give way to the pain of a broken arm. He reconnizes the tangled thought processes. They'll curl themselves into knots—

certainty-uncertainty, recollection-discovery, familiar-unfamiliar. All she knows is the pain.

Joe Paul Martin adjusts his EMS cap and smiles, pattin' her thin white hair.

Right there with you, ma'am, he thinks. When that metal filin' flew into my eye, it was me bein' hauled off to the ER. Patch comes off tomorrow, but I won't be forgettin' the pain any time soon. Be awful not to see—even in one eye. The singin' is a bit unusual.

Fine with me if it makes you feel better, he thinks. Musical like Nana. An ooze of blood has marked the old lady's fall; he bends for a closer look.

Scraped her head, looks like, he tells himself. Amazin' how scalp wounds bleed. This one's not too bad. Hurt if she moves that arm though.

Joe Paul gets an antiseptic wipe to clean the cut and looks at the patient. Older version of his grandmama, the person he loves best in the world. Lucy Jenkins raised him two towns over, and she's a real woman, a real woman in a man's world.

"Lucy Jenkins, present" is always in the secretary's notes for the Council minutes, and that's longer than Joe Paul's been livin'. Plays the organ at the Main Street Methodist Church, and the whole church relies on her. Preachers come and go, but not his Nana. She's the one and only church musician, everybody's advice giver. You can hear the respect when they say, "Miss Lucy." She's "Nana" to him. "Nana" is a lot of things—mama and grandma, confidante, coach. Friend's in there too. Nobody says "Nana" but him.

On top of it, Nana changes her own car oil. He knows because he taught her. She likes the way it saves her money, and she doesn't care a bit if it gets her hands dirty. When he was little, she taught him how to pat his head and rub his stomach. Took him a while to get it goin'. The exact minute's clear as yesterday. Like playin' the organ, she said. She knew what she was talkin' about.

Jugglin's that way too, Joe Paul thinks, smiling at the old lady. How many organists in the whole wide Methodist church can juggle?

This old lady favors his Nana. Cousins maybe. Nana will know. She carries all the county families around in her head, the kinfolk and connections—everybody down to the cousins once or twice removed, even three times or whatever, plus the ones married in. He can't figure it out, but she can. She has it all straight and she can explain it.

"You just lie still, Miz . . . uh, Miz Faber," he says, scanning the clipboard. "That arm won't hurt you so much if you just be still there. We'll be pullin' into the hospital pretty soon now. Dr. Welhelm says he'll be waitin'."

He pauses, wonderin' if she heard. He can't do anything about a hearin' problem.

"You sure do have some nice flowers in your yard, ma'am. I was on your street the other day, and I told my Nana about 'em. They're real nice. 'Course I don't know one from another, but yours're real nice. You must of put a lot a work into 'em."

To encourage the old lady's brain onto a sidetrack, Joe Paul smiles into the faded blue eyes peerin' up at him. One of 'em looks different. Funny thing. He's sure the eye wasn't what got hurt when she fell. Almost missed that cut though.

The eyes are wide open. Joe Paul meets the stiletto stare and waits.

"Young man! They're prize roses from the . . . uh, the gardens. What's . . . what's their name? I'll think of the name directly. Prizes! They got prizes for the fragrance. When my Frank was alive—he was the president of the State Rose—uh . . . group, some kind of group. He got rewards for the best smelling roses in South Carolina. That was after we came back from New York.

"Now—well, *now* . . ."

Her eyes narrow and she's whisperin'. The pain has moved to another universe.

"*Now* Col. Mitchell won't leave 'em alone! Col. Mitchell? Died at the Battle of Malvern Hill in Virginia . . . died fighting the Yankees. It's not right what people say around here! People think the Yankees hanged him from a tree in my yard, but that's not right. He wasn't a spy atall. He died in Virginia in that battle. He was not caught and hanged for a spy! Not the correct history. No, he died at the Battle of Mulberry Hill . . . died! Think that makes a difference to him? No, not a whit of difference! He came home like the rest, and now he can't stay away from my roses! He just loves them."

There's a pause while she catches her breath. Joe Paul watches as she gulps the air. He needs to breathe too.

"Young man, did you know Lunita Murray?"

"No, ma'am. I'm afraid not."

"Well, Col. Mitchell was in love with Lunita Murray, and she was my great aunt or was it great great? I don't know right now . . . can't remember.

"Anyway, she said she'd marry him when he came back from the fighting. She'd be waiting with roses in her hair—you know, waiting for him to come back. Well, when he did, she was dead too. Didn't matter. What he needs is roses; mine are the best in town! He wanders around looking for her, and she wanders around looking for him. They just wander around looking for roses, and they can't find each other or . . . or anything! He comes around every night looking. He smells 'em and smells 'em. Can't get even one. He smells the fragrance right out, and *nobody* can do anything atall about it."

Joe Paul takes off his cap and scratches his head. Interesting story, but the details aren't real clear.

"Being a ghost, he's can't deal with those stout canes. Even with his cavalry gloves, he can't grasp the thorns. They just poke right through 'im. All he can do is smell 'em and grieve, smell 'em and grieve. That he does, night after night. Nobody can do *a thing*, not even the maestro of the Metropolitan Opera!"

She tries to pull herself up and hollers out in pain as the elbow shifts inside the strap across her body. Humming a little tune, Joe Paul reaches over to quiet her. It'll be calmin' for a patient who doesn't seem to understand every little thing happenin' to 'er. He likes this old lady.

"Now you just lie still, Miz Faber, ma'am. We'll be there in about two seconds. You tell me some more about Col. Mitchell, please ma'am. I heard he was a real hero in that war. You say he likes your roses? I sure wouldn't blame him. They are pretty."

"Young man, are you on the Council?"

She sniffs. The question replaces a groan forming in her throat. The urgency of her tone says she's forgotten the pain.

"No ma'am, 'fraid I'm not."

"Well, I'm glad you said that because I want you to make me an appointment with the Council. I have to report that crowd of ghosts smelling the fragrance out of my roses. The other night I went out to check. Couldn't find one, not a lily either. Now that they've sucked up all my rose . . .

"What do you call it? My rose . . . what is it? I can't think of the word. You know, the nice smell. The ghosts suck it right out, and I can't do anything atall about it. Now it's the lilies! They did something to the lilies! Not one of them left!

"But I was talking about Col. Mitchell. Col. Mitchell would obey a town. . . a town, you know—a town *ordinance*! He's a law-abiding man. He carried the flag when they drilled. Cadet at the Citadel before they shut it down for the War. As everybody knows, it was flag and sword, sword and flag. He would mind that, and I wouldn't have to keep after him. You be sure to tell the Council I want an ordinance. No, tell 'em to put me on the agenda. I'll talk to them myself—next meeting!"

She stops to gulp in another breath and glares at the friendly face bending over her. The eye patch gives Joe Paul a rakish air he likes. It's not much help on the job though.

"But . . . but wait, I forget! You're not the one on the Council! You're a pirate, and you're wrong to be kidnapping an old woman! You should know it's not respectful and it's not nice. The sheriff will be at your door! I'll see to it, young man—in New York, a policeman on a horse! Maybe they have those around here now. He'll come to your door, count on it! It's wrong to be a pirate . . . the wrong thing to do in this world! God will be the judge. GODWILLBEEEEEEE—"

Her voice rises to unknown decibels. "The glass-crackin' range," Joe Paul called it. His scalp prickles, and every hair stirs to attention as the ambulance swerves, careens inches from a ditch on the wrong side of the road. Jerkin' the wheel to straighten his wild compensation, the driver struggles to regain control, swingin' 'em clear of oncomin' traffic and just missin' a good-sized bread truck comin' in from Wesley.

"Oh Lawd!"

The voice from the front seat expresses Joe Paul's feelings exactly, though it's been a while since prayer presented itself as the thing to do at times like this. The old black lady knows all about this patient, but the shatterin' screech tilts even her rock-solid steadiness. Maybe just nervous about the driver.

The ambulance slows, rounding the corner into the medical campus as the ER ramp comes into view. Joe Paul's moppin' his forehead and talkin' to himself.

No need to worry about being heard. The wailin' cry covers all sounds, even the squealin' brakes and the driver's vivid blue language.

"This isn't bullets, but I'm sure sweating," he mutters. "Have to change my shirt and it's not even noon!"

The joltin' decibels stop, and Joe Paul looks up as the ambulance inches toward the ramp with fine precision, backup beeps soundin' softly as they move in. Not a bit too soon. It's clear to this EMS medic that he's runnin' out of options. One thing for sure . . . nobody can say what might happen next in this vehicle.

Yeah, he tells himself, I may be competent and compassionate, but I'd rather not be dead! And this too—I better call her pastor to come visit. Maybe Nana, on top of it. They'll know what to do for this little lady. She sure does need somethin'.

It's me again. Here's the next thing that happened—this phone call, I mean. I can deliver the verbatim because I have my pastor husband's phone video-bugged and Shirley does the same at their house. She's lookin' for the best time to talk to Moish about what's on her mind, and monitorin' his study may help her find out.

When Miz Hamilton committed suicide, I saw like lightenin' from on high that my Ricky needed backup. He's not a woman . . . let me tell you what, baby, Rick is not a woman! Anyway, sometimes, a woman needs another woman to talk to. Men don't know how. I could've helped Miz Hamilton, and I determined with every ounce of grit I could sharpen my teeth on that what was needed was a listenin' ear on the pastor's telephone. (The church still has a land line.) If I knew what was goin' on, I could help.

So far, it works pretty well. I don't know what will happen if Ricky finds out. If Moish knows, Shirley'll have a worse problem than me, you can be sure! She's a kind person though and agrees with me about the proactive. She's placed the bug so well I get to hear the rabbi's breathin' even. Learned that from a Mossad buddy. She got the video bug from her Shin Bet brother-in-law. They're smart over there and they don't like suicide.

Because of our little intervention, this conversation was just like here. Personally, I think my husband shouldn't be so hard on his childhood friend the rabbi, but sometimes Moish asks for it. Ricky still has his two old buddies, but Quentin's another matter—for Moish, 'specially.

This is what's goin' on: The sun is streamin' in the rabbi's study window, and he's just made a call to my baby, the Rev. Richard Parker Apricot III, pastor of the Union Street Baptist Church of Beulah, SC. It's the late '90s, and we all live in this little South Carolina town—well, everybody but Quentin. And the T-shirt fella. More about that later and the rabbi too. I know 'im like I know my own hand because his wife's a close friend of mine. Believe you me, he's as worried as he looks and that's all the time.

"What must I do to be saved?" Moish says. I hear his long fingers tappin' the big Hebrew Bible. He's smilin', but worry lines furrow the forehead.

"You know very well, you son of an Egyptian."

The voice on the phone is somewhere between a growl and a welcome. "Open up that *Stuttgartensia* and read Isaiah 53. You know you won't do it."

"I'd rather be the adopted son of an Egyptian than the son of a pagan!"

Levy takes a breath, congratulatin' himself on the neat dodge. But Rick's in-your-face assurance gets under his skin. This is just today's version. The two of 'em carry on a theological scrap they regularly escalate.

"Love and hate, twin brothers," he's mutterin'. "No, not hate. I don't hate him."

He's talkin' to himself, the phone on mute as he looks around for a pencil to sharpen. Shirley says he does that when he's frustrated.

"The Isaiah thing took me by surprise," he's mutterin', "but it was crude to say 'pagan.' Rick knows what he's doing . . . loves to slip in Isaiah. He's usually not so obvious." Moish is thinkin', next time, Richard. This won't be the last round! He's got his pencil and goes back to mutterin'. "You more than deserve it, Rev, whatever I come up with. But maybe it's just fishing . . . looking to be thanked for this Hebrew Bible?"

"So, Moses, you want to talk about adoption—?

"Listen, Rick. Never mind all that. I have a question."

Levy's cuttin' in before the aggravatin' voice can quote Paul and all that Romans stuff about grafted-in gentiles, and the "rich olive stock." He's reachin' for any brake available to jolt to a stop the old debate my Ricky's ready to drive forward with his usual energy. Baptists just don't know when to stop jokin' around, he's thinkin'. Adoption, Isaiah 53? The prophet's name is grabbin' at his composure, chokin' that famous ability to deliver the perfect comeback.

"I promise to answer with a question," Rick's sayin'.

"Stop. I'm needing to be . . ." Here, the rabbi sharpens the knife-edge of his tone instead of the pencil. He's pitchin' his voice in a lower register, talkin' more softly. The change is s'posed to be noticed. As far as my Ricky's concerned, he shouldn't start off with a theological salvo . . . and yeah, he deserves what he gets. Rick loves this man . . . like a blood brother.

"Okay . . .."

"You know the Feinemanns," Moishe says.

"Sure. I bought my wife's last birthday present there. Diamond earrings, in case Felix didn't tell you."

"Well, never mind that, though I concur . . .. That was better taste than you usually show up with."

"All right. Serious or not? I'm busy."

"*Mea culpa*, Father Apricot. Listen. You know how depressed Miriam's been."

"Sure. She didn't do it, did she?"

"No. Well . . . but I don't know what kind of danger she's still in. Give me your take on something."

"Shoot."

"Please. Try to rein in the humor. It's never been that good. Black doesn't suit you anyway. Leave that to the papists."

Bringing out the pulpit voice, my Ricky lowers his decibels by half. "Go on," he says.

"What do you know about laughing? I mean, in your experience, does it fit in with anxiety and . . . well, anxiety linked with depression? You know . . . all the things chasing themselves around in Miriam's head this spring."

Here my husband, the Union Street pastor, angles his frame comfortably beyond the desk and unclenches his right hand. It's takin' him some effort not to bust out laughin'. What he's thinkin' is this:

Moish is going on, I'm in the dark, and he's scoldin' me for black humor! Now what's this about laughing?

Rick adjusts his knees to a better position. All those rabbis and their folks, God love 'em. The pain's all tangled up with joy—a quip, in the middle of it. Laughing and crying, always both. Better not go there (my Ricky's got a tender heart). Yeah, empties my tear ducts every time, he thinks. He knows Moish'll come through with the details, and he needs him to know he's still listenin'.

"Well, I'm not sure I know much, but go on."

"She called—"

"That's a new development?"

"No, wait. She called, said something happened yesterday, and then—Rick, as the Lord God lives—"

". . . before whom I stand."

"Yeah, before whom I stand, too . . . she couldn't talk for chuckling. Then she was laughing. Before she could say any more, Felix came in and she hung up.

"What do you make of that? Could hardly talk, barely get her words out. Should I be worried? Rather be relieved, but I'm not sure it's realistic. What do you think?"

"I think you're wondering if she's better . . . maybe worse?"

"Did you see anything like that when Mrs. Hamilton died?"

Levy hears himself mention that suicide in Rick's congregation, but he won't go so far as regret it. Today he needs perspective. Something about this Baptist clears the air for him. Nothing like an old friend. This one has a good head and a good heart, as well—Christian or not.

"No, just Psalm 88 all the way," Rick says. "After a while, she stopped giving it up to God. Don't think she knew the psalm, but it was like that . . . darkness and more darkness. Then God just wasn't in it anymore."

See what I mean, darlin'? Miz Hamilton just needed somebody to listen to 'er. Could've been Ruthie . . . me, I mean.

Rick goes on, "Were you . . . maybe wrong about the chuckling? Sound coming over the phone, wasn't it? Was she . . . crying?"

"I asked myself that. No, she was laughing, right out of her corset . . . her middle, I mean. Wasn't hysterical laughing—just seemed delighted. I don't know what to think."

"Maybe Felix . . .?"

"I'll call him later if he doesn't call me first. I need somebody else's take on how this sounds. But you didn't hear how it sounded, so what do you know? I guess the ball's irretrievably in my court . . . still."

"I'll pray."

"You would."

"So should you."

"Let's don't get into that right now. I'm verging on worry, friend."

"Okay. Let me know."

"Maybe it's nothing. Okay, see y'."

"Yeah . . . but wait. Something just occurred to me—"

"What?"

"Quentin's coming in tonight. He knows more about suicide than anybody should . . . you remember all that."

"Yes."

"Hold on a minute. I have to go get something."

The silence on Rick's end makes space for the past to rush in and take over.

"Rick has to bring up Quentin," Moish mutters. "Never misses a chance. When it was bikes and softball all the time around here, who'd guess we'd lose touch. Our lives just went different ways."

Moshe switches the phone to the other hand and clicks to wake up his computer. He's thinkin' about Quentin. Shirley says he thinks about him all the time lately.

"Who could get over a son's suicide?" he's mutterin'. "Don't know how Quentin's life is shaking out now, but I know how it was—Schoolhouse Branch, South Carolina creek-bottom dirt under our toenails. We didn't know we were Jews and gentiles. Curious fact: Jewish families in the South don't lose their southernness, old friends either. Most of the time. Is "southernness" a word?" Thinkin' out loud.

It's okay. Ricky's not around to hear 'im, just me listenin'.

"Any way you put it, it's a real thing," Moish tells himself. "Rick and Quentin and me . . . Southern to this day if Rick's right about Quentin. Why not? They've kept in touch. He probably knows."

The computer's slow. Levy gets up and walks over to look toward Miz Faber's house. Discouragin', the changes in their neighbor. Easier for 'im to think about the past.

"Rick and me . . . changed?" he mutters. He's thinkin' about seminary—the heavy studies, professional hurdles. "No," he says. "We're still Southern Americans. None of it's changed us—not the languages, not the counseling or the finances. Liturgics, budgets, bar mitzvah prep . . . none of it."

He turns from the window and paces around his study droppin' the phone in his pocket.. He'll know it when Rick returns. Bookshelves, desk, the computer. Levy picks up a pad next to the Hebrew Bible. He wonders what Rick went to look for. Somethin' about Quentin. The name irks 'im. Easier to remember the Quentin back then than think about Quentin now.

Quentin sat in as many classrooms as we did, he thinks. Running his own now. Changed him? Well, he has other reasons to be changed.

"Rick and I got to work," he's mutterin'. "Fund raisers, committees, sisterhoods, visitation. Rick's got prayer breakfasts, I've got bar mitzvas. Have to stay relevant with the youth. Tough for Quentin too, I guess—Anglo-Saxon, all that other obscure stuff—dissertation, PhD, tenure track. Different kind of corporate ladder. It's all an overlay. Rick and me—still Southerners," he tells himself, "still friends."

Moishe's doodlin', makin' circles in a row like bullets on a list. I can hear the pencil scratchin', but the pad's not big enough for the list of all the things he and Ricky do. Amazin' how alike their lives are.

"I'm back," my Ricky says. Moish fishes the phone from his pocket and sits.

'Took me longer than I thought," says Ricky.

"Okay," Moish tells 'im, but he's still thinkin' about Quentin and he's wonderin', did I miss something? Did Rick say something else? Drifting thoughts are a symptom. Is something the matter with me?

See what I mean, darlin'? Moish is a worrier!

"Yes, go on," he says to Ricky.

"He wrote something about it."

"You mean he wrote you a letter?"

"No, a manuscript . . . what I went to get. Has to do with suicide."

"Well, if he's still teaching, I guess he might start writing. Most English profs write on the side, don't they? 'Publish or perish.' Did he broaden out into psychology or something?"

"No, not psychology. It's still English, but he's at Agnes Scott now—you know, Atlanta. Not USC anymore. This isn't a journal piece. It's fiction—or supposed to be. Could be personal experience, uses his own name. Some sort of writer's ploy to keep the pump primed, he told me. Says he'll edit himself out later. I'm not sure what he's planning to do with it, if anything. Had a purpose once. May be enough for now."

The rabbi's listenin', not wantin' to. He doesn't like admittin' the loss of that childhood threesome—he and my Ricky and Quentin—best buddies. That's how it was, and Beulah, South Carolina, was a different place. I've heard 'em say it, over and over.

Rick goes on explainin' about what Quen wrote.

"In the piece, he's on a train . . . having this conversation. Could be his fictional self or his real self. You can't be sure. Some shrink started it, writing therapy or something. Anyway, if you want, I'll ask him if he's okay with letting you look at it. Like I said, he's coming this weekend. I can say something's happened . . . um, you're hassling some issues he gets into. It'll stop there unless you want to talk to him yourself . . . or . . . tell him why you're interested. You know . . . ask him about the experience. He may not want to talk, but it's been a few years since the suicide."

The rabbi's readin' between the lines. Several things goin' on here. He's not sure about the drift.

"I can give you my copy," Rick says. "You can read it before he comes . . . isn't long. And if you're worried about saying . . . uh, saying too much about Miriam Feinemann, you don't have to tell him any more than you want to—I mean, if you decide to talk to him about what's on your mind . . . or the piece itself."

My Ricky's painted himself into a corner and he's not sure what to do. Moish feels the ice formin' somewhere in the region of his heart, the place caution sets up a station and all the worries hang out. Rick can be trusted, but Levy doesn't like the sound of all this. He knows Ricky's fine with confidentiality. Private's private with him. But how should Miriam's rabbi look at this conversation? He's already broken trust by talking to a Baptist minister! She'd be horrified. Felix, livid!

Think about that later, he says to himself.

"So, you think I should read it?" Moish gets around to askin'.

"I don't think it's private, and you're his friend too—or . . .."

There's a long pause. Levy waits, lettin' his Baptist buddy moil around in the difficulty he's made for himself.

Uncomfortable spot and I don't care a bit, Moish is thinkin'. Rick got himself into it; he can get himself out of it.

"About the suicide issue," Rick says, chargin' ahead. "In the piece, he's feeling some pretty strong emotions. At the same time, he can't avoid talking to this stranger . . . has to be civil. What he's feeling isn't related to the conversation—not at first, anyway. Suicide's in the background. A player, you might say. Could shed some light on whatever's going on with Miriam. Not much about laughing, but out-of-place laughing comes up at one point. Anyway, you said 'chuckling,' didn't you?"

Rick plunges on before the rabbi can answer. Moish doesn't care. Listenin' is better. Besides, my Ricky needs to get off the phone. Workin' on a sermon. Moish has a sermon to do too and his is Friday.

"But you say," Ricky puts in. "I'm headed to the post office, can drop off the manuscript if you want. I need to return a call from Quen before he gets himself driven over here tonight. I'll ask if he cares."

There's a pause. Ricky seems to be thinkin'.

"The piece might help fill in the gaps since you saw him last."

"Okay," says Moish. "Bring it if he doesn't mind. Writers know better than psychologists sometimes."

"Yeah, and you're right about Lit. teachers," Ricky says, "profs like Quentin, anyway. They do write, according to him. Guess he's no exception. Incidentally, he'll be here more than a few days . . . his spring break. Coming to see his aunt and won't go back for a week or so. Want to have lunch . . . like on Tuesday?"

"You mean with you?"

"Well, with me and Quentin. Coffee Shoppe at noon."

"Uh . . . it's been a long time."

Moish tries to squelch the loud inner warnings. There's a thunderin' debate threatenin' to break out into this phone call. Better watch what he says. The rabbi doesn't relish seein' or talkin' to Quentin! Agreeing to read the piece is one thing, lunch is another. He could read Quen's story then just not get around to seein' him. Caution's yelling, but there's somethin' else too. I know because I've heard him and Rick argue this very point. Ricky's always tryin' to get those two back together.

"We've looked into the yellow woods . . . taken different roads," the rabbi mutters to himself. He's hit the MUTE button so he can think. It helps to think out loud. "Mine and Quentin's diverged a long time ago. Too long? Probably. I don't have to see him. But what about Miriam? No . . . it's not what I want to do."

"Yeah. He said more or less the same about you," my Ricky tells 'im, "but he quoted Frost."

"Probably a busman's holiday sort of thing," the rabbi tells 'im. He's really jangled by that coincidence. Feels like it may be a sign, but won't admit it to himself. "Well," he says and thinks some more. "Okay. You can bring the piece."

"All right, I will if Quen agrees. And Moish . . ."

"What."

"Moshe," says my Ricky, "this isn't some cheap ploy. You've heard the straight stuff from me plenty of times. You know I'll pick up the gloves in a heartbeat. But I'm here to tell you, this manuscript wasn't written secretly for you or secretly for anybody, and I had nothing to do with it. Quentin wrote it at a bad time in his life . . . trying to survive. It was for his own sanity, not your salvation. I'm just warning you ahead of time in case you get narcissistic on me. Just letting you know. You can take it or leave it."

"Okay. Yeah, I said I'd take it. And I get the disclaimer, so you're safe enough if you're worried about sharing the blame. And . . . all right, I'll have lunch. I'll do that too."

To himself he's sayin', Christians! What will they think of next?

The two hang up huffing, the rabbi shakin' his head, wonderin' what to expect. He has nothing to fear from their evangelism—ploys or no ploys, goys or no goys. Right now, he's got a sermon to finish and it's Wednesday. Still, his interest is piqued. He trusts Ricky, and he can't deny he loves him like a brother.

Quentin? Well, Quentin was his friend. The thought of seein' him again hasn't arrived as an eventuality draped with dread, surprise, surprise. He can't stop thinkin' about Quentin. Now that he's off the phone, he's talkin' to himself again. I don't even need to listen hard.

"Quentin McJabe . . . *McJob*? Doesn't the *Mc* part mean *son of* . . . like *Quentin, son of Job*? Losin' a child would be like that . . . and suicide, very hard even if he didn't raise him. He's qualified to talk about it. Who would think it when he was winning football games and all the crowds were yelling . . . and who'd guess he'd go blind?"

I hear it in his voice, baby. Years of fierce anger are easin', vectorin' away toward a vanishin' point and he goes on mutterin'.

"Have to feel sorry for a guy whose sight shuts down after his son commits suicide, especially when nobody knows why—either case."

The blindness may not be permanent, but the whole thing's shakin' up everybody, I can tell you. Some shrink might know, but my Ricky doesn't . . . Quentin either. No obvious cause, nothing physical. Moish mulls it over from time to time, just like me. Quentin's a puzzle.

"How does it feel for the lights to go out . . . without warning," Moish asks himself. "Hope it isn't contagious. I don't need blindness!"

He rips off the page of doodles, tosses it, and drops the pencil into that obsidian cylinder on his desk. Rick's bringin' the manuscript, and Moish thinks he better listen for the doorbell. He picks up the cylinder. It's black . . . reminds him of Capernaum, like he told us that time he showed it to me and Shirley.

Will Quen let me read it? he thinks. He could easily say no.

Here I am again. I like to get into people's heads. With Moish, it isn't too hard. He has furrows across his for'ead the size of plowed-in sweet potato rows and his voice is worried, worried. As they say, "It takes a worried man to sing a worried song." He sings a worried song, let me tell you. At this juncture, he's real worried.

The rabbi likes his study. It's a haven—scholarly wanderin's, sermon prep, counselin' sessions from time to time. Today, none of that. Questions are sproutin' like weeds. He's got problems and no answers: Quentin, Alice Faber next door, the sermon, Miriam. He's weary. Feels good to look out the window and think about nothin'. A long gaze takes in the two yards, theirs and Alice Faber's backin' the Levys from Applebaum Court.

"Have to speak to the yard man," he says out loud. "Bushes need trimming. Young Murdock's dropped the ball on the shrubbery, but the man knows roses. Ought to be paid more."

Levy polishes his glasses and puts 'em on again. He does this all the time. When I can't hear 'im doin' anything or if I'm not lookin' at that video or Shirley either, I know he's polishin' his glasses. He keeps an eye on the yard work, but he can't increase Murdock's pay. Finances are in other hands. More worries.

"Not much in her life to enjoy now," he mutters to himself thinkin' of Miz Faber. "Murdock's got to be in the budget. Augusta doesn't do roses."

Miriam's call has overlaid the back and forth he's just ended with Ricky. Can't forget either conversation. Clip within a clip. When Miriam called, he was standin' at this window . . . like now. He saw the *Feinemann* ID and thought, *the voice*? Maybe Rivka.

"Rabbi?"

Not Rivka.

"Yes, good morning . . . this is Levy. Just going out."

The put-off sounded lame, but she would miss the dodge. A miniature shout's invaded his ear. Not *the voice*, not Rivka.

The phone hand attached to the shout would be propped on a table next door to the den. The den is Rivka's station. She's hackin' out a piece for that Jerusalem newspaper and hasn't seen her mother press the button marked *Levy*.

The moment has him. Moish feels his hand grip the phone. Ripples of anxiety are tightenin' the rest of him. Every muscle's awake, taut as physical therapy.

"Change my phone number?" he says to himself, rememberin' this call. "No, not ethical."

By his tone of voice, I can hear he's horrified even thinkin' it. The day of the call, he didn't acknowledge the caller, but she knew he knew. Should've said, "This is Miriam Feinemann. Is this a convenient time for you to take a telephone call, Rabbi?"

"Not in this century," he's sayin'. She can't hear, of course. Just in 'is memory.

"Rabbi . . . Rabbi!"

Now he's makin' the sound of Miz Feinemann's voice.

"It's . . . I have to tell you something . . . important. It's—"

A blank to be filled, but he didn't do it. Refused to say, "Yes, go on." The caller plunged ahead anyway.

"Yesterday something happened . . . .."

Shirley says he loves this family, but he's distraught. Can't think about Miriam without frettin' and worryin'. She could do herself in any time and he's her rabbi. Puts him on the spot.

"Those empty pauses should be in caps," he crazily told Shirley one time. "Dots are dots unless they're standing watch over Miriam's next thought. Then they're fully armed, like land mines. 'Pause'? Utterly inadequate! 'Ellipsis' doesn't work either. More like *selah*. 'Pause and think about it,' Brother Rick likes to tell me—as if he has to translate! Baptists are so blasted sure of themselves. Gentile chutzpah if there is such a thing. Whatever, Rick has more than his share."

Shirley isn't too sure about tellin' me all this, but it's okay. Makes me think more of Moish. He has a heart, no two ways about it. Ricky's got his share of chutzpah, but he's gentle with it—to everybody but Moish. Then it's "Katy bar the door."

"Have to wait out the pauses," he told Shirley, huffin'. "Armed units guarding the airways. Denying access. Miriam owns command and control! Guess the next word? Interrupt? Unallowable intrusions . . . presence of a hostile! There it is. You just have to wait. Enforced listening isn't conversation. The laughing made it worse."

The day of the laughter he paid attention though. It's his duty as her rabbi.

"Go on, Mrs. Feinemann," he said. "Tell me what happened."

Wrong thing to say. Could be on the phone an hour.

"Rabbi . . . Raa-aa-bbi, Rabb . . .!" Again, that excited female-ish voice, his version. Shirley's pretty good at conveyin' Moish-as-Miriam.

"Then a tiny sound like a gasp in the phone," he said. "What was that sound? 'Can't be a *chuckle*,' my good sense was yellin'. No, no, no . . . not suicidal Miriam. She can't be chuckling. Weeping?"

Shirley said he switched the phone to the other ear and took a breath. "No, it was laughing," he said, "and it was still coming."

Moish was revisitin' the details as if he was testifyin' in a court of law, Shirley said.

"I told myself, no chuckle, not even a faint one, can be coming out of this telephone! Then whatever it was rolled into something that nailed my attention. I could feel somebody's diaphragm shaking. I could see the belly laugh coming on, baby cousin of a guffaw or something. An earful from the other end made the hair on my neck prickle. Too much of it, you'll say. Yeah, I know it's time for a haircut. But hear me out . . . this voice couldn't be Miriam's! What in the world! Did some teaser grab the phone to see how long before I'd say, 'Who is this?'"

"Was it someone else?" she said. "Not Mrs. Feinemann?"

"No. I called her by name and she didn't correct me. Then she said Felix was coming in. And I'm not slipping," he told Shirley's look. "She may be!"

At this, he started pacin' back and forth across the kitchen.

Like I said, the rabbi's a worrier.

"A deeper level of the depression?" he said, makin' tracks in straight lines, there and back, on her newly mopped floor.

"Maybe manic depressive?" Shirley said. She learned quite a bit in the IDF. "Bipolars . . . hard to diagnose."

These days, calls from Miriam Feinemann make something go wrong in the rabbi's mid-section. He has to stop and take a breath, make himself breathe.

"I'm wound up, tight as a scroll," he told Shirley. "Be preserved for centuries like some horrible Pharoah-mummy. Worse, it's the new normal!"

Awful development. No rabbi concerned with the smooth runnin' of a congregation deserves this. Everybody needs his guidance, and Mrs. Feinemann's gobblin' up his time. He's sure he isn't helpin'. What if she . . .?

"Breathe out," Shirley says. "Breathe in. The tightness goes."

The day of the call he didn't say, "Are you doing all right, Miriam?" To stick a toe in the door of that quasi-conversation wouldn't be a good idea, and his voice might betray him. He knew the landmarks. More than once lately, he'd found himself wanderin' around in the neighborhood of panic. Same street, same address, same orange zigzag lightnin'. How to prevent a suicide? Was it even possible?

"That laughter was like a body blow," he said to Shirley. "Should I hang up, blame a broken connection? No, better just listen. She said something happened."

He waited, thinkin' she'd tell 'im what. It got worse.

"Oh, Rabbi . . . I can't talk now. Here's Felix . . .. He's just come in, and . . . he's giving me some kind of signal. I think he's saying . . . what is he saying? No, Miriam? Why is . . . he say . . . ing that? I have . . . to . . . to stop now. Thank you so much, so . . . so much, Rabbi. You are truly . . . our rabbenu."

"She was laughing out loud, gasping," he went on. "Did she overdose . . . on coffee maybe? Sounded giddy! What in the world! But wait, don't people in deep distress laugh sometimes? A new development? Is she worse? Couldn't tell. Then she broke off the call."

"I just managed, 'Yes, Mrs. Feinemann . . . yes, goodbye, Mrs. Feinemann.'"

"The line went dead. I stood there, phone in hand, picturing the Feinemanns. The only Feinnemann who doesn't wind me up into that scroll is Felix! Certainly not Rivka! Nothing's easy when it comes to Rivka. She whispers for attention and gets it."

"*The voice.* Worst distraction of all," he told Shirley. "Italics . . . she talks in italics! The mother blasts away in shouting little caps, but Rivka? It's something else entirely. Her voice is from another world! The words swing around in your head, back and forth, back and forth, zany arcs and diagonals. When Rivka talks, she makes you look at the words! The words don't just communicate, they confront . . . like a work of art, the way art confronts! Always takes me by surprise. A battle, like something to be mastered.

"Mastery. Yes, Rivka needs to be mastered," he goes on, exasperated and worried. Now he's in trouble.

"There it is. Mastery—that's the notion I've been struggling to bring into this world. Crazy androgynous times. I just gave birth . . . like a seahorse! *HaShem*, preserve me," the rabbi says, not exactly prayin' but knowin' from Shirley's uplifted eyebrow he's reached thin ice. This is chauvinism plain and simple. Yes indeed, he's in need of resources beyond his own. The rabbitzen's eyebrow says it all. I've seen 'er do it. She's goin' for the uzi.

He was stuck in his sermon prep that day, same day he was talkin' to my Ricky like I told you. He took the mop to clean up after himself after he made tracks on Shirley's perfectly washed floor. Nice like that. I think she decided against the uzi.

He was worryin' about the sermon, concerned he'd miss Ricky and the manuscript, so he went back to his study. Shirley put up the mop.

Under the window in the study is a puzzle spread out on a library table. Back in there, he picks up a piece. Then he puts it down. I've seen him do it. Another distraction. The puzzle fixes some things because the pieces are mostly alike.

"They're teasers," he told my Ricky one day. "Like the Holy City . . . a minyan of shapes, same look-alike problems she's shoved at us for millennia. Whole world feels it! One day, this puzzle mess will be a beautiful view of the *Kotel*, but right now . . . just the jigsawed edges of another distraction. Colors and curves and corners—if they didn't distract, they wouldn't do their job."

This day, the rabbi and my Ricky were comparin' notes on how to help the perplexed. Shop talk, you know.

"The puzzle beckons," Moish tells him. "Some just want oil for the troubled waters. One or two need psychological intervention. The rest want me to pick up the frayed ends . . . of whatever. Everything's as monumental, on a personal level, as the problems of the City, ancient and modern. Sometimes I can make a difference, sometimes I can't."

I call that commendable candor, hon. My Ricky could learn a few things from his rabbi friend.

"If discussions reach an impasse," he says, "the puzzle offers a break, a moment to reflect and not talk—not all at once, anyway. I stand, take a few steps toward the window, mention Jerusalem. There's some chat, some de rigeuer handwringing about the City's future. Then I find a way to be standing by the table, fiddling with puzzle pieces. The wearier person joins me. Where's the rest of that rosy stone, that blue or white, that little *magen David*? When a match turns up, everybody's happy. I feel the sigh even if I don't hear it. A few minutes of this and we can talk again, emotions defused. When enough peace is restored, we can go on with business."

He can't fix everything, but he does his bit.

"To everyone's surprise," he tells Rick, "there it is, some reasonable path toward a solution. A bit of encouragement, hope. We could actually work things into an better something else."

The rabbi told Shirley, who's a great cook, that he imagines a long plaited something; the strands are comin' together (with a few interruptions) into another thing entirely, something more appealin'. The unformed disorder and twisted raw materials are changin' into a better whole, just so . . . and if it's not perfect, it's better—like helpin' someone make a Shabbat *challah*. Whatever it is, starts bein' different, almost beautiful. He wants that to happen. Sometimes it does. Sometimes it is beautiful, and when the change happens, he feels alive. It seems there's a fire within him that's on the point of kindlin' and leapin' to life, but it rarely blazes. Still, things are better—at least for a while. I don't think he'd say all this to Ricky.

Right now the rabbi's pickin' up a piece, lookin' at it. The mate's right beside it. He didn't see it till just now. Conversations in this study can take a turn like that. The puzzle has its benefits, but right now it isn't helpin'. He's stuck. Work. But his mind keeps wanderin' off onto irrelevant things.

Rivka's in from Jerusalem and the situation's complex. Questions about Miz Faber's yard are nothin' by comparison. Rivka isn't impressed with a Jerusalem puzzle. What she wants is an answer: What is going on with Miriam? What is being done to help my mom? Felix wants answers too, and the old jeweler isn't interested in puzzles! Last week's conversation invades Moishe's thoughts. As usual, Rivka's voice dominates.

No. Reruns won't do, he says to himself, back at his computer. He turns off the desk light to look at his sermon. Best off. Just makes dots of light on the screen. Another distraction.

Levy eases two long fingers across his closed eyes, trying to shut out *the voice*. He can always hear it when he thinks about Rivka. Her words hang in the air like they're in print. Gettin' a look, if only in imagination, is finalizin'. It's like remembering a word—the exact, right one.

Does *satisfying* say it better, better than *finalizing*, he asks himself. No, even if *finalizing* turns the thought to jargon.

The word drops down with a thud, straight from the innards of some twenty-pound government manual. But it's exactly right. Conveys his dithered efforts to be done with every distraction. Try not to think about Miriam or Quentin, or battle *the voice*. Rubbin' his eyes and mentally wanderin' back to the bureaucratic pit he dug some extra funds out of as a college student, he's losin' more ground. Random musin' takes over.

In that office, he's mutterin', "Back then, I indulged private fantasies about other employees. The place was dehumanizing! Slaving away in that environment took the proclivities of a literate cannibal—some species not discovered yet. Human letterheads! They ate books. Smacked their lips over that alphabet soup everyone joked about. If you X-rayed their insides, you'd see ten encyclopedias of verbal fodder, worse than the stuff lawyers live on. Ugh! After hours they secretly devoured the obsolete documents. No shredding needed around here!"

The rabbi shakes his head and looks at the sermon. "Distractions" . . . a better topic this week?

Y'know what, babe? I love these Feinemanns. My daddy's passed away and my mama lives a long way off—for South Carolina, that is—and they're so nice. They take in stray kittens and they've been nice to me. Miriam told me all about this conversation. I'm passin' it on the way she said it . . . well, almost. Give me some latitude, won't you? Like I said, I enjoy gettin' into people's heads.

While the rabbi worries, distracted by the reruns in his head, Felix and Miriam are sittin' in their kitchen talkin'. Today, the weekly prayer group meetin' at Feinemanns' Jewelry Store stayed only an hour, so the proprietor, that's Felix, closed early. A slow day. Now, as he often does, Felix is about to describe an odd encounter; he has an eye for the human-interest story. Chats against the backdrop of diamonds and rubies are sometimes amazin'. Miriam missed this one, at home with Rebekah, cherishin' the precious hours before their daughter returns to Jerusalem. Rebekah prefers her Hebrew name, Rivka.

"You were telling me . . . she brought in the cufflinks," Miriam says to 'im, smilin' and stirrin' her tea. The jasmine aroma's nice.

Her smile is the genuine article, he's thinkin'. I've told her a thousand times. That night—rush week, it was—the smile caught me. So shy, not enjoying herself. I went over for some rich details to tell the brothers. Later, we'd laugh. Why not? She wouldn't be invited back. Right now, someone was coming to talk to her. Just that, so she smiled. Then I couldn't forget the smile. She certainly wasn't Miss Congeniality! For sixty years now . . . that smile.

"The missing stone . . . she asked you to replace. A cat's eye? You said it was . . . a cat's eye. Go on, Felix," Miriam says. She told me one time he can lose his train of thought. He's pretty old.

Felix goes on. "Then the lady said, 'Maybe it was a petrified cat.'"

"You are telling me . . . she said those words. The very words?"

"That's what she said, my love, 'a petrified cat.' I was holding her husband's cufflinks in my own hand, and I was wondering, what happened to the rest of the cat?"

"Ruth, dear, the wrinkles of his face were branching out like . . . ancient rivers and streams. His eyes . . . two wiggly lines. Felix looks at me . . .. I return his gaze. We look at each other . . . three seconds, eight, ten. His lips curve down, that droll way of smiling he has. You know, my dear, how some mouths bend down—the corners, you know. His eyes squeezed shut again, he saw . . . my shoulders. Shaking. Yes, my shoulders were shaking . . . a petrified cat?

Try to picture it. There they are in their kitchen, and they're lookin' at each other. Something's happenin' that Miriam's tryin' to keep in control of. The laughin's silent, but her midsection gives her away.

Felix feels something in the tabletop runnin' in his direction; the surface is shiny polished, and it's lyin' perpendicular to the stripes of her blouse. A tiny vibration is signalin' the front of his starched white shirt just above the belt buckle because he's leanin' toward her. For a minute, the alarms jangle and he looks at his wife. Miriam's really laughin' now. It's real, uncomplicated waves—yeah, pure enjoyment—some sort of eruption gatherin' strength and force till the table between 'em shakes so much he can't miss it.

Felix resists, but the urge can't be stuffed down.

Across the table, Miriam's wipin' her eyes and gaspin'. Six decades of experience tells her Felix is losin' ground and all his efforts at decorum are failin'. She gets it, but she's not prepared for the roar that busts out with the power of emotion brewed, bottled, and corked throughout half a year's worry.

Now Felix can't look at his wife. His eyes are shut tight. He throws back his head and rests it on the back of the kitchen chair. He's too weak to hold it up. Even the hair on his head feels limp. (I know. Sometimes I laugh like that).

What do people think about when they laugh? This is how I see it. In a real fit of it, laughter rules. Do heart patients wonder about all that exertion? Does any surgery patient think he'll come apart? He's fightin' the pain all that laughter inflicts on his stitched-up insides! Does a woman listenin' to her man's belly laugh ask what would happen if he actually lost his breath? No, nothin' bends the moment. It's the laughter that rules, baby. Just that, nothin' but that.

Pain reins in the mood, and Felix steadies his breathin' to gasp out a question. He thinks changin' the subject might settle 'em down.

"You didn't tell . . . the rabbi, did you? Did you tell hi . . . m, him . . . . I mean, did you on the phone just now . . .?"

"N . . . oooo . . . oo. I didn't ge . . . t around to it . . . A round tuit . . .! And don't you tell him, do . . . on't you ei . . . ther, not if I . . . can't."

He's wheezin' with laughter and so is she.

Miriam puts her head on the table as Felix gets up, lookin' for relief. He crosses the kitchen, eyes on the floor. He catches the sunshine of late afternoon; the sun's jiggling bars and squiggles of brilliance across the shiny surface of that floor you could eat on. Like I said, he's catchin' the merry shakin' of all that light, and now he has a wild new reason to laugh. Felix is an old man, y'know. This old jeweler puts out an arm to steady himself, leans on the island in the middle of the room, and reaches for a tissue. The built-in tissue holder was a good idea after all, he's thinkin'. Miriam had it right once again.

Felix dries his eyes and blows his nose. He'll be sore tomorrow. How to explain that in town? He'll groan or somethin', and the whole store will say what's wrong? He decides he better not go in at all.

The thought of stayin' home in bed is deliciously funny. He'll be lyin' there among the pillows, a big bandage around him. Dr. Wellhelm will be packin' up his rolls of gauze and the oil of myrrh and stuff. Then he'll shake down his big, just-invented house calls bag. Dr. Well's breakin' every protocol of modern medical practice by meetin' the crisis at 29 Applebaum Court in person. He'll peer through those thick, black glasses of his and murmur, "Well, well . . . you must have rest. Rest is the essential thing if you intend to get well, Felix."

Has to catch himself, Felix is thinkin,' has to keep himself from murmurin', "Well, well . . . rest in peace." Felix's had open-heart surgery, has reason to think like that. Today he might just come apart like Raggedy Andy if he keeps on laughin' that way.

The butcher-block island is reassuringly solid. Felix clutches his achin' sides. Across the room, Miriam is gaspin'.

"Sto . . . o . . . p, stop . . . you're kil . . . ling me." She stands up, pushes her chair back, and moves unsteadily toward his outstretched arms. She's strugglin' to catch her breath, but his heavin' chest sets her off again.

"We can't te . . . ll him, we ca . . . n't, can we . . .?"

"No . . . we must not tell hi . . . m. No . . . t now, not yet, anyway. He might have a heart attack."

"I t . . . old you . . .. Stop it . . . sto . . . p it!"

This happened in *our* kitchen. I'm leavin' it just the way I had it when I decided to write it all down. Like I said, give me some latitude; I'm doin' the best I can, and nobody knows the details better than me. You have to have the context.

Voice. That's a word you use if you're a teacher, but the real voice is that voice inside your head. You're the one who makes the adjustments, 'specially in a story about voices. The main one's Miz Faber's voice, of course. She's the opra singer and it's the real thing. But Rivka's and Miriam's are pretty amazin' too. I should also let you know that when I talk, I don't talk loud. People have to get up close. That's why I do it. I like people right up close, babe.

"You cook good, hon," says my husband. He's the six-foot-five pastor of Union Street Baptist Church of Beulah, SC, and he's finishin' his pancakes. I tell 'im the milk went sour in the fridge so naturally I made pancakes.

Whatever, he thinks. I can it tell by his blank look.

As long as they come out like this, he's not complainin'. I look at things so they seem like destiny, Ricky says. God's in his heaven, all's right with the world—most of the time.

"Watch your grammar," I tell 'im as I take the bottle of sorghum from the table. "I bet you ignore those wavy green lines even . . . .."

"What are you talking about?"

I shoot 'im a fierce look as I wash the sticky drippin's from the bottle. "Sure enough, Rickybabe," I say. "You need to be more careful. Baptists get a bad enough rap as it is without bad grammar."

"Who gets a bad rap? It's not any Baptists I know bleeding members all over the countryside. That's the liberals," says Ricky.

"Well, you may like to think so, but Mother said her pastor told 'em from the pulpit they were actually down, lower attendance than at any time in the past five years and it's a trend."

"There are things that should be happening in that church that aren't, and they have nothing to do with grammar."

"You're right about that," I say, "but anyway—how about tellin' me, 'Thank you, Ruthie . . . thank you for takin' such good care of me, feedin' me pancakes, correctin' my grammar, all before seven-thirty in the mornin', never mind usin' the milk when half the women you know would throw it away!'"

"Mama, you take good care of me!" he says, reachin' over to snag me around the waist. I'm makin' a move to cross the room behind his chair. Pulling me over, he brushes my hair aside, or tries to, and tangles it up in his glasses.

"So much hair," he puffs, smilin' at my efforts to get away. "So much hair, and I'm the only one who gets to get all mixed up in it. A woman's hair is her glory, says the Bible . . . specially yours."

I laugh and extricate myself as he puts the glasses on his nose. Then he takes 'em off again to untangle the hair. Like I said, it's red. No, it's really more like orange—pumpkin orange, pumpkin-on-fire orange.

Like the sun itself, Ricky tells me. He's more poetic than me. By now my hair's in its usual, unmanageable state.

Putting away the cookbook, I look over at my husband. He's examinin' that hair caught in his glasses. Any minute now he'll put it in his pocket! Crazy man, I think, lettin' myself gaze. That's right. I'm gazin' like I'm tryin' to map the lines of his face. There aren't many. His hair is bushy and gray years before it was 'sposed to be that color, years after it should start thinnin'.

I've married a movie star, I think, and he's a *Baptist*! I just have to make the most of it. And yes, there are things that should be goin' on in that church that aren't. It's Baptist.

Ricky's phone rings. He fishes it out, shuttin' down the *1812 Overture* before the cannons start.

"Pastor Apricot," Rick says. It's his pulpit voice, sugared with a little how-can-I-serve you?

The voice on the other end belongs to Moish. I can tell from across the room. Nobody talks like Moish. He knows how to e-nun-c-iate.

"Rick, Mrs. Faber fell and broke her arm. Thought you'd want to know."

"Thanks, buddy. How bad is it?"

"Nothing besides the broken arm. Could have been worse. She was running out to her roses and stumbled, fell on the arm. Bruises and scrapes, little more, but they're keeping her for observation. She cut her head when she fell and can't explain much, so the ball's in their court for answers."

Rick hears *business as usual* in his friend's tone. Too bad about the broken arm, but it's minor compared to the troubles now closin' in on Miz Faber. The Levys are back to back with her place. Not on the front lines of care-givin', but all that neediness tangles them up too. Augusta has to have backup; she's old as Alice Faber. Be lost without 'em.

So would this pastor, Rick told me once. Miz Faber's on the Baptist rolls, but he doesn't know 'er like the Levys. Shirley's almost a daughter. Little by little, they've turned into the daily go-to. Available. Not sure how it happened; it just did. The Levys have no child and now they have Alice. Her dementia's a given. If the rabbi and rabbitzen are gettin' used to her sorrows, they won't be faulted by

Ricky. Crises one after another have a levelin' effect, he says. They're better than good neighbors.

"How's she taking it?"

"Well, you know Alice. I think they're having to engage in some truth gymnastics to keep her from bolting."

"Truth gymnastics."

"Some medic, or maybe one of the chatty nurses over there brought up Col. Mitchell. Faber's made the leap she's some place where she can talk to him. She's going on about pirates. New development, I think. As long as she can rail at Col. Mitchell about pirates or ordinances or whatever, they may get her to stay in that hospital bed. See what you think. We're all she's got, you know. That daughter doesn't concern herself except to have her accountant pay the bills."

"Yeah, I'll write *Alice Faber* on my list."

Ricky waves toward the blue pad and pencil I keep with my cookbooks and I hand 'em over.

". . . calls here in town this morning," he tells Moish and writes the name.

"I'm headed to the hospital now."

"Okay. We'll compare notes later."

Ricky drops the phone in his pocket and I grab my chance.

"Baby, let's pray before you go."

"Sure. Anything in particular?"

"Well, we laugh at Miz Faber, but it must be scary to be driftin' away from yourself. She's not the same person she was. Better pray for the rabbi some more too. Shirley says people are askin' about 'im. There's some rumor he's become a Christian . . .."

"Yes . . . Mrs. Faber. That was Moish. She's got more problems." He hands me back my blue pad and pencil. "Fell and broke her arm out in the rose garden."

He looks up. What I said just sank in.

"Moshe . . .?"

"One of the Beth Shalom folks said they heard it, then somebody else told Shirley the same thing. She's sure it isn't true. He isn't actin' different. But it's made a problem. It's messin' with Shirley's timing, the moment she was lookin' for. You know how it is. They think they're the only one in the world and it can be hard. She was lookin' for the right minute, and now she's waitin' for him to say something."

I ruffle my hand through my hair. In the sunshine of the kitchen windows it'll look like breakin' into flames. I like the way it makes Ricky open his eyes, like he's about to call the fire department. Then I go on.

"She wants 'im to *tell her*. Break the ice or somethin'. If there's anything to it."

"Don't you think he would've told me?"

"Not if he hasn't told Shirley. Maybe he'd think you'd get too much satisfaction. You know, like you'd won or somethin'."

"Nonsense! That's not the way it is and you know it. When it happens, you want everybody to know. Think back, baby."

Here my Ricky makes that cute, worried face, and I want to kiss the wrinkle between his eyes. Rick's the opposite of Moish Levy. He does not worry. But when he does, he's just . . . well, it makes 'im look like a sexy Supreme Court judge deliberatin' on a case and he's the tie-breaker. Takes my breath away.

"Still," he says, "I've been pretty blunt with Moish lately. He may want to sort things out on his own before he tells me . . . be sure it's the real thing and not just something I pushed him into."

"Nobody pushes Moish into anything, Rickybabe."

I can see Ricky's replaying the latest of his all-out battles with the rabbi. Things are more civil now that they're grown, but he'd like to take back half the things he says. He's frownin' and lookin' out the window. The sunshine's nice.

Rick's not one to admit mistakes. I have to grab the opportunity when he gets himself together to look into his soul. Teachable moment, right?

"Yeah, Ricky, you're sweet to everybody but the rabbi. You need to step back sometimes, shug. It won't do much good to kill 'im on the way to a decision. The Lord isn't askin' for his head on a silver platter!"

"Sweet uh?"

I know what he thinks of *sweet*. It's no compliment to this Baptist, but about now he needs to hear it straight like everybody else. The stuff he says to his rabbi friend is way over the top sometimes. I've heard the phone conversations, and I wonder how those two can go on talkin' to each other for years and years. Old friends? Who needs enemies! There's gotta be a limit. I've told him so, over and over. He won't listen. Just says doesn't everybody fight with their brother?

Pastor Honeybabe's caught my John the Baptist slam but decides to let it go.

Too nice a morning to fight, he's thinkin'. I've just put on my schoolmarm thing; he knows I'll be shaking a big spoon at 'im next.

Somethin' in the pancakes, he's tellin' himself. Better change the subject, pull out some pastoral dignity. Things could get out of hand.

That's what he's thinkin'. I know my Ricky.

"Paul went out into the desert for years," he solemnly says, like a Sunday school teacher. "He wasn't in a hurry to talk about what happened to him. First had to get things worked out with the Lord. Maybe that's what is going on with Levy. Best to wait and see. If he's been knocked off his horse in the noonday sun, so to speak, he'll come around, tell me eventually. Doesn't have that much pride. Nobody does. He'll have to tell me."

"Okay," I say. "Just keep prayin'." It's too nice of a day to be fussy.

"We should pray for Quentin," he says. "For Moish and Quentin and all that . . . also for Miriam Feinemann. Her depression has Moish worried."

See what I mean about the rabbi? Everybody knows it.

"Okay," I say.

My big man sits down again, me across from 'im. His long arms reach across the table and he grabs my hands. We sit there waitin' then Ricky begins.

"Lord, Ruth and I come before you with a few things on our minds. But first we want to remind ourselves who we're addressing. And yes, you're the Shepherd of sheep that do some serious wandering from time to time. Thank you for the cross. Thank you for forgiveness and for bringing us into your family. We remember, and we're bringing before you some family matters. Thank you that you've made us family—all the sick people I'll be seeing today, all the dear saints who keep this church going while I'm out. Thank you for my Ruth, dear Lord. She does take good care of me. I am grateful for her. She's a wise lady.

"Father, open Moishe's heart if it isn't already and Quen's, too. Please heal that breach. And Lord, take care of Quen's eyes. Who understands that blindness? Nobody but you. Help him let go of whatever's making his body react like that if that's what it is. We don't know why . . . nobody knows but you, and you healed all those blind people. Please deal with his fears and griefs. Lord, have mercy on Mrs. Faber—that broken arm too. Guide the folks treating her. We ask you for healing—for Miriam, as well . . . the depression that's so troubling. Rebekah's going back to Jerusalem. Protect her. Give Miriam and Felix assurance that she'll be all right."

A pause then he goes on.

"Never mind that she's not a Baptist. Help me to remember to keep on bringing her name before you, Lord. Thank you for hearing our prayers and meeting our needs. We love you, Lord Jesus, and we make this prayer in your name. Amen."

I repeat my *A-men* and get up wipin' my eyes. Have to smile at my husband. He really is one of a kind. Now I'm wonderin' who it was when he said, ". . . never mind she's not a Baptist." The Lord can sort it out.

"You better get goin', honeybabe," I say, steppin' up to be kissed.

". . . or better yet, take a bite out of you, Mrs. Apricot."

He bends down and wraps his two arms around me, kisses the top of my head, my cheek, then gets to the real business of kissin' me.

"Mmm, mmmmm," he says. ". . . I'll see you later."

The rabbitzen knocks on the door and in the same motion, pushes it open.

"Miryam, Miryam and Felix . . . Shirli."

Footsteps announce Annabelle. She comes in smilin' from somewhere in the house. Her distant Haitian ancestry is clear in her posture. It and her politeness hide her age, but right now, the formality's nowhere to be found.

"La, Miz Levy, I'm happy t' see *you* this mornin'. Somethin' has happened in this house. It's wonders upon wonders 'round here. Wait'll you hear."

Shirley smiles as Annabelle hurries on, stoppin' to catch her breath as she spills it all out. It's takin' some work.

Shirley listens with that intensity of hers. She's thinkin' how easy it is to love Annabelle. She hasn't known many African Americans, and everything about Annabelle stirs her interest. Shirley's an Israeli, but she's been in America long enough to catch the emphasis on *African* when the words get put together.

"Diverse city," she told me one time. Smiling when she said it. "Diverse like Israel."

To Shirley, the emphasis falls on *American*. For her, gettin' to know Annabelle's like sunshine burnin' off the mornin' fog. Annabelle's part of this family. No other way to put it. Right now, she's also thinkin' about something else. I'm explainin' to her the fine point differences among Christians over here (better me than Ricky) and now she's wonderin': The second blessing? Miryam and Felix? **כבוד מות**!

"That, too?" she says to Annabelle. "Come . . . we will dance!"

They embrace and join hands and they're laughin'. Then they raise their arms, they turn and sway. They're hummin' the same little tune. The gentle turns get faster (she's an old lady, remember) and tears streak Annabelle's cheeks. They shine like streams of light on her dark skin, and when she stops, puffin' from the effort, she says to Shirley, "La, la, honey . . . who woulda thought!"

"Still praying . . . . They are still praying?"

"S'pose so. Prob'ly still at it."

"I will not stay. Call me if I should come later."

"I will, honey. I sho will. You go with God. But wait . . . . You nevah tol' me why you came t'day. You want me to tell 'em somethin'?"

"*Ken* . . . uh, yes. Say that Mrs. Faber has broken her arm . . . to be praying for her."

"Sho will, honey. I'll tell 'em . . . bye now."

"*Lahitraot, chaverah.*"

"Yeh, that's right." The old woman follows Shirley to the door, chucklin'. "Tha's right, tha's right . . . and you still beh'd not tell 'im 'cep t' pray—not yet, not 'less you think . . . ."

"No . . . not yet."

CHAPTER TWO
Words

HAZEL VON GELFOND AND GLORIA FINKELSTEIN ARE
surprised to run into each other at the Camellia Grille. Hazel's finishin' lunch,
Gloria's just coming in from the Beulah Flower Shop. Hazel feels like dessert,
lookin' around for the server when she sees her friend. The Grille's crowded.
Gloria's about to leave, but Hazel catches her wave. Gloria speaks to the hostess
then makes her way to the one empty place in the dinin' room. After windin'
around purses, brief cases, and chair legs that man with the belly hadn't pulled up
to the table, Gloria sits down. I'm at the next table and give 'em a wave. Ricky says
I shouldn't listen in, but why not? It doesn't hurt anybody.

"I'm having dessert, but I haven't ordered," Hazel tells her. "You can when I
do and then have this table when I go. Where else would you sit?"

"Thanks. I am hungry. Thought I might miss lunch altogether in this crowd.
What's good today? I don't have much time."

"I like the shrimp and grits."

Gloria laughs. Kosher isn't a thing of the past, but she has some latitude now.
Hazel, likewise. Food has a new dimension.

The two chat about this and that, Gloria waitin' for the right moment to
spring some news on her friend. When the orders go off to the kitchen, she delivers
her bombshell and sits back to watch. The gasp she expected isn't long comin'.

"That's what she said. I was down there getting flowers for Max's funeral. That's what Susan said."

"Gloria!" Hazel opens her eyes, tryin' to put herself into the scene. She can picture her friend leanin' in to catch Susan's every word, but the news was unbelievable.

"That's right . . . that's what she said."

"Has he told anybody?"

"Well, Susan knew it. Somebody had to tell her."

"But how could she be sure? Wouldn't we know . . . I mean, sermons or hints in casual conversation, or something—wouldn't he tell somebody?"

"Not necessarily. You remember how it was at first . . . the only Jew in the world and all that."

"All too well."

"Maybe it's too soon. Getting used to things maybe. Just have to wait and see."

"The rabbitzen? Wouldn't she say something to somebody?" Hazel wants to know.

"Not if he hadn't told her."

"Not told her and she's his wife?"

"Well, maybe not. At first it's a strange feeling, as you know yourself, Hazel."

"So true. I didn't tell Harry for a month."

"I wasn't too thrilled about the funerals either. Sam might have just thrown me out. I didn't know what to do at first," Gloria says with a chuckle.

Hazel laughs. "That's right . . . what to do? What could you do but just pray maybe."

"Well, I guess we don't have anything not to tell the rabbi after all."

"Looks like he has something to tell us."

"Shirley should let us know . . . assuming *she* knows."

"Don't be ridiculous, Gloria. She has to know something." Gloria's diggin' in her purse for the prayer needs list when Hazel interrupts.

"I heard that Alice Faber is in a coma."

"What happened?"

"She fell, hit her head. They're saying she may not live." Hazel is whispering.

"Has anybody been to see her?"

"Not if she's in intensive care!"

"Is that where she is?"

"I don't know. I just heard she's in a coma. She wouldn't know it if you did go to see her . . . if they let you. Probably wouldn't if it's intensive care. Just family, you know."

"Poor Alice," Gloria says. "No, she wouldn't know it, coma or no coma. Hasn't been herself for such a long time. But what family?"

"So true. A blessing she has the Levys. They're so kind. Not anybody but them . . . well, and the Baptists. They look after her, too, I think."

"Yes. The Levys, very kind . . . for years now. I'm going to the jewelry store when I'm done. I'll add Alice to the list. Isn't Rebekah good to keep the store?"

"Yes, but she's going back to Jerusalem, isn't she?"

"Soon, Felix says. He's not so worried about Miriam, but Jerusalem's a long way."

"I'm still not used to calling her Rivka," Hazel says.

"That's what *Rebekah* is."

"Well, I may know it in my head, but it feels strange coming out of my mouth."

"Me, too, really. Unusual girl. I guess *Rivka* fits."

"Felix says we can pray in his office. He's keeping the shop this week, not Rebekah. Miriam will tell him later. He prays when there aren't any customers . . . all the time, she says. I mean, unless he has a customer. She's keeping the list now . . . if she can. You know how depression is. How will a person be from one week to the next?"

"Better, God willing," Gloria says.

"Yes, G–d willing."

"Such a man he is . . . a good man, the rabbi. He's been so worried about Miriam."

"Are you coming?"

"No. Appointment with Gretchen in an hour. I'll come next week. After sixty we need help with the hair, you know. Under the dryer, I'll pray."

"Without ceasing, I'm sure."

Gloria smiles conspiratorially and they laugh, both thinkin' that prayer's a new experience—this kind of prayer, anyway. Who would have guessed? The thought brings memories stretchin' back through half the year. In a way, an eternity. Prayer, so different now. Maybe that's it.

Babe, the Feinemanns' Jewelry is the perfect place to pray. Quiet. Nowadays you have to look to find a quiet place. People even drive around this town with their cars like loud speakers! Beulah used to be so peaceful.

"Tell Miriam about the rabbi," Gloria says. "Felix, too. Rebekah probably won't believe it."

"She's at home typing . . . something for that paper in Jerusalem."

"Odd how she works on her stories even when she's here. Doesn't seem to relax a minute," Gloria says. "Maybe it's why she stays so thin. Doesn't need to hear about the rabbi . . . wouldn't be interested, I think. But that's the Feinemanns' decision."

"What an odd daughter. Can't say I envy them."

"You have to admit she's successful. Can't fault that."

"Of course not," Hazel says.

Gloria looks at herself in a compact fished from her purse and decides not to put on lipstick.

I can tell by the way she's lookin' around that she's wonderin' about catchin' the server's eye in this hubbub. Might not get to eat after all.

While Rick Apricot is chattin' with his friend Quentin, on the other side of the Square, four blocks from Union Street Baptist, Jonathan Stein is on the phone to Judge Solomon's office. This isn't a friendly conversation. The problem is the judge's late-comin' lunch order. The Palmetto Street Deli's the new kid on the block, and the proprietor wants happy customers, especially if this one's the old judge.

The frustrated Stein is tryin' to get his head around the particulars of the botched order, and right now he's strugglin' with a peculiar voice, maybe from behind a wall. He isn't too sure about the setting. Judges' chambers in small-town

South Carolina are a world away from NYC venues where he delivered, then sent others with deliveries when he became the boss. They might be the same, but they easily might not.

Somehow, the sandwich came with a slatherin' of horseradish instead of mayo. One big bite was all it took for the judge to concur with his inner advisory board on the question of bellowin' for help. This much Stein can make out, but the rest is impossible. The clerk was out to lunch, all three paralegals too. So was the judge's personal secretary. The wiry old bailiff, Petersby, was the only one around and he can't hear very well. When he finally determined the direction of the hoots for help, he knew his duty—first responder! He was the one. Stein can picture him boltin' down the hall, the knife-edge creases in his impeccable browns scissorin' up and down at such a rate they could cut his legs off.

Unfortunately, the courthouse stalwart, this one fully armed, is well beyond his best boltin' days and didn't reach the judge's chambers in time to prevent some significant damage to the judicial dignity. The mouth of his honor wasn't burned badly, but his ego was altered, an effect as tellin' as if he'd been temporarily emasculated. The ink stain on the Oriental isn't temporary, a lastin' result of some wild sweepings of the air and mighty flailings about by the arm of the law.

As Stein listens, the scene plays itself out to a mixed conclusion somewhere between comedy and cataclysm.

Jonathan Stein has a vivid imagination. At one time he entertained hopes of a movie script from his own pen, but when he tried to market the piece, nobody was interested. The Beulah Petersby resembles one of the characters more than a little, but Stein isn't thinkin' about him right now. His creative juices are always on tap, and who can blame him for addin' some fiz to the drama of this impossible phone call. He can't hear most of it!

Why is the judge's secretary talkin' like that?

In Judge Solomon's distress, the formidable Marli-Pearl has been called back in. Nobody else can deal it.

Returnin' to her duties as the judge's go-to and go-for person at the courthouse, Marli-Pearl put on some speed, but she isn't entirely pleased about missin' her full lunch break. The leftover grits and moon eggs, that side of blackened turkey bacon are gettin' cold on the kitchen table. Have to be thrown out this evening.

The warmed apricot nectar is coolin' where she left it and the thought makes her grumpy.

Good thing I decided against the extra egg whites, she's tellin' herself. The wide swathe she makes comin' back in is consolation enough to salve most aggravations; she barely notices an effect she usually enjoys.

Everyone at the courthouse, attorneys to zip-drive locators, gives her wide berth and not just on grumpy days. The entire population, not includin' Judge Solomon, exerts themselves Monday through Friday in a vigorous attempt to contain a very real if unacknowledged dread of 'er.

Nobody wants to bump into the judge's secretary. In private and at a distance, they're her disciples, every one of 'em, though nobody admits it. They've stuffed their admiration so far down they're unaware of it themselves. If confronted they'll never confess, even in the privacy of midnight bedrooms, to any connection with Marli-Pearl.

Truth be told, they model her methods. They find occasion to consult her in private when they need information. The whole place benefits from her informal intelligence operations. She's as much of an institution as Judge Solomon: Marli-Pearl, collector and purveyor of secrets. This woman's the best-kept secret in Beulah!

To the judge, she's more than a convenience. She has the title Amanuensis, and as a secretary she's first rate. Marli-Pearl also carries around in her head an entire Rolodex of human error, every bit of it generated on the local scene—broken laws and statutes (federal, state, and county), abused city ordinances down to the smallest infraction (letter and spirit), even a list of buildin' code violations or wrong choices of hardware in the area of doorknob selection at registered sites of the historic downtown. Substitutions for real S-hooks and window shades of a non-period color are a special annoyance to Marli-Pearl. She's interested in architecture. Saggy pants and belly shirts make her apoplectic.

As an amateur genealogist, Judge Solomon sometimes requires this or that bit from his personal secretary, and he pays her for the trouble, pays 'er well. He also receives from Marli-Pearl's research the whiff of an impression—some family's personality or inter-connection with some other family, its overall reputation, even an occasional parole history going way back. Officially, he consults Marli-

Pearl as any judge consults his secretary, but the oblique gleanings he now and then gains from 'er prove useful to the Bench, in a quiet sort of way.

The judge would like details (her MO, for example), but he's impatient with things like that. Marli-Pearl's the details person. That's the difficulty, and the thought gives him a headache. Anyone poking around for Marli-Pearl details will be confronted with their own case file she carries around in her head—three times the number of details. One or two, actionable.

Judge Solomon's questions about sources and how she acquires 'em are lively as his theories on her methods. Like lawyers and judges, she seems to generate ill will in many quarters just by breathin'; nevertheless, he tells himself, some foul reputations stem from mere sheer jealousy.

Doesn't everybody hate lawyers? But when they have a problem, they go looking for one. Lawyers don't make money by stealing it! They have comfortable incomes because people pay 'em!

Judge Solomon hates lawyer jokes. Marli-Pearl's name won't be mixed in with such tripe—not in his chambers! Won't allow it. In the end, she seems no worse than a dozen attorneys he's played golf with for years. When his suspicions fail to spring out anything specific, the judge just stops askin' questions about how Marli-Pearl does things.

He long ago stopped expectin' a celebration of honor and integrity to smooth the jagged edges of her reports, but the information she delivers is valuable. Reference material. She knows what she's talkin' about. Her accuracy and precision are in the public record, causin' the judge to wonder why Marli-Pearl never considered the law. Certainly smart enough.

She probably dreams in closin' statements and briefs, he tells himself, marveling and shakin' his head. Yes, thinkin' like a police detective is part of the skill set even if some lawyers lack it. For Marli-Pearl, the required qualifications leave no gaps and that's all the time.

Marli-Pearl takes special pleasure in rattlin' every person she comes across, and right now she's findin' Jonathan Stein's fully focused attention an easy playground to saunter around in. Stein can hear only a good-sized bit of what she's sayin', and he isn't too sure about that. The struggle to put in place all the pieces of the actual problem is makin' him sweat and she knows it.

The unsuspectin' deli owner has never in his life been confronted with a whispered complaint. Arm wavin' and shoutin' come with the territory, but Marli-Pearl has left out those details. Her personal style is like a secret invasion by intergalactic aliens. Now, as always, she's talkin' so softly that Stein needs to supply, on his own, a good half of every sentence. For Marli-Pearl, this is just as it should be. It weights her threefold case—first, the negligence of the businessperson she's addressin'; second, the medical implications of the judge's sufferin' ("his honor is also allergic to bee stings"). There is, in addition, an actionable relationship between all this ineptitude and Stein's personal worth.

Stein has a newcomer's disadvantage. He's only heard the woman's name once or twice—nothing more, not even from his wife. Oy vevoy, what's he supposed to do?

Nobody whispers, not in Jonathan Stein's experience, and he considers himself a man of experience. Six months after comin' to the Sun Belt from the Big City he's just beginnin' to feel comfortable. Southerners are odd and they talk funny, but they eat, same as any other human bein', and they like his food. Right now, he's confronted by the wildly unexpected. At this moment, Beulah, South Carolina, appears to Jonathan Stein as odd as the Amazonian jungle or the backside of Io, neither of which he can come close to imaginin', even with all his batteries charged. He's heard that the Amazon has some kind of twelve-foot snakes hidden in all that green stuff, and who knows about the tuckus of Io? It's becomin' altogether too clear that this little town has its own lurking hazards. Where he comes from, people speak their minds. They talk so you can hear 'em. There aren't many whisperers in New York City!

"Horseradish . . . you're telling me horseradish?"

"Horseradish, Mr. Stein."

Six syllables barely loud enough for a whisper, but the veiled threats come through loud and clear. The softer the voice on the phone, the louder his own, but his increasing decibels fail to prime the pump. It's like an audio seesaw—his volume goes up, the voice on the other end goes down. Infuriating!

Inadvertently wrapping himself in the long cord of the deli's ancient telephone, Stein is puttin' physical effort into the dual tasks of understandin' and workin' himself free of the phone tangle. He hasn't yet learned that the whole town of

Beulah lives with a similar predicament. Everyone wants to tell Marli-Pearl to speak up, but at the same time they're afraid she might. It makes no difference. She ignores her one friend's timid hints about bein' heard, and Marli-Pearl puts no stock in doin' unto others as she would have them do unto her.

Susan Satterthwaite at Beulah Flowers supplies Marli-Pearl with Venus Fly Traps. It's a profitable friendship for the florist, but she's given up suggestin' to the judge's secretary that she talk louder. She shouldn't feed the hungry little carnivores so many hamburger bits either . . . it's the end of 'em!

But it's good for business, Susan tells herself. If Marli-Pearl kills 'em and has to toss 'em out, that's one more she'll have to buy from me. She can afford it. Sure doesn't listen to me. Does she hear as softly as she talks? Deaf people talk louder, not softer, don't they? But who can figure her out anyway? Certainly not me, and I don't know why she wants my spiders. She's no scientist, even if she is so smart. I bet she doesn't know anything about how strong those webs are. But maybe she does . . . maybe she wants to sell venom to the anti-toxin labs just like me. Ugh! Competition, just when I'm getting my other business started.

Susan shakes her head with frustration. She's just breakin' even with the new venture. If somebody else around here comes into the market, profits will drop.

"Be just like Marli-Pearl to horn in like that! She's so finicky and precise she'll probably be better at it than me," Susan says, talkin' out loud in her frustration. She snips off three rose stems. "On second thought, she may just want 'em because they like hamburger." The Jones wedding order goes to PAUSE as she pictures the guy who fed a black widow hamburger till it just rolled over and died.

Like Marli-Pearl for the life, Susan tells herself. Maybe she saw that black widow in the State paper before I even mentioned it. I bet that's what happened. She'd like watchin' black widows kill themselves gorgin' on hamburger. Likes money too.

The florist finds her occasional companion more intimidatin' than enjoyable, but she doesn't know how to get free. Like Stein, she's entangled, has a business interest. And she knows more than he does about the hazards of getting that woman's attention.

I know what she can do if she decides to get irritated with somebody, Susan thinks. Marli-Pearl likes to eat and she likes to feed things. She knows more than anybody ought to about this town's appetite for gossip. She does love to help the hungry! Feeds some kinda hunger for her, too, I bet . . . the public on steroids when it comes to gossip. The difference is she knows how to manufacture it to begin with. Doesn't just pass it on! What she does to a story's an art form.

Susan Satterthwaite has her suspicions, but she's never, not in the privacy of her own thoughts, spelled out her view of Marli-Pearl's tactics: She repeats the news and adds theories of her own. In every rag of a whispered rumor, she sees a disturbance of the peace lurkin'. Has to defend the common good. So what if her speculations turn into some unsuspectin' citizen's big problem? Person's probably guilty—most are. Besides, her explanations are as likely as anybody's—guilty or not. An explanation's needed, and Marli-Pearl has a store of possible misdeeds and transgressions to fit every frame.

That a theory is taken for fact doesn't worry her. If folks miss the "might" or "could've," if they get in a hurry and misquote or turned a possibility into the real thing, why should that chicken roost at her house? It's somebody else's problem. She can't help it that people like gossip! Not her fault when telephone chats and chance grocery store conversations get muddled. No one questions her accuracy. Ask Judge Solomon!

Susan Satterthwaite also knows the morsels of this and that Marli-Pearl gathers and drops around Beulah have an effect as telling as the bits of hamburger lethally teasin' her favorite houseplants. More than one family has tossed it in and left Beulah for who knows where when Marli-Pearl found a potential scandal linked to their name. When her offended respectability got through with 'em, they understood the main points, but the particulars, whirrin' around like a cloud of bitin', invisible sand flies, were too vague to unscramble, the suggestions too horrifyin' to talk about.

Marli-Pearl has an uncanny ability to shade even the casual chat with a hint of dire and shameful consequences. Puttin' a special slant on the story to be spread around is a skill she hones. Her style developed early. As a child, Marli-Pearl was told by her mother, "A soft voice is a fine thing in womanhood." That was the day she overheard an entire phone conversation and mostly understood it.

"Mama," the five-year-old Marli-Pearl said. "Why's it bad for somebody to have . . . you know, what you said to Miz James on the phone. Why's it bad?"

Mrs. Prake stopped waterin' the begonias and looked at her daughter. What children hear when you least expect it, Linda Prake told herself. All I said was, "Bless her heart, she had a noisy mother . . . .." Now I'll have to explain. Try to, anyway. Marli-Pearl won't let it drop. She's always creepin' up, listenin' to my phone calls!

Mrs. Prake knew all about the local celebrity, and she's shared what she heard. The details of Alice Faber's life and career, as well as the whispers about her daughter, are established fact, thanks to Linda Prake, who has a cousin in New York. The old lady hasn't sung for years, but she doesn't need to. Her reputation has gone before her like a blast of that curly, three-foot shofar guardin' the mantle of the Faber livin' room.

"No, it's *Faberge´*, " Linda's cousin insisted. "They shortened it to Faber during the war. I think her husband didn't want to sound like some sort of Vichy guy—you know, those French Nazis? They say Faber, but it's really *Faberge´* . . . like that perfume. It isn't 'Frank' either. His real name's François."

Marli-Pearl's mother didn't admit it, even to herself, that she sowed, watered, and fertilized all the hearsay that came her way. She'd polish the details; then, with the story down pat, she'd perform it for friends, neighbors, interested newcomers—especially the newcomers. The pastor heard her favorite line when he visited her at the hospital once, "Bless her heart, she had a noisy mother!" Always a part of the story.

Linda Prake enjoyed the juicy crop of narratives that came back in a form very different from that original healthy stock she planted then got tired of. The new version was ten stories, each sproutin' others, each with its own exotic fruit. But to explain what she meant by the detail Marli-Pearl overheard was a headache.

A noisy mother. Marli-Pearl won't let that one alone, Linda thought. I'll have to come up with somethin'. A child just can't understand a thing like that. It's odd how the pastor didn't either. Just looked at me funny.

Linda Prake could fix most things, but she couldn't fix what she didn't know. The missing detail was Marli-Pearl's fear of the "P's." The story Marli-Pearl overheard scared her, scared 'er bad: Miz Faber grew up in a Pentecostal church!

"I didn't know she was a Pentecostal," Linda Prake's cousin said to her on the phone. Pentecostals? Marli-Pearl had to know, and Linda did the best she could.

Thereafter, to Marli-Pearl, the famous singer was a "P." The "P people," whoever they were, were noisy and did somethin' with snakes in church. The thought made her freeze. The whole thing wound itself into a consumin' fear too awful to talk about. Some night, the P's would sneak in and put a snake under her bed! Mama said there were plenty of P's in Beulah. There was a church full of 'em on the other side of town.

Marli-Pearl thought about that bad, noisy mother. She said to herself, Mother says ladies speak softly and Mother knows everything. Some day, I'll know everything too. I'll speak softly, just like Mother. I won't be like them.

These discoveries turned into a lifestyle—for one, makin' people feel guilty. Right now, with Jonathan Stein, Marli-Pearl was succeeding on all fronts. I heard all this from Sarah Stein. She prays at the jewelry store and I do too. It wasn't as bad as Jonathan thought, but he was pretty worried.

"Don't tell him?"

"That's what I said."

"Speak up, Jonathan! Why would the rabbi want to know about a sandwich?"

"Not the sandwich!"

"Oh, you mean . . . ."

"That's exactly what I mean. Don't *tell* him . . . it's not time yet. You'd have to say something if you asked him to pray, right?"

"Well . . . I guess you know best."

"Yes I do, thank-you-for-remembering-it!"

A smile angles itself across the narrow lips of Sarah Stein, who loves her husband and catches every tilt of humor in his occasional gruff communications. But sometimes things are confusing.

She has to admit it. In the confusing times, she tells herself, I *am* fortunate to have my hearing, unlike Aunt Rena. I don't know why I can't always catch his words. It's the phone connection or something.

Sarah worries about her husband. Jonathan is starting to mumble.

Nobody can make out what he's saying, she thinks. Odd thing for a grown man. Is something wrong with his throat? He should see a doctor, but he won't.

Men don't. Mm, the doctor . . . funny name. It was . . . *Wellhelm*. Yes, Dr. Wellhelm. Not Jewish though. That won't help him with Jonathan.

Deciding not to fill in the pause when Jonathan put his usual clampdown on extra words, Sarah says goodbye without askin' him to repeat. Just do what Jonathan wants. She knows what that is, despite the mumbling. She reruns the conversation, making sure she has everything right.

Jonathan was going on about horseradish and the judge or something, and all at once he stopped and said not to say anything, and . . . well, I better not think about what he said not to say, she tells herself. If I form the words in my mind, I might say them out loud later. Jonathan said to call the others but not him. "Don't tell him . . . not yet," he said. Then he couldn't talk anymore, in a hurry. That was all right. It was tiring to try and catch his words, but I can follow instructions. Have those right.

I'll call the others then pray, she says to herself. Amazing . . . South Carolina does have telephone service.

The Manhattan skyline rises in her thoughts and she wishes she were home. Why did Jonathan want to leave New York? Why here? She can't understand it. Better pray about that, too. Not necessary to go around sad. And Jonathan can still joke. That's a blessing.

The meditations bring a sigh of relief, a string of happy thoughts to shut out the irritated panic of her husband's voice still echoing in her mind. *Verklempt*, he was. Anyway, he was mumbling less, that higher-pitched voice. The skyline of her beloved city fades a bit as she prepares to raise the prayer alert. It will be nice to talk to somebody who doesn't mumble.

Pulling the list from a drawer, Mrs. Stein asks herself if it's proper to think of G–d as "somebody." Would "S–y" be better?

For a long time we didn't know from . . .. But how could we miss something so important, she asks herself. Wasn't it plain from Torah? But we weren't reading the Bible so much then, she thinks, fiddling with her wedding ring. But it's all right now. Yes, it's all right—well, everything but the sandwich.

Looking down at the list, she hums a tune and puts her finger on a name. It will be all right, she tells herself. Everything will be all right.

I like Quentin's aunt. She's old-fashioned and old, but she *cooks*. She's good at it too. Her best friend is Lucy Jenkins. She's my aunt, but she doesn't live in Beulah. Most of the gossip I know comes from Aunt Lucy. This little look inside Miz Martelote's head I partly imagined, but I'm never wrong, not even about the dignified talkin'. She's from the older generation, really older. Aunt Lucy's told me the same stuff she told Miss Evelyn, and I've wondered about it just like she's doin'. She's a lot like me.

Almost ten-thirty. Time to get settled for the night. Puttin' down the telephone, unpinnin' the antique cameo at her neck, Evelyn Martelote tells herself that thanks to Lucy Jenkins she has plenty to think about if she can't sleep.

John Solomon collapsed from some dire disease of the jaw? Surely not cancer! A jaw tooth? Did Lucy say "lockjaw"? How could that be? Isn't everyone inoculated for tetanus?

I have heard nothing about the judge's health, Evelyn thinks. Everyone says the judge will outlive us all. Heralds of the fact never mention which generation he will survive, but it doesn't abrogate the point. Lucy must be wrong. She's over there in Calhoun! Why is she spreading something like this if she doesn't know? And what about the other thing—Mrs. Stein's secret? She knows something she wants to tell everyone but can't—not yet, she says. Whatever it is, she's pleased about it. You do have to shout at her. And the rabbi, a Christian? Who could believe that? Still, stranger things have happened.

The old lady looks into a black ocean of trees and leaves and sees a shinin' panorama of spring green that will appear with mornin' light. The scene is more park than yard. Even in the dark, she feels that big expanse of grass, trees, flowers, and leaves and it's green. The thought clears her head.

"Speculations," she tells herself. "Lucy always did like her bit of gossip."

The old lady doesn't hear herself murmurin' out loud. She's been doin' that since her seventies. This night, Aunt Lucy's latest newscast is wearyin'.

"Lucy has it all wrong," Evelyn thinks as she unbraids her hair for bed. "As everybody knows, John Solomon is upstanding, right living, and healthy—especially healthy."

This crazy man is somebody else I now know, but that's a later part of this story. He sure does love the Lord. Ben's an English professor like Quentin, and I hate to mess with his style. Style? Yes, I hear style and I like words. Be a shame to tell it any other way. Just be patient and give 'im a break. I know he's not as interestin' as me. He's an English teacher. They get poetic sometimes, 'specially in letters like this one we just got from Jerusalem. His *mirepeset* has a voice. The second floor veranda, that is, speaks to 'im, and calls 'im out to gaze at the south wall of the Old City—the Jaffe Gate and Bethlehem Road, pointin' like a thin finger in his direction. The Arab village below has its own voice, callin' to prayer five times a day. He's told us about all this.

from Gilo

Ben Steingaard here. I'm pondering the scene, trying to describe it to you two dear folks of the Apricot household. Most of my efforts are still scattered around on the table inside—too many pages, too many words.

The Almighty does sunsets just to set off these ancient walls. Evening by evening, the stones turn rosy as darkness approaches . . . every night. Clouds rarely get in the way. I'm taking off my watch. The air is cool on the sweaty ring around my wrist. Time. So little of it, so much to do. Tonight, Leviticus—"Called," in the Hebrew. The title is in the first line of text: "And the LORD called Moses, and spoke to him out of the tabernacle . . . ."

Called. The word sounds a shofar blast. It rings with my name, puts my spirit at attention. Coming into the arms of the King, and after that to Jerusalem, I entered another world and I knew it.

I'm reruning the memories. Everything is still so new. I'm still trying to understand why it feels like a marriage—spirit, body, and mind fully united for the first time. When it happened, the union was complete, like lovers perfectly matched—the stuff of legend, the famous lovers. It felt like that—my whole being united. No other way to put it. But you two, unlike some, will understand. Yeah, I know. I should have said "Ya'll."

Spirit is feminine in the Hebrew, *haruach*. This is a marriage of three. The great rabbi from Tarsus said, "When it pleased God, who separated me from my mother's womb and called me through his grace to reveal his Son in me . . . ."

God revealed his Son *in* him! Somehow Paul knew. He perceived the Presence. I struggle to understand . . . yes, my spirit was where it happened—my spirit, His Spirit. God, the Incarnate God, willing . . . not just willing to *be* that, to be human, but willing to make a human heart his home.

The thought captivates me. God . . . *God the Son, the Son of God* was willing! Yes . . . and only by the blood.

Oh my Redeemer, that you should have been pleased to live in me!

I'm watching as the sun sets a little to the left beyond the roofs of the City new and old, washing the Temple Mount in crimson—a stunning panorama stretching beyond what I can see.

The blood is all over Leviticus. All those sacrifices make a point. It can be avoided, but it can't be missed. People stay away from this part of the Bible. Blood is everywhere in Leviticus and it's offensive.

History, ancient law? They're boring, people say. But they love history; in the millions, they study the law. What does it mean, this book? It's clear to any reader willing to see it.

"It is the blood that makes an atonement for the soul." Chapter and verse say themselves in my mind because it's my birthday. I don't forget the numbers.

I think about the words. They're astonishing, easy to memorize: "The life of the flesh is in the blood. I have given it to you upon the altar to make an atonement for your souls: for it is the blood that makes an atonement for the soul. Therefore I said to the children of Israel, No soul of you shall eat blood, neither shall any stranger that sojourns among you eat blood."

The words circle around inside me as if winding around in my DNA, angling up to be doubled, tripled, then circling off into eternity. One eternal circle turning inside me, uniting me within myself, moving me through my teaching day. If I come across someone who will listen, my day is made. One more open ear, one more eye to shine with understanding, one more person, one more heart— Arab hearts, Israeli hearts, the hearts of Druze and Danes and the new British immigrants, American Jews who'll stay and those who won't, gentiles, visitors from Asia, tourists from everywhere—anyone who's willing to listen.

Paul said to Timothy: "Be instant, in season and out of season; reprove, rebuke, exhort with all long suffering and teaching . . .." Not just to open hearts. No, it's all the time. "In season and out of season," Paul said.

Chance encounters happen. I have to take care to be courteous, remember the prickly laws against proselytizing. I know myself—I'm friendly, cynical, still too worldly. Habits of years aren't easy to shake, but I make use of all that. Conversations begin a hundred ways, each with its own opportunities.

I have to tell you about the first Israeli cop I met—a square-built man with gray hair, pictures of his family inside the uniform cap—his family on the top of his head! What a statement.

Communication is easy. Everyone speaks English, and I'm coming along with the Hebrew. The *ulpan* is a challenge, but it works. The money side of things is manageable, even in this uncertain, expensive place. The inflation I can hedge. People say, "Simplify your life." *Simple* I can deal with. University pay isn't much, but it's enough, and the Right of Return assures my place here.

Daily I'm thanking the Eternal for a Jewish mother and father, people I never knew. My Jewish parents were the ticket God put in my hand, even before I knew I'd ever want it, even when I was cast onto the mercies of Roman religious after the accident. I'm here at last in Jerusalem, home at last.

In fact, what problems do I have? I search my mind for needs and am amused to find, one more time, the oddly certain but perfect provisions of the Almighty. They're puzzling sometimes, but right, always right. *Adonai Jireh* . . . God-my-provider. Even the health worries are a thing of the past.

I'm standing here with my eyes closed for a minute—sense of contentment huge. My only problem is the one Isaiah had. Who will believe my report? But if belief fails to take hold, I just go on to another and another.

Thou, LORD, seest me.

I pray Hagar's prayer sometimes. God sees me! The Lord of the universe sees me . . . and loves *me*? Yes, loves even this wasted, half used-up semi-Jew raised to be a Roman, who spent years mocking, looking for who knows what—acceptance, meaning, a place in the world? The Lord of glory saw something else.

The telling thing is *God's own love, his own lovely Son.* He looked at me and because God is love, he could only look with love. It was his own Beloved he saw . . . and he saw it with the eyes of love. God the Son made his residence by the Spirit in my body, and God the Father could look at me with love because . . . well, just because—

How to understand all this? I certainly don't feel lovable. You'll find out when you know me better!

Every time I look across at the Old City it's like experiencing all this for the first time. I'll stand here a minute longer. I'm still remembering what it was like.

It was like being discovered, like squirming little Israel, lying by that path covered in her own blood.

Me too, I'm thinking . . . me too.

"And when I passed by you and saw you struggling in your own blood . . . .."

The Spirit speaks to me in Ezekiel's voice, in the voice of God, "I said to you in your blood, 'Live!' Yes, I said to you in your blood, 'Live!'"

Before that was I lost from God's sight? Can you say, God discovers a person? Probably not, but Paul knew what he was talking about. He was apprehended. Exactly . . . *apprehended*.

When the Lord apprehended me, I was snatched from death . . . like a rescued newborn left by a path to die—Oedipus or one of those girl babies in China. Only now they abort. I was taken up, washed in the blood of God, washed clean forever, and made to live.

Leviticus is calling more persuasively than the evening air or this stunning view. The eastern sky over toward the mountains and wadis of the Judean wilderness is getting darker, shading off into lavender. Glad I'm not having to find dinner out there in that desert!

Now I'm hungry. Better see what I can find.

Something easy. Get it done. Get to the Book.

Reaching into a pants pocket, I find my small Hebrew Publishing Company Tenach to put next to my dinner tray. I'll balance a plate and read.

Still some beet salad. Maybe an orange. Flatbread.

Doesn't matter. What matters is to get the Book propped so I can read while I eat. So much catching up to do. All those lost years when everybody else studied the Bible. I didn't and I didn't want to. Now I can't get enough of it . . . maybe even in Hebrew after a while. The thought's exhilarating.

The Word . . . *God the Word!* How did I miss it all my life? Well, I can blame—

No, no point in that, I'm telling myself. I have the Book now, and I can make up for lost time. I've spent years with books. I know how to hold a book. I know the feel of it in my hands, what it's like to devour a page. This Book is different.

It reads the reader. Quentin said that and it's true . . . so strange. I go away encouraged, even after being examined—heart, mind, and soul.

I'm reliving my first experience of divine scrutiny. I was having breakfast on a train, and I wasn't the open book back then, not open to other people, anyway. It was him. He said, "I learned about the suicide" and I was stunned. I was looking into the open gash of one man's mortal pain. The raw wound was laid bare . . . impossible not to see.

At first, that jewel business was just a quaint, far-fetched metaphor, nothing more—just some lush imagery from a literary man whose suffering bought him the right to be poetic. Silly and sentimental.

No, the man was right. I saw something else, even then. St. Paul called it "the indescribable gift." I began to see it, even when I couldn't think what to say to a grieving man with a heart big enough to be polite to a stranger. He must have wished for privacy and solitude!

Breakfast on that train: my terrifying heart condition, that chitchat about academic theories, all that biblical bantering. What did I know? Nothing at all, it seems.

Oranges in a bowl on the table. I'm looking for a knife, glad I thought to buy oranges.

No . . . two, I'm thinking. I'll have two.

Turning an orange in each hand, I'm looking toward the veranda. Night is falling, lights dotting the scene, and I'm remembering Quentin and that train. For him, the sun had risen on sorrow, but not black darkness. There was something else.

All that grief and pain open to a stranger's eyes. My eyes. What to say? What to do? You know him. This was my first encounter, and I had no idea . . ..

It was like this: *I* was the one with no place to hide. His words took on a different timbre, as if two voices spoke together—as if this professor wasn't the only one speaking. Then the other voice was speaking alone, inside me and in my ears as if, in the cramped, public clatter of a train, there was no one but me in that gaze, that welcome.

The walls of the Old City are dark now. I'm still holding the oranges, remembering the golden apples of fairy tales. I could live on oranges.

In the kitchen, I'm getting a plate, a glass, a saucer, washing my hands, peeling an orange.

Delicious juice . . . all over my hands.

It wasn't that my heart was healed. No, I had a whole new one—*whole*, new.

Have to wash my hands again. *Supremes* . . . chefs call orange segments supremes. A dish of golden supremes, better than salmon any day, even dressed up with parsley potatoes and eaten on a train. I have a whole new heart.

Here's flatbread and beets, a block of cheese. I'm carrying the tray to the table by the sofa. Something to drink? Wonder what I have.

I was like the Hebrew people, divided within myself. God said, "I will give them one heart, and I will put a new spirit within them and take the stony heart out of their flesh that they may walk in my statutes and keep my judgments and do them, and they shall be my people, and I will be their God."

Does oneness mean that—to be whole and complete? I'm thinking about the *Shema*. Hear, O Israel: the LORD thy God is One.

. . . their God, my God.

I'm on my knees now. When you get this letter, please pray with me. In God's timeless order of things, we're in the same place, in the same minute in his presence. Join this worship. I can't do anything else right now, the confession of Thomas is filling my heart. The words belong to me. I have a healed heart. If I put out my hand, I can touch the hem of that garment, breathe the fragrance.

It's later now. Looking toward the *mirepeset*, I see nothing but dark, a black rectangle where the door opens out onto the night.

Time to eat. Get that done. Tomorrow, I'll speak with that *chasid*.

He'll be hot with questions. That's good. He's angry and he's listening. I'll show him John 6 and Leviticus 17:11. He'll incandesce.

"Eat the flesh of this rabbi you call the *Meshiach*! Eat...? Drink his blood? *Meshuggah*! Crazy . . . you're crazy! Gross . . . gross! Crazy and godless!"

Something like that. He'll lapse into his comfortable old American vernacular then try to get on track again. This Elihu will engage—fireworks and dynamite. He'll be so worked up he can't hide his New York origins. Anything can happen.

Elihu is the man hit by a car I told you about. I reached out a hand, but it didn't help him much, and the car was already around the corner out of sight.

It was Rosh haShanah. He had some injuries, and I spent the whole day in that emergency room. A robed and bearded rabbi came in to blow the shofar.

With that blast, he unknowingly commissioned me to sit with Elihu if he'd let me. I said I wanted to practice my Hebrew. He agreed.

There were weeks of healing. Then the man disappeared into his community, but other talks followed.

Now the anger keeps us at it. We both have to be right, to vanquish the other and win the duel. Truth is at stake. *Truth*!

"Bring it on!" I tell the night air as I roll up my sleeves. Have to unbutton the collar of this pink shirt, undo the necktie. You'd like it, Ruth. It's striped, orange and blue. Be done with it! It's too hot.

Now I have to stop everything and tell you . . . something you've experienced yourself, I'm sure. A delicious sweetness is taking over everything—memories, supper, studies, the heat of this small apartment, tomorrow's challenges. Some words, just a few—

The servant of God must not quarrel but be gentle to all.

And now I'm forgetting everything—what to eat, what to drink, whether there's still a bit of wine around here. I'm rummaging through the books on my makeshift blocks and boards bookshelf for another Bible. I sit down, flipping pages, looking for the chapter. This is it. ". . . be gentle to all, able to teach, patient, in humility correcting those who oppose you, if God perhaps should grant them repentance to know the truth . . .."

When you read this, please pray. The time and distance differences are nothing to God. What he'll think about is that we're in agreement. It's a promise.

It doesn't matter if I've already talked to Elihu. When I ask for help, God gives it. Time doesn't matter. To God it's right now.

"Dear Lord, my Beloved. Please don't let me make a mistake tomorrow. You know how I am . . . the heat of the moment. Please, give me the words to say."

I know you've prayed because now I'm content. Peace is spreading over me like a golden, evening cloud. It's better than food.

Your brother in Christ,

Ben

CHAPTER THREE
"The Jewel"

I LISTENED TO THIS "JEWEL" BUSINESS, THE WHOLE thing. The rabbi is like Quentin's Aunt Ev, that's Miz Evelyn Martelote, like I said. Moish, like Miss Evelyn, has begun to talk to himself, and he reads out loud when he studies. That's all the time. All Shirley and I have to do is listen. Piece of cake. I'm never wrong.

The rabbi tries to get comfortable. He adjusts the ottoman, stretches his legs, undoes the top button of his shirt. Nothing works. Beginnin' of arthritis maybe.

Dinner is over, Shirley's out. He has the evenin' to himself—just him and Quentin and suicide.

"Fictitious Quentin or the real thing," he's askin' himself. "Could you know? Rick said Quen is coping, but Quentin could always cope. Could've invented it. Poise is Quentin's natural habitat . . . like water for a fish."

Levy opens the envelope, takes out a handful of typed pages—the window on suicide at close range, a´ la Quentin. Might clarify the Miriam situation. Moish's thinkin' about Felix, thinkin' about suicide. Quentin knows about suicide. Knows all about loss.

Cover sheet—title, font, total number of pages.

"I wouldn't have cared if he refused," Moish mutters to himself. "But Quen wouldn't refuse. He'd blunt the corners of the *no*, but he couldn't prevent Rick's candid delivery. Rick the blunt, Quen the polite—the friends of my youth. Politeness is worse than a straight *no*."

He moves a leg from the ottoman. Feels better. Now, time to put it all aside for the more recent Quen.

"I'm reading this for Miriam's sake," he says to himself. "For all the Feinemanns. Laughing and depression? Maybe Quentin knows something."

Picture it, babe. Memories of Quentin are writin' themselves all over that page in his hand. The person fillin' his thoughts is a tall early teen, captain of junior high football the year of Moishe's bar mitzvah—almost tall as Rick. Beat 'im to the growth spurt. Who'd guess Rick would get taller in college!

More ways than up, Levy's thinkin', recallin' one bout or another Rick lived through before he met me. " . . . atheism, unrequited love, even mononucleosis. All the same thing maybe. Bed rest might fix it all, even the atheism," Moish is tellin' himself. "Maybe all an atheist needs is some bed rest. Company helps." I've heard 'im say it.

Rick landed me. Moish married Shirley. But Quentin? Well, that's another story . . . not something he wants to think about.

"The Jewel," Levy says out loud. He moves his legs to another position, starts to read. Curiosity's replaced the discomfort.

The Jewel

Quentin sank unsteadily into the booth and opened the menu, sure his eyes wouldn't focus.

I'm a derailed train, he thought. Three hundred bodies mashed into the coaches, scattered on the ground.

It hurts so much, something murmured. Someone was screaming. The train crash—yesterday? Dates on the calendar, wounded and twitching too?

He squinted, avoiding the rush of images sluicing past the window. Eyes, too tired to work.

A stack of English papers at home was waiting to be graded—another hundred next week. He weighed the degree of eye strain: which was greater, grief or grading papers? His eyeballs hurt, but they were focusing and the jewel was still there.

Maybe it's the points . . . a diamond grinding me, he thought. Better get as much protein into myself as I can. Hedge against exhaustion.

Diamond? Maybe sapphire. Sapphires are almost as hard. The blue would hurt more . . ..

No, the jewel box held the smoothest, most iridescent of pearls . . . only one, a pearl with value he couldn't guess.

The face of that jewel merchant, Kaleda, rose in his imagination: India . . . rubies for his inventory. Did he die in the train wreck? A jeweler's eye was an asset, but it wouldn't help in a train wreck.

No . . . no, he told himself, Kaleda is fiction. That derailed train happened.

The jewel was still there, but he couldn't clear the train wreck from his mind.

It's mine, mine. Mine, a pearl mine . . . at the bottom of the sea.

The thought of slowly surging ocean currents was soothing in the clatter and clink of breakfast conversations all around him. The arguing joy, the feel of that jewel still snugged into its velvet case somewhere inside him steadied the impressions sweeping crazily by. The velvet was *noir absolu*.

Snugged. That's what the plumber said. In spite of himself, Quentin smiled at the local expert, as fine and fitted, as old-fashioned as his language and the pipes he left behind. In his head, a map of the town grid, every line and bend. He knew where everything was, when it was put there, where replaced. And he could fix it.

"Dr. McJabe, you don't tighten down the faucet too hard. That'll cut the gasket. Just snug it down easy, don't you know."

My heart needs a gasket, Quentin thought. Then, chagrined by the poetic drift, he pulled his gaze back to the menu. No, I'm not a wreck yet, just some dangerously swaying cars.

A hint of nausea moved over the leaden heaviness of his inner landscape like a poisonous smog complicating the cloud cover above crowded city streets the day of an earthquake.

Maybe we're having two nights now, he thought.

The gray morning light was wrong. He managed to shave, change his shirt in that astronaut paradise of an everything-a-foot-from-your-elbow sleeper. The bed was all right, but it didn't give him sleep.

Face it, he told himself, that was more weeping than any healthy American male should indulge if he means to look at himself with respect, ever again—in any mirror.

Something was yelling, "Heads up!" He could feel his sensibilities bolting in disarray. Defeat was in the air. Time for food and coffee, protein and caffeine.

The dining car full of chatting people, unnerving. Talk, food, family, friends. They were idly perusing newspapers, idly looking out windows.

Does a thick lens magnify swollen eyes, he asked himself. Red as nightmares. I'll scare people to death.

He was glad to be alone. Too bad he had no book, but reading at the table wasn't allowed, even in a room full of strangers.

Nonsense . . . a vestigial verboten from day before yesterday. Polite? There was no purpose. No decorum. All that was passé, like life itself.

I'll eat and beat it, he told himself . . . eat and beat it, eatandbeatit, eatandbeatit, beatand eatit, eat and beatit. The rails took up the rhythm.

What if I start laughing, he thought, panic coming in with cymbals, clashes and clangs, to scatter the few valiant thoughts checking their flight to stand firm.

Grief laughter. That's all I need. Not just a red-eyed monster but a lunatic—that's me. As bad as . . . "a blue trip slip for an eight-cent fare. Punch, brothers! Punch with care! Punch in the presence of the passenjare . . .."

No. Get yourself together! Have to order, talk to that server coming. Force some steadiness. I have an excuse to . . . to act sane. Twain certainly won't help, Somerset Maugham either.

"Yes. Coffee please and this one . . .. Yes, the eggs with cheese, sausage and pancakes, extra butter. Could you bring a carafe of coffee? Thank you—yes, cream . . . not non-dairy creamer, please. I prefer cream."

The red carnation in its heavy vase was nice.

I nearly said, thankyouthankyouthankyou, he thought. Should be a law against clicking rails.

Why didn't I see it? All the signs were there . . .. Suicide rode into my life like an army with banners.

Quentin was fumbling for the pearl. He found it, the cool surface there, right there. An outspread, sweaty palm reached for the folded napkin to his left. Get whatever help he could.

Yes, yes . . . an army with banners. Yes, and the jewel, still there. Yesyesyes.

I will make it through this day, he told himself, surprised. It will happen, though not by my generalship or my own jewel merchant's savvy, certainly not by my vast supply of quotes from the literary canon!

Quentin smiled bleakly. There was always someone with a vaster supply. And the pearl had nothing to do with it, nothing at all. It belonged to the plumber, as well as to him. To the plumber, most books were a waste of time. Maybe he was right. King Solomon said something like that, and he knew just about everything, at first anyway.

The crummy buildings, cows, cars and dogs, fields, gas pumps and trees rushing past the window were creating aftershocks in his stomach. Better look somewhere else.

"Uh . . . may I join you."

It wasn't a question.

Quentin's thick glasses swung around, swiveling up to fix on black-framed Windsors three and a half feet above his head. A broad smile, white polka dots on a red tie.

Hang it, he thought, edging the pearl back into the velvet.

"Of course."

"Thanks. Crowded place today."

"Um."

The silence marching back and forth across the table marked off the two men from the clatter of the Amtrak dining car rushing thirty-five people in considerable comfort toward Washington, D.C. The waiter, bringing a menu for the guest he'd guided to this table, now stood waiting.

"Hot tea. Extra lemon. Some water. I brought salmon for the chef to do for me. He can cook it now. Potatoes with it . . . not fried. The chef knows. Put extra parsley on the plate."

Quentin drank his coffee.

Has to be Emory, he told himself, struggling to rein in the annoyance. He was losing the war with pain. The troops wouldn't hold their position in a stranger's trivializing gaze.

I have to be civil, he told himself. Can't have him quizzing me because he knows something's wrong. What if he's a psychiatrist!

A wacky picture plays in his imagination: the frightened breakfast crowd backing toward the doors, waiters scurrying around to create a couch from two booths as his breakfast companion pulls out a pad, draws up a suitcase to sit on, and adjusts his glasses.

Dr. Freud and the Fried Onion Rings . . . no, the Fried Green Onions. Not tomatoes. They've already been used. Let's see—Freud, Freight, and Fried Green Onions. Might work as a title—freight for baggage . . . that's good. I'll have to think about that one. Could be a story there.

"You have contacts in the kitchen," Quentin offered, groping for casual.

"I just have to watch what I eat," the stranger said. "Had a heart attack last year. Amtrak can be cooperative if you ask ahead—and bring what you want."

Another silence while Emory looks out the window. I've come up with a civil gesture. Now this unwanted guest at my table can do his share.

Guest. The word hangs in the air.

Yes, this man is my guest in a way, a fellow traveler. Maybe he's going to a funeral . . . probably not in that red tie. Going to his own funeral he thinks and he certainly will eventually. Obviously worried about dying. He's had the chef make special food!

The perception walked across his consciousness as if in black crepe. Quentin took off his glasses and rubbed his eyes.

Rubbed eyes look red . . . good smoke screen.

When he put his glasses on again, the person across from him seemed different—a man who was going to die. Maybe soon. Did he have a jewel in a velvet case, something to take with him . . . or just a velvet case to be buried in?

My son will be buried . . ..

No! Can't go there. Lord, show me who this guest is. He's your guest, like me. Give me something besides an emotional storm . . .. Help me welcome him.

Bent on control, Quentin remembered his natural scowl, lips, a natural downturn. I look bleak even if I feel friendly, he told himself. Consciously create a difference . . . now. There's a guest at my table.

The man turned from the window and looked directly at him.

"Joel Schiffman. Danville."

A hand across the table. The voice was firm and confident.

Had plenty of sleep last night, Quentin thought as he took the offered hand. Ready to greet the day. But he knows he has a limited number, and he's making the most of each one.

"Quentin McJabe."

"MENSA?" Schiffman said.

One more time Quentin told himself grimly: Quit the Phi Beta Kappa key, your father's gold watch chain. Bad form, pompous and vain. Lord, you're not finished with me yet!

"No." Quentin managed with a smile. "I just got into studying."

"Can keep the black dog from the door," said Schiffman, shrugging his shoulders.

"And black marks off probation lists."

"Phi Bet's don't worry about probation lists," Schiffman said.

"I did worry about grades at one time."

"But not after a while . . . which is interesting," Schiffman said.

"You're academic?" Quentin was attempting without success to fire a spark of interest somewhere in his numbed senses.

"English. Military academy near Danville—The Grove."

"Pretty place. I was there for some special drills in the late '80s."

"Before I arrived. What do you do besides swing around that Phi Beta Kappa key," Schiffman asked, smiling so ingenuously Quentin couldn't take offense.

The waiter was offering hot tea, more coffee. For a few minutes the two men adjusted glasses, cups, napkins.

"You were at The Grove," Schiffman said, pouring tea from the small Amtrak pot, squeezing in some lemon.

"I went with a friend. His son—neighbors, you know—his son was receiving an honor. Went up for a weekend."

"Hampton's a nice little place. I like a bigger town myself. Danville has what you want

. . . isn't that metropolitan yet. Not too much traffic."

Quentin was casting about for what to do with this conversation. Something more substantial . . . .

More personal? I have to talk to him. Might as well make it count.

The challenge, a kind of relief. It felt good to dodge out from the black cloud of misery that, beginning yesterday, blocked everything from view. Coffee helped.

Quentin remembered the man's question, "What do you do . . .?" He hadn't answered. The horrors of the last twenty-four hours were backing off a little as curiosity rose. Who was the man across from him?

Volunteer some information? Safer if I choose the details, he told himself. I don't want a barrage of personal questions.

"I teach English too . . . University of South Carolina. Have to say, I prefer small towns to cities, even medium-sized."

"Well, well. We're in the same secret society."

"English Departments actually do paint the job with that brush these days."

"You bet. Only it isn't just 'these days.' I can hardly remember the so-called New Criticism. In fact, when I got baptized into it—even then, it was a stream out of the forest primeval!"

"You studied where?"

"Emory. Brooks and Warren BA, MA; Duke for the doctorate."

"So you got the new wave right from the horse's mouth. Since we're off duty, I won't clean up the metaphors."

"Be my guest. Yes. Right from the horse's mouth . . . yes, yes, yes, in fact."

Quentin let the beginnings of a smile crack the mask of his face. He recognized the Derrida mantra. "I don't think I've ever told anyone this, but I'll confess—"

Schiffman laughed out loud. "You're making me your Father Confessor (hear the caps) . . . before breakfast?" He poured tea into his cup.

"This is it: Mea culpa," Quentin said. "I never got through *Ulysses*, even in graduate school."

Schiffman shrugged. "Don't think it really matters. Deconstruction hit our profession in more places than Joyce research."

"True enough."

"Some gains in the whole thing though. All that managerial truth stuff, to borrow your word. All but obsolete in the '60s, but it took Derrida, sweating out those weeks in the Harvard library, to spotlight the words themselves.

The last vestige of the Enlightenment got a gentle death, thanks to him."

"What did you make of Allan Bloom's critique?"

"Oh, he's just sore because he and his precious old literary canon got left behind. Probably planning to retire and write a meta-narrative."

Quentin laughed in spite of himself. The guest at his table was engaging. The Grove's loss if he had another heart attack, if . . . he died. Anybody could . . ..

Anybody could die.

Space. He needed space and there was nowhere to go. The aisle was crowded with diners; here and there servers in black balanced trays of steaming food, hot drinks. Sit right here, the only option.

Lord, it's your call. This wasn't my idea!

A server approached with food. It looked like theirs. Standing next to the table, he presented the plates—offering them as if for approval. The salmon, potatoes and parsley—perfect heart food. His sausage, cheese eggs, pancakes—the extra butter, the real cream—all the protein he should need after a sleepless night.

Protein isn't everything, he told himself, but it might help the exhaustion. Picking up a fork, he decided not to bow his head and thank God for the food.

Schiffman turned down the salt. He generously peppered the salmon, squeezed on the lemon. The food smelled good; Quentin's spirits were lifting. He would keep up the conversation. Food and talk, better companions than the searing grief.

"No meta-narratives? That's the current myth, actually. Better still, the current Bultmannian myth."

"Bultmannian?"

"Bultmann—yes, when Bultmann first cut a broad swathe across meta-narratives, he demythologized the Bible first, Albert Schweitzer right after him, but—"

"Oh. You're talking about all that 'historical Jesus' stuff. Actually, from what I've read, the Jesus Seminar is interesting. We're finally getting to the truth of the whole hoax—or, in case you're a Christian, the whole self-hoaxed first century, which isn't much better, now that I think of it. The denials and fabrications of those people! Worse than Washington—Clinton's Washington, anyway. What a mess."

"I guess you mean Bill." Quentin turned to signal for more coffee.

"The less said about Clinton the better—both of them."

"Yes, I am a Christian. The real Bultmannian myth turns out to be the naïve view that the Bible can be deconstructed. The Higher Critics gave impetus to that; others have kept it up . . . for a couple of centuries. The Bible always comes back. But wait a minute. I thought you were just saying last rites over objective truth. The Jesus Seminar's 'truth'—is it just truth for them?"

"Truth for them? Interesting. No. I think they're onto something. To deconstruct things further," Schiffman grinned. "Let's say—though I don't really believe in meta-narratives, definitely not the Bible—let's say that their version of the Jesus story makes the most sense: local hysteria, emotional reports of women, disciples trying to save face, never mind the overlays, the retellings for two thousand years.

"My parents were Jewish, but they died when I was a baby. I grew up Catholic. I know how stories can proliferate—Mary sightings, visions, statues that weep. I gave it up long ago. Protestants are no better! All those rumors that brought us the witch burnings! Give me a good, practicing Roman Catholic any day for a flat-earth Calvinistic fundamentalist!"

"Flat is a good place for two feet," Quentin said.

The rabbi puts down the manuscript and stands up, walks around his study. ". . . good place for two feet," he's thinkin'. The firmness of the floor feels good.

"The story's all right, but it won't sell if that's Quen's idea," he says to himself. "Has to be writing therapy. Academic types talk about Lit., but don't write it. The Jewish fellow in that red necktie's authentic enough. Schiffman . . . a real person? Maybe just fiction. Wonder if Quentin remembers my red tie. How long since I've seen him? No. I never wore that tie when he was around. The polka dots on that Emory fellow, original. Fits the story well enough.

"Rick has a point about some of the details here—that shock of suicide for Quentin, his efforts to shift gears when the stranger joins him, his torn up emotions. What about the Quentin I'll see tomorrow? Did this really happen to him?"

Deconstruction Theory It's a curious approach, Levy's thinkin'. He knows a little bit about everything. Now he's reachin' for a page he dropped on the floor. "Derrida . . . a Mediterranean Jew, who agreed with the Palestinians. Odd," he says.

He sits down and starts readin' again.

> ". . . any day for a flat-earth Calvinistic fundamentalist!"
>
> "Flat is a good place for two feet," Quentin said.
>
> "You're not . . .."
>
> Quentin laughed. "Well, I'm an Episcopalian. Not often accused of fundamentalism. Thanks for the compliment, even if I'm misreading the text you've put on the table."
>
> "Holy smoke. I think you're serious."
>
> "I'm quite content with the biblical meta-narrative. It's a better read than *Beowulf*."
>
> "Oh, you can have *Beowulf*. Who wants to learn Anglo-Saxon. More proof of our Teutonic

connections. There's a meta-narrative factory for you! Besides, if language is only signifieds and signifiers anyway, why lose sleep hassling a language deader than Latin?

"What I'm into is our new course: *Lit and Technology*. We use *Star Wars*. The cadets love it. That Force business has some heavy truth—truth-for-everybody, if you will. It's not exactly new, but Shaw's or Bergson's idea of an 'Emergent Evolution'—you know, the 'striving of the Life Force'—makes pretty good sense to me."

"So, since you're into *Star Wars*, would you classify yourself as a Richard Rorty deconstructionist? He seems more comfortable with technology than Derrida and Caputo, at least with NATO's use of it."

"Well, of course it's all Stanley Fish at Duke. But yes, I don't see how an American riding on a comfortable modern train, headed for an even more comfortable rental, up-to-the-minute laptop in the brief case, mobile phone, etc. etc. . . . I don't see how people like us can knock technology with any kind of integrity. But I'm forgetting. Fundamentalists don't believe in technology."

Quentin smiled, the intellectual give and take was a surprising relief. The impulse to communicate with this man was growing and he welcomed it.

"As a deconstructionist, what's the basis of your integrity," he offered pleasantly.

"Integrity's just a word," Schiffman said. "It doesn't even have the same sound as soon as you get to another linguistic environment. Integrity is what a community agrees it is. Our world is technological; technology gives us what we want. I admit it. It's a big part of my 'truth.' I'll exchange it for church any day, never mind rosaries, candles, dissolving meta-narratives—no offense, of course."

This conversation could rock along for hours, hypnotic as the train, Quentin thought. He watched his companion eat, amazed that a passenger-hungry Amtrak let the chef make a custom breakfast—salmon and parsley potatoes, at the busiest hour. Schiffman clearly meant to stretch out his life. Quentin decided to turn up the heat. He knew how.

"I guess you follow the advances in cardiac technology . . . stay up on the latest."

"Well, I'm not thinking about by-pass yet. Just a mild heart attack. The doctor says that I can do a lot by diet and exercise. Even diabetics can sometimes reverse things with diet. It's something I watch—a lot, in fact. When the diet-exercise angle stops working, I'll rely on technology. Breakthroughs will come. I figure on many more years, ever-increasing numbers of English papers to grade. . . and more chances to shun the meta-narratives."

Quentin chuckled, "To get back to your dissolving meta-narratives—an interesting expression, by the way. I find this arresting . . . and maybe you didn't know: The Bible is always on the bestseller list. They don't advertise the fact; could blunt the edgy, hot-news feel—the new thing this week and all that. You can imagine. Having it there all the time, week after week, wouldn't be news. Change the effect. But whatever . . . it's the number one bestseller of all time."

"But who reads it? Surely not your average brainiac who sports a Phi Beta Kappa key for jewelry!"

"Nonsense. The greatest thinkers of the Western world have taken the Bible as plain text. It's only in recent times its authority has been widely questioned.

"Western science, Western civilization, technology—it all emerged from a conviction that the universe was created by a larger intelligence, one that gave us mental resources close enough to the designer's to learn how it works. Jacques Derrida got into Saint Augustine, as you know. He's a flat-Earth fundamentalist if ever there was one."

"Well, I'll give you that. But Derrida reads Augustine with a *difference*."

Quentin laughed. The French pronunciation was straight from Paris, maybe North Africa.

Schiffman went on, "Are you modern or pre-modern . . . certainly not postmodern! I can't read Christians. Half the time they talk like Charlemagne's chaplain, the other half, like Isaac Newton's apprentice. Where do you come down? You a rationalist?"

"Well, faith—Derrida calls himself a man of faith—faith isn't exactly Cartesian. But the Bible matches what I know of myself and what I see in the actions and reactions of people around me. History? The Bible was there first. Example: Not any time soon will you find a more convincing 'Exhibit A, Passing the Buck,' than the Clinton White House. When Hillary rationalizes Bill's philandering ('It's from child abuse at four'), like Eve, she's making the *not-responsible* case straight out of Genesis 3."

"So that makes you . . . what, a pre-modern?"

"Well, you have to have faith even to get through the day . . . to get on a train, for instance. I guess you heard about that crash in India—three hundred people killed, two trains colliding head-on.

"To have biblical faith is to go on taking risks because you have a firm basis for doing so. People act the way the Bible describes them—whatever the century. It describes me to myself. There's a hometown quality to the supernatural, as the Bible describes it."

Schiffman guffawed. "Hometown supernatural . . .. Now I've heard everything. What do you mean by that? Not Mary sightings, surely. What's your firm basis?"

Quentin was warming to his topic.

"It's just that biblical supernatural is recognizable. It isn't so different from the way things work out in daily experience. I had a friend—a minister, fellow from Scotland. He was a Nazi prisoner, Second World War. One day a verse from a psalm came to mind. He knew God was telling him to escape."

The waiter had returned with checks to sign. Quentin stopped the story to take out his pen. Breakfast done, the two men stood to leave the dining car, each in a different direction. Schiffman watched him closely, looking for more, it seemed.

"These sleepers are pretty tight, but you're welcome to join me. My compartment actually has two seats."

"They sure don't waste space around here!" Schiffmann said, laughing. "But yes, I think I will. I have a few more hours on this train. Might as well have company. Thank you."

They moved beyond the door, through the swaying corridors. At Quentin's number, they found the sleeper made up, in order: two close, but comfortable seats, two big windows.

Quentin motioned his guest to sit.

After a few minutes, Schiffman said, "So, what about your friend in the Nazi prison camp?"

"He escaped. It was that simple. The psalm was inspiration. Details worked out along the lines of what you might expect from the verse he noticed."

"What was it?"

Quentin reached into a jacket pocket and pulled out a battered Bible in faded maroon leather. He began Psalm 71 at verse three.

"Be thou to me a rock of habitation to which I may continually come. Thou hast given commandment to save me. For thou art my rock and my fortress."

He closed the book.

"So?"

"He and a friend escaped, somehow reached Gibraltar, which was British. Still is."

"A good story. I've heard such stories from World War II, but I never knew anyone who . . . experienced something like that."

"Well, experience isn't the only test. It's the correspondence, if you will, between the Bible and human experience—my own and what I see and hear in the lives of other people. It wasn't an abstract ideal, some idea about truth my friend had as basis for his risk-taking. He took the risk, trusting a human record—well, human and more than human—a testimony that was recognizable to him. The Bible's full of deliverance, from all kinds of enemies. What he needed was deliverance!"

Schiffman sat looking at Quentin. After a while he spoke.

"It seems to me, though, from what I hear, people I talk to and the stuff they say, you know, the exclusivity of it—it's very off-putting. That's the problem with meta-narratives. They belong to a people, and they make use of the meta-narrative to . . . totalize violence, if you will."

He paused then continued, "Since we're talking Derrida this morning. You know as much about the Crusades, the Inquisition, as I do . . . more, I'm sure, if my hunch is right and you're a medievalist. I mean, who else talks about *Beowulf* at breakfast? Even if you're not, you know about the Middle Ages . . . all those good church people who spent their wretched, petty lives doing good deeds in order to salve their consciences, pay the church, escape purgatory, reach the pearly gates. How different are fundamentalists—or to be more polite—Bible-believers? In fact, I'll coin a new term: Neo-medievals. Stress on the '-evals.'"

The troops were rallying . . . good breakfast, good fight. In spite of himself, Quentin felt better.

"Okay, the faulty meta-narrative first. What people, what culture can you credit with the Bible? Is it Mesopotamian or Egyptian, Canaanite or Davidic monarchist or a little Samarito-Assyrian, some lapsed Judean with Judeo-Babylonian thrown in? Or later was it the product of Hellenized elite Hebrew Christians or kosher (if unsophisticated) Galilean fishermen mixed in with some very non-kosher, Roman-sympathizing tax collectors? Or what about this: the not-easily definable work of a rabbinical-Pharisaic-Roman-Tarsusite-Gamaliel-trained, sometimes Gnostic-sounding, bondservant of Christ, who thought of himself as a 'Hebrew of the Hebrews' and said, 'All things are lawful'? I mean, whose culture is it?

"And what about now? Isn't it odd that the Bible appeals to Americans and Sudanese, Israelis (yes, Israelis . . . Israel has its Christians—Messianic Jews, I mean)? What about the Norwegians, the Chinese, Algerians? The rich and poor, persecuted and—"

"Fine. You can stop right there. Yeah, what *about* those persecuted people? How does your meta-narrative deal with that? Your God is supposed to be good, isn't he? Some of us do

good, go to church or mass or synagogue, but
. . . well, the rest of us, we're left to
muddle through!

"One woman, a psychologist I was reading
a few weeks ago, claimed that people are so
damaged from childhood they wouldn't understand
God if he called 'em on the phone. They aren't
thinking straight. A lot of hurting people out
there! And not just that train wreck in India.
Besides, what about the ones who never heard
of the Bible or Jesus or anything a church
peddles? What *about* all the suffering in the
world? Jesus Christ!"

No more, Levy thinks. He puts down the manuscript and stands up. The story's too heavy. He can't read it. Who needs reminders of suicide and suffering? But the conversation with Miriam still bothers him and he remembers something odd.

"You are truly our rabbenu," she said.

That Hebrew mistake brings up the bat mitzvah controversy. Not a cudgel he was ready to pick up in seminary.

Levy mulls over the changes. Feminists made their point, even with him; in fact, he's guided two bat mitzvah girls in the last year. "Impossible for Miriam Feinemann's generation," he mutters. "The grammatical goofiness of 'our rabbenu' wouldn't come from a mouth properly schooled in Hebrew—enough for a bat mitzvah, anyway. 'Our rabbenu' is like 'seraphims' or 'cherubims', but usually people who make those mistakes aren't supposed to know any Hebrew. You have to forgive 'em."

He's started thinkin' out loud again.

"I shouldn't let Mrs. Feinmann get to me this way," he tells himself. Meditating crankily on the verbal faux pas is a relief, a way to deal with that ghost of anxiety wrappin' itself around him like an incubus. What if . . .?

He looks at the phone across the room and feels like messin' with it.

Break it, he tells himself. "Telephones . . . ugh! Cell phones are the worst. You can't get away from 'em.

"That call was like some exotic crustacean, brought in steaming. It coaxed me to crack the shell and pop the dreadful tidbits into my mouth. What a surge of insufficiency!

"'Goodbye, Mrs. Feinemann' . . . satisfying, that hasty hang-up." Levy feels his fingers release the phone and drop it in the stand. I can see 'im movin' his hands around.

"Attack Miriam's problem like a lobster," he tells himself. "Crack the shell then pick the thing apart bit by bit, throw most of it away."

A sharper realism and a deeper compassion say *no*. Like I said, Moish is a good man.

"No, what it needs is patience and plain, homegrown stubbornness. Seminaries don't cover things like this. You learn it on the job. She meant to tell me something then didn't. Then she thanked me! Absurd conversation.

"The Feinemanns . . . married fifty-three years, a solid marriage. The best it seems, her sudden decline hard to explain. Weeks with doctors, grim moods, questions, dark frustration. Felix suggested that trip to Israel, said they could visit Rivka, see the Land. Then he waked from a nap to his wife's efforts at squeezing herself from an open window of that Dead Sea resort. Ninth floor.

"The Land is calling me, Felix . . . leave me alone!"

Levy knows the story by heart. Everybody does. Felix is puzzled and afraid. What's happening to his wife? They took 'er from the window and hurried off to a doctor. Then the suicide watch began. A psychiatrist in Columbia is seeing her now, the best Felix can find. He takes the suicide threats seriously. Can't mess around.

"*We* can't mess around," the rabbi tells himself.

"Female hysteria? The womb—an unknown, a mystery," he mutters, imagining a long line of puzzled males scratching their heads and silently mouthing, 'Women!'

Ha ha!

"I'm overreacting," he tells himself. "But how can anybody talk about suicide one week and chuckle in your ear the next? Antidepressant maybe. They're adjusting the medications. Psychotropics have to work their way through the system. Maybe that's the problem. Or a different med. How in the world did she talk Harry into changing 'em?"

The Hebrew Bible is open on the desk in front of him, ribbon place marker stretches out from the pages like a little road beckoning 'im. One step, two. The rabbi moves forward then stops at another puzzle—that *Stuttgartensia*. What to say to Rick?

"I have to thank him," he tells himself. "Such beautiful script. The bottom of every page has notes on the codices, not Christian commentary—should be harmless enough unless you're somebody like Rick. They'll be a challenge for a Christian fundamentalist.

"That's him," Levy mutters. "But he's smart . . . just distances himself from all things intellectual."

The text of the open Hebrew Bible's easy to read, the letters crisp—every serif. All those jots and tittles . . . .. Yes, babe, I know about all that. Rick's told me, and so did my dad before he died. That was in th' Emmanuel College days. I miss 'im a lot.

"Jesus said that, didn't he?" Moish says. "Jots and tittles."

Levy knows the words; he doesn't need Ricky to tell him the name 'Jesus' is Aramaic, run through Greek-Latin-English-transliteration-translation channels. He congratulates himself on knowing a few things about Jesus, but he won't say ישוע like Shirley. He stops at educated and tolerant, thank you very much. *Yeshua* brings the whole thing up close and personal. For Israelis, Yeshua's just another startling young rabbi with a followin'. Far in the past and wrong-headed maybe, but he was a *sabra*. The name *Yeshua* doesn't bother 'em.

"The jots and tittles," he goes on mutterin'. "Perfectly clear in this Bible. The type is right for hours of reading, better than a computer screen. Won't need to lean over when my eyes are tired. Might even improve Isaiah."

The rabbi rubs the crease between his eyes with two long fingers.

"People say I look severe," he tells himself. "What can I do about that? You play the cards you're dealt! When my face is relaxed, I look threatening. When I concentrate, I scowl. Time for new glasses maybe."

Tomorrow at the Coffee Shoppe he'll thank Rick for the Bible. Right now he's gotta finish Quen's piece. The author'll expect some kind of comment.

Moish sits in his chair and picks up the pages. Looking for his place, he rubs the creases in his forehead and stretches both legs across the ottoman. He adjusts his glasses and glances at the paragraphs. Let's see . . . Schiffmann was talking. Here.

> ". . . What *about* all the suffering in the world? Jesus Christ!"
>
> Quentin closed his eyes. Waves of sorrow washed over a consciousness taken by surprise, a tsunami. Aaron's voice came at him like a sheet rending in a gale: "Quentin, what's it all about? What's life for? Why do I have to live this way?"
>
> Quentin looked at Schiffman. His chance companion was no longer an intruder. They'd traveled and talked all morning; he was invested. The man didn't know he'd brought with him a measure of relief and Quentin was grateful. If he could, he would point this man away from his fruitless hope, all those health obsessions and academic fads.
>
> Quentin gripped the pearl. The jewel was round and smooth, the value of it beyond estimation.

> "I'm glad you brought up that name. Jesus
> Christ is the answer to every part of the
> question you just asked."

Moish puts down the manuscript. "Here comes the onslaught," he says to himself. "Rick warned me. I really can't blame him. This is Quentin's writing and it's not for me. Odd, the confidence of Christians—all stripes, not just the Baptists. They're in love with death, not life—unlike us. They're guilt-ridden, compulsively set on some sort of pie-in-the-sky-by-and-by substitute for actual engagement with this life! It's all about there, not here. But I can't convince Rick. Worse, he's persistent as well as confident.

"Quentin has lost his son. He's the father of a suicide. *HaShem* . . . don't let this happen to Felix. Don't let it happen to Miriam."

He looks at the page.

> ". . . Jesus Christ is the answer to every
> part of the question you just asked." Quentin
> stopped, took a deep breath, and added, "My
> own, as well."

So—Quentin actually has questions, Levy thinks. Well, I guess he does. At this point, his son has just committed suicide! And Quen's not Rick.

He drops his glasses on the floor, rubs his eyes, and goes on with the manuscript, wondering where the story's headed. Shirley says his new readin' glasses are better. He fishes the new ones from a pocket, puts 'em on and looks at the pages.

"Let's see . . . the compartment. They're crammed into that little space, Quentin's had a rush of grief, but he's still talking to this fellow."

Levy finds the place and goes on readin', quickly gettin' back into that emotional moment he thrust aside. The grief of an old friend isn't easy to dodge, even after years. "Years and years," he mutters to himself.

The two men sat silently for several minutes, one shifting a little in his seat, the other holding his gaze. Schiffman caught the emotion, as evident now as if another person, a dangerous person, had just entered the space. Quentin was searching for words, control coming within reach.

I will engage this guest. Have to address his questions.

When he spoke, his voice was steady.

"It's essential to factor in wrongdoing . . . yes, *and* suffering. The negatives are real—your own case, for example. You're dealing with the givens, taking the negatives straight, following your doctor's plan . . . enjoying it, I think. I admit I've wondered what it took to get Amtrak to fix that custom breakfast!"

Schiffman smiled, eyes never moving from Quentin's face. "Not easy. I know some people; so does my doctor . . . and too, I covered the costs—a lot more than overhead! Go on."

The silence held for a minute and Quentin continued.

"All right. Wrongdoing is a negative; you have to take it straight, looked at full on, no denials. Christianity isn't just good people going to church, lining up for tickets into heaven. The Bible is clear: not one unaltered human being will stand before God, the God who is holy . . . pure, and powerful.

"But you're right to bring up Jesus. Whatever people know about him, most remember this: he was radically loving and he had power. The record says he lived an irreproachable life—and died for no demonstrable reason beyond jealousy, ambition of the leaders, and fear of Rome." He paused.

Am I preaching, he asked himself. This man is as well informed, as soaked in the secular, as anyone I know. What's he thinking?

"So, who got deconstructed—the power structures or him? By all I can tell, he got the worst of the deal. Are you suggesting that we continue to deconstruct the Jews who crucified him?"

Moishe takes his feet off the ottoman, sits up straight, turns back the cuffs of his white shirt, and picks up another page.

"Always comes down to a castigation of the Jews," he tells himself. "I'll hurry through the rest of this stuff. Quentin's not talking about suicide here." He's ready to be done, but he finds the place and reads some more.

"No, it wasn't just the Jews. The Romans were there. And so was everybody. The universal relevance of the cross is a foundation stone of Christianity, but it took a widely known, first-century genius, Saul of Tarsus, to figure it all out.

"Jesus said, 'The Father and I are one.' This Saul, the Pharisee and Bible scholar—now

Paul the disciple, but Bible scholar still—it took this Paul to see that if Jesus really was one with the God of Israel, he couldn't be bound by time. He had to be that 'one whose coming was from of old.' He acted in a timeless dimension; his cross fits every case.

"It wasn't just first-century scholars and friends of Jesus who validated all this. That odd and aristocratic wild man, John the Baptist—he hardly knew Jesus, though he was related to him—he called him the Lamb of God, who takes away the sin of the world. Saul knew this . . . everybody in Jerusalem knew it. John was the son of an important priest, who offered incense in the temple! What his wild son declared out there in that God-forsaken Judean wilderness people came miles to hear. They came and they listened.

"John prepared the people for Jesus' ministry. Two of his first disciples were ready-made, as it were—disciples of John before they followed Jesus. They remembered what John said: 'This is the Lamb of God, the one who takes away the sins of the world.'

"Then Saul or Paul spent years poring over the Scriptures, the Hebrew Bible he knew well, and he saw that what the Bible said corresponded to the life of the one John described. The Man who flattened him on that Damascus road was the man on the cross, that perfect man John called 'the Lamb of God.' It meant something to him, to Saul or Paul, because he knew just about everything there was to know about the ancient sacrifice system—the law, the Passover, the sacrificed lamb.

"It made sense to him as it probably wouldn't have to another living soul at the time. He'd studied it all for years. The connection with Jesus was the last piece of the puzzle, as it were.

"After the Damascus Road and after he studied the new picture for years—*years* by himself in some desert—he saw that when Jesus confronted and took him, he entered a different kingdom. He was *apprehended*, and he had dual citizenship—the Roman citizenship overlaying his impeccable heritage as an Israelite, a Pharisee and student of Gamaliel; but also now, he was a son of the heavenly kingdom. He was the subject of a monarch, who wasn't Caesar, because a lamb—the eternal Lamb of God—was sacrificed for him . . . for Paul himself, for Paul the individual. Now the God of Abraham, Isaac, and Jacob accepted him, though he couldn't keep the law, not perfectly, as God required. The Lamb had taken him up, made him righteous and clean. He was more than a subject; he was a child of the King.

"No one but a hairsplitting, punctilious . . . law-troubled and guilt-obsessed Pharisee like Paul could have understood it so well. It was easy to do wrong! He knew what the Law said about wrongdoing. From what he could see—and that was very clearly—it all pertained to him. The Messiah of Israel had come, and he brought a better deliverance than the deliverance from Egypt. Because he came from God *as God*, his act mattered in every generation."

Quentin stopped. Time to regroup, but he could see that Schiffman was listening. He had to go on.

"'Every generation'—the psalms are full of the phrase. What God does is relevant to every generation. Paul understood it as nobody else could, and he explained, for his time and everyone coming after, what the life and death and resurrection of Jesus means."

"I find him convincing," Quentin said, lowering his voice, adding an edge that could be taken for steely. He hoped not, but grief was very near. He could give himself no quarter.

"Well. You certainly sound convinced. I can tell you like teaching. Funny though . . . even in this little closed-in space, you haven't scared me yet. Maybe I'll revise my opinion of flat-Earth fundamentalists.

"But I can't quite get it together: you talk like a rationalist. This Paul was a scholar, you say. St. Paul is all I remember. Somebody churches are named for, etc. etc. But you say it's because of a connection . . . the Bible, us."

"Yes, it's the correspondence. Christians aren't idealists and we aren't blind. The biblical record is realistic; it fits human experience. It also gently encourages us to believe, invites us to take a little taste . . . to see that God is good.

"There's a certain peace, as well. It helps to know . . . to have the habit of peace. We know our sins are forgiven. Not because the holy God suddenly turned nice old forgetful grandfather, a senile, nice old gentleman. No. It's because the Lamb's blood was as acceptable—light years more acceptable—than all those temple sacrifices God ordered in the first place to prepare the world for what He would to do through His Son. If it's enough for God, it has to be enough for me. He shows me every day He's satisfied with the sacrifice, even in my case. I just have to remember."

"I guess the cross meant a lot of suffering," Schiffman said quietly. "The Catholic school I went to—well, some of the teachers . . . were very clear about that."

"They were right. And when you look at it straight on, not denying anything, you know God suffered that day—the Father as well as the Son. The Bible says it somehow happened through the Holy Spirit. So God knows what it is to suffer. And of course, the suffering wasn't for nothing. It lets me sleep at night, though the exception . . . well, it proves the rule.

"Sleep in this world is all the disconnect I'll ever know. I won't go to sleep never to wake up . . . or worse. No, I'll wake up with God because he made a way in his own human body for that to happen. He carried his body right across the line of death and walked back out of where it took him with Death left defeated behind. That's a rock as real as the one my Scottish friend escaped to!"

Weariness was overtaking him. Quentin couldn't suppress a yawn. Schiffman looked at his watch and stood.

"Speaking of sleep . . . I meant to have a nap after breakfast. It's almost ten. We'll be in D.C. around eleven-thirty. Guess I'd better see what I have to do before I get off this train. Headed for D. C. too?"

"Yes, I am."

"I'm seeing my godson graduate from college. Not in English. Magna cum laude in microbiology. All the grad schools wanted him. I guess it's better for him than Shakespeare . . . make more money. The Bard never had a chance once Joe discovered the biology lab. You're going to a . . .?"

"There was a death—"

"Oh, I'm sorry to hear that. Someone close? Maybe I shouldn't ask."

Schiffman waited. Quentin's eyes were fixed on the window.

"My . . . son. I learned about the suicide . . . yesterday."

Quentin spoke to himself more than to his companion. Now he turned and faced him. For a moment, the only sound was the clatter of the rails as the two men stared at each other. Schiffman broke the silence, his voice barely above a whisper.

"I'm terribly sorry. I've been . . . well, something of an intrusion today. You've treated me like a guest. I'm sorry."

"No, I think we're here at the pleasure of another Host."

"How . . . how can you deal with this, this—" Schiffman's voice was a breath trailing to nothing.

Quentin looked down. He was drawing on the resources of another; he had none of his own. Tears . . . but somehow his voice was holding. He looked at Schiffman. He'd opened the door of the compartment and was standing, one foot just outside in the swaying corridor of the train.

Quentin stood. As he spoke, his voice gained resonance. "I'm not sure how to describe it— the life of the Lord, the life He's given us as a gift . . .. There's one of Derrida's words again." He paused.

"The truth is, the eternal gift . . . we it take with us. If Jesus Christ . . . if the Spirit of Israel's Messiah comes to live in a person, that mortal human being has His life. We don't go empty-handed; we don't live empty lives. We have that life. It's a kind of treasure . . . like a jewel. And all anybody has to do is ask for it. Forgiveness comes and a different life comes with it. That's all . . . you just ask."

Quentin's glasses had fallen to the floor. He didn't remember taking them off. Now he bent to retrieve them. His guest was leaving.

Schiffman was silent, staring. Several seconds elapsed before he said, "Your son then . . .."

"No, not my son."

Light and shadows swept the tiny space as the two men braced themselves to match the jolts and bends of the track. The train was traveling at speed, and the countryside swept by in a blur. Neither spoke. A long blast of the whistle signaled a station and broke the pause. Quentin spoke, remembering the one thing left to be said.

"Thank you for the opportunity to tell myself one more time my sins are forgiven."

```
The train lurched and Schiffman steadied
himself. They were silent, as if a chasm had
opened between them. Then he was gone. A few
steps away, he paused and spoke, his words
just above the clatter of the rails.
    "Thank you."
    Quentin sank into his seat, knowing the
porter would wake him. Sleep came easily.
```

Moshe drops the last sheet on the floor, leans back in his chair. His eyes are tired; he's tired. Emotions are draining.

"Maybe strong emotions could be prodded out and sold in a weight-loss program," he mutters. "The sign reads, Visit Our Salon. Scaring Off Weight Our Specialty. Pound a Week. Guaranteed."

Silly thought. Levy closes his eyes. The leather chair's comfortable. Minutes pass before a ringing phone jars him awake. He rubs his eyes, stands up, and goes to answer it.

"Levy."

"Rabbi? Do you . . . you do have time to talk?"

"Rivka . . . ."

He suppresses a yawn. *The voice* dithers his thinkin'. Capturin' Rivka's content isn't easy. The music of it takes over. Everything else out there's irrelevant.

"Your mother . . . is something—?"

"Strange, and not herself. She's not herself."

"Not . . . herself?"

"She's following Felix all around the house."

"Something wrong with that?"

"My mother's never done a thing like that. She doesn't ever follow dad around."

"How's he feeling about it?"

"Loving every minute, it would seem."

". . . loving it?"

"He isn't staying at the store so much, and . . . well, he's kind of laughing to himself."

"And you're concerned about that."

"It's just not like them . . . not like them at all."

The rabbi catches the soft, breathy syllables and gropes for an open-ended question. Keep her talkin'.

Rivka came back from Jerusalem, and I quit dreading the phone, he's thinkin'. When she called, *the voice* curled into my ear, could have been the first time. Doesn't talk like Felix . . . or Miriam!

I mean! Rivk's somethin' else.

Tantalizing vistas are spreading out in front of him. He told Shirley it's like an eternal spring that's also autumn and the pomegranates ripenin'. Orange blossoms like a sky at sunset, blue-gray bars of cloud knifing the orange-gold above him. Bushes and fruit all around—an open pomegranate, pips sparklin' red in the evenin' light, each one a bit different to the taste. Shinin', oddly shaped seeds. You know, like with random facets, smooth-cut like jewels. Big bushes heavy with those orange flowers and fruit—reddish blush on the outside, little crown at one end. It's a wonder she's not jealous. All this describin' Rivka's voice!

His mind's taking off—back to the Land, forward to Paradise . . . .

"Foolishness," he tells himself, still muddled with sleep. He isn't thinkin' straight.

"Rivka's talkin' about her mother and I'm lost!" he later said to Shirley. "Couldn't let this happen. No one knows more about Miriam than Rivka. Miriam's following Felix around, she says. That's as strange as the laughing!"

He's managed to get back into the phone call. "When did you start noticing?" he says to Rivka. "Are you afraid?"

Fear. That's the heart of it. Nobody wants a suicide, especially if the one at risk is the oldest member of the sisterhood!

"Afraid? You want to know if I'm afraid?"

The question draws a big circle, big enough to include him.

I'm the one who's afraid, he's thinkin', astonished. Why did I ask her that? She noses around Gaza on her own, fades into the background, forays into murky corners chasing stories, sees all sorts of people—parents of children training for suicide missions!

He might be readin' her resume: Israel since nineteen, familiar with the territory, all the territories. No naive bumblin', no missin' the hazards. Resourceful and savvy almost from the first. Did the homework. Moish knows all this because Miriam reports Rebekah's journalistic escapades in minute detail every time she gets a letter. No. Fear isn't a part of this picture!

"Well . . . afraid for her."

"They're gazing at each other as we speak."

"Gazing?"

"They look like they could eat each other up."

"And that's something you're worried about . . . or not? But you mentioned laughing. You said 'Felix' though . . .."

"It's like a little joke, a secret joke."

"What about her?"

"That's something else. Try to imagine this: she's burrowing down into his arms and, and . . .. And then she—"

"Starts to laugh . . . Felix, as well?"

"Well, yes. Perhaps you've seen . . . you've seen it, too."

"I don't know. They've been married a long time. Still, it's not their standard approach to each other, and the laughing . . . sounds a little different from standard depression if there is such a thing."

"It's not depression now . . . not anymore."

"People don't get over depression in a few hours, Rivka. What about her meds?"

"No, clearly it's the opposite of that—not medicine, not chemicals at all."

"So. Bottom line. You called to tell me you're not as worried . . . or are you worried?"

"Not worried. I'll be leaving in a week."

"You're sure she's out of danger?"

"Come and see. Find some excuse and come."

Not an invitation I'll turn down, Levy's thinkin'.

"Tomorrow about four?"

"Tomorrow afternoon. Come by at four. You'll see, you'll see yourself how things have changed."

She never says goodbye, just shuts down the phone. Brief and abrupt like Hebrew. *Rivka*'s a natural switch from *Rebekah*.

CHAPTER FOUR
Questions, Few Answers

LIGHTS CUT PARALLEL BEAMS. IT'S WARM AND STILL.
Shirley's drivin' in from the music group. Nights of the late spring, Levy's thinkin'. No pomegranate autumn-spring in this universe, but spring has its charms.

Standing at the study window, he notices the black outline of the Faber house. Of course, no one's there.

"Cool nights won't last," he tells himself. "Alice in the hospital, no shrieks tonight. The ghosts can do as they like. Maybe smelling is drinking for them. Smelling till whatever it is shrivels up and dies. Imbibing the fragrance like iced tea or sangria or something. They get drunk on it, apparently. Combat with intoxicated ghosts . . . or one drunk old colonel! Makes a good story, whatever the version. Now, the bottom line's a broken arm. Should we move to another neighborhood? No, not convenient . . . the synagogue's close."

What can anybody do about it? Ricky and I often wonder.

The rabbi doesn't like waking at 2:00 in the mornin'. Shirley dresses and goes out to check on things. Some sort of bond. She'll go, night or day.

The sitters don't share her sentiments. They come and go, but sitters have to be there. Old Augusta can't do everything, though she lives in the house now. The ones who put up with Miz Faber are afraid of ghosts. Those who laugh at 'em can't handle an old lady who bolts outta bed in the middle of the night and runs for the garden. Easy to persuade the new ones. What do they know? She'll say, "Open the French doors. I need the air."

"Scream of the banshee. Scarier if you spell it right—*b-e-a-n s-i-d-h-e*?" the rabbi's mutterin', wondering if he does know how to spell it. "Anyway, Faber's not an Irish name. Frank was a Jew . . . our French Jew. I'll make a quiet suggestion . . . tell 'em to keep those French doors locked! Rick's responsibility, as well. Might listen to two of us. What a problem. The turnover's like popcorn. Wonder how long she'll be hospitalized?

"Nobody can tell Mrs. F. it's the deer. No, ghosts are out there again. Somehow, Col. Mitchell's now a crowd of 'em. Who can say?"

He thinks about Miz Faber and that glass eye. "Yes indeed, it's enough to convince a bedpost. Too bad it doesn't work on deer."

Shirley's coming in from the garage, singin' to herself. To the rabbi, the words're odd, but I know 'em. Why is she singing about Hitler and the Pope, he's wondering. Knows the tune but not that line.

Well, I don't know *Fiddler on the Roof* the way Shirley does, he tells himself. Can't match her musical knowledge. Alice Faber does though. Probably explains a lot.

Shirley says an insane picture's been driftin' through his mind lately. She's the cantor, replacin' that guy who passed out cold blowin' the shofar in the middle of a service. She's steppin' right in to fill the void. The thought horrifies 'im, Shirley says. Accordin' to her, Moish imagines the scene and describes it to Shirley like this:

"'He will not be coming back,' you're telling me. 'Poor man,' you're saying, '. . . a bad heart.' " Moish is modulatin' the vowels the way Israelis do, like "behk," not "back," showin' Shirley how she sounds tellin' this story.

A female cantor! He's scandalized. Could happen. What in the world? Worse, he's beginning to think in Israeli, bending that *a* toward *eh*. *Shirli* . . . it's all her doin'.

"Shirley!" he says aloud, lovin' the sound of her name and wonderin' how he managed to catch the eye of this person.

"Moshe?

"I'm in here," he says. "Wondering how long the peace and quiet will last."

Shirley's standing at the door—hooded gray-green eyes, a smile curlin' her lips. She's laughin'. All around her, he thinks, the springtime night's waftin' in like a diaphanous muumuu. Night-bloomin' flowers seem to dot that auburn bush of hair. No, that's too Greek. Sabras are prickly pears!

Good thing she can't see with my eyes, the rabbi thinks to himself. Could be reading my mind though. The thought's unsettlin'.

Shirli, my song.

"*Ken*," Shirley says, lapsin' into Hebrew in the comfort of home. "Alice is worse in the full moon, Augusta says. What will the hospital do?"

"The ghosts too maybe, but they aren't noisy."

Shirley laughs quietly. He loves her laughter—can hear it any time, even across a crowded room.

An enchanted evening, he thinks. No Alice!

He follows the rabbitzen upstairs, noticin' a little discomfort in his left leg.

Baby, you're gonna say this is none of my business. Yeah, I know, but Shirley told me every detail. Israelis are pretty up front, if you know what I mean.

The rabbi wakes up. The pull of Shirley's thoughts is nudgin' him to semi-alertness. She hasn't said anything. Sleepily but with interest, he's openin' his eyes. One corner of her mouth edges up, then she smiles.

"What is it . . .?"

"*Baali*, about Miryam . . .."

"Look," he says, reaching to smooth her hair on the pillow. It looks uncomfortable. "I know what that means, so don't call me *Baali*. Well, I am, but not . . .."

"Enough. You . . . too sleepy to talk."

"Okay, you say the sweet nothings. You're right. Too early in the morning to fight. As you know, I'm a morning person. Always win if we go at it before first light."

"Ha! Morning person! But that sounds nice . . .. Let's go at it, *Baali*."

"For sure we will if you keep that up." He mutters the charade of a threat, running two fingers along her arm.

"Oh grrrrr, grrrr. You don't scare me . . .."

Covering her lips, he shuts down the sarcasm. *Shirli*, my song, my song . . .. But what was it about Miriam?

"Okay. What . . .."

"What?"

"What? You started something about Miriam. Out with it. And don't keep smiling like that. You know where it leads. Gotta get up and get to work."

"Work?"

"Well, maybe this week you write my sermon, Madam Rabbitzen."

"You've done the week's work already."

"Think so? Have I still got to deal with you . . . you *and* Miriam Feinemann?"

"You're taking Mrs. Feinemann to bed! I'm getting a divorce!"

He groans and tries to break out a quip then thinks better of it. What can you say about eighty-somethings on a second honeymoon? Following her husband around the house?

He's a heart patient, Levy remembers. Better read up on heart surgery and sex after eighty then have lunch with Felix, give him some quiet, rabbinic counsel. Such a problem! What in the world?

"Well, well, well . . . she *is* quite a lady!" he mutters theatrically, then more seriously, "Rivka told me . . .. But what about Miriam?"

"Not to worry. She is all right. She'll be all right."

"How do you know?"

"I know. Not to worry. "

"You've talked to Rivka?"

". . . to Miryam. She is . . . *b'seder*."

"Well, I'll see for myself. I'm going at four. Rivka said to come and see. She agrees with you, but I don't know . . .."

Shirley has pulled away and looks toward the window. He studies her tanned skin, lovin' the curves, wonderin' all over again at the pleasure of wakin' up to find a woman in his bed.

I'm promisin' you, darlin', Shirley's told me every bit of this. He's said all of it to her and she likes it. I don't think he'd like her tellin' me though. But a girl has to have a friend. You tell your girlfriend everything.

I'm still seven-and-a-half, he's thinkin', rememberin' the day he began to speculate about grown men and women who shared the same bed.

But what's this shaking?

Puzzled, he glances over the line of her shoulders . . .. Weeping? An enchanted evening can do that—never mind the dawn delights. It's beyond him. He feels more like shouting or lifting weights or running a mile—after he wakes up anyway. Sometimes she just cries. Now?

"*Shir-li.*"

She turns to face him. Her eyes are shut, and laughter's comin' from the bottom of her tanned toes. The merriment's infectious. Laughing?

"What . . .?"

"You' . . . re f . . . ull of ques . . . questions this morning, *Ba . . . ali* . . .."

She's barely managin' the words, tryin' to breathe.

"Shirley . . . what is it, what in the world?"

"You're so worr . . . ied about Mir . . . yam. I've ne . . . ever seen her better! She is . . . I promise you, she's fine . . . *b'seder*! Avraham and Sarah . . . that's what they are. Maybe there will be a, a Yitza . . . ak."

Laughter's drowning him, no escape.

HaShem . . . what in the world! Is this thing catchy? Maybe laughter's catching! Contagious, like a disease? We should all be so lucky . . . die laughing.

He can see himself struggling with the obit: ". . . Miriam Feinemann, beloved wife of Felix, died happy . . .." Won't do. "Mrs. Felix Feinemann, beloved wife, mother, stalwart of the sisterhood, passed away in her eighties after succumbing to an unaccountable fit of . . .." Won't work.

Forget it, he thinks to himself. All this laughing is crazy . . . me next. He reaches to pull his wife over to him. The shakin' of her breasts against his skin takes his breath away, makin' him chuckle involuntarily.

A few minutes later, the two of them lie there exhausted, wipin' their eyes, pushin' each other away, vaguely hopin' to get the day started. They can barely move. What in the world?

A crisis? He's sure of it. Rabbi and rabbitzen, overcome by laughin' . . . can't cope!

Has to pull himself together, at least by four—no, by noon! He'll be seein' Quentin then the Feinemanns. Stayin' in bed till two, phone off, won't work today. Lunch might help though he'd like to beg off.

"Don't exp . . . ect them to tell you all abou . . . t it, Rebbe. They won't tell you. I hope by then you'll . . . you . . . 'll be awake enough to be dis . . . cree . . . eet." Shirley's trying to catch her breath, still laughin'.

"Listen. You'll see," she says softly.

"Come and see," . . . Rivka said.

They're in the Beulah Coffee Shoppe. Quen looks older, babe, quite a bit. Moish knows he's starin'. The man opposite he hasn't seen in years and Quentin can't see him now. The rabbi's not about to ask how he is, and Quentin's too polite to bring up the past. Moish thinks he'll want comments about that "Jewel" piece since he's read it. Neither one of 'em knows I've heard every line. I feel so sorry for Quentin, for Moish too. It was hard on Miss Evelyn. But all that's for later.

Moish is havin' trouble admittin' to himself Quentin's piece was interestin'. He's tellin' himself, that " jewel" business doesn't work. Too obscure . . . no explanation till the end. Then what do you have? He remembers the jeweler's glass Felix has and imagines looking through it at Quentin's "Jewel." How would that help?

Sure enough, Mr. Feinemann pops that little glass into his eye and there he is, the Injun colonial, regulation monocle and all. That's the way the British say it: Injun. Levy's picturin' himself with a jeweler's glass in his eye, but in the blank gaze from across the table, eyes don't really work as comedy. This should be the direct line of sight! Forget the standup routine. Not appropriate. Rein it in, he tells himself.

No, it's not just the years, Moishe's thinkin'. Suicide has taken a toll, never mind the blindness.

But I digress. Better let 'im tell his own story. Moish is a pretty good storyteller, even when the whole thing gets filtered through my pal, Shirley. She has 'im down. Told me about it after it happened. This is what Moish told her as I wrote it down.

Quentin's blindness is soberin' at close range, but all that laughter is like an ebbing tide that crashed him into something, breakin' 'im up into little bits of himself, each one quiverin', dithered by the waves. He hasn't laughed like that in years, and the urge is still on 'im. The early morning romp did damage; he's strugglin' not to yawn.

What in the world? This can't go on, he tells himself. Whatever it is, I've got to squelch it. Quen might feel he's the butt of some joke. He hasn't been sightless long . . . probably still uncomfortable with it. He might feel like the target if I let go and laugh. Always was sensitive, more than anybody. No, I'm here to research depression, Levy reminds himself. Have to be ready for Miriam.

Miriam at Four . . . Sounds like Book I of a sappy Victorian novel: cliffhangers set with heavy drapes, potted palms, tea cozies . . . dra . . . ama. One-a drama, that's a feast—*Hamlet* maybe. Two-a drama, it's a beast. Two humps that one, and it's got on silk pajamas.

He shuts off the nonsense and goes back to worrying.

With an English prof, I can bring up Dickens, he tells himself. Have to talk about something. Odd how Dickens avoids a fully maudlin sentimentality. Sentimental, but it's bearable. Could be that river of poverty and misery running from his pen.

Quentin knows suffering . . . first-hand. Maybe I'll mention Dickens if nothing else presents itself. Dickens should be safe enough. But Quentin's a medievalist, and I've forgotten anything I ever knew about that bag of bones. Too close to the plagues and Crusades to suit me. Better let Quentin lead the way. It's actually rather good to see him—surprise, surprise.

"Reuben sandwich for me, please—sweet tea."

Rick never has trouble placing an order. Baptist seminaries probably have a course for that—Decision Making 401. Have to pass it with honors before you graduate. Wimps need not register. Do they let wimps into Baptist seminaries?

"Other things on the menu, Father. Always trying to impress me . . .."

"Okay, but since you haven't ordered, I recommend the honey-baked ham . . . fresh daily. They do the pigs out back. You can hear 'em squealing any hour, day or night."

"That would be Mrs. Faber, Richard—chasing the ghosts from her roses. You should lend her your shotgun and explain about the deer. Give your deacons a break."

"I'm sure you've already tried to tell her. Somebody needs to explain to you that even an act of Congress—"

"I'd like the turkey club . . . extra bacon," Quentin says to the server. "Coffee with cream—I prefer cream to non-dairy creamer—and would you cook the bacon well? I'd appreciate it. I like it crisp. . . .. A movie about crisp bacon? No, I don't believe I've seen that one."

The server looks like she can't tear herself away.

Quentin, Quentin, Levy thinks. Blindness makes you more appealing than ever. What was that movie? Something with cheese . . . and that Ortolan fellow. Still polite. Quentin's secret, maybe. Still knows his own mind, I see.

The contours of a face he once vowed to avoid forever hold his gaze. The rabbi didn't expect to enjoy this, and he's not real comfortable with the feelin'.

Not supposed to be this way, the past is yellin'. He tries to dismiss the caution, but it doesn't work.

A tricky moment, no question, he tells himself. I guess the blindness makes it easier. He can't see my face and I can see his. Still the same classic features. The patina of decades just complicates lines too perfect for a teenager. Quentin always had good bones.

Moish keeps on starin' though habit says *Don't*. The lines in that face are as fine as the flourishes on an invitation to a state dinner, he thinks. Quentin's been through a lot, but his expression's not morose. He's looking around this place, trying to picture it. He's seen it . . . built before the blindness set in.

Levy glances past Quentin toward the back of the room. A server balancing a big tray is hurrying from the kitchen. To his left, across from Rick, another is tidying a table while a third puts down a fresh white cloth and a vase of freesias . . . Shirley's favorite. He'd know the fragrance anywhere.

The rabbi thinks about his wife. What she's doin'? Unable to resist, he again studies the face across the table. Quentin is unfolding his napkin. That's a lapse, Levy thinks. Quentin doesn't do that till the food is served. It's the rule. Then he sees the waiter comin' with the orders and understands . . .. That sense of smell, keener now without the vision.

Quentin took his good time ordering, Moish says to himself. Now he's staring out the window as if he can see it—town square, opera house, storefronts . . . probably playing out the old memories. They would include a Jewish kid and a Baptist. I'm like a double image on what he's imagining. My face is on all the memories . . . a face-over? Same with me; his face is on mine.

The thought is unnerving, and Levy catches himself wonderin' how Quentin pictures him. A sixteen-year-old, a twenty something? Can't be older than twenty. What year was that? Doesn't matter. We haven't seen each other for half a lifetime.

Levy thinks about the town he hardly noticed growing up. The questions then had nothing to do with new stores or old, shopping or town politics, certainly not the Beulah Opera house. Just games at first and the widening freedoms . . . then the whole scene changed as they made forays into some strange new territories, widening inch by inch.

Who started shaving? That guy grew *half a foot*! No . . . he was snowin' *who*? . . . nobody's snakin' *his* party doll! You can't be serious!

A few years will pass before these intensely interesting details fade to a comfortable, accustomed manhood. Then the back and forth will feature war, war and college, marriage and pregnancies—with or without.

"You mentioned Mrs. Faber," Quentin says, looking toward Rick.

"Remember her? The Levys' neighbor. Physically healthy, but declining . . . some confusion, dementia. She thinks Col. Mitchell's ghost is smelling the fragrance out of her roses. You remember him."

"A ghost does that?"

"Well, I mean . . . the ghost is breathing in the fragrance or something. Moish will help you with the theology. Beyond that, you'll have to ask Mrs. Faber or Augusta." Rick smiles wickedly as he glances past Quentin at Levy.

"I'll take you by her house and you can ask her, Quen. She'll tell you all about it. If she gets you to say you're on the Town Council, she'll make you put her on the agenda. She wants the town fathers to make an ordinance or something. One or two things have changed around here, all for the better!"

"An ordinance . . . against ghosts, I suppose."

"Well, yes . . . and when they start allowing bow hunters to shoot deer in the town limits—to scare 'em back into the woods, you know—that'll take care of her problem."

"So it's really the deer."

"Probably, if anything. My wife says roses don't smell the way they used to. Just the older types."

Rick addresses his sandwich, and they eat for a while in silence.

"Did Rick give you my manuscript," Quentin asks unexpectedly, pausing to look across the table as if he can see Levy's face. "He said there's some question about grief and laughter."

Across two sandwiches, freesias in the green vase, a few square feet of invisible tablecloth, Quentin seems to search for something like eye contact. Levy meets the sightless glance and the blind eyes turn away.

He smells the freesias . . . even if he can't see them. Feels my gaze, Levy thinks. Maybe it's just hard talking to me. We wouldn't be here except for Rick. What a jumble of emotions! My eyes are prickling . . ..

"Depression and laughter," he answers, fighting off an impulse to leap up and shake Quentin by the shoulders. He feels angry, sad, frustrated and gropes for indifference as Miriam's face comes into focus—Miriam, potential suicide.

"It's rather odd. Something's causing the depressed person to laugh inappropriately. Rick caught the connection in your piece—grief and laughter. Other connections? Depression . . . can it bring on laughter at the wrong time?"

"Grief can be expressed as laughter. Yes, it happens. But depression?"

"Laughter's the issue and it isn't hysteria. But laughter's become a contagious disease around here." Levy smiles irrelevantly and goes on. "With this person, the laughter's pronounced, depression as well."

I'm a hypocrite, the rabbi tells himself. He reaches to retrieve his dropped napkin and winces with the effort. His rib cage aches. Where did that comment come from? Well, I can't deny it; I'm sore from laughing!

"The laughing is pronounced?" Quentin says.

"Yes, but in this case, the depressed person is also . . . unexpectedly taken with her husband. As if they were on their honeymoon or something. She's laughing a lot, doesn't seem depressed right now. The couple's in their eighties."

"Sounds like a spark to encourage. Won't they benefit from a little honeymoon vim and vigor?"

Rick laughs. "'Honeymoon vim and vigor,' is it? That's good. I'll have to work that into a sermon," he says between bites. "Text from Genesis."

"I don't have that *Stuttgartensia* with me—thanks for it, by the way—so I'll just have to agree and wish you luck with the preaching . . . on what, Onan?"

"So," Quentin says, "it's laughter in the context of depression. Grief isn't a factor?"

"That's right."

"Well, *risus dolore miscebitur et extrema gaudii luctus occupat . . . .*"

Half smile, same look . . . . Top this, buddy!

The old Quen, challenging me in Latin, Levy thinks. The old rivalry! He's amused in spite of himself. Okay, you asked for it

Picking up the gauntlet, calculating the exact spot under Quen's nose to throw down the contra, he says, "גם–בשחוק יכאב–לב ואתריחה שמחה תוגה". Since Israel, he likes the modern, Sephardic sounds and wonders if Quen will catch the different pronunciation.

An old video flickers—my house, those nights before my bar mitzvah when Quentin helped me practice Hebrew. Quen learned quite a bit, as well, the rabbi tells himself. Then we vied with each other for Latin prizes in high school. People noticed how that Jewish kid was getting into the Latin. They thought it was all Hebrew.

The memories muscle in, smotherin' him. He feels like the guy who till this minute can't admit he's gettin' old. But there it is: cake in the middle of the table . . . black party napkins, fifty-three candles smokin' up the room.

Unable to dodge the admission, Levys thinks, Quentin was a good friend and, yes . . . I guess I've missed him. It's the canoe in the living room . . . bigger than a fifty-third birthday cake, load of candles and all.

"Okay, enough you guys. I'm sitting here too. And yes, I know you just said, 'A merry heart's as good as medicine.'"

"Wrong proverb. It's actually 14:13, not 17:22," Quentin says. 'Laughter is mixed with sorrow, and in the end, grief may overtake joy.'

"That wasn't Abraham and Sarah!" Rick counters with a big smile, shaking the water from his ice tea glass. "But I think something's happened to your laughing depressed person, Moish. It's some new factor you haven't found out about yet."

This is Rick the clergyman, I'm hearing, Levy thinks. You listen when he dons that mitre. Influence. Union Street for years. Even in the hometown, Baptists can send you packing overnight, but it won't be happening to Richard.

"New factor? Like what?"

"Something's happened. There's some new thing you aren't considering because you don't know it."

"That's actually what the person said . . . 'something has happened.' Then got off the phone before telling me what."

"The depression, is it serious?" Quentin says.

He has more reason to be interested than Rick, Moish thinks, and I should be careful what I say. But this is a safe enough forum. Quentin was never one for loose talk and he'll leave for Atlanta. Rick's like a tomb with pastoral confidences. Still, this is a public restaurant. Better keep it *sotto voce*. Servers spread any shred of gossip that comes along. Part of the job description. I need to keep an eye on other diners too—anyone in hearing range.

Levy scans the room and sees Judge Solomon's secretary two tables over. In the noise, she won't hear anything . . . not close enough.

"Suicide is a threat."

"I see."

"You'll see for yourself soon enough," Rick offers, biting into his sandwich, not hearing himself repeat Quentin's odd verb.

Rick isn't thinking about blindness, just eating and looking at the big Seth Thomas ticking loudly on the wall in front of him. "Sounds like no immediate danger."

"You may be right. By the way, Quentin, was that train guy fictitious? The Schiffman fellow . . . was he your creation or a real person?"

"I had that conversation, but 'Schiffman' is fictitious. His name is Benjamin Steingaard. We still talk."

"Doesn't happen a lot . . . train chat turning into a permanent thing. No doubt the conversation was different from the way you wrote it. Like giving him more color—that red polka-dot tie, say? I've always wondered how much personal experience a writer puts into his fiction. Not autobiographical, was it?"

I've reached a forbidden edge, the rabbi thinks. Unlike me, Quentin won't intrude on the grief of another. That suicide . . . like a ghost that just showed up to take the fourth chair. I admit, demands of curiosity speak louder than the politeness telling me to quit asking questions.

Politeness isn't everything.

"Mm . . . well, he made a point of looking me up at Carolina while I was there. We've stayed in touch. Ben comes to Decatur . . . flies into Hartsfield off and on. No, no added color. Just the way he is, red tie and all . . . chutzpah." Quen smiles as if to reestablish a former given, the inner circle of mutuality that salutes from a distance the odd things about a buddy's culture—peculiarities observed and appreciated, but not one's own.

Levy wants to avoid the icy, wintertime path separating their lives, but he's asking himself, is Quentin hearing *thaw* in my voice? Blindness is an odd facilitator; still, the man I distanced myself from wasn't blind. He may hear *friendly*. Do I want that?

"Still teaching at The Grove?"

"Actually, he isn't."

"Moved on to higher ed . . . university?"

"He's teaching in Israel—teaching and preaching, as he describes it."

"Preaching in Israel!" Rick puts in.

Does *he* know this man—this Stein-something, Levy asks himself. No, probably not. Rick's just curious about "preaching in Israel."

The sketch of an ambush is drawing itself faintly across his suspicions, but he decides to let it go.

Rick and Quen . . . ambush me? No, it's a little soon for that. Wouldn't happen in a place like this. Quentin's troubles have sobered all three of us. Besides, Rick's openly obnoxious about "witnessing," as Baptists put it. He doesn't need the aid of somebody like Quentin. Quen's an Episcopalian! May not even know the word. Set in that frame, the scene looks harmless enough. Whatever, it's a challenge—Quentin across the table and Rick to my right. It's been a long time.

"Preaching. Then he's not an agnostic anymore. You made him sound theologically hostile . . . if friendly otherwise. Not exactly into your take on things, as you were putting it to him."

"That's right, but I was surprised when he wanted to get into it more deeply. He'd drop by my office; we'd go to Starbucks. His questions were . . . interesting. He looked into teaching at Emory and was in and out of Atlanta. Nearly took the position; it's his alma mater. He's exposed all my blind . . . uh, the blind spots in my case. I guess his own . . . blind spots came out, as well. He's changed his mind about a number of things. Ben's become a good friend."

Quentin's loss of sight is still a tender spot, Levy says to himself, trying not to be pleased. Quen's never lost control . . . never, not even in adolescence. That slip about blind spots gave him away. He's struggling. Still not dealing with it, never mind Rick's assurances to the contrary.

"A good challenge never hurt anybody," Rick mutters, wiping his mouth with the big cloth napkin and clinking the ice in his tea.

"Well, I couldn't just tell him to make a decision," Quen said, smiling in his direction. The poke finds its target. Rick lifts an eyebrow Quentin won't see, finishes off the tea, and lets the server replenish it.

"Ben bristled with objections at first . . . taught by the Jesuits, you recall."

"That should have given him answers, from what I hear," Moshe offers, fighting off the sense that, in a minute, he'll be wondering why he pursued all this. "They're the Roman answer men, aren't they?"

"Depends on the answers you're looking for," Quentin says. "Apparently, the ones they gave Steingaard brought more questions than resolution. His ideas about the gospel writers and what they're attesting were . . . as tangled as—well, I'm about to wander off into a lecture."

Quen smiles and finishes his sandwich in a final bite.

Seems the bacon was crisp enough, the rabbi thinks. Bacon. Who can like it?

"Go ahead. What lecture?" Levy asks him, glad for an academic diversion in a conversation tilting toward theologically uncertain. Quentin won't be lecturing on theology, he feels sure.

"Well, I almost said 'as tangled as Faulkner's syntax,' and since you read Faulkner, I'll go ahead and say it, but . . . I apologize for the drift."

"Tangled questions."

He's unaccountably drawn to the door opening a crack in Quentin's chitchat . . . theological confrontation? Coming from Rick's mouth, something like this would send up red flags. But this is Quentin, the scholar, the stuffy Episcopalian who couldn't offend anybody . . . not unintentionally.

No, let's have a donnybrook, a real Irish shindy, Levy tells himself. A knock-down-drag-out! *Erin go bragh*! I'll fight both of 'em. Rick's been spoiling for it. Maybe Quen and I can ambush him. We'll have a real one. We're still ten, after all . . . ten and sixteen and eighteen. Wait for the moment and jump in.

Revisiting the old memories makes him smile. Won't register on Quentin, he tells himself, remembering the boyhood fights. Now one, now the other . . . ally or foe. The wars just toughened our friendship. The Beulah Musketeers! All for one and one for all—black eyes, scratched up legs and arms, busted lips. No broken bones, fortunately.

Bring it on, he silently tells the company.

"One thing he wanted to know was why the Savior of the world had to be Jewish."

"Well?"

Rick's being awfully quiet, Levy thinks. Is he inviting Quentin to trot out some intellectual gospel talk? Probably no such thing in this case, but Quentin seems into it. Maybe not. These things could be connected with the Lit. he teaches—language, the logic. Certainly the Bible's good literature.

But that "Jewel" piece . . .. What if it's more than fiction, not just some shrink-driven psychology? If this conversation gets out of hand, I can duck into Dickens . . . Dickens of the delicious preacher parody! And why doesn't Quen answer? He brought up the "Savior of the world" business.

"What did you say?"

"I told him that truth, like gravity, has to be taken into account. It's powerful, unified. We know about the creation of the world, we know the ancient covenants, the sacrifice system at the heart of the community, we know the Book and they're in the Book . . .. I'm talking about *your Book*, Moshe."

The rabbi says nothing. A tide of emotions is rolling in . . . annoyance, anger. Better to listen, not give away anything.

"Since all this is the truth," Quentin says, "—you know, truth the way gravity's the truth, break your bones truth—it stands to reason that the prophecies," he pauses to stir his coffee, "the predictions of a Messiah who'd deal with the oppressors—that person, would have to be Hebrew. I don't have to tell *you* to check Deuteronomy! When the Northern Kingdom was deported and all things Hebrew changed to *Judean* and *Jewish*, it meant that . . . well, yes—the Savior of the world had to be Jewish. The Babylonian captivity confirmed it. The exiles returned to Judea. I'm telling *you* these things, Moshe? But this is rambling. Occupational hazard of teaching, I'm afraid."

"Why *of the world*?"

Exactly how much history of Israel is this academic into? Do I need to hear any more of this stuff? Still, one gentile's take on Deuteronomy, etc. in answer to some half-gentile's questions is . . . well, I don't get it every day.

"It's what the prophecies said."

The button's been pushed; the lecture will go on . . . ho hum.

"You know all this, Moish, but I had to tell Ben. All those passages—the psalms, Isaiah, others that reference the nations—it's clear that *gentiles* would eventually worship Israel's God. Only the Jewish Anointed One fit the prophecies God only gave you—'your people,' I mean. Context would be Jewish, fulfillment for everyone."

Levy watches the server refill Quentin's coffee cup. A detail from "The Jewel" is drifting through his memory.

"Tea sip" . . . . The Ben guy in that train conversation really was an Emory tea sip, and he had salmon and parsley potatoes for breakfast!

"How's his heart?" Levy puts in, glad to find a way to dismiss the non-Jewish topic.

"He's been healed."

"Healed?" Rick puts down his iced tea glass, splashing drops of water all over his side of the table. "What happened?"

"Ben had prayer for healing at St. Philips in Atlanta and he was healed. He doesn't even eat salmon anymore."

I should push the point, Levy thinks. He'll fire up Rick if that look proves anything. Could be a metaphor. Maybe when he said this Ben fellow's heart was healed he really means "heart," or "healed." Christians do that.

"Not everyone shies away from the subject of miraculous healings," Quen says with a smile, turning toward Rick. Levy notices the challenge and Rick's fidgeting. A theological version of Faulkner's syntax is closing in, but he shoves the thought away. Rick's question has exposed an interesting weak spot.

Quentin, what about all those months you've needed healing, he tells him silently. Your self-assurance looks intact. Maybe so, maybe not. But you couldn't say "blind spots." When you describe this guy's healing, there's a catch.

It's odd. Episcopalians are into the next social event, latest stock market report, charity balls, fundraisers. Experts in white linen and shiny brass, flowers and elocution. Whisky-palians—they call *themselves* that! And what's all this? Quentin sounds like a fundamentalist . . . worse than Rick? Didn't he drop "fundamentalist" into that train conversation? This Bible stuff—is it literary or what?

Biblical literalist? That's absurd. If the three of us had a round, whose side would Quen be on? Fundamentalist and fundamentalist against a well-informed rabbi, or the educated views versus Rick's kind of literalism? Quentin has a PhD, for heaven's sake! Surely not Rick and Quentin against me!

Levy surveys the battlefield, checks his arsenal. Still, he tells himself, I'm just not sure I want to fight a guy who's blind.

"It doesn't matter what Episcopalians believe," Quentin says unexpectedly. "It's a truth thing. The Bible is very clear about healing; it was common during the ministry of Jesus and later in the church. Some Episcopalians don't read the Bible at all, some read it but don't take it seriously."

"You do, I suppose," Levy puts in quietly, instantly regretting the edge on his tone. Sarcasm wasn't what he intended.

Oughta come up with a different tone, he thinks. Quentin will leave soon. Be in Atlanta, back only now and then to see his aunt. That doesn't mean we'll get together . . .. It certainly hasn't for a long time. He seems friendly enough. And he's part of my past. The affection . . . well, it's still around here somewhere.

"I take it you're not lumping yourself with Episcopalians who don't believe the Bible, as you said just now."

"No. I'm not lumping myself with them or with anyone who dismisses the Bible. It's as reliable as gravity, as the calculations supporting gravity as Newton saw it or loop quantum gravity, or string theory, or causal sets . . . or chaos theory-fractals, wormholes, all the recent conversations in astrophysics I know you've read. They're built on a firm, mathematical foundation. The Bible has a basis just as firm. The book itself is a firm basis."

No vulnerability here, the rabbi says to himself. It's Quen's physics talking. Unusual guy—turned on by physics and literature, both at the same time. Maybe now more than ever. We always knew how smart he was. Any minute he'll pull out a yellow pad, fill it with equations. Probably has a calculator in his pocket, all the scientific functions. Still into physics, I see. Can the blind write equations?

"But not relative? You don't agree with 'culturally relative,' I take it."

"No, not culturally relative."

Moishe stops. This isn't a place to push Quentin. The long list of cultures. Quen trotted out for that Joel Schiffman or Benjamin Stein-something, whoever he is—not what I want as a fixture in my memory, he thinks. The subject chafes, and the *which culture* question is annoyingly persuasive. I won't go there, rabbi though I am—or since I am, he tells himself.

The Bible's a Jewish book, isn't it? But we don't get into it either—any more than the Episcopalians, if Quentin's right. Where's this going? The whole thing's like a speck in the eye.

Yes . . . Your theology eye.

The thought drifts by. To himself Levy says, no, we didn't create the Bible. Happened in spite of us. It survived despite the way we treated the ones who wrote it.

Isaiah's death legend flickers in his imagination, the miseries of Jeremiah next. Some kind of voice-over—outrage and decibels, a Jewish lawyer delivering threats. *You put my client in a pit!* Words crackling with indignation; a well-manicured hand shaking gold-rimmed glasses at him, face scowling as the other hand's shuffling around in a stack of papers, stopping just long enough to scribble something illegible on a long yellow pad. *Actionable! You'll be hearing from us!*

He shuts down the video, reluctantly admitting it wasn't just King Ahab who deemed Elijah a troubler of Israel. Moses was right . . . no, Samuel, or so Rick thinks. Quentin too, apparently—anybody who takes the whole thing seriously: attributions, authorship, dates, all that quasi-historical stuff, the King-David-wrote-all-the-psalms people, carried away with the "sweet singer of Israel." Always a question of education. That's the essential thing or you fall into all kinds of silly errors.

But no, he tells himself. we never did treat the prophets well. After they're out of the way, we make saints of 'em. Bad as the Romans—gave 'em that precedent maybe, like the sword-point conversions that brought us King Herod!

Ah, Israel . . . woe, woe, woe! And oh yeah, I'm counting on Quen's brand of Anglicanism not to include mind reading, as well as gifts of healing.

The expression makes him smile.

I reckon a Jew should say *Oy vey*, not "o yeah," Levy tells himself, saluting some real, homegrown chagrin. *I reckon?* Where did that come from? Jews aren't ever rednecks, are we? I certainly am Southern, nearly as Southern as . . . well, as I am Jewish. And Judea was the Southern Kingdom, double credentials! At Passover I wait for Elijah like everyone else. I lift Elijah's cup, listen for the knock at the door. It came one year. Everybody laughed when that six-foot-eleven Duke basketball player turned up. Another old friend.

Do we expect anything? Jews or Southern Baptists or Episcopalians—do we expect a prophet . . . the Messiah?

Prophets are safer at a distance—past or future, the *very* distant future. The Messiah too. The famous rabbis have a one-word answer for all queries: When will the Messiah come, Rabbi? Soon, they say. Soon . . . soon.

What to make of this stuff, Levy asks himself. Rick, maybe Quentin, too— both of them think they know all about it. Odd. It's "Soon!" for Rick, but with a difference, and I sure didn't expect a sermon from an academic. Ignorant notions from a professor make no sense. Some sort of neurosis?

He watches the other two, now deep in conversation. Rick's taking a few final gulps of tea, Quentin's crumpling his napkin against the plate, turning his fork over to show the server he's done. He stands, grasps his cane, and maneuvers himself beyond the chair.

Maybe it's time to drop the old rough and tumble, Levy thinks. The way to the old rivalries bristles with question marks, but the ice is melting. I can feel it.

Rick's cell phone rings, and they watch as he turns away to answer.

Time to get on with the day. Food and talk . . . some doors opening. I could decide to keep up with Quentin, Levy thinks, like this Ben fellow. The climate's changed a little.

Quen . . . well, what can you say? Quen—old Quen or new Quen, he always was interesting to talk to. Let bygones be bygones maybe. Can I?

He turns toward Quentin, surprised that he wants some more chat.

Rick set up this lunch, and I couldn't think of a dodge, he says to himself. Odd how things have worked out. Can't account for the heart. Maybe Solomon had it right—a nearby friend really is better than a far away brother in a day of trouble. But I'm not the one in trouble. That's Quentin . . . and Miriam. Rick never seems to have trouble.

"By the way, what did Schiffman's, I mean that Steinman's Jewish friends say about whatever it is he's preaching? I suppose he has Jewish friends. Didn't seem much of a Catholic. I'm guessing he isn't preaching Judaism."

"Oh, you mean Steingaard. In fact," Quen says, fiddling with his credit card as Rick grabs the check and heads toward the register, "he went back to his Jewish roots for a while, but found more questions than answers there too. One day in a Starbucks he said something that surprised me."

"What was that?" Levy says. They're alone. The comment Quentin left hanging begs for an answer.

"He told me he wouldn't tell his rabbi . . . wouldn't, absolutely. Whatever happened to him theologically, he would not tell his rabbi. I'm not sure he still feels that way. He talks to everyone now."

"Preachers do," the rabbi says, barely suppressing the sardonic flavor nestled like an after-dinner mint along the edges of his tongue.

"His rabbi had a heart condition. Ben knew something about that."

Honeybabe, Moish has been livin' with some awful memories. That's probably why worries hang on--next-of-kin to awful memories maybe. Anyway, he's told Shirley about Jerusalem, but about now, he's decided to write up everything connected to Jerusalem plus all that stuff stirrin' in his spirit.

This is Moishe's story. I wouldn't mess with it for the world, too intense. Funny though . . . even when he was beginnin' to face all this and deal with it, he still couldn't bring himself to say "I" and "me" and "my." Still too painful, I guess. He's kind of pretendin' all this happened to some "he" and "him" guy . . . can't fully put himself into the picture yet. Yes, I know. I'm a pretty good psychologist. You don't have to tell me.

The walls and bookcases of the study whisper *Quiet. Be still.* **Levy can't keep** his eyes open, can't even make out the time. I have an hour, he thinks. He angles his legs across the ancient leather ottoman, leans back in the chair. Lunch and laughing have done him in. The Feinemanns in a little while. For now, just rest the leg. But nothing's comfortable. Pulled muscle maybe. Nap and forget about it . . . just one hou . . ..

Shirley looks in. The antique clock marks off seconds with a hollow tick-tock as if to mark every degree of irrelevance between twelve and twelve. Time comes and goes, doesn't push or pull. It's just there.

The day is warm, and the scent of old books, old leather, sandalwood, and the lemon oil rub Annabelle uses for furniture drifts with the dust motes on shafts of light from the southwest window. Sleep holds him as if in a gently rocking boat. The neighborhood is quiet. Levy moves his legs but doesn't wake. Ten minutes, twenty, twenty-five . . ..

Sting of sand, a whipping wind shaving his left cheek. Sand swirling all around. The sun is turning the air to molten copper . . . zahav, v'shel nehoshet. Gravestones at his feet, swimming in the radiating blasts of heat as if they were side-by-side oven doors too hot to open. Sand, every grain transmitting, doubling the light, broadcasting the obvious. Who needs to hear it?

Clear skies, temperatures in the triple digits. Hot.

Hot tombstones. Who would think . . .?

Don't look. I'm here to look, to . . . look. Ebenezer . . . no, not a stone of help. This is me looking at the end of the world. A whimper after all, not a Big Bang . . . Big Bang—it was a big bang. No . . . no, no.

The click jolts him awake. From another place, another time, he peers through slits just wide enough to see his wife's face at the study door.

"*Motek,* four?"

"Is it that . . . already?"

". . . thirteen minutes past."

Watchmaker Israelis, even fix the driftiness of our clocks. Some kind of blindness we have . . . we see but don't get what the hands mean.

HaShem, you put eternity in our hearts. *Melech haOlam . . . .*

The rabbi gathers his limbs from the chair, rubs his eyes, walks from the study. Miriam and Felix and Rebekah, he says to himself. I've got to . . . figure out something.

No one expects us to be on time, he tells himself, ringing the doorbell.

"Oh, it's you, Rabbi. Right on time. I said to Felix, 'He's always right on time . . . such an example to us, such an example.'"

"Miriam. Well, I didn't expect you to think of this as an appointment," he says laughing in spite of himself. He's walked into a cloud of lavender accented with ancient star shine—a different Miriam.

She's smiling broadly. Her round face radiates a welcome he can't miss. She's wearing perfume! Delightedly wringing her hands, she hurries on.

"It's so, so good to see you, Rabbi. I was telling Felix just now, 'Felix,' I said. 'The rabbi is a wonder, don't you think? He is always right on time, and he always has a good sermon. Don't you think so, Felix?' I said to him. And do you know what he said in reply, my Felix? He himself is a wonder. He always says something so wise. Wise he is, Mr. Feinemann. He is so wise. He said, 'Yes, Miriam, the rabbi, he is our example. Always a good sermon, no question.'

"Please come in and take a chair. I will call Felix. Rebekah is here somewhere. So thin I don't always see her. What do you think, Rabbi? I should be worried? Rebekah is too thin, thin like her father. I said to Felix, 'If she's too thin, the rabbi will know. He will know what to say.' And do you know what Felix said? He said,

'Yes, he will know what to say.' Such a wise man Felix is, so wise. And a good man too. He is a very good man, have you noticed, Rabbi?"

"Actually, I have. You are speaking a truth, Mrs. Feinemann. But don't disturb him if he's having a nap. Be good for him, I expect."

"A nap? Yes . . . he was nodding at the lunch table. He will want to see you, I am sure. And Rebekah—Rivka now, you know, Rabbi—Rivka made her special cake. Felix said we should have some special cake because the rabbi was coming. Felix is such a considerate, kind person, don't you think, Rabbi?"

"Indeed he is, a kind, good person. If he's sleeping, don't disturb him for my sake. If there's cake, he should get up for that, of course."

"You know . . . the kind with little apricot pieces, apricot pieces and almonds. She got the recipe from her Sonja Zolte recipe book. You know Sonja Zolte. She wrote *A Year With The Wonder Pot*. In Jerusalem, everyone uses it . . . all the best recipes, all the right things to put into your food. You will like it. You will see. Rebekah will cut it. My hand shakes too much now. Felix says I will cut myself. Such a considerate husband, my Felix.

"Felix . . . Feee-lix, the rabbi is here, Felix."

Still calling, she edges her wide body past him and into the next room. The words carry with surprising resonance.

Moshe Levy feels more than hears the new quality in her voice. The words surge like tiny ocean swells, rolling back and forth along the passages of his inner ear. A voice he's dreaded.

"So here you are, in fact. I knew you'd come."

All at once Rivka, as if in answer to his thoughts.

"Rebekah-Rivka. Thanks for suggesting a visit, and I'm . . . seeing the changes you mentioned."

"She will find Felix. Won't come back at all."

Moshe laughs in spite of himself. The thought of afternoon delights among the seventy-eighty somethings has taken him by surprise. Applebaum Court . . . another wonder? He thinks of the "Wonder pot" and laughs. I love these people, he says to himself.

The daughter is thin, thin like Felix, though thinness isn't so noticeable in an old man. Rivka? Poster child, but no model. Well, maybe Twiggy. How to account for *the voice* in a body so thin? She should be voluptuous. Dismayed at his thoughts, he shoves them away, but a rebuke is rising like a wraith, moaning imprecations against the crass body judgments he's indulged.

LORD, your gifts—how oddly distributed! How do you decide? Wonder upon wonder. Some beauties, some world-class sopranos. Some with energy or sharp, creative minds, some with big breasts, some with nothing but courage, angles, and bones . . . and astonishing voices. Strange world.

Unnoticed, Felix has come in smiling, looking sleepy. Miriam's with him, a cat under her arm.

"Rabbi! Good to see you . . . just the moment for a visit by the rabbi. I fell asleep reading Torah. I was reading the Torah . . . ."

The words trail off, his smile fading toward the tentative as if he thinks the rabbi won't believe him.

"Source of all wisdom, Felix. Try to stay awake next time." Levy smiles and extends his hand. The jeweler takes it, causing Levy to wince. Quite a grip for a sleepy man in his eighties.

"Wisdom, yes. Also humor . . . .."

"Humor?"

"I opened the Bible and there it was, the prophet Elijah and some ravens. Isn't it strange? God sent unclean birds to feed Elijah. Scavengers, no? Did they bring him dead meat? Shocking. But God sent them. What do you think, Rabbi?"

Felix and Miriam are both chuckling. Rivkas exchanges her quizzical look for a smile then laughs with them—a glassy, brittle laugh like ice cubes tinkling in a water-beaded tumbler on a hot day. Hot day in Jerusalem.

"How do you interpret this strange thing, Rabbi? Give us your understanding," Felix mutters breathily. It's taking some effort to rein in the laughter.

The Applebaum shule, Levy thinks. What in the world? Yes, it is funny, and no, I dare not think about it. We'll be laughing our heads off!

The rabbi runs his hand over his head, warning himself irrelevantly not to knock off the kippah he knows isn't there. Ravens. At all costs, no texts with ravens! I could have a laughing fit on the bema. Couldn't control—

His thoughts are tumbling . . . a thing unwanted and unbidden is rising, like a stalker no longer seeking the shadows.

Control . . . have to control—Blocked and ambushed, he feels the color drain from his face. Ravens . . . .

That street . . . the air convulsed. The world is coming apart.

Screams obbligato violenceviolas cellos-of-hell, arias raucous in sirens sforzando, sound waves breaking in my eyes.

The words pair crazily in his head. *No, no . . . no. I'll be blind the rest of my life* . . . a voice sounding like his, flat and final—*the verdict, eyes like pebbles.*

Hunched in an alley of the New City, acrid . . . smoke blowing all around him. Ragged, choking clouds block his view, fill his lungs. Shock like rigor mortis fixes the curve of his back—bones, nerves, and senses struggling to tell his locked-down brain the thing the rest of him understands.

Not the café . . . had to be somewhere else, another block.

The facile reassurances drift away, powerless to catch and hold. In the hot half breeze, the smoke is clearing. His eyes are stinging and straining, as if growing out on stems. Try to see . . . no, must not. Can't look, not anywhere. No. I have to see . . . .

The better to see you with, my dear—a mocking voice murmurs. No, I'm thinking like somebody in a cartoon. This isn't real . . . .

In the radiating heat, the street writhes and shudders. Here and there sirens wail—the sounds are random, no direction or purpose. Louder and louder, complicating the screams and cries—shouting, everywhere shouting.

She won't be on time. Not ever . . . not today. No.

Running. Thoughts tumbling out onto the street.

Meet for lunch she said. Tomorrow? It's the wrong day.

Resolve the irresolvable—have to get closer . . . they won't allow . . . . It'll be blocked off with police tape.

Now he's staring. On the pavement, just there—a finger, the nail neatly painted with a natural-looking pink enamel, a ring with a blue stone, blue and cool-looking a yard or so beyond. It lies where it rolled and rolled, beyond the trail of blood.

A voice, still his own, speaks in a matter of fact tone—

They will come, the ravens from the shules. They will do their work. They will serve the community. We will be grateful . . . .

No, no, no, nonononono . . . no.

"The rabbi . . . a drink of water, Rebekah. Go and get it . . . not too cold. Cold is not so good when a person is . . .."

Waving her hands back and forth as if to fight off something, Miriam releases herself from Felix's arm circling her waist and cuts short her usual caution about ice cubes. Rivka has left the room.

"It is too hot to make calls, Rabbi . . . too hot. Even young persons have strokes. My cousin Esther was only twenty-seven . . . that story is not for today. Shirley must make an appointment. Go and report this to Harry. You are pale in your cheeks—pale, very pale. A cold cloth on your forehead, Rabbi? I will get a cold compress . . . right here in the powder room, a small towel with cold water. Have him sit down, Felix. You've thought of that, dear husband . . .. Yes, that's right. He should sit."

Rivka's hand is steady as she holds the green glass to his lips. Water, no ice cubes.

Moshe drinks a little, glad to be dealing with a domestic hubbub in the quiet comfort of leather, glass, wood, and bronze, pictures on the walls, prints of Jerusalem at dusk shouting to him that the city's still there, still there. Rivka will return in a few days . . ..

Brute force. He forbids the images. Speak! A level voice . . . now!

"Thank you very much. No, I'm fine, just didn't sleep much last night, actually . . . just a little tired. The water's fine, what I needed . . . really. May in South Carolina, what can you say? It is hot outside; I should drink more water."

Rivka will notice the artificial voice booming out reassurances. Miriam and Felix will hear the words, won't catch the phony. If that plastic timpani is all he can muster, it's time to leave.

Levy finishes the water, puts down the glass, and stands. Thrusting away the insistent videos of death, he tries to smile. Rivka lives with this and she's returning. The hazards for him are nothing but flashbacks . . ..

This was supposed to be about Miriam, not me, he tells himself. Must go on talking or they'll be sure I'm ill. Have to . . . do what I came for. She does seem better.

"I won't stay. Rebekah, thanks for making the special cake. Please . . . a rain check; we'll have it next time Shirley and I are in the Land—"

"Rabbi, you didn't walk in this heat?" Felix cuts him off. At just-turned-eighty, he can put a considerable rasp in his voice, and he knows how to file the edge of it.

Like an ancient, biblical instrument . . .. He can sure tune the pitch to sharpen a point, and there's no modern equivalent.

Levy's exerted himself to be exact, but misses the crazily mixed images. Right now, an unmistakable scorn fills the airspace all around Felix Feinemann and it includes him. A tonal quality no one could miss, speaks eloquent commentaries on the careless excesses of youth and irresponsibility. From where he stands, Moshe salutes the man's efforts, the kindly concern, the reasonable disdain.

"I'm only a block away, you know, Felix, and with the trees . . .. But I don't want to forget why I came over today. I came by to ask you to see Oscar about our portfolio. Time to do an evaluation, meet with your group. Be so kind as to add my thoughts to your discussion—some notes I've jotted down here." He manages to get out the words as he hands a leather-bound folder to the old man.

"It's time we thought of investing in Israel. There's growth. The country's doing well. No better place to invest."

"I will, Rabbi," the jeweler says softly, concern etched in the wrinkles of his narrow face, an ancient script dimly decipherable. "And you will see Harry. They will work you in. Don't get overtired. We can afford a roller-coaster portfolio, but not the crisis of a rabbi's—"

"He will be fine, Felix, you will see." Miriam interrupts her husband as if to block an evil word, a stray malediction escaping unbidden. "Go and make a visit to Harry, Rabbi. You will need to have a check-up though men don't want to go to the doctor, not my Felix either. Everyone should be examined by the doctor at regular intervals. I've always said so. And when the need arises. You will visit Harry's office, Rabbi. It is for the sake of your people. Shirley will tell you. It is for Shirley as well you must go."

Miriam takes a breath and goes on, the general haranguing her officers.

"Felix, we will not let the rabbi walk home in this heat. Rebekah will take you in the car. Go and bring the car, Rebekah. The rabbi must not walk on a day so hot. You will drive him to his house."

Rivka is gone before he can argue. He walks to the door, and the two old people follow, frowning and tutting about the heat— dangerous, risky this time of year to walk about in it.

Moshe shakes his head, battling the oddity of health advice from these two. He'd come to see about them . . . Miriam, certainly. That issue is off the table, it seems.

She hasn't even thought to tell me what happened, Levy says to himself, opening the door. She's forgotten whatever it was she called about. Have to keep an eye on her though. Wait a week or so and look in again. Rebekah's return to Jerusalem will be upsetting. Harry will shed some light. I have a need to know. An excuse, as well.

My aunt and cuz, as you know, babe. I'm in the loop. Cud'n Joe Paul. I'll have to call 'im that. He'll die of embarrassment.

"Nana, is that Miz Faber in Beulah our cousin?"

Joe Paul licks the delicious crumbs of fried chicken from his fingers and smiles at the best cook in the world. She's eatin' chicken too, not concerned about the fat. Doesn't have any herself.

"Not a close one, darlin'. But she was Papa's mother's sister's . . . daughter's child, Papa's cousin's child, don't you know. Around here it's always appropriate to say 'cousin'—Cud'n Alice, you know. She won't understand now, bless 'er heart— whatever you call her. Was she in a lot of pain?"

"Yeah . . . but I got her talkin' about Col. Mitchell and the roses. She sorta forgot it."

"Good for you, son. You're a good man. Pass me the tomatoes, please."

"You'll be gettin' some good ones this year, Nana."

"*We*, you mean."

"Well, I didn't do that much."

"I always 'preciate the tilling, and you did plenty of it . . .. Those hot peppers are comin' along. I hope you know what to do with 'em."

"Yeah . . . and another thing South Carolina grows is weeds. You'd think a garden would be weed free after you'd dug it up the winter before."

"That would be nice. You're right though. Weeds grow in the dark around here . . . all winter long."

"Clumson pro'bly has a course in weeds. I bet there's somethin' you can do with all of 'em. We just don't know what yet. Weeds . . .!" He shakes his head and laughs, thinking of a few weed people who seem to get worse and worse, year by year. Wonder what you could do about them . . ..

"Nana, you can't keep on with those tenants over in Mayville. They're takin' advantage of you."

"Well, they've had a bad time, son. Jolene was in intensive care, and James is preaching at his church and workin' two jobs. Baptists do that, you know. They're good people. I love 'em like folks. They'll get around to payin' the rent. If they don't, I'll go over and talk to 'em."

"Pray, too, I betcha."

"Nothing wrong with that."

"Nothin', nothin'. You know I didn't mean a thing."

A long pause while they chew meditatively, both measuring the quality of the store-bought tomatoes with the real ones coming in soon. Lucy Jenkins won't buy tomatoes in a grocery store, but these were from the Jordan's produce stand. They're ripe, more or less . . . open fields in Florida prob'ly. They'll have to do.

"How long's it been since prayin' was something you did, son?" Miss Lucy fixes her still-brilliant green eyes on the young man she loves as if she'd borne him twice instead of raisin' 'im by default.

"How long?"

"Well, you're right . . . not too recently."

"Is Jesus real to you, Joe Paul? Is he as real . . . as day?"

Two green lasers pin him as if to a gurney. He's listening.

"Is he real . . . *in* . . . *your* . . . *heart*?" The words fall like big water drops in a baptismal font.

Joe Paul dodges into another image as her second finger takes the lead. Percussion. Her band. Tapping out the syllables, her fingers make the words pull like music. Nana does amazin' things with those fingers, amazin' musical things.

Right now she's makin' music just tappin' on the tabletop, Joe Paul complains to himself, wishing she'd chosen to keep the beat on somethin' a little less embarrassin'.

". . . uh, don't be askin' me that all the time, Nana," he hedges, hoping to avoid anything else on the subject. This woman can be persistent. Then remembering what he wanted to ask her, he breaks in, relieved to think of a less aggravatin' topic.

"Nana, is Miz Faber—I mean Cud'n Alice . . . what is she anyway? I thought you said she used to sing at the Assembly of God. Is she that or a Baptist? Or somethin' else now?"

Lucy stops tapping and curls three fingers around her fork. Spearing a tomato slice and shifting her eyes from his, she reaches for the salt with the other hand.

"Shug, when she went to New York to do her opera career, she seemed to stop bein' anything for a while. That's what I heard. But after all that, having her voice crack up and all—that daughter, too—she came back here. The Baptists have been good to her. I'm pretty sure she's a Baptist now. Her house—you know, the big one over on Applebaum Court. It's close enough to the Baptists to walk. Evelyn says she did walk once. Why're you askin'?"

"Well, she still has a voice, you might say, and she kinda scares people. She started screechin' when we were takin' her over to the hospital, and you shoulda seen Bill Allen tryin' to keep the truck on the road. It took him by surprise, I tell y'what. If she starts that at the hospital, they won't know what to do with her but knock her out, I guess. Can they do that?"

"Could be . . . but maybe not, not the way things are right now. Betty Berttison said on the phone a little while ago that she's taken a turn for the worst. They thought she'd be goin' home, but her heart acted up, so she'll be there a few more days and then they'll send her over to the nursin' home . . . rest and some kind of aerobic exercise if they can get her to do it. For a while anyway, see how bad it is."

"Somebody oughta tell Pastor Rick at the Baptist Church. He'll know how to calm 'er down. If he doesn't, I don't know who will!"

"You go over to Beulah and talk to him, son. That's the thing to do."

Joe Paul wipes his mouth with the cloth napkin Nana always finds necessary to provide. Then he stands, picks up the supper dishes to prep 'em for the dishwasher. For such a good cook, he can clean up the kitchen and love doin' it.

Across the table, Lucy Jenkins smiles. A *fine* man, she thinks. A fine man and I'm proud of him. Just needs to get right with the Lord.

Is that the way a Methodist should say it? She doesn't care. It means what she wants it to mean. A heart thing, like Wesley said, and it's not completely clear that Joe Paul's heart is where it ought to be. Joe Paul likes that Baptist preacher though. He'll know what to do. Maybe not just about Alice Faber.

". . . happy birthday to you, happy birthday to ya'll . . .."

One voice then another rises over the hubbub and laughter.

"Hurry up and blow out the candles! Are ya'll waitin' to get old? Yeah, waitin' for a few more to show up on that cake!"

". . . those trick candles?"

"Course not, bozo . . . that's not what I meant! I mean the kind that just pop up out of nowhere like mushrooms when you take too long to blow 'em out. Didn't you even ever hear of that kind?"

"I sure didn't. I bet you didn't either!"

"Anyway, they're gonna be seventeen before we get a piece of that cake!"

"Maybe they're waitin' t' get legal! If she waits long enough, she'll be eighteen while we stand here. Maybe they're magic candles."

"Maybe she thinks it's bad luck to blow out candles. Out goes the flame, and poof—"

"Shut up, stupid! Who thinks that? You superstitious or somethin'?"

"Not as bad as you are, Zero!"

"Don't get your hair in the cake . . . Davita! Moish, what are ya'll doin'?"

"Somebody . . . push it out of the way! No, not like that. You'll catch her hair on fire!"

"Jimmy, will you stop it?"

"What am *I* doing?"

"You're shovin', that's what! Get over, y' big lug. I can't see!"

"Davita! Moish . . . make her blow out ya'lls candles! Hurry up! Don't you want to make a wish?"

"Can't you just do it? I want some cake."

"Count 'em for her, Quen. You're the math whiz. Maybe she's trying to figure out how old she is! She's forgotten how to count! …sev-en, eight, niy-un, ten, e-le-ven, twe-eh-lve…."

"Hush, Moish. You're making me nervous! Are you finally ready to blow out the candles? You're supposed to too!"

The dark-haired girl looks across the flames at her twin, challenging him to be the good host, her eyes daring him to keep up the banter. She's well able to squelch his mockery and he knows it.

I'll stick this in the flame and blow it over on you, smart aleck, her eyes say, as she stretches a black curl around her little finger and lifts both eyebrows very slightly. He stops counting and meets her gaze, giving in, loving her spunk.

Twenty teenagers crowd around the table, all talking at once, jostling, pushing each other, shouting this and that, everything from good-natured insults to instructions almost serious, a few boomed out commands of a quasi-fire marshal. Every one has an opinion to be declared at top voice. In the middle of the crowd, Davita Levy faces a huge white cake, brilliant with sixteen candles and she is taking her time.

The tiny flames reach radiant little fingers to the face bending toward them as if to meet a kiss. At the moment, her twin seems the only one getting through to her, though the whole room senses the glow of embers smoldering somewhere within Davita's core. One person, only one, can articulate the growing warmth she scarcely understands herself, and that person is not her brother.

Moishe's taunts dealt with, Davita takes a deep breath and shuts both gray eyes. Then, her mouth a red O, she opens them again to look around at the room full of friends and at her twin, still grinning across the table. Not waiting for a joint effort, she moves her face closer to the white candles and with a mighty puff extinguishes all sixteen, raising cheers borrowed from the pep rally and bonfire earlier this evening.

"Well, finally! I didn't think you could do it."

"Why didn't you help me then, Moish?"

"Because I'm too old for such nonsense. I began my seventeenth year twenty minutes ago, remember?"

"You'll die first too, old man!"

Davita swirls her black mane of hair in the direction of her twin. Smoke from the candles swishes in spirals toward a ceiling festooned with clusters and clumps of balloons and crepe paper streamers swaying this way and that, as if they too were courting the candles' blaze now extinguished and filling the room with threads of pleasant smoke.

"Leave him to his own mischief, Davita. Let's go outside. Too smoky in here."

"Moish, you get to cut it. It's your birthday cake too. I'm leaving."

Reaching out his hand, Quentin grasps the girl around the waist and guides her through the crowd of young people now gathering up plates and forks, gibing the other twin as they goaded Davita to action a moment before. Everyone is hungry.

"Moish . . . that's not big enough. I want a bigger piece."

"Who'd you say made that cake? Henry's mom?"

"If she made it, I want two."

"What's gotten into ya'll? You'd think birthdays were every day you're so slow! You bored with birthday cake or somethin'?"

The night air on the patio is cooler, and the girl angles her face toward the darkened sky as if for nourishment as her tall companion pulls her close. She turns and stretches out both arms, smiling and lacing her fingers at his neck.

"Happy birthday, Davita."

"I made a wish."

"I don't know how you could with all that going on."

"I made a wish about you."

". . . about me?"

". . . and me."

"What did you wish?"

"I can't tell. It wouldn't come true."

"Surely, you don't believe that."

"Well . . . if I told you, you'd know."

"So. That's why I asked you, silly."

"I sure won't tell if you call me 'silly'!"

"*Silly* means *blessed*. Did you know that?"

"No."

"What did you wish?"

"Well . . . that it would last forever."

"What would?"

"Your arm around my waist . . .."

"But I didn't have my arm around your waist."

"You were thinking about it though, weren't you?"

"Well, yes. But . . ."

"And now your arm's around my waist. Let's stand here forever."

"Kiss me, Davita."

"Forever . . .."

The noise of the party is growing faint as the crowd of young people disperse with plates and cups, looking for places to sit or sprawl—sofas, chairs, corners of the floor. One or two voices are approaching, and Quentin releases Davita from his embrace as Rick edges out the door, balancing a cup of punch and a plate with two pieces of cake.

"*Apricot* . . . can't you see these seats are taken?"

"What seats. You think you're in a movie or something? You probably think you are the movie!"

"Get lost, will you? I have business to talk over with Davita." His friend grins and slides a long leg back over the threshold, slowing the swing of the screen door.

"Okay, okay . . . I'm going!"

Alone again on the patio, the pair stand silently as if trying to restore a moment the interruption dispelled. The casual tilt it took with the appearance of their friend corrects itself, coaxed by the beckoning of a small night breeze that stirs among the backyard pines, causing the spikes of starlight to blink on and off like overhead fireflies winking at their fellows flashing signals to each other above the blades of well-trimmed grass. On the calendar, early fall . . . so sweet, and the South Carolina summer still hanging around.

"Davita . . ."

"Mmmmm . . ."

The head resting on his chest seems fixed and content, a permanent arrangement. Say something and wreck the moment, again?

"Davita, I have something for you."

The girl stirs and looks up to lock her eyes into the gaze fixing her face . . . as if afraid of losing sight of it forever.

"What is it?"

"You have to see."

"See . . .? Let me see."

Quentin reaches down to kiss away the command as he draws a small box from the pocket of his dinner jacket. Not moving from her lips, he finds the fingers of her left hand and presses the gift into them, still holding her in the kiss till she begins to squirm.

"How can I see if you're doing that?"

"I'm reconsidering. You can look next week. Didn't you say *forever*—?"

Holding the box, she again reaches up both arms and returns his kiss, stroking his neck with her free hand, accepting the challenge. Then, knowing she's gained her point, she releases him and looks down.

"Que-nn . . .. It's so . . . small." Davita breathes the words as if in awe, hesitating.

"Open it."

"Now?"

"Of course, silly."

"I'll let you call me that if you always say it that way."

"*Silly* . . ."

She looks up at him, then down again as her fingers push aside a bit of antique satin string and press back the spring-loaded top. Inside, a ring with a blue stone greets her gaze, causing the girl to breathe in, to hold her breath then release it in a long sigh.

"Quenn-tin . . ."

Without speaking, he draws out the jewel and slips it on her left ring finger, smiling. "You can read about sapphires in the Bible. They're mentioned several times."

"Quentin . . .. Quen, it even fits."

"I love you, Davita."

"Quen . . .. Oh . . ."

The girl looks at her hand, then holds it up to admire the stone in the dim glow of one small light at the back door of the house.

"What . . .?"

"It was my mom's, Davita. Aunt Ev brought it out last week. I said I wanted it, and now I want you to . . ."

Nothing more tonight, I told myself miserably. I was seated in my study. Samantha's last audio has wound down unattended. The old movie playing in my head has blocked out everything . . . extended run. Seems to be a hit. Too bad there's no revenue, I was thinking. Has to be some way to shut this down.

Read a little . . . the new braille book. Go to sleep reading. If I can.

I followed the string from my study door. Down the hall, the bedroom. But searching fingers found no book. Still on the desk. Follow the string back to the study.

Gaining the study without stumbling, I felt around on the desk—audios to be graded, tapes, recorder, pens, pencils. Writing is so strange now. I winced, thinking how it must look. Sometimes I must make my mark, whatever that turns out to be. I fingered the Katz translation . . . *Solomon's Song*. No, not tonight.

Work might do it. Maybe get into the plans for that new tutoring program—something useful and complicated, might drown the mind.

Drowning my mind? Is that what it needs? Think about something else. No. The images aren't fading . . ..

An hour of Ben's wisdom would be great, I told myself. He'll quote St. Paul—that renewal of the mind business. But the mind isn't my problem. More like heart medicine. Ben's an expert on that. Too bad he's so far away. Email? No, not emailed sorrows . . . a non sequitur.

I grasped the string and again made my way out the study, down the hall. Better pray . . . nothing else for it, I was thinking, undoing my tie and unbuttoning the top buttons of my shirt. They're all white now. No braille for colors.

I'm tired, dear Lord.

Unaccountably, I thought of Moshe. An irrational impulse was rising. Scratch around in my memory for a phone number, punch in the digits . . . at this late hour? The thought overtook me without warning and nearly convinced me the rabbi would like to chat.

Moishe . . . I miss talking to him. Moish and me, and Davita . . . Davita.

One weekend when Quentin was over here to see Miss Evelyn, he described this moment to me and Ricky . . . 'bout broke my heart. Pore ole thing! This is pretty much it . . . pretty much as he told us.

CHAPTER FIVE
"Wuss"

IT'S A GOOD THING I HAVE FRIENDS ALL OVER TOWN.
Cindy was at the nurses' station, and she passed on to me these horrible details.
Poor Moish. He told Shirley all about it. Couldn't tell *what* to do.

Finding the old lady asleep, the rabbi decides to slip out, but she jolts awake.
Now she's glarin' at him with round eyes. No escape.

"Col. Mitchell says you have to be saved . . . saaaaaved!"

Levy shifts in his chair. That Baptist better hurry up and get here, he thinks.

"Col. Mitchell says you have to be saved or you'll go to hell . . . hel-ll . . . lll.

With every syllable, the decibels increase by a power and more are on the way.
Rabbi Levy adjusts his tie and smoothes a wrinkle in his trousers, then moves his
hands to the arms of the chair, gripping it with long fingers. His palms are damp .
. . next minute the anger will show up. He can feel it coming, fright too.

A fragrance . . . his wife's perfume? It's all around him. Somebody's brought a
vase of freesias. Shirley? She isn't here now.

"Mrs. Faber, can I get you a drink of water? Your pitcher's almost empty. I
suppose you don't want ice."

"Ice, ice . . . ice. Yes, I want ice. Ice is cold. Hell is hot. It's HOT! You . . . don't
want to go to hell . . . to . . . HELLLLLL!"

Mrs. Faber begins to wail, causing the rabbi to leap from his chair and knock
it with a clang onto a cabinet.

"Just a minute. I'll go . . . I'll get your water."

He bolts from the room toward the nurses' station, almost colliding with Harry Welhelm, MD.

The doctor! Yes, the rabbi tells himself, the excuse I need. This is perfect. I'll talk to Harry about an appointment. Perfect solution!

Miriam Feinemann's fixation with his health will reach crisis levels by Shabbat. She'll look for a report. These days, her age is moving in reverse. Everything increasing—intentions, determination, physical strength. Benjamin Button all over again!

The depression's a memory, and except for the nagging questions about her laughin', as far as Levy can tell, Miriam's low moods have melted like a mornin' mist. In their place are all those things missin' for months—persistence, strength of purpose, zest for life. Now she's better, better enough to come after him about that doctor's appointment! Focused as a pit bull, maybe just as strong. He has to get out of here right now. Anything will do, anything to get 'im far as Mars from Room 53 and Alice Faber.

Yes! Harry . . . right in reach, just when I need him. I can tell Miriam I've talked to the doctor. Won't be an opening any time soon. Somebody else can deal with Alice. In over my head there.

"Harry . . .." He extends his hand.

"Good to see you, Rabbi."

The doctor takes his hand in a limp grip. He's bald as an egg. The black-rimmed glasses magnify gimlet eyes black as marbles made of jet. He angles his thin lips into a chilly smile and murmurs.

"We can ease our concern about your neighbor. She's doing well, well . . . a little time for that arm to heal, just a little time to be entirely well."

"Good news."

"She'll go home in her cast this afternoon. You would do well to let the neighbors know. She is well-supplied with help at home, I believe."

Home! My street . . .!

The rabbi comes to the fact as to an armed adversary. Faber next door again!

"Yes, she'll be glad, I'm sure . . . back to her roses."

He tries to smile as the doctor peers at him over a large envelope then adds it to a thick pile of charts cluttering the nurses' station. Somewhere behind them and to the left the wail rises in pitch, getting louder. Nurses are hurrying from several directions.

"Fifty-three," someone shouts.

Good. Somebody will see about her . . . somebody besides me, Levy thinks.

"I'm glad I . . . ran into you," he mutters in the doctor's direction, rallying a casual tone and a noncommittal smile. "I guess I'll have to have that physical I've been putting off. Can't live with my wife or my congregants if I don't do it. They're making an Olympic sport out of worrying about me."

"Problems?" the doctor murmurs, drawing out the syllables, hypnotic black eyes making a target of his face.

"No, they're . . . uh, just worriers. I've come, uh—you could say, I've come into range."

"Well, my office just called with a cancellation. Tomorrow morning. Nine o'clock."

Adjusting his glasses, Dr. Wellhelm turns to walk toward X-ray. Negotiations? Nil. He nods to a nurse—code, no doubt, for call-my-office-immediately-to-fill-the-cancellation. The deed is done. Here's the appointment card.

Ugh! I'll have to go tomorrow . . . nine o'clock, Levy thinks, regretting the foolish assumption that Harry wouldn't see him for a month, maybe two. Blasting himself for assuming, he glances toward the end of the corridor. Rick Apricot is coming in. Levy greets the sight with something beyond relief.

Turning to a nurse smocked in rollicking pink and blue teddy bears, he says, "Mrs. Faber needs some water. Her pitcher's almost empty, Room 53. She does like ice."

All he can muster is a silly, conspiratorial whisper. Forced? To his own ears, yes it is. But right now, he has to get out, leave it to the Baptist.

Pastor Rick, the good shepherd, he thinks, wondering where the expression came from. He'll know what to say to her. I certainly don't. Probably shouldn't do this to him, but . . . isn't she a Baptist? Baptist or Roman or whatever, the differences aren't too clear to this rabbi!

Levy nods to the pink and blue and flees the nurses' station. In the hall, he barely acknowledges his Baptist friend and surrenders the watch. Gotta be somewhere else, somewhere besides this hospital, and he doesn't want to think about that blasted physical in the morning. Maybe Shirley can come up with a reason to cancel.

No, Shirley will be on their side. Can't serve up hope on that plate.

They lie in bed listening to the rain. The sound isn't peaceful . . . bullets peppering the roof.

Just as he thought, Shirley is all for the physical. She's treated him to one or two clipped Israeli speeches about unsuspected high blood pressure and diabetes. Then came an uncle, a war hero who, with a yearly physical, would be alive today. The cancer was advanced when they found it. Too late. He died a year before they expected. Tragedy. His country needed him.

This woman should be in politics, Levy thinks, dodging the assault. Missed her calling when she married me.

He can picture MK S. Levi haranguing the full Knesset—a clattering barrage of complicated improvements in their already functional healthcare system. She'll fix every problem, real and imagined. Now, she's blistering the opposition with her special brand of *sturm und drang*, demolishing every argument till the whole governing body pleads with one another to hurry it up—anything to get this woman busy doing something besides scorching the air and waving her arms! Their ears can take no more. Audible groans, but the vote is hers, overwhelmingly.

When I die, she can run for office—high office . . . could ectually be prime minister some day, he thinks.

No, no! I won't say it like that.

It's a linguistic virus or something, he tells himself, turning over. Can't get comfortable. Last week I talked redneck, this week I sound like a mom and pop selling flatbread and hummus a block from the Old City.

Drifting toward sleep, he feels the Israeli bending of *a* toward *e* wiggling its way out of some English tutor's mouth. He's a goateed chap who glares and shakes his black wayfarers, murmuring, "Ehctually, you must ehdjust your enunciation more precisely, Moshe. A valiant attempt, nonetheless. Theht will be all for today."

Lingering hint of the British and it's creeping up on me. No, I'm an American and a Southerner. Thanks very much, ya'll. This Moses says *actually*.

He's too sleepy to lecture himself. But the sounds are easier to wrangle than the thought of Prime Minister Shirli Levi.

She certainly has it in her. Yeah, and she'll change the *y's* back to *yod's*. Another certainty! Her name has a nice ring. There they are, the electorate, talking happily among themselves, telling the neighbors to vote for her.

"Shirley Levy, Shirli Levi—she lived in the United States until her husband died. Leading rabbi, you know. We are again electing a woman, a new Golda!"

Half awake, he lumbers listlessly over the scene. He's already dead and buried. There's . . . the tombstone, lettering precise, perfectly executed Star of David. The Jewish section of the Mount Magnolia cemetery, cool and shady . . . big white blooms dotting the shine of deep green leaves, edging the breeze with that lemony scent . . . horrible. Will she come back to weep at his grave? No. Too busy running the country. Might even remarry—

Of course! She'll marry some IDF brilliant who sports an eye patch and potters around in his house shoes, knife between his teeth in case of attack. Named Moshe.

The rabbi groans, feeling the pressure of six feet of dirt on top of him.

"You sleep with too much cover, *hamoodi*. Stop *fighting* it . . .."

Remarry? Yes, be magnanimous. I will be dead, dead and gone, gone for . . . for good.

"I . . . what?"

Dozing off. Now Shirley's distant remark nudges him back into the dark room.

The rain has strengthened to a storm and the wind is howling—the sound, straight from Alice Faber's mouth. Her white hair is streaming in the wind, little wisps of it blowing out behind her like a trail of smoke. Ancient banshee on the loose.

Saved . . . saved, saaaaved.

No . . . I'm still asleep, he tells himself, wallowing in waves of semi-alertness like a waterlogged swimmer, at the same time struggling with a real-world need to estimate the exact number of inches falling from the sky. A cataclysm of rain, the whole world over.

"You are moaning. What *is* it, darling?"

Two or three more speeches are waiting in the winds . . . no, in the wings, in the wings. She's hastening me to my doom . . . the clinic, 9:00 a.m.

Too sleepy. Can't . . . tell my wife I will not bother with a silly appointment a few hours from now. No sleep and I can't come through it with . . . flying colors flying in the wind . . .. No, with a perfect bill of health because I'll be so—so blasted not myself. Can't sleep. I'm too wrought up! What does that do to you? Probably makes your heart race.

He relives his visit to the Feinmanns, a moment now recasting itself in surreal outlines à la Poe. This Poe has a Salvador Dali mustache. The rabbi turns over again and straightens one troublesome leg.

What in the world? Should I tell the doctor? No. All it takes is some little thing like that. Doctors get all excited. Harry will skewer me with those black eyes then murmur exactly what his med school trained him to murmur.

There he is, peering into my soul! "Well, well . . .." He'll order a series of tests . . . could go on till summer, even into the fall! Ugh. Won't tell him . . . I will not tell him.

Shirley is awake. He can feel her looking at him. Now, something about the cover.

"What is it, Moshe?"

"Nothing . . . uh, not a thing. Think . . . I was dreaming. Storm? Didn't hear a storm forecast."

"Tornado warnings on the late weather report. Surprise, surprise . . . you went to bed already, *motek*."

"Tornado . . .? Tor . . . nado, tor . . .."

He's running from a fiery chariot with fiery horses—running, feeling the heat behind him, hearing the rumble of hooves thundering upon him, nearer. A loud crack of thunder pushes him over the edge, the sense of forces more powerful than he confounding his resistance as if by the wave of a hand. The rabbi falls into deep sleep.

In the dark, the rabbitzen mulls over the health issues.

Moshe, Moshe . . .. What an ehss about doctors my man is. Typical. Think they'll live forever.

In the storm, the bed is cozy. She thinks about those strange little nursery songs that work by shushing the babes with terrors, making them feel hidden and safe in their beds. Ruth has had told her . . ..

Scares 'em to sleep, prob'ly, Ruth said.

Shirley is drifting off, losing the train of thought carrying broken up cradles fallen down from treetops, dead old gray geese, rabbits caught for their skins— buntings to wrap the babies in. Buntings. What are those . . .?

If I die before I wake . . ..

Ruth's voice murmuring scary American lullabies blends with the crash of the storm as the room, illuminated brilliantly by a flash of lightning, falls again into darkness now covering her like a blanket. Without prelude, a familiar voice in her heart mingles with Ruth's then fills the night, calling her briefly to semi-alertness and worship.

Shir-li, my song . . . my song.

Curling next to the rabbi's sleeping form, she reaches toward the welcoming Presence with words more accessible than the lullabies. Words she learned in childhood come unbidden . . . like comfortable old friends.

"Blessed art thou, Lord our God, King of the universe, who closes my eyes in sleep, my eyelids in slumber. May it be your will, Lord my God and God of my fathers, to grant that I lie down in peace and that I rise again to life. Hear, O Israel, the Lord our God, the Lord is One . . .. Blessed be the Lord by day; blessed be the Lord by night; blessed be the Lord when we lie down; blessed be the Lord when we rise up. The Guardian of Israel neither slumbers nor sleeps. Into thy hand I commit my spirit; O Lord, faithful God, you have saved me, for in thy Salvation I have hoped, O Lord."

. . . precious Name, the precious Name, she thinks in English as the Hebrew of the prayer blends gently with concerns too heavy to bear alone.

Adonai, let him be healthy, and I need him to . . .. Please, let . . ..

Lapsing into Summerian, a blend of thanksgiving and praise, petition and drowsy rejoicing, the rabbitzen falls asleep beside her husband.

Shirley's makin' biscuits. Moish likes biscuits and she's taken up the challenge.
Israelis don't eat biscuits . . . just the ones who used to live over here.

"Breakfast? With gravy? Biscuits are sweet!"

"You've never eaten a biscuit?" Moshe said. "No, not sweet . . . unless with jelly. Or you can put honey on 'em."

Ken, Uri talked about study sessions, biscuits with honey. He ate biscuits . . . at Harvard. So, not the British kind. Not biscotti. Not sweet.

Moshe went on, "American, Southern—big and fluffy," he said. "They're proof the South will rise again." That meant what?

"Probably nothing," she explained to me. "Teasing. Moshe, the comedian."

"Doesn't the whole world like our music?" he said that day. "Everybody eats biscuits. It's a credential—you know, fried chicken, sweet tea . . . cooked vegetables, biscuits."

Shirley's gettin' the American/American South distinctions, but the passion? Why? "Vegetables . . . soft from overcooking? Moshe's Yankee Green Beans speech, a stand-up routine, follows. 'Like apples,' he says. 'The crunch is audible!'

"No cooking advice from him," she told me that day.

Right now Shirley's takin' the pastry cloth and rollin' pin cover from the 'frigerator and rememberin' Biscuit Lesson Number One.

"Shirleyhon," I told her. "You havta get a pastry cloth for biscuits . . . and pie crust. You don't want extra flour in the dough. Not the thing. A little bit of flour's on the pastry cloth. Just stays there from last time, not enough to mess up the dough.

"Another thing: pretend the flour's gunpowder. If you work it, it'll blow up in your face. Well, I don't really mean blow up—"

Shirley's face looked white. Just some flour maybe.

"If you think that," I went on, pretendin' not to notice, "you won't fiddle with it. The thing is, Do. Not. Develop. The Gluten—that's the gluey stuff, makes bread dough sticky—you know, elastic. With biscuits, it's what happens if you work the flour too much. Not what you want for biscuits. *Thou shalt not develop the gluten:* that's the 'leventh commandment. If the gluten kicks in . . . well, you don't want that. Y'want 'em light, not tough."

RuthAnne "Mishmish" Apricot, that's me . . . her key to a strange new world. As wives of old friends, we see each other more than most wives of pastors and rabbis. Tel Aviv and the South Carolina Upstate are pretty far apart and bridgin' the gap was slow. Then somethin' happened.

One evenin' as she lighted the Shabbat candles, Shirley started wonderin' about the friends of a rabbi's wife. In a kitchen across town, the woman soon to be her best pal was talkin' to herself and makin' the coffee. "Girlfriend," I was tellin' myself, "who *is* the pal of a Baptist *minister's* wife? Can y' tell me that, Ruthbaby? Who is it?"

The rabbitzen smiles when she thinks about me. Right now she's dustin' flour from her hands, thinkin' she's found the sister she always wanted. Some benefits to that—biscuits, for example.

"Cut the shortening into the flour?"

No mystery for this Southern biscuitiere . . . how's that for makin' up a word (and you say that, "bis-cutier"). Shirley had just crashed into Biscuit Necessity No. 1, and I was right there to help.

"You get out your pastry blender," I said. "Gotta have one, honey. It's like th' pastry cloth. Things just don't work right if you don't."

Today, Shirley's siftin' the flour, thinkin' about Biscuit Necessity No. 4, the sifter. That's after No. 2, the pastry cloth, and No. 3, the rollin' pin cover.

"No," I told 'er, "don't let anybody say, 'no need to sift.' That's baloney. If you don't sift, y' get extra flour."

So that's done—she's sifted the flour, measured, resifted with the rest of the stuff—salt, baking powder, soda. The shortnin's cut in, buttermilk added. And she remembers her first biscuits. A true *balagan*, let me tell you. A *balagan's* bigger than a snafu, like a snafu that gets named it's so big—like a hurricane, y'know? Those biscuits were big, yellow, and tasted . . . there was no word. Not even in Hebrew.

I was at her house soon after. In one hand, she held up baking powder, baking soda in the other. "Both, *chaverah*?" she said. "The same, these two?"

"*No ma'am,*" I told 'er. "Not the same thing! Sometimes one, sometimes both, but if you get too much soda, it will rise real high, whatever it is, turn yella, and taste like soap."

Shirley's eyes were round. Three full seconds.

Q? Simple A: the soda!

Shirley hadn't mentioned the big yellas, but now she was curious.

"*Balagan* . . . last week. Moshe choked. I was calling Wellhelm."

"The recipe has half as much bakin' *soda* as bakin' *powder*. Did you reverse 'em?" Ruthie, the fountain of knowledge!

"Moshe," Shirley said, "is telling me everything American. But Moshe is a man. He likes biscuits, he is not making them. Baking powder? Soda? What does he know about too much soda? Or buttermilk?" She'd thought of somethin' else I said.

"Just make some if the store's out," I told 'er one day. "Tablespoon of vinegar in a cup of milk. Let it sit out for a while . . . you know, so the curdle'll work. Or lemon juice." When Shirley forgot to pick up buttermilk, she tried out my advice. The kitchen was hot. Right away, buttermilk! There it was. Shirley remembers Biscuit Lesson Three, maybe Four. The recipe said, "Incorporate the buttermilk with a few swift strokes."

" . . . 'a few swift strokes'? I stroke a cat."

"They mean *maneuvers*, stirrin'," I told her. "It's a few 'cause of the gunpowder. You don't overwork anything with flour in it unless it's bread, Shirleybabe . . . well, for sure not biscuits, and watch the soda and bakin' powder!" From her look, I finally got it that to mention gunpowder wasn't the thing.

She's now a biscuit chef, not an apprentice—hummin' and spreadin' the pastry cloth on that solid walnut table Moish's grandfather willed to 'im. It's just right for making biscuits, *buhseder*. She eases the dough from bowl to cloth. More flour? Only a little. Dough won't stick on this cloth.

The friendship has other benefits beyond Southern cookin'. With the oven at pre-heat, Shirley's relivin' some other things I said. When we knew each other well, I told 'er about Naomi and SIDS. Shirley knew about grief, fresh as yesterday.

"More babies?" she asked

"We're prayin'," I said, "but the Lord isn't tellin' us to go for it. Not yet."

She told me her story. One miscarriage. More. Then we talked about Moish and Rick. Not much to say about lost babies. They grieve, but they don't talk. For us, friendship's a *haven*. We share . . . pain and trouble and questions. We have each other. Like a mirror.

Shirley's wonderin' if I'm makin' biscuits. Two ways to do it, I've told her. I guess that was Lesson Five. Some like 'em thick, others thin—crunchy like crackers. Moshe wants thick, she tells herself. Knead for thin.

After a while our chats became easy. Reasons to see each other came more often. Some commonality's deeper than grief, but we didn't get it at first.

"In life, we can't be gunpowder," Shirley's told me. She's easin' the rollin' pin over the floury surface and thinkin' about that.

We're not biscuits, we are bread dough—kneaded and kneaded. *B'seder* . . . the Baker knows what he's doing. *Jeremiahu* went to the potter. Potter, baker— they work clay and dough . . . roughly. Something beautiful comes. *Tov m'od*. Ruth and I laughed . . . cried, our arms around each other. The green line was crossed. Friends? Sisters now. We had a commission . . . as with IDF. We are under orders. She is speaking openly, taking care of her big man who is preaching to the Baptists, also to others coming by—even rabbis. The common thing is this: In our hearts, a throne. The Messiah of Israel reigns. *Yeshua HaMeshiach*, I say. Ruth says, "the Lord Jesus Christ."

Shirley's twistin' the biscuit cutter, takin' out the doughnut ring, and she starts pressin' circles in the dough. Hot oven, the pan ready, timer set . . . biscuits for lunch.

The right time to lay out the sweet truth to her husband hasn't come. She's felt the acid rain; now she just circles the topic.

"The time was right for me," she's explained. "Everything came together. A visit home. Tel Aviv. Batya is saying, 'Beth Evenezer in an hour? Want to go?'"

"Yes, some time with my friend . . . nothing else to do. Even now, every detail—fresh, as if yesterday. *Ken*, the time was right."

But the right time to tell Moshe . . . when will that be?

I've told Ricky and he's glad for an ally. For Moishe's fifty-third birthday, he thought of that Hebrew Bible. Inspired! Be a bridge maybe.

But Moish parries every thrust; he throws up walls, smothers openers. He comes at 'er with scholarly reasonin', jokes, work. Rick's used to it. Shirley's not.

"We'll talk about that later," Moish says and there's no later.

Shirley's not easily shaken, but all this has set her back. She cannot get inside the iceberg castle Moish's made for himself. When she says the name *Yeshua*, the North Wind blows.

"Shut up, shut down, shut out!" Shirley's told me.

She loves her husband and she's gettin' nowhere. Better to pray and wait. At the moment, she's certain of just one thing: Moshe Levy and Yeshua? No.

Now, biscuits in the oven, Shirley's about to call. Time to tell me about Alice. Miz Faber's a Baptist and she's gotten worse. My phone's ringin'.

"Mishmish, we must pray for Ahleece. She is having a behd time."

The Hebrew for "apricot" is her salute to the friendship, not the fruit.

"Shirley, it's you," I say. "I'm glad . . .. I was about to call *you*. She may be comin' home tomorrow, Ricky says. Augusta knows and she'll be ready for her, but I'm not sure they oughta jerk Miz Faber around anymore."

"Not going so well, Mishmish. The arm's better, but she is more frail, Moshe said to me . . . the shock of the fall, probably, and she's afraid to die. A change, even to come home, is not so good. Moshe says the fall did harm. Her problem, more than the broken arm. She is not coming today, Mishmish. We will pray, you are starting. Also for Moshe."

"All right."

I love to pray with Shirley. Feels like livin' back in the Old Testament—Deborah and Miriam and . . . that Abigail.

I put down the blue dishtowel and sit. Telephone prayers with Shirley are nothin' new.

"Dear Lord, one of the last things you did on the cross was look after your mama. She had to be pretty old, and in the middle of all that pain you thought about her. And there was that young disciple, John—the one you loved best, and he was brave enough to stay around when the rest of 'em didn't, and you put 'em together, mother and son. Thank you for that, Lord. It's still amazin'.

"Shirley and I are rememberin' that and we're thankin' you for your care and your compassionate heart, Lord Jesus. We have no idea how to help Miss Alice, pore ole thing. She's scared and her arm's been hurtin' her so bad. When will she be comin' home? When she does, we don't know what to do for her.

"We have to rely on you because we just don't know yet . . . her pastor and me and the neighbors, we don't know exactly what to do. Make her be comforted . . . not afraid anymore. And please help Augusta. Give her the strength to do whatever it is. She's old too, and she'll need all the backup we can think of. Please help us think right.

"No. Wait . . .. That's not it. Lord, what Miss Alice needs is *You*. She needs you to walk into that room and take away that fear. She needs to know you're where your people go—you're our dwellin' place, like Moses said . . . I mean Moses in the Bible.

"Thank you in advance, dear Lord. We need to know what's goin' on with the rabbi, too. In Jesus' name, A-men."

I stop and Shirley prays.

"Our Messiah, I agree. I am asking for wisdom—for the rebbe, to help Ahleece. We are thanking you for your power and compassion. You will bless us with a complete blessing."

"A complete blessing . . . yes you have, dear Lord!"

"*Ken!* . . . yes! *And let us say, Ahmain* . . .."

"AAA-men!"

"Mishmish, who can reach her?"

"I don't know . . . the Lord, for sure. Get into all those tangles, make her remember who she is in him."

"Yes . . . *b'seder*. We will be praying."

The connection drops, and I sit there thinkin', phone in hand.

Better keep on prayin' for Augusta. Pore ole ladies! But you'll help 'em, Lord, I know it. But what was that about the rabbi? Shirley didn't mention anything.

Annabelle moves slowly from her chair to answer the knock at the breezeway. She's never moved fast, not even at sixteen. She sees Augusta and reaches to open the door. With Miss Alice in the hospital, less to do maybe. Don't hafta watch her all the time, Annabelle thinks, not really wonderin' about the visit, just glad to see her friend. She'll have some news for the folks. Always does.

"She sca'ed, Belle."

"Whose sca'ed?"

"Miss Alice, tha's who."

"Why she sca'ed? She's takin' tuins now, uh. Her tuin to be sca'ed?"

"Could be. Whatevuh th' case, she sca'ed . . . real sca'ed. We needs t' pray."

"Wait. How you know this?"

"I know, an' besides, I feel it. Miz Apricot came by . . . hurryin' to the hawspital with some stuff she picked up to take, and she say to pray. I say, 'Miss Alice wuss?' an' she say, 'Miss Alice real concuin'd an' anxious. Y'all pray f' her.'"

"What's she anxious about?"

"She fraid a dyin,' I think, but that's jus' me. You know how Miz Apricot don't be real fowud an' all . . . play'n it down. 'She anxious,' she say."

"Well, that's new."

"New or ol', she sca'ed, an we havta pray."

"This here's a prayin' house now, let me tell you. Y' come to th' right house."

Not wantin' to interrupt the prayers down the hall in the den, Annabelle motions her friend to a chair. The two sit for a minute, close their eyes, cover their faces with their hands, and began to pray.

"Honeylambtail . . .."

The Rev. Rick Apricot loves hearin' my voice on the phone, but he never knows . . . well, I better let Ricky tell you this part. He has this thing about names I can't do justice to, know what I mean?

I can never tell what pet name she might lay on me. Ruth has an arsenal, and the strength of her creativity is powered up by my bewilderment! Worse, she's never satisfied. Every week since the Saturday we got married, she's thought of one or two new names—once, a string of outrageous flower monekers. "My darlin' Rickyrosebush," for example. Later, just "Rosebush." Then, the coup de grace. "Listen, Nastyturtium!" Angrily.

The names are natural as breathing, but the day I became "Sharonyricky rosebush," I asked what was going on. This one sounded like me, legal and undisputed, but what was that "Sharony-" part? When I probed, Ruth sputtered, blue sparks flying from her eyes, causing me to check the door out. Open . . . nothing to block an escape.

Nossir, she could not make out why I'd cause her to be self-conscious! It was like askin' the old man if he slept with his beard in or out of the covers . . . downright irritatin'. I'm sure you get the picture.

In the end, I had to content myself with a contrived theory: to be a "Sharony rosebush" was something like calling yourself a Christian. The adjective was okay for you; the real name was the King's, the real Rose of Sharon.

"Well," she huffed, "you don't expect me to call you the name of the Messiah of Israel, do you . . . as well as the King of Jacob, I hope!"

In the following weeks, she churned out combinations of "Shorty," "Shug," "Shugga," and "Sweetheart"—sometimes "Sweet-Shorty," sometimes just "Shorty," at other times, "Shorty-Shugga-Sweet" or "Shorty Shuggababe" then all tied together in various other horrors like "Sweet-Shorrtee" or "Shorteeshug." "Sweetee-Shorrtee" rhymed with Congaree and Santee and Hory; they were the SC-Native American items, I guess. Knew better than to challenge her. No grounds, no hope of a cessation. She would make up names for me, and I'd have to . . . well, like it or lump it.

In fact, I almost liked it . . . on the inside of my heart anyway, the place where I think of my small, little Ruthie seated next to the King, that mighty arm lovingly drawing her close, where he sits on his heavenly throne and she sits with him, glorious orange hair poofing out all around his shoulder like a cloud of fire, fire gathering up fire.

The Lord has promised me a new name, and Ruth's the earthly agent, apparently, giving 'em out in cloudy bucketfuls, loaded with divine inspiration. Have to live with it. Good thing there's a rule about pastors' wives not serving on committees! She might come up with some name in an unguarded moment. The thought chills me to the bone.

"Ruthbaby, what can I do for you?"

"Lammyluv, you hafta to go see Miz Faber again. Y' know how she got that idea that some way she's goin' to hell, and now she's had a heart attack. They don't know what to do with her over there. Martha Ann just called and she's desperate. Dr. Well can't get her to listen to a word he says. You know how soft he talks. Then she opens her mouth like she's gonna holler and everybody just clears out.

"Dr. Well can stand it, but he can't get a word in edgewise—nothin' she's willin' to listen to. She can't hear the best, an' what she can hear she's not takin' in. See if you can go over there . . . right now? They're thinkin' with a heart attack and all, if she goes into another screech, she—"

"I'll go. Thanks. See ya later, baby."

"Bye, Sweetpudd'n. I love you."

"I love you, too . . . .. Save up some kisses."

"Stoppit. You're bein' a pastor right now, remember? Somebody might hear and not know it's me."

"Okay, MRS. APRICOT—avoid the appearance of evil and all that. See you in a bit, MY DARLING RUTHIEBABE. I'm heading over to the hospital, and I said that out loud, I guess you heard . . . as well as everybody else."

The line went dead and I put the phone in my pocket.

"'Gusta, you 'n me gotta to go to the nussin' home. We gotta go now. If we want to do what we need t' do fuh Miss Alice, we gotta do it now."

"I know it's true. I feel it. Let me get m' hat. You drivin'?"

"'Co'se I'm drivin'. You think the rabbi go'n take us?"

Augusta laughs with her. What they're doin' Rabbi Levy doesn't need to know. The thought of lettin' him in on it horrifies 'em though neither one cares to pursue the point. Chuckles are enough.

"He know you goin' out?"

"He's sleep . . . takin' a nap. Besides, we won't be out long. Miz Levy's in the house. Lunch is ovuh. She knows."

On a Levy day, Annabelle has to to tell 'em somethin'. She can't just waltz out. Doesn't do that at the Feinemanns' either.

"No need to tell him then, is it?"

"We don't need. 'Side that, he tuinin' into uh fuss budget. We don't need that, do we?"

"Sho don't! Don't need no fuss budget."

"You say Room 53, same as the hawspital?"

"Thas' right, same as the hospital. Easy t' remember."

CHAPTER SIX
Light

MY FRIEND, THIS POLITE OLE QUENTIN, GETS HIS SHOES shook when he talks to me. He does do that. I'm such a shock he can barely deal with it, so he has to give in and talk. It's good for 'im. I guess I learn a thing or two just like he does. This is what he told me . . . in his own stuffy words. Man, he can be borin'. Pore students. This was some day, let me tell you, darlin'.

Blindness fixed the habit. I often stood in the doorway of Buttrick Hall and ran my fingers along the Gothic contours. When blindness descended, Edwards' architectural details formed a link to the classroom building—familiar even when I couldn't see it. The lines were pleasing. When my eyes could feast on the curves, swirls and parallels, my memory took note . . . made a record. It would orient me in the dreadful, uncharted waters of the strange new journey. I couldn't have guessed.

Dangers were everywhere even as the way, like the Gothic contours of this building, became more familiar. Unexpected hazards, wildly dismaying surprises . . . every day. But as my confidence grew, I learned the path from class to dining hall, from campus to my house—there and back again, as Tolkien has it.

Just now I was thinking about William Augustus Edwards, architect. Did students know about this South Carolinian, my ancestor? Edwards wasn't an uncommon name at home, but I hadn't heard of the man myself till that random online search when I should have been doing other things.

Not entirely random. And I learned something. Came away with questions. "An Edwards connection?" I queried Aunt Ev. "Wasn't my mother an Edwards?"

"Yes, darling . . . an Edwards." A long, bewildering, genealogical recitation followed. I listened, but I wouldn't remember. My lack of interest pains Aunt Ev, and I've learned to avoid the subject. This time I did my best to look interested. I was, a little.

Then, as now, I was looking for an escape; it felt better to think about the architect than all the horrid questions pressing in on me. An imagined Edwards, the feel of his Gothic angles and curves at Buttrick doorways—the subtleties of style dictating these particular lines and smoothed stone edges—were a dependable and effective distraction. Today old William Augustus wouldn't dismiss the worries he was supposed to replace.

Leaving Buttrick with white-knuckled determination, I gripped my cane and made my way down the steps to the accustomed brick walkway. As usual, I was commandeering every resource to get around the Agnes Scott campus unassisted.

In five years, these walks had become as familiar as the daily path around my house—a familiarity that would save me. At home, the guiding strings a friend put up to help the blind man were a true lifeline. But now, the cane was replacing them, even at home. Joined to my newly awakened senses and more than reliable memory map, the cane was beginning to do it all.

Somehow I have to get around, I told myself those first black days. And I have to do it alone. Who can relate to sudden blindness? Nobody. The answers have to come from me, and they'll have to be there every day.

Deliverance beckoned from within the darkness. Materiel was stored in abundance somewhere within myself. That would be the battleground, the place of victory or defeat. My inner landscape was a strange new terrain, embattled, and now it was all I had.

The house is only a block down and on the college side of the street. Traffic is heavy on Candler Road, the street Agnes Scott faces on the east, but that crossing I need never make. The school fronts on College Avenue, and a tunnel under the street provides a sidewalk in the direction of Decatur; after a while, I ventured that far. Once Samantha walked with me.

As I made each determined new foray into the routines, I found the way opening before me. I could not doubt that the Sovereign Lord I've known since boyhood was helping me. And the Lord eased my mind: No, this isn't pride; it's not vain self-reliance.

What I faced was the stuff of pure necessity. Others might not understand, but I knew the Lord of Hosts was in it with me. I was encouraged and the coping projects succeeded. The sense of divine approval was unmistakable.

Verses from Isaiah sprang to life with the blindness, giving me perspective: "The Spirit of the Lord shall rest upon him, the Spirit of wisdom and understanding, the Spirit of counsel and might, the Spirit of knowledge and of the fear of the Lord. His delight is in the fear of the Lord. And he shall not judge by the sight of his eyes, nor decide by the hearing of his ears."

The decision to trust my own resources was the basis of another choice when a plan was gently pressed upon me, the offer of permanent assistance. At first, the school's designated helper guided me everywhere. The need was undeniable, but when the dean offered to hire someone permanently, I said no. Several students offered. One was Samantha. I said no.

In time, I became accustomed to the cane at home. On campus, I found I could trust another set of clues, this other familiarity. I had by heart the path from Buttrick classrooms to the library next door. In my sleep, I could get to the dining hall beyond the library, around the corner on the same side of the one-way drive winding through campus on the north side. I could find my way to the chapel next to Buttrick on the other side. The buildings I frequent are on the same side of the street. My internal map of faculty offices showed me the door of every administration friend, every colleague. The men's room I could locate.

How would a student help me with that one? The question gave the dean a chuckle; my firm, sardonic tone sealed the *No, thank you.*

Though I was prepared to point it out, I didn't need to remind the dean of the school's recent restructuring of curbs and stairways, a considerate provision executed long before accommodations for the handicapped became a mandate with the backbone of law. Thanks to a very civilized ethos around here, I could go just about anywhere without fear of stumbling at a curb or falling down stairs. Where there were no ramps, I found elevators. A lifetime away, though actually the very recent past, I privately mocked the elevator folks. *I* would walk up stairs and have a healthier heart, keep off the extra pounds, as well.

When the blindness came on, the metamorphosis was like waking in some grim prison cell to find myself Charles Darnay facing the guillotine. I fought despair with the blind piano games of my youth, but found little relief. The doctors gave me academic muddlings, nothing more.

Blindness and the psyche? The subconscious, emotions, anxiety . . .? The diagnosis wandered off in that direction. No, no physical cause. We just don't know. We're gaining on the issues, but . . . still at ground level with the psychosomatic effects.

Who could have predicted it?

"I will make it," I told the dean in that conversation. Then I said, "Thanks for your time," picked up my cane, and as if to prove the point, got up from my chair and moved confidently toward the door. The dean couldn't know how much it helped to hear footsteps approaching in the hall. The dean wouldn't guess I was praying earnestly, "Lord, please don't let that person have two full cups of coffee!" Coffee wasn't expected so I felt safe enough. And yes, I made it through the door without crashing into the bookcase on one side or the person who wasn't bringing coffee on the other. I left the dean and made it out of the building without mishap.

Like ancient lighthouses, sounds rose here and there, becoming essential sensory points to orient me in the darkness. But my cane was the marvel. As I caught the fine points of using it, the thing began to see with eyes all its own, and memory supplied me with auxiliary aid from my internal map of the outside world. Faculty friends made an improvised braille map of ramps and elevators. All of it helped.

I am grateful for what others did, but the problem was mine.

Blindness is the frame, whatever images rush in to fill the space. On this day, coping skills aren't in the picture. I've made it through one semester with Samantha in my class, but today none of my best interventions succeed. Resolve is eroding. People are more interesting than architecture and dead architects, even ancestor architects—but Samantha? I am capitulating and I know it.

I cannot shut her out of my thoughts and it's not just Samantha. It's both of them . . . Samantha Edwards, Davita Levy. But how can that be? Wouldn't perfumes be different after twenty years?

Not in this case! It was the same. I'd know the fragrance anywhere.

Questions are answered in the vivid new signals from other senses, a surprise advantage with loss of sight. Senses awoke, senses I took for granted when eyesight dominated my life, but unwanted discoveries have followed. One of them, the intrusive power of perfume! The fragrance was Davita's.

When Samantha approached my desk bringing a paper, the air curled itself around me like an olfactory feast.

the same, it was the same.

I had to grip the desk to steady myself. Would she notice? The person in front of me, the eyes that would perceive my chagrin, did not fill my gaze; I couldn't see the students in the room—not those on the back row, not the one at my desk. I was alone, in a dark place. Control required a strength I doubted then found. I consciously loosened the tension in my fingers, smiled with conscious welcome, and consciously greeted my best student, assuring her I'd enjoy looking at her paper.

The words were habit, habit and euphemism. What I meant was this: I will listen—in her case, with pleasure.

Somehow, the plan to record student work was a success. Everyone was willing—students, staff, others helping behind the scenes. Everyone was ready to fall in with the project. The kindness of the school amazed me. When the black darkness shut me off, a committee from the Departments of English and Psychology consulted my doctors and afterwards, with better understanding, sent a recommendation to the dean. A procedure was in place by the time students arrived, all of them curious about the prof suddenly gone blind. The horror moved sluggishly toward a new normal; things went on somewhat as before, thanks to the combined efforts of many good friends. Thanks be to God.

But there was no provision for the hazards of fragrance . . . or Davita's face. It swam into the darkness like a misty presence in a persistent dream, sharpened with the seeing of memory. It was an image I wanted to escape, yet dreaded losing. Davita, Davita—

Emotions I was locked in with were easier to control, but Samantha is perceptive. She would see into any drummed-up determination. Sensitivity like hers wouldn't miss my confusion. Undergraduate though she is, she could be teaching the course herself! Her observations lack the depth of scholarly experience, but the things she sees in the works we read reveal such keen perception that I forget how little she actually knows. Her previous schooling was excellent. I've known graduate students not so well prepared. There's more. It's as if she's personally acquainted with the authors, a confidante in all their inner joys and struggles. Where did that understanding come from? It's the stuff of wonder. It could become an obsession.

Aunt Ev talks about "unflinching candor," a trait she admires. She's taught me to admire it. I must be candid. Samantha is an obsession.

I will not guide her Independent Study, though it would be to her benefit. I cannot trust myself. I will not help her with all the fine point questions about graduate schools certain to come up in the fall. Someone else will have to do it.

Samantha . . . anything about Samantha is a troubling thought. She restores Davita. Yet Samantha is making a place for herself, her own place on her own terms. Even worse is that absurd blanket of felt disloyalty settling about me, a ridiculously irrational accusation heavier than every caution I level at myself as I rehearse all the verbotens, the ethical hazards of falling in love with a student. Disloyalty?

Yes . . . unaccountably, I feel disloyal to Davita.

I don't want to leave the college, but I may have to. I've been at Agnes Scott only five years, and the position is advantageous in every respect—perfect, in fact, except for Samantha Edwards!

On that day, on the steps of Buttrick, Davita's face filled one huge wall of my inner screening room, but now the face has two names, not just one, and there's another face, as well.

For the twentieth time since black daybreak, I tried to dismiss the only other question keen enough to make me feel worse than the drifting sense of Samantha-Davita edging a permanent place into my life. The face of Davita's twin obscures everything, forces an unwanted blend of memories and present realities.

They're all connected. I have to deal with the muddle, one person at a time. If I succeed, I may regain the peace I'm losing, at least some of it. Blindness is challenge enough.

Only a few more weeks of the term, I was telling myself. I have to sit down with him, just him . . . but what will that be like? Maybe afterwards I can deal with what Samantha is doing to me . . . but an *after Davita*? Is it possible?

And what if it is? Even if I can start life over, it can't be with Samantha. If with her, it can't be here! Still, the meeting I dread will have to come first. That much is certain.

Life after Davita seems worst of all. Maybe there won't be an *after Davita*—Samantha's appeal, perhaps, is the appeal of the impossible.

No, I tell myself. She has an appeal all her own, and it makes me feel disloyal to Davita? Davita's been gone more than a dozen years!

I feel muddled and old and weary. The effort to live with blindness accounts for some of it. Students and teachers are polite; I know they look out for me—avoid collisions, choose not to cross in front of me or do anything to make me stumble. When I fall into bed at night, I am exhausted, just glad for one more step toward the goals I've set myself. Thoughts of Samantha and Davita edge in upon my sleep, and soon the twin is there, as well. I wake miserable. This morning, it all came to a head.

I will not put this off, I told myself, injecting the admonition with icy severity as I made my way from the classroom building to the chapel.

Though the alarm clock proclaimed dawn, there was no light to tell me so. Psalm 50 struck me where I live, bringing to the forefront all the tangled issues I've try to avoid. Words of today's psalm from the Scripture CD have dogged my path and stationed themselves to collide with me on the school's brick walks. Headed for class, I heard them as I cautiously made my way into Buttrick and down the wide hall. They waited at every classroom door. One line of the psalm iterated a command in every conversation. The words filled my head and spoke to my heart.

> Consider this, you who forget God, lest I tear you in pieces, and there be none to deliver.

The syllables echoed in my mind. They derailed the Chaucer lecture. I could hardly think. There was no class discussion. I cared so little about what I was saying I could spring out no student comments, not one.

The chapel would be empty. No one to interrupt me. I'll bother no one, I told myself. The term was coming to an end—students off somewhere worrying, cradling neglected textbooks in library carrels or labs or dorm rooms. They wouldn't be coming here.

I edged myself into one of the side pews and knelt. The posture honors God and hauls my recalcitrant flesh toward reverence, a humble acknowledgment of who I am and the one I'm addressing. Though the habit of a lifetime, kneeling is a decision, and the choice fulfills its purpose. For a moment I thought about the worshipers who have prayed and sat quietly here, quietly as if in a rocking chair.

How can they do it, I asked myself. Has to be a different culture. I know some very reverent and faithful—

PRAY, I told myself. You are not the judge! From habit, I shut my eyes.

"Almighty and most merciful Father, we have erred and strayed from thy ways like lost sheep. We have followed too much the devices and desires of our own hearts. We have offended against thy holy laws. We have left undone those things, which we ought to have done; we have done those things, which we ought not to have done. But thou, O Lord, have mercy upon us. Spare thou those who confess their faults, and restore thou those who are penitent, according to thy promises declared unto mankind in Christ Jesus our Lord. And grant, O most merciful Father, for his sake, that we may hereafter live a godly, righteous, and sober life, to the glory of thy holy name."

My straying thoughts edged toward submission. Heard by my own ears, the familiar lines from the *Book of Common Prayer* woke my heart. It helps to pray aloud. Touch of the Shepherd's crook, I was smugly thinking.

. . . nice, poetic figure.

Recognizing the tilt of pride and the twin whispering *I don't care*, I shoved them away, ordering my mind to be still. I would approach the Almighty in my own words.

Just talk now.

A command, but I welcomed the desire to pray. It comes from outside me.

"Lord God, for years, I've swept aside your reminders. You want me to make things right with Moshe, but I haven't. You've opened a door; he may be willing. When we were together, he seemed . . . what? I felt openness. Openness in me too. Help me. I want to make things right. Give me wisdom. Please give me the words and the heart to say them. You've shown me that I love him. He was once like a brother. I miss the things we did together—talking, studying. We've been distant too long. Help me with the timing, the place. Every place and every time are present to you. You promise wisdom when we ask . . . and without reproach, gracious God. We're sheep, foolish and wandering. Thank you for your merciful care."

I felt a check and continued the prayer within myself. The Lord would hear.

Lord, Moshe and Davita —memories of one ignite memories of the other . . . and what about her? What about . . . *Samantha*? Lord God, I need you every hour. Thank you for the cross. I need a Savior every hour. Yes, every hour.

Time to attend, to be done with poured out petitions, even the heartfelt words of easy thanksgiving. They were right, but it was time to listen.

The coolness of the place, the familiar smell of old wood and old books, brass polish, flowers and dust, even a suggestion of perfumed hand lotion or fingernail polish surrounded me like heralds of the incarnation—comforting, a sort of response. They suggested, no promised, the bracing words I waited for: instructions, commands. Nothing quite clear, just a sense of burdens lifted, answers on the way. I had to speak my thanks. Words are my business.

Thank you, Lord . . . thank you for who you are, O most wonderful.

Call upon me in the day of trouble; I will deliver you, and you shall glorify me . . . .. The one who offers praise glorifies me, and to the one who rightly orders his conduct, I will show the salvation of God.

The lines drifted around me like an enveloping mist on a warm breeze. Words of the psalm that arrested me like a daybreak sergeant spoke healing, as by a steadying right hand, for the bruise inflicted by a jolting left. They suffused the deepest corners of my concern, melted the fear, offered resolution and the settled rightness of spirit I longed for.

Lord, you are merciful!

The response of my heart was like the next necessary breath, the thing that had to be if life would go on. For several minutes I knelt. I was relaxed. Just a curve of bowed head and bending shoulders. Peace was coming on, a real breathing peace.

Then, with eyes still shut, I felt for the cane. I would stand then make my way out of the chapel. No footsteps, no intruder on the quiet. I hadn't interrupted the spiritual business of anyone else.

Last night, I laid out a handkerchief to pocket with my keys. When I exited the house, I gathered my cane, briefcase, books and audios, then hurried out, leaving the handkerchief. Now my face was wet, but I hardly noticed. I was beginning to see light.

"There's that cat again!"

Debra Quarles, my canoein' partner, is peerin' around the nurses' station as the marmalade slithers into a room far down the hall, way too far to chase.

"Somebody's sure takin' advantage of that new rule about pets. The tomcat's

visitin' everybody now. Hope he does some good," Debra fusses.

Jessica Lynch, the charge nurse, looks up from a chart and clicks her ballpoint. While the discussions were still ragin', she was vocal about the No Pets rule, predictin' bites, allergies, ringworm, cat scratch fever, disasters of every kind, never mind trouble with the therapy dogs. They're supposed to be here!

But the home office said *Allowed*. Branches of the nursin' home chain have discretionary choices over some rules, but not this one. Pets, includin' cats, will be allowed. Accordin' to the new doctrine, they make residents feel at home, a bit of home away from home—comfort, companionship. Besides that . . . well, it's the rule now. But how can you be sure a cat isn't a stray? Beulah's full of 'em and they get in.

One staff meetin', an odd Internet item came up. The table explodeded when somebody remembered the cat that predicted deaths. Staff members who weren't so computer savvy saw the news item on TV or in the papers. Everybody had an opinion. The topic nearly destroyed an already packed agenda; Jerome nixed it before it could get goin'. Then they forgot about it . . . mostly. Jessica says it hung in the air for weeks. Then the administrator firmly banned any mention.

Now, fewer people theorize at break about the Internet cat; the item has lapsed as a subject of conversation. Only the cat lovers find a reason to keep up the talk. But now, a new thought is formin' in two heads on duty at the nurses' station.

Maybe we should pay more attention to what that orange cat is doin' around here, the charge nurse says to herself. Is he visitin' people who're about to die . . .? Still, if he makes Mrs. Faber screech again, he'll be out of here!

For Debra Quarles, the notion of a death-predicting feline is creepy. It makes no sense, not scientific, but we better keep an eye on that tomcat.

At the door of Room 53, where Alice Faber now lies motionless, the marmalade takes three cautious steps, sniffs loudly and begins to purr. In one smooth bound, he reaches the old lady's feet and slowly begins an investigation that include several possibilities—edgin' forward, or stoppin' stock-still, frozen where he is, fixed and immobile as a ceramic mantlepiece cat, or a third and more likely option, of breakin' into immediate flight.

Findin' the sleeper undisturbed by his presence, he follows the outline of a thin leg and halts. He listens to the shallow breathin' and waits for developments, readyin' himself to leap into the air and off the bed at the slightest hint of anything that doesn't suit 'im. The warmth and stillness are reassurin', and he crouches tentatively then sits, lettin' his tail arrange itself along the leg. Cautiously, he settles full-length, next to the sleeper, and stretches out his forepaws Sphinx-like in front of him. Then he relaxes, still purrin' loudly. In a moment he's sleep.

Unnoticed by him, one ancient eye opens a crack, then the other. Then somewhere in that jungle of nerve endin's, jumbled thought paths, misplaced impulses that register needs, wants, and memories, a dim sense of the familiar begins to form. A purr...?

Purring . . .? It's my Angel Puss purring! Angel, my kitty! Where has she been so long? It's her, sleeping by my leg! Angel Puss is sleeping with me. She's guarding my bed. Sweet old kitty.

Thoughts but no words fill the silence of the room, and the cat continues his drowsy purr. The figure on the bed is immobile as the cat, unwillin' to disturb the visitor or reveal the fact that it's under scrutiny.

Alice lies absolutely still, listenin', feelin' the warmth and pressure of the small feline body. It's her ninth birthday, and she's had Angel Puss one year. Every night the cat guards her bed. There's no sleepin' without her.

"My kitty . . . my kitty! She's back," little Alice tells herself delightedly. "I missed you, kitty. I missed you so much!"

The voice speaks so softly it cannot be heard over the clatterin' of dishes on supper carts wheelin' from the kitchen toward the west wing. Little Alice lies quietly, thinkin' about the day she tried to baptize Angel Puss. Angel didn't like it, not a bit.

I was practicing, but Mama said just to think about it . . . not do it on the kitty. Little Alice remembers her mother's voice. It was sweet like always but firm.

My birthday was on Sunday, and I was baptized that day too, she tells herself. The water was cold, and my mother wiped her eyes when the pastor welcomed me into the church family. Papa looked a little embarrassed and dug around in a jacket pocket for the handkerchief he always has.

I knew what he was doing. Sometimes he lets me look at the handkerchief in church. He always has a handkerchief in his pocket; he lets me hold it and run my fingers over the raised stitches. Mama says she embroidered it for him before they married. She embroidered a bunch of 'em—sheets and pillow cases, and towels—all of them with her new initials.

In his pocket, Papa always has a folded, clean white handkerchief with his initials. At church I can ask for it. I guess he has it the way he has a tie. Neither one is for anything but to look good, and they both look good on Papa. At the baptism, the handkerchief got a purpose. He wiped it over his glasses like dusting 'em off, but I knew . . . .. I'd never seen Papa do that. Mama gets wet eyes now and then, but not Papa.

Little Alice is relivin' the day the Morgan girls have told me about. This is a family story all Miz Faber's folks know. They tell it over and over, the day of her first solo in public. She was glad to make Jesus happy that day. The grown-ups explained everything so she understood . . . well, mostly. The main thing was that now she knew when she was bad that Jesus knew it too. It made him sad, but when she told him about it, he would always say he'd made it right already.

She knew what it meant for somebody to get in trouble on her account, in trouble instead of her. That happened once and it was probably an accident. It wasn't that way with Jesus. He took the blame on purpose.

Somehow, he made it right on the cross. That was in the Bible storybook at Sunday school. I knew that everything was all right now. Jesus was King, and he could do anything he wanted. I could be baptized if I wanted to. Being baptized is a way to tell everybody. That's how Mama explained it and that was all right.

I *wanted* to tell everybody. Baptism . . . and nine years old, the same day!

"It's two kinds of birthdays," Miss Janie told me. "You're testifyin' that you're born into Jesus's family, and you're nine years old, both birthdays today." I wasn't sure I knew what Miss Janie meant by that, but she's sweet and I like her. In honor of the baptism, she read the story of Nicodemus to the Sunday school class.

Nobody was being baptized but me, little Alice reflects, tryin' very hard to lie still and not disturb the cat.

The door to Room 53 opens a crack wider, and a dark face peers around it. The light from the hall spills in, makin' a white triangle in the shadows on the floor of the room, a triangle widenin' toward the sleeper and the cat on the bed. The marmalade's awake now, measurin' the escape route, uncertain how to make a run for it with two humans he doesn't know blockin' the way out.

Little Alice stirs, aware the cat's unsettled. She opens her eyes, but not in time to see him jump.

Strangers or not, he is exitin' the scene! They have to make way.

The marmalade leaps from the bed, startlin' Augusta and Annabelle as they come into the room. Like an orange streak, the cat's gone, racin' down the hall as if his tail's on fire. The staff at the nurses' station look up and shake their heads. What's this business comin' to?

"Crazy decision somebody made . . . .." The thought has sidetracked Debra's concentration on a stack of forms, and it feels good to say it out loud. An orderly nearby smiles, rememberin' how his old cat comforted his mother when they took care of her at home three years ago. His ol' mama and that ol' cat . . . .

Little Alice looks sleepily around the room and sees two helpers she loves almost better than her mother. Lula and Maude! They've come to get her to bed. It's been tiring to be baptized. She's ready to go to sleep.

I won't fuss tonight, she thinks. They'll brush my hair and fluff up my pillow. Maybe Maude will sing to me even. She smiles a little and looks at the two dark faces peering down at her.

I'm already in bed, she thinks. They must've done that already. Must be time to go t' sleep. That'll be nice.

Not entirely sure how to approach the old lady, though she's been keeping her house for years, Augusta begins to hum softly. This situation's dif'rent.

F' how many years, she asks herself. Now she real sick . . . somethin' beside all that confusion goin' on inside her head.

> "Jesus love me, this I know,
> Faw the Bible tell me so
> Little ones to him belong,
> They aah weak but he is strong."

Annabelle softly joins in, varying the music till it's a chant and a tune and a murmur, soothin' and sweet and melodic, nothin' like the music in a church hymnbook, but sweet and gentle and soft, the words familiar to all children, whatever age. At a pause, the housekeeper says to the old lady, "Miss Alice, honey, we here to say a little prayer with you this evenin'. We go'n bring everything befo' Jesus. He'll hear ou' prayer. We'll pray now, Belle."

"Yeh, it's time. Let's pray."

"Lawd Jesus, you see this chile here this evenin'. She be needin' your presence right now. We seekin' your face to be a comfort to the downhearted and a solace to the needy. Miss Alice and us is waitin' on you to come into this room and manifest the Presence to one and all. We wait before th' throne in honor and in respect because you a mighty King and you our Savior. If Miss Alice need to be born anew, we axe you to bring her into that buith right now. If she yo' chile, we axe you to help her as only you can, blessed Lawud."

"Yes, Jesus. You know, you know . . . yes, Lawd."

"Be present in our midst, dear Lawd our Savior. Please give Miss Alice peace and rest in her soul. You the God of all comfort, and you, the Father, the Son, and the Holy Spirit can do what nobody else can do in heaven and upon the uith, dear Lawud. Be upon her heart in Spirit and in Truth. Let her know it is you, the Father, the Son, and the Holy Spirit, please dear God."

Augusta begins to hum, swayin' a little with the tune, but Annabelle has caught the eye of the old woman in the bed. A smile is beginnin' to turn up the corners of the thin, creased lips. Annabelle smiles broadly and reaches down to stroke the wisps of white hair lyin' this way and that upon the pillow. She hums with Augusta, and soon little Alice is singin' with 'em, carryin' the hymnbook tune in a strong high notes, clearly singin' out every word:

"Jesus loves me, and he died
Heaven's gates to open wide;
He has washed away my sin,
Let this little child come in.
Yes, Jesus loves me,
Yeeehs, Jesus loves me.
Yes, Jesus loves me.
The Bible tells me so."

The room is quiet now, and little Alice speaks confidently into the dark countenance holdin' her gaze

"I was baptized today! I was baptized and I'm nine too. Miss Janie said I had *two* birthdays today! Isn't that nice, Maude?"

"Who…?"

"Shush, 'Belle. She think you Maude," Augusta whispers. "It's okay. You be Maude f' right now. She happy."

"Yes, honey. You did have two kindsa birfdays today. Id'n that nice?"

"I'm sleepy now. Tell Mama, I'm coming to her room after a while, maybe in the mornin'. Tell her, please Maude . . .."

Alice closes her eyes as Annabelle reaches up a sleeve to dry her own.

"Yes, honeylamb. I'll tell 'uh. You go'n t' sleep now. You go on t' sleep."

The two old women stand silently, watchin' and wonderin' as the person they'd come to see begins to drift off. The old lady or the child? It doesn't matter. What matters is that she's not afraid. She's lyin' still and peaceful. They've done what they came for.

When a few minutes have elapsed and no muscle stirs, they edge toward the door, pullin' it mostly to behind them. The sleeper, more frail but not much older than her visitors, does not stir.

No one notices as the marmalade tom slides through the narrow crack and returns to his spot on the bed while the two old women, now outside, close the door of the Beulah Nursing Home. Still drying their eyes, they head for Annabelle's car. In Room 53, the purr of a cat winds itself in a complex counterpoint around the shallow breathin' of the sleeper.

Now and then little Alice, not yet asleep but not quite awake, murmurs bits of a song that come from somewhere in the depths of who she is or who she was or who she will become. The words are soothin', and the rhythmic whisper pleases the dozin' cat.

Yes, Jesus loves me—yes . . . loves me. Yes . . . the Bible tells me so.

These two ole ladies told me so too. I didn't figure it all out till about a week ago, babe, puttin' stuff together after I heard about that angel and the bathrobe. My. Isn't the Lord wonderful?

Five-thirty a.m. The rabbi's standin' in the kitchen gropin' around for a wine glass. Somehow he's managed not to wake Shirley as the nightmare turned into a wide-awake sense of encroachin' doom. Couldn't rest. Either awake worryin' or muddlin' his way through that horrid dream, a surreal version of his encounter with Dr. Well earlier in the day. Wake or asleep, he's miserable.

Harry the Horrible, he thinks. Nine o'clock yesterday morning. Now I can't get away from those black eyes. He's impaling me on some sort of medical spit, whispering, "This will not be painful." That's when he jabs the pointed shiny thing into my leg.

I managed not to mention the Feinemanns, and that swelling behind my knee wasn't anything! I wasn't thinking about that. Of course Harry had to find it . . . whatever it is. Is it really something unhealthy? Well, fat isn't healthy. Has to be fat. I won't obsess over it!

Why does he talk like an undertaker? That voice is right out of some black-and-white horror film, 1934.

Holding the wine bottle and replaying the office visit, the rabbi listens as Harry's voice shudders through his imagination. The sound is runnin' a chill through every inch of him.

What does *liposarcoma* mean, anyway? Whatever it means, it has nothing to do with me. Still, I should understand the lingo.

He's afraid to search the term online, afraid not to.

Didn't Harry say the lump might not be anything? Whatever the case, tests have been ordered. No backing out.

In the dream, his name is on the chart outside Room 53. The chart reads, MOSHE LEVY. Alice is well now, at home fighting the ghosts. Room 53 belongs to him. Harry insists on looking in every half hour to check on the leg.

Odd how those round black glasses turn his pupils into black beads, Levy thinks. His voice is like a sweet weasel. He hisses every *s*.

"Room 53 . . .. Well, well, liposssssarcoma," he says when he comes in. "We won't know till . . .."

Harry doesn't say *till what* or *when*. He peers at my leg. Then he points with the shiny thing, says the words, goes out looking worried. But first, he wipes his fingers and those horrid black glasses on a handkerchief—a big white handkerchief embroidered with strawberries! Look like giant drops of blood.

Just a dream . . . but it does no good to tell myself that.

In the nightmare, I've decided I won't tell anyone, Levy's thinkin'. I made Harry swear on his Hippocratic oath he won't say what's going on inside that leg. For some reason, Harry keeps repeating, "Room 53 . . .. Well, well, well . . . Room 53. Room 53, 53, 53." It's a part of the pact, some sort of a mnemonic device to seal the covenant.

A tumor growing behind that knee?

The rabbi blocks the image, banishes the word. He won't say it, even to himself. Circumstances might make him, but he can fence off circumstances.

I'm fine, Levy tells himself. I feel fine. I'm just gaining a little weight. There's some extra fat back there behind that knee. It doesn't hurt. Not even sore. The pain when I walk? I don't know . . . has to be a strained muscle. Too much tennis with Shirley.

He reaches for a wine glass, drops it, watches it shiver into tiny shards and needles all over the floor. Unforgiving pavers . . . the wrong decision for a kitchen!

He goes for a broom and dustpan feeling clumsy but much too alert for 5:33 a.m. Awake, weary . . . and he is barefoot.

Joe Paul swings into the church parkin' lot and nearly collides with my baby, the Union Street pastor. He's just arrivin' in his new truck—dark gray, about the color of asphalt. The medic jumps from his older model. Ricky's holdin' a coffee mug with one hand, with the other, gatherin' some papers. Unfoldin' his long legs from the cab, he exits, slams the door, stows the papers under an arm, and sticks out a hand.

"Well, Joe Paul! You trying to kill me, son?" he says, smiling broadly.

"I'm real sorry, pastor. I didn't see you drivin' in. How y' doin' these days?"

"I'm fit and counting. The Lord could return at any time! How about yourself? You and Miss Lucy keeping the Methodists tied down over in Calhoun?"

"Well, I guess we try. They can be a pretty rowdy bunch."

"Not that I know of. I never saw a rowdy Methodist in my life. They're mixin' around with those upstate Pentecostals, are they?"

"No, sir. I don't think so." A wry grin angles his lips. He isn't quite sure what to say next. Who knew what Pentecostals might do? Certainly not me, Joe Paul thinks, hopin' the Baptist pastor can hit on another topic for discussion.

"Coming to see me or thinking about courting my secretary one of these days?"

"Well . . . no."

Joe Paul laughs, tryin' to fit himself and Betty Berttison in the same picture frame. It's a struggle. She's single and beautiful, but so nosey and bossy she'll still be lookin' twenty years from now. He remembers her well enough from when they were both in youth group about five years back. That was when the Methodists didn't have a youth group, and everybody turned Baptist for a while.

"I just wanted to tell you that Cud'n Alice—I mean Miz Faber, I mean she seems to be in pretty bad shape, and since she's a Baptist and all . . .."

Avoiding eye contact with the pastor, Joe Paul rubs at a spot on the finish of his truck. He isn't good at lyin'.

"Let's go inside. We can talk better in there. It's hot out here."

"Okay," Joe Paul murmurs, wonderin' what he just got himself into. Maybe it wasn't such a good idea to come over here after all.

The two men cross the blazing asphalt and go into the church. In the office, Joe Paul nods to Betty. She looks up surprised but doesn't stop her hundred-a-minute to speak or acknowledge his greeting.

"Any messages, Betty?"

Not missing a stroke, she glances toward the pastor. She's hurryin' to finish a report for the Baptist Association day after tomorrow. She hopes he won't find anything else to change. Already the third round.

"Yes, sir . . . just ten," she murmurs as she reaches the end of a paragraph. She stops typin'; her fingers hang over the keys as if to keep the words from escapin'.

"That funeral on Wednesday . . . funeral home called; some Miz Brown from over in Carlisle is movin' here and wants to come talk to you about joinin' this church; the chairman of the deacons wants to know about lunch next Tuesday. He may be out of town and wants another time; the beach retreat chairman is needin' to talk to you about how many are going this year; the deacons are worried about whether we'll need a new fridge because the old one is 'bout to give out; the rabbi called, wants you to call him back; and Miss Ruth said to remind you of dessert with the Elliots this evenin' at eight. I took care of everything I could. Here's your phone numbers so you can call 'em all back if you want to."

She takes a breath and snatches a long yellow sheet from the pad in front of her; it's covered with scribbled notes and numbers. Holdin' it out for the pastor, she turns and looks up at Joe Paul, impaling him with her violet eyes.

Less messages when Pastor Apricot takes his cell all the time, she's thinkin', well aware of what she's done to Joe Paul with that look. Never mind the number's private, she tells herself. I'm still the one on duty.

"Thanks. I always rest easy knowing everything's covered," the pastor says, smilin' at her and wavin' his visitor toward the study to their left. They go in and Rick shuts the door, leavin' Betty to stare after them a full twenty seconds. She lifts two well-shaped eyebrows and rearranges some papers then returns to the typin'.

Joe Paul Jenkins, handsome as ever! My, my . . . and look at that mustache! He sure has grown up, she thinks, reachin' for a breath mint. Curiosity is stirrin' up a serious challenge to efficiency.

What's that Methodist doin' in here, she thinks. Have to find out some way.

Inside the study, the pastor motions to a chair, drops his jacket on the desk, and goes over to the window. For a few seconds, he looks out into the hot afternoon then turns toward his desk. He loosens his tie, unbuttons the top button of his shirt, and exchanges his sunglasses for frames with clear lenses. These he carefully cleans before they go back on his nose. It's a hot day. Even his glasses feel sweaty.

"Tell me about Miss Alice," he says as the silence stretches out.

"Well, Pastor, we're related to her, my Nana says, but I didn't really know her till she fell and we got called . . . 911, y' know, sir. I was on duty when we went over to 'er house and got her to the hospital. She sure has a powerful voice! I've never heard anything like it, and . . . well, Bill Allen nearly drove the truck into a ditch when she went off. Lucky we were almost there, and we could turn 'er over to Dr. Wellhelm. She's in kind of a bad way, bein' confused and all that, and my Nana said I should mention it to you . . . since she's a Baptist and all. Maybe you can go over and see 'er or somethin'. I don't think she knows where she is even . . . .

Here Joe Paul pauses. He's laid out his business. Now he can't think where to take the conversation.

What he really wants to know, uh . . . is well, what did Nana mean when she skewered him with her green eyes and asked about Jesus bein' real in his heart? Can't forget her question, and it's botherin' him quite a bit. How to put it . . .?

Rick Apricot senses something but can't quite make out what. It's not clear yet, not enough to satisfy him. He's also prayin', a prayer more like listening than asking.

"Maybe a bit concerned about where she's *going* to be," he observes casually.

". . . goin' to be, sir?"

"Someone at her age isn't long for this world, son."

"You sure can't tell it by 'er voice!"

"What do you know about Miss Alice, Joe Paul?"

"Not much, Pastor. I just found out from my Nana that we're related to 'er . . . some kinda cousins. Nana said I should call her 'Cud'n Alice' . . . you know, 'Cousin Alice.' 'Cud'n's the way they used to say it, y'know. That's the way Nana says it. I slip up sometimes."

Joe Paul grins as if caught. It's not a bad thing to be like his Nana, but she's a little old-fashioned. My Rick remembers his own Manny Ma's lectures right here in Beulah when he was a boy.

Manny Ma was big on family. She had two or three encyclopedias of family history in her brain. She knew, he says, the exact year and day when the Levys came over from Europe. Old Levy gained everybody's respect and trust, and when his grandson, Moshe, wanted to become a rabbi, the whole town cheered him on.

Rick knew about the quiet chats around breakfast tables and dinnertime talk over collard greens and corn bread, fried chicken and banana puddin'. When they thought about Moish later, with sweet tea and supper sandwiches and ice cream, they were still cheerin' for him. Whatever it was he needed to do, it'd be all right . . . and he'd succeed at it. Everyone was sure about that.

Smart kid, somebody said and heads nodded. Nobody knew what it meant to train for a rabbi, but the twins—our kids. They belong to us; their folks're nice people. Moish and Davita, children of the community; everybody wished 'em well.

Folks at Congregation Beth Shalom agreed. Ricky remembers the stories. Some years passed and the synagogue, drawing from the few Jewish families in Beulah or one of the nearby counties, needed a spiritual leader. Rabbi Moshe Levy? Would he come back?

The question was tossed around in every household—even Baptists, Methodists, Episcopalians. With breakfast batter bees and sorghum or hominy grits with bacon and scrambled eggs, everybody wondered. Later, with the country-fried steak and macaroni pie, green beans and homegrown tomatoes, they speculated. When it was time for cereal and peaches at supper, the topic was still number one.

Different?

"Naw," somebody said. "He'll be the same ol' Moishie."

Yes, Moish could come back, Ricky remembers. He heard it again and again: "We'll be glad to see him. It's not like you have to worry about a rabbi being a sheep stealer," somebody quipped. "Leave that to the—"

"Well, we won't be nasty," another voice breaks in. "So sad about Davita though."

As he mulls over the past, Ricky makes a show of shufflin' papers, absently doing his best to be offhand and nonthreatenin'.

"So, Joe Paul . . . you're related to Mrs. Faber," he says, bringin' himself back.

"Yes, sir. I'm s'posed to say 'Cousin Alice' . . .. I mean 'Cud'n Alice.' I guess it's the same thing. *She* might hear the difference."

"Son, she'll do well to know the voice of her closest kin now'days . . .. The confusion has progressed quite a bit. She's different from what she used to be. Did you know about Alice Faber's opera career?"

"No, sir, I did not."

Joe Paul lifts both eyebrows and, with hands on knees, he angles his chin toward the floor as if to brace himself and leans forward a few medical centimeters. His eyes are frozen in the wide-open position. "No, I certainly didn't."

"She was known for the range and power of her voice. One New York critic called her 'Faber of the crushing crescendo.' The term, 'Faberized,' was in common use. It meant something like 'at top volume and getting louder.'"

The thought made him chuckle. Ricky Apricot isn't a steady reader of the *New York Times*, just now and then. I like it though. "That's a good thing," he tells me. "Gets you out of those worthless murder mysteries and spy thrillers."

"What's 'crishindo,' Pastor?"

"It just means 'louder and louder.' You've had a taste of that."

Pastor Apricot looks up and grins, at the same time noticin' sweat marks on the arms of the chair. Joe Paul's sittin' up now. He's begun to squeeze the chair arms with both hands. His knuckles are white.

"Yes, sir," the medic agrees, laughin' too loudly, shakin' his head. "She still has a voice, that's for sure."

My pastor husband allows the comment to pass while he loosens his tie a bit more and slips the sunglasses into a pocket of the coat slung over the desk.

He means to keep the conversation on Joe Paul's chosen sidetrack as long as this young medic wants. Holdin' the direction of their talk just steady enough to avoid alarmin' him, the pastor watches Joe Paul push his wristwatch round and round, smooth the hairs on his arm, move one foot, then the other as if he can't get comfortable.

Now, without fanfare, Ricky Apricot—pastor, teacher, preacher, and evangelist—comes with the deftness of experience to the unspoken question weighin' down the room with a heavy silence. Joe Paul wants somethin'.

A quiet prompting in his heart says, NOW RICK. When he speaks, it's in obedience and his voice is gentle.

"I'm guessing Miss Alice isn't the only person around here wondering . . . 'where will I be when my day comes.'"

Joe Paul lets the comment hang in the air. The long pause is like a full stop, words posted on a sign.

"You and Miss Lucy . . . is it something you've been thinking about, Joe Paul?"

He says it quietly, in a tone so casual that the silence makin' itself felt behind and before 'em seems to fade away like somethin' imagined. The soft voice imposes no emphasis, no interrogatory heat, but Joe Paul breathes audibly and shifts his feet.

". . . where will I be when my day comes? Uh well, no—well, maybe me and Nana are a little concerned about her, about Miss Alice—I mean 'Cud'n . . .. Maybe a little. And well, I'm . . . but Nana seems—and she's gettin' older, too."

The medic stops. To rearrange all that, to catch those derailed thoughts and scrambled up emotions tumblin' out of control is a task he won't pick up. He wants to say that Nana is completely sure, but even that he can't venture. To admit that she knows with certainty where she's going might suggest he doesn't. Even that will take some doin'.

Joe Paul draws a hand through his thick, sandy hair then presses it down as if to smooth out the cap marks and stuff down any thoughts tryin' to escape. Can't trust his mouth. Can't even trust the top of his head. Maybe it won't just sit there like it usually does. Might start shootin' out questions like Roman candles. He wishes he hadn't left his cap in the truck.

His mustache is beggin' for attention. It feels good to run his fingers over it. Nailed again, he tells himself, wonderin' how this pastor can look like he knows exactly what a person's thinkin'. Nana does that. How do they know? He shoulda kept his cap on . . . but no, y' don't wear a hat in the house, especially not in a church. It's not respectful, Nana says. He feels bare and exposed.

"How are you with Jesus Christ, son?" The voice is gruff with authority, but gentle and soft, and the man who straightens and turns up to face that shinin' window is too . . . well, he's just too *there* to ignore.

Way too . . . big to risk passin' off with some kind of chitchat and too nice to get mad at, Joe Paul's thinkin'. Gave me some relief to see him shufflin' around with those papers, but now he's gettin' into the questions . . . .. At least he isn't lookin' this way.

The medic feels nailed again as the pastor turns from adjustin' the window shades to face him, his eyes kind. He's smilin'.

Heck! What am I gonna do? Joe Paul asks himself, panic squeezin' at his chest, his gut, the fingers of both hands. Even his feet are sweatin'.

In a flash, he knows that everything is up for him. It's over . . . .. Right here in this church office, he's losin' it completely. Inside, every bit of resolve and stubborn procrastination and common sense cynicism is turnin' to jelly along with his whole body, his brain even. He leans over and puts his head in his hands, tryin' to steady himself. Not much better. He might fall right out of the chair! Tears are beginnin' to run all over his face and through his fingers.

The room is quiet as a summer dawn—dew on the garden, roses just wakin' up, and a young Miss Alice Faber just emergin' from her house, bendin' down to sniff the biggest one, smilin' and hummin' to herself.

The picture flashes across Joe Paul's mind before he has time to wonder who it is standing next to her. Now that Person is standing next to him, and he's knowing without a breath of a doubt that everything is goin' to be all right. He knows who this is, and he knows what he wanted to say.

The pastor puts big hands on his desk and leans forward as if tryin' to decide about sitting. Then he straightens his tall frame again, and stretches his back against the window. With all six feet, five inches of him outlined by the light, he waits, watchin' the shoulders of the blond medic shake with sobs. There is no sound. Rick wants to cross the room and take the chair beside Joe Paul, lay an arm across his shoulder, or just sit and wait. But thinkin' better of it, he stands there, not sure what to do. He has time. Joe Paul isn't thinkin' about him.

Ricky's aware of a throne . . . coming clearly into view now, fillin' the room, the universe. A Voice. Within his spirit, the sound of its crescendo is fillin' heaven and earth. The sweetest music, the sound of many waters . . ..

The Healer—Joe Paul's brother in that, Ricky thinks and decides to sit at his desk. The Lord of Glory, my dear Lord . . ..

The sound of a familiar chorus comes softly from Betty's desk, the words clear. "Shine, Jesus, shine . . .." The song goes on, bringing into the study the Father's glory, the blaze of the Spirit. Anderson station.

Joe Paul stirs, fumbles in his pants pocket for a handkerchief, finds it, and dries his face.

"Sorry about that, sir . . .."

My Ricky says nothin'. A full minute elapses before Joe Paul speaks again.

"Nana asked me if Jesus was real as daylight to me."

The block of silence is like pure gold.

"Real, Joe Paul?"

"Yes, sir . . . he's real. I've heard it all my life, but now . . .."

The young medic has to shove fingernails into his palms to hold down the feelin's surging around somewhere inside him. Another flood of tears is ready to break. The memory of a starlit night in the back of his truck confronts him like a bailiff with handcuffs. The thought has troubled his dreams for over a year, and the person he hurt cries all the time, somewhere off in the distance. It doesn't matter where he is or what he's doin': that cryin's out there. She moved away, and he can't do a thing but feel bad. Now that scene, and a lot of other stuff, he offers to the Person standing there with him.

Lord, here it is . . ..

There is no weight. His hands are empty. His arms feel nothin' at all. He's standin' there, holdin' 'em out there empty as if . . . as if that Person whose eyes are so inviting has taken everything away and now is spreadin' his arms to embrace him.

Me, too . . . will you take me too?

The question frames the picture and then it isn't there anymore. Nothin' there but a sweet new peace circlin' him all around . . . and underneath, the everlastin' arms.

Just like the hymn says. Nana's favorite.

"I really know it now." The words are just above a whisper. "Real as daylight."

"He'll be the Light of the City, Joe Paul. No more night. He brightens our darkness . . . .. Says to anyone with ears to hear:

'Your sins are forgiven. I have paid the price.'"

The long silence sets its own duration. Neither wants to break in. For Joe Paul, the truth he just spoke fills his mind and spirit. Jesus Christ is who he said he is, and this medic belongs to him. Rick is rememberin' the *selah*, that emphatic pause punctuatin' so many psalms: pause and think about it.

We have to pause to let you in, Lord, pause and think, then open the door.

One more thing. With the better part of a silent minute gone, the question must be asked.

"Have you been baptized, son?"

Rick knows he's edgin' toward uncertain ground here. Methodists take a slightly different view of things in this area. Still, you obey the command: ASK.

"I'll have to check with Nana about that. She'll know. I don't remember."

"Do that, Joe Paul. I'll be here when you want to talk. And be sure to tell her that—"

"That Jesus is real as daylight to me now? Yes, sir, I'll tell her. My sins are forgiven! I couldn't keep it to myself."

Joe Paul smiles for the first time. He's catchin' the strength of a discovery just now breakin' in upon him.

There is no shame in tears. Shame has gone from your life . . . Never again.
There is now therefore no condemnation to those in Christ Jesus.

"Real as daylight, Joe Paul, not the sun, but just him . . . Jesus Christ, shining in that City."

Ricky's still speakin' softly. Only a tickin' clock marks the seconds of a new life findin' itself here at last, alive and well—the freshness of spring rain or the measured rise and fall of breathin', a beautiful child restin' after the struggles of birth—now a second time.

Joe Paul gets to his feet a little unsteadily.

"Pastor, I think it's time I got home. Want to talk to Nana."

The pastor picks up a pen and fiddles with it. He's tryin' to mask the confusion-laced problems his own emotions are loadin' on in full measure.

I know what just happened, he's thinkin'. Had very little to do with me!

Bits of Scripture drift through his thoughts and a measure of self-control is settlin' the flood of joy threatenin' to break out.

ONE SOWS, ANOTHER WATERS, BUT IT IS THE LORD WHO GIVES THE INCREASE . . . .

NO ONE COMES TO ME UNLESS THE FATHER DRAWS HIM . . . .

I AM THE RESURRECTION AND THE LIFE. HE WHO BELIEVES IN ME THOUGH HE DIE,
YET WILL HE LIVE . . . .

Ricky absently taps his pen on the desktop then drops it from his fingers as he gets himself together to grip Joe Paul's hand. Then he thinks of a better gesture, walks a few steps away from the window where he's been leanin,' and spreads out both arms. Joe Paul accepts the offer as if he's hungry. He doesn't remember his parents, never knew a fatherly hug.

As he reaches the door of the pastor's study, the medic tries to say somethin' conclusive, but no words come. He's gripped by an awe he can't deny and doesn't want to. Still gropin', he thinks of the one thing he knows is right. The words come out just above a whisper. He's smilin' with his eyes and every muscle in his face.

"Thanks, again, Pastor. You were . . . well, you were a big help."

"Remember to ask Miss Lucy about your baptism . . . and tell her I said hello."

"Yes, sir. I will do that . . . . Both of 'em."

He turns toward the door and leaves, hurryin' out before the beautiful Betty Berttison can see he's been cryin'. There isn't any shame, for sure, but Betty might not know it yet!

Now the pastor's grillin' himself, not sure where this is goin'.

Apricot, he's tellin' himself, you can't be breaking down, even if some exhausted young searcher gives up and falls into the arms of the Lord right here in this office. Okay Rick, do you have what it takes? This job . . . it takes unswerving steadiness. That's what it's all about. Is this you? A grown-up, functioning, Baptist pastor's gotta have it. What about it, Richard?

Not an easy question, but there it is . . . demandin' an answer and not the first time. The self-directed spotlight shines in black and blindin' white on an image of inadequacy, vulnerability even. Before he can fully frame the question or form an answer in 'is head or heart, one word turns his thoughts in a different direction.

Listening.

He isn't alone in these thoughts.

"Yes, I have some self-control," he hears himself sayin', "but you give it to me, Lord. I have to ask for it."

Needy? Yes, but not forsaken. I have the heart to care and the ears to hear, but they come from outside myself.

"Please don't take those away. I need to hear you and them."

Received.

Call the rabbi, Rick thinks, a little more ready for the next thing. Betty said he called. He picks up his cell phone, punches three keys, and waits. His spirit's full of the scene he's just witnessed. The Bible talks about a "divided heart," and it's a bad thing, isn't it? Well, yes, but maybe not right now, he's thinkin'.

Where I am right now? This is a divided place to be, he tells himself. Good thing Joe Paul wasn't paying attention to me. Had his own concerns, lucky for me. What would he think if he knew how much I was struggling. I'm not sure Moish has to deal with things like this. Better not get into it with him right now. Can't trust myself to talk much. Is it bad to feel this way?

"Whatever it is, it's the facts, ma'am—just the facts."

Ricky tells me everything. I don't need a video bug for stuff like thus. To be in two places at once feels strange to 'im. Two faces fill up his inner screenin' room, Joe Paul's and the rabbi's. He knows what one wanted. What about the other?

"Rabbi Levy."

"Moses, Rick. You called." Short, the only possibility.

"Rick . . . thanks. Where . . . uh, where are you?"

"At the church. Long day, friend."

"Could you come over here after . . . after you leave work? Could you do that? I need to see you, and . . . I won't keep you long."

"Sure, buddy. I can do that. See you in about forty-five. I have to lock up. Betty's gone already. That okay?"

"Yeah. Six forty-five. My house . . .."

The phone went dead.

Ricky stood at the Levys' front door for all of two seconds. Moish must've been waitin' by some window. He came right away, waved Ricky inside. Ricky told me the fading daylight made the foyer and specially Moishe's study seem like nighttime was here already. The two friends looked at one another. Levy pointed to a chair in front of that wall of books and Ricky sat. He was wonderin' about the electric tension cracklin' around the corners of the room. He could feel it and Moish was not sittin' down. He was pacin' this way and that, pointin' his long fingers like two five-barreled shotguns at the floor. Looked like he was blastin' away at an army of invisible Lilliputians wagin' war all around his feet.

My pastor husband's watchin' these maneuvers, not sayin' anything. Moish hasn't said a word since the two syllables he didn't say at the front door. Now Ricky's wonderin' where Shirley is. Time to be done with preliminaries.

"What, Moish . . .."

A pause.

His friend stops and turns around on his way to the other side of the room.

"Do I look sick to you?"

"Sick?"

"Well . . . yes—sick. Do I look like something is wrong with me?"

"You're limping a little."

The rabbi just deflates, falls into the nearest chair and stares.

"Limping?"

"Yes, you look like you don't want to use your left leg as much as your right. You been trying to defeat Shirley on the tennis court again?"

"You can see that I'm limping?"

"Look . . . I know you like a brother! You couldn't lose two or three ounces of weight or get a splinter in your toe big enough to hurt without me noticing. You're limping, ol' buddy."

"Did you notice it . . . before today?"

"Did I . . .?"

My Ricky's lookin' absently at the bookshelves, tryin' to recall.

"No, I don't think I did. But that's quite a display of your walking abilities you're putting on right now. I'm not apt to miss a change in your stride, even a little one. We 've known each other forty years, right?"

"Thirty-eight and three months."

"What's going on with your left leg, Moish?"

"Harry thinks he's found something besides fat behind my knee. The leg's a little sore, but I'm thinking you're right . . . too much tennis."

"But Harry doesn't think so."

"No."

"What's he recommending?"

"Tests, of course."

"Soon?"

"He's sending me to Columbia to a specialist . . . tomorrow."

"Shirley going with you?"

"Haven't told her yet."

"You have to tell her, Moish."

"I don't need somebody to go to Columbia with me! I just want you to keep an eye on Alice Faber while I'm out of town. Everybody's concerned about her. If I'm not here and something happens, they'll wonder where I was. I don't want a bunch of questions about all this . . . not till I know something, you know . . . definite. Harry's his usual pessimistic self, of course. I don't want the town grapevine diagnosing me or saying I've succumbed before the doctors even find a problem. You understand?"

"Sure, buddy. But tell Shirley. You have to."

"I'll get around to it. She's out right now, but maybe when she gets in—"

"What can I do besides keep a watch for Mrs. Faber's . . .?" Ricky said he couldn't think of a way to finish the sentence.

"Nothing really. Thank you for listening. You always do."

"A friend's job."

"You better get home. You've gotta be hungry. It's past suppertime."

"Okay. Call if you need to . . . and tell Shirley! Don't put it off."

"Yeah, I know. I should tell her, but I don't know what to say. Harry isn't sure about anything—just sending me to this specialist. Is it that important? Why should she worry?"

"Be realistic, Moses. Would you want her to keep you in the dark if some doctor found something suspicious in her breast? She'd come over and talk to Ruth, sure—but would you want that to be all? No support from you while she's battling the questions crashing in on her? I mean, Shirley's strong, but we all need another person at a time—"

"Yeah, but she's—"

"Don't say 'a woman'! You know better than I do that she was one step from a brilliant IDF career when she married you. She's some sort of grit that's not even invented yet. I can see it now! You don't tell her, and she'll have your—"

"Sometimes they have to cut off a leg, Rick."

In another room, a telephone rang. In the distance, a siren spoke: two notes, up and down. Somewhere brakes squealed.

Rick said Moish looked like he wanted to suck the words back in, but the door he'd opened couldn't be shut. Neither one wanted to cross that threshold, specially not Moish.

Dammit, it's my leg! What am I supposed to think? What am I supposed to do? The questions were written all over his face. But he caught himself before he started raging at me, Ricky said. He's got better self control. He'd taken a big step, and I was the friend there with him when he pulled up the edge and looked at the thing full on. He knew I deserved better.

His head was also full of Shirley--incandescent and beautiful, those amber, angry glints in her eyes. Rage? Better to rage at himself than me . . . or give Shirley cause. No, he couldn't close the loop with her on the outside.

"I know I have to tell her," he said to Ricky, " . . . but after supper. It's salad night. Won't take long."

Moish followed Ricky out the study, down the hall. Outside, an unexpected shaft of sunset brilliance, was washin' over their faces like gold. From the corner of his eye, Ricky saw Moish glancin' at his face in that gold-framed mirror in the foyer. Moish smiled like he was lookin' at a healthy man.

The glow of health, he was tellin' himself. For a second or two he believed it, Ricky told me.

He put a brotherly arm around his friend's shoulder.

"Call me, you know . . . any time."

Rick got out the words then clamped his tongue with his teeth—hard, pain sharp enough to deflect the assault his heart was launchin' at his tear ducts. My pore baby. Has such a soft heat. Not here, he was tellin' himself. Can't happen, not here—

Had to get himself outta that grip of grief threatenin' to draw both of 'em down to the pit. That's the way it felt, Ricky told me when he calmed down. Out—get out of here, now.

He saw his friend standin' in the doorway, painted gold by the sunset. The emotions backed off, but not for long. Ricky was bitin' his tongue harder.

Makin' a silent appeal in the direction of that beautiful sky, he got into his truck. Then he lost another squadron of ground troops. Tears. Streamin' from his eyes.

"Lord God, You love him! Do something—"

All my husband could do was pray. Good idea if you have to drive.

Richard Parker Apricot III, pastor of Union Street Baptist Church of Beulah, SC, put his head down on the kitchen table in our house on Church Street and gave it up.

He's a big man, and his vulnerability of heart is about the same as his shoe size. Few get a close-up of this defect, but I know. The sun was settin'. Unnamed new colors shone through the window. I bent over and covered whatever part of 'im I could. For a fragment of a minute, seemed like the room was catchin' fire with that sunset light on my hair. I'm not as bad as he is, but I couldn't do much but just cry too.

After a while, I said, "Baby . . . baby, what is it, honeybabe? What is it? Can't you tell me? Come one, baby. You can tell your Ruthie. Come on now . . .."

That plunged Ricky into more weepin'. I stood up, shook back my hair, and wiped my eyes on a stray napkin. Then lookin' down at 'is shoulders still shakin' with sobs, I stretched my arms over that troubled bulk and kissed the back of his head.

"It's all right, darlin' . . . it's all right. It'll be all right."

That night I wrote in my diary, "The light faded into grays as the sun edged below the horizon and spread a blanket around the two of us as if to lay on a shield against new sorrows."

Sometimes all you can do is resort to poetry.

CHAPTER SEVEN
The Ripples Spread

MORE STUFF FROM BEN. WHAT IS IT ABOUT ENGLISH profs? They make long sentences and use big words, but at least this one knows how to dust up a little drama. And too, they still write letters.

It was one of those small Jerusalem groceries they'd call a mom-and-pop store in the States. I'm about to fly out of Ben Gurion, and I wanted to pick up Turkish coffee and rice, some packaged milk for the colleague coming to apartment sit, but the lentils caught my eye. The mounds of small circles looked like coins—shades of brown, some almost black, others bright orange. Different taste, the orange ones?

Lentil stew. Esau called a dish with lentils "that red." He was willing to sell his birthright for it. No, not now, I told myself. I'm going away. Wait till I get back—

Turning toward an aisle with coffee, I didn't see that shopper hurrying toward me—a very thin young woman. She approached almost at a run clutching several items. When we collided, everything spilled from her arms and crashed to the floor. Something broke, and a brown syrupy liquid began spreading in sluggish streams right in front of me—a jar, now surrounded by pointed fragments of glass.

I'd barely missed stumbling to the floor myself. She wasn't so fortunate. This person was thin, so thin I wondered in the shock if it wasn't some part of her broken into pieces, not that stuff, that . . . whatever it was. She wasn't bleeding.

Huge blue eyes bore into me with punishing alertness and held as if to set me in stone. The face was oddly attractive—narrow, pointed chin, good bones angled as if by a diamond cutter. I reached out a hand.

"*Bevakasha*! Are you hurt?" I blurted it out in English, groping for a Hebrew word, something more to the point than *please*!

"American. You are American."

I caught the words—a simple statement of fact, murmured through gritted teeth from where she still lay on the floor. She said it with a trace of emphasis, maybe scorn. The exact label wouldn't come, scorn more likely.

At any rate, I couldn't let her be cut by the glass, and Hebrew or not, I had to get help. She'd be injured if she put her hands in the wrong place or slid on the slippery liquid.

"Let me help you!" I said, feeling clumsy and foolish, wondering how she could know I'm American. Telling myself Hebrew would be the *first priority of my life* from this minute on, I gripped the hand she held out. She got up, grimacing at the mess, then stood picking glass from her palm and scowling at a tiny red mark. It matched the color of my chagrin. Cuts were an issue. Waving my arm, I motioned for the clerk. Hazard another foray into Hebrew? No, scaring up the right words from my limited supply wasn't an option. I could botch it altogether!

Have to get vocabulary, I told myself. Vocab's the key! Got to have it.

A young helper—maybe Arab, maybe Israeli—appeared like Ali Baba or the sorcerer's apprentice from out of nowhere and began to work his magic with broom and mop. The young woman pulled another glass fragment from her hand and turned her attention to dark swatches of dust and sticky debris the collision had streaked across her khaki slacks. She swept hands over her legs as if to dust herself off, then stopped, wincing with pain from a bit of unnoticed glass. Something had to be done.

The proprietor, a man of forty or fifty, seemed to be venting his ire on the employee. He was hovering around, scolding his helper in what I recognized as Hebrew.

Clumsy foreigners! What's a man to do?

Listening to the unmistakable cadence of the language, I caught a word here and there, and thought irrelevantly about an odd comment in an American novel on the Six Day War. Yes, Israelis do rattle away in Hebrew when they talk. Accurate description. I guessed the writer didn't speak the language, just recognized it when he heard it. Meaning doesn't get in my way either. What I hear is the sound . . . that rattle.

"*Bevakashah*," I lamely offered again, trying to smile. Receiving no response, I turned to the crisis at hand. Do something . . . right this minute.

I should pay for her purchases, I thought. Go to the checkout and leave the young woman looking at her hand or stand there with her? She seemed to be someone who should be watched. Might get into more trouble! Ugh. An American mom-and-pop store would stock Band-Aids. Probably not this one.

Dark blue eyes, narrow face, sun-bleached hair pulled back in a severe bun. She wasn't a person I'd even notice on the street. But now, her electric gaze was pinning me to the spot. I couldn't pry myself loose. Groping in my pocket for some bills, I stuck them into the proprietor's hand, pointing to the broken glass, then to the young woman.

Money's magic, I thought, as the shopkeeper slid past me and went to the front to open an ancient cash register. The clean up, rudiments of first aid, and grocery transactions completed, I now held two bags filled according to her specs—bottles and jars rattled off in Hebrew to the proprietor. Then I followed the unfortunate shopper into the blazing heat of the store's front sidewalk.

"Can I get you a cab?" I said, still wanting to do something as restitution for the trouble and the cuts—anything to make it up to her.

"*Lo*, she snapped, unintentionally pleasing me with a word I knew.

Okay, I thought. No cab . . .. But I have the stuff. I can call at least one of the shots! English, keep on with the English. She guessed I'm American . . . said it in English.

"What can I . . .?"

The young woman was fumbling around in a large leather bag, a camera bag, by all appearances. She produced a cell phone playing "Dixie" and smacked it against an ear.

"Yes, I am here, go on and talk to me. Yes, I can hear you well here, Miriam."

I looked away, taking pains not to listen.

Why am I being polite? I said to myself. Isn't politeness up to the phone person? She sure isn't exerting herself for the sake of a clumsy, chance companion holding her bags as if guarding 'em with his life on this Jerusalem sidewalk. I'm the one looking foolish!

"You say that Alice Faber died today? No, no . . . please do not cry. Yes, I can hear."

More uncomfortable by the minute. I made a point of turning away as she stood there clutching the phone. What to do? Did this new information demand something else of me? Should I offer assistance . . . again?

Alice Faber? American name? And "Dixie"! Was the phone call a crisis for her? I wished I had a better word than "her." The intimacy of names came to me like a revelation. To know a name is to know the person, even if in a bare, rudimentary way. The name makes a way . . .

Lord God! You've given us your name . . . several of 'em and the best, the very best!

The words came to me like breathing. Another realization brought me up short. I hadn't prayed in these increasingly odd circumstances. At least that could be amended.

Lord, God, I said silently, help me know what to do! Should I offer help again or just leave? She's learned of a death. Who is she? Is it right for me to want to know? Please give me wisdom . . . *bevakashah*, and thank You, dear wonderful Savior!

The young woman walked a few steps in the opposite direction. Her back was turned, making it easy for me to plant my feet where I stood holding the bags with her replaced selections. The shop owner had thrust them at me as if they were mine. You paid, he seemed to be saying.

She'll have to come back and get the stuff, I thought hopefully, wondering if she noticed the chauvinism. An American woman fluent in Hebrew, who clearly knew her way around this place, would have brushed shoulders with more than a few condescending men. This shopkeeper wouldn't be the first.

I won't be one of them, I said to myself, gritting my teeth in frustration. Maybe if I just stand here, she won't feel threatened.

I couldn't dismiss the degree of interest this odd encounter was generating. In spite of everything, I was fascinated. Today I didn't need a distraction, but here it was.

Who is this person? A "Dixie" ringtone? The thought amused me. Who would catch it here? Americans, maybe. Yes, a few of us. A Southerner? Has to be. Trace of Southern accent? I couldn't be sure. She'd said almost nothing in English.

As I watched, she put the phone in her bag and approached, frowning. I stood there with her parcels behind my back. Seeing the advantage of the position, I decided not to produce them. She might take possession and hurry off down the street. I really didn't want that.

Grocery purchases were the last thing on her mind. Seeing her expression, I prepared myself to be left standing on the sidewalk of this ancient city, two bags full of who knows what in my hands. The purchases, mine only by proxy, belonged to a person whose name I didn't know, maybe never would. The thought fascinated me, and I moved my fingers to be sure I had both bags. I didn't need this stuff! Couldn't even identify it—not by appearance, not by Hebrew label! What I needed was—

"I need . . ." she paused, then went on dramatically, "a plane for home four hours from now." The words came out breathlessly, falling on my ears with the shock of puzzled discovery. "And I must get this EPROM I have here to Gilo on the road to Bethlehem."

In her hand was a tiny flash drive, fished from the depths of her leather bag. The information seemed to escape unintended. Now she scowled as if she'd been caught off guard in something she should have kept to herself.

That's it! It's Twiggy and her voice is glittering gold.

I greeted the discoveries like brave new worlds. The voice abrogated every other demand. There was no heat, no schedule, no departure, no plans for today or questions about . . . anything. It was simply necessary to do whatever I could to prompt another word, something else from her mouth! It seemed to drip gold, to make palpable and delightful long sparkling ranks of sound, waves rolling into my head like gleaming breakers on the shores of Paradise. Incredible!

It's a gold stream, I thought, by default groping around in my English teacher's muddle—simple necessity and a crazy longing to be accurate.

There it is . . . glinting right there! Where she's standing is the bank, a gold-laced stream and it's Twiggy, but not British.

"Gilo?"

The two syllables never sounded so sweet. I said them with amazement, savoring the winsome vowels, not wanting to let them go, yet needing them to fill the air and move that voice to say something else.

"I'm headed there. I have an apartment in Gilo," I offered, unable to keep the information to myself.

Then gathering up my good sense and some courage, as well, I went on, annoyed that I'd defaulted on a commonplace courtesy. Unacceptable.

". . . and my name is Benjamin Steingaard. I'm sorry about causing you all that trouble back there. I really am sorry. I teach English here, and if I can help you get to Gilo, I'm at your service. Believe it or not, I have a car, and I'm headed there right now, actually. If you wait for one of those Egged busses to get you to Gilo, you won't make it there by nightfall—or to Ben Gurion. A cab might, but it'll cost a fortune. Sorry. I'm sure you know all that. Please let me help. I also have to catch a plane four hours from now—believe *that* or not."

I stuck out my hand with the parcels, hoping the young woman would see me as friendly and unthreatening if reeking with male superiority. I half expected her to grab the bags and bolt. Would she think me forward? I wondered about the T-shirt.

She looked like she could take care of herself, but I knew nothing about her. Maybe she carried MACE in that bag—MACE or some other kind of pepper spray or lemon juice. The Margaret Atwood variety. I was floundering around in silly questions. Deep, swirling waters and I can't swim worth a dam' I said to myself. She could have a revolver in that bag! Maybe I'm the one who should turn and run!

I waited, tried to suspend judgment as she took the parcels and transferred an item or two into the camera bag, then faced me, blue eyes leveled as if looking past a gun sight: no pepper spray, no pistol . . . no nonsense.

I think she'll leave that bag right here on the street, I told myself. No. No Israeli would leave an unattended parcel. Israeli? American? Who is this person? She's fluent in Hebrew and knows her way around. She won't abandon bags for the cops to blow up though she looks like she'd enjoy leaving me to deal with two or three units of *meeshtarah*!

"Please take me right to Gilo in your car. I can arrange the other things myself."

I stood there holding out my hand as if the bags were still in it. The syllables curled around in my ears as if to test every tiny bone and synapse. It was like trying for something in a new language. The golden voice was all I heard—at first, no signifiers. None. Just the sounds.

Then we were making our way through the crowded streets, crazily dodging traffic and pedestrians, zooming around the lumbering Egged busses crowded with Israelis going every way but her way.

Who was she? My offer of an introduction prompted nothing. I drove wildly, frustration fueling the haste. Question marks seemed to stand along the streets in big shining letters—bronze, tall as hotels.

How can I make her say something . . . make her talk? No. *Persuade* her to talk? Not that either . . . somehow get her to, coax her gently to talk, beg?

As though deep in thought, this thin young woman sat there quietly, looking out the window of my rusty Citroen. The tumbling self-interrogation on my side was about as illuminating as old neon, flicking on and off in faltering reds and blues. The towering questions flashed by in dizzying sun and shadow. I couldn't do a thing but watch for drifty pedestrians and chide my blustery male forcefulness. She didn't speak.

Will I find out . . . anything, I thought, mentally shaking a finger in my own face. Might as well be chiding a bad little boy . . . who's deaf. I had to hear that voice again. I needed it like a drink of water. It was a hot day and I was sweating.

At the corner of Jefferson Davis and Second Street, my Ricky's anglin' his gray truck around a turn as he heads toward Calhoun. The new family out Highway 17 wants a visit. Twenty minutes to get there, twenty to get back. Play that tape. No tape player in the truck, but an antique model's turned up in a Sunday school supply closet. The Miller Presbyterians don't do CDs of sermons. Probably can't afford it.

Little churches . . . no money for high tech, he's thinkin'. This preacher serves two, the tiny Jones Memorial Presbyterian Church of Miller and an ARP on the Anderson side. The folks could visit at the other church on off Sundays, he's thinkin', but most will eat breakfast late and wash their cars. My Ricky knows little churches. Pat Palmer . . . what kind of preacher is he, Ricky's wonderin'?

"Pat dropped in last winter, the day of that terrible cold," Ricky said later. "I wasn't going out on a frigid morning—43° outside, be colder when the wind picked up. Canceled my appointments, planned the day around the new sermon series."

Yeah, my Ricky wouldn't waste the time, any time he could snag from feeling sorry for himself. I put in my two cents when he tells me somethin' like this.

"Courage would be the topic—courage today, courage of the Old Testament and early church saints, the courage of the Lord. Calvary to coincide with Easter. Research, a detailed outline, the main Scripture passages, the illustrations. That was my to-do list.

"It didn't happen. Instead . . . I was face to face with a healthy looking old man. Apple cheeks polished by the cold, blue eyes sparkling. Didn't know whether to be astonished, or irritated, or just glad for the interruption.

"G. Patterson Palmer," Betty said, reading the card in her hand. "He's a Presbyterian." She raised one eyebrow.

"The man bounded into my study, provoking a silent growl on my side. My my, I was telling myself, th' granddaddy of the Gerber baby. For sure, a jolly ol' elf.

"I commandeered a smile and put out my hand, not entirely pleased to be confronted by a radiant face and a web of wrinkles squeezing two sparkly eyes. 'Plowed in by laughter,' they said to the world. I sure wasn't in the mood for upbeat. On a bad cold day, hale-and-hardy was somebody else's frame. I did not feel like being friendly.

"This isn't pink-with-fever, I was thinking. That glowing countenance could light up a room—just ordinary good cheer, no question. Shone from the man like sunshine on an ice field. I was surprised by the thought and had to admit to myself, if self-pity was a person, he'd be outta here in a huff, one flushed face sent packing by another!

"We'd met but hadn't chatted in the privacy of a study. Got through the preliminaries quick enough, fine points of getting to know each other, as well. I was warming a bit to my guest—wry wit, odd passion for Hebrew, fondness for small town South Carolina.

"More than I'd realized till that day," Ricky told me, "this Baptist pastor was ready for a new friend."

The minutes of his day, all that give and take with church members, flow like a branchin' stream in all directions: instructor, coach, and marriage counselor; advisor, legal agent for the state, and SBC representative; church administrator and educator; prophet, spiritual director, and comforter; personal confidant and father confessor; funeral director, sometimes even pinch-hit janitor. "All that is me," he said, as if I didn't know. And more on top of it.

"With the youth," my Ricky went on, "I need the talents of a stand-up comedian, and every hat's a crown from the King." Now he's smilin' at me.

"He's laid on one more assignment," says Ricky. (To be an alert and teachable husband, I'm thinkin', but he says somethin' else.) "These are my orders: to be the passionately engaged leader the spectacular RuthAnne Marigold Wilkerson Apricot deserves—my friend, as well as my wife. Not many others."

You guessed it, honeybabe. When Ricky tries to explain somethin' like that to me, I tear up. Not as bad about it as he is, but give me a break! It would take a woman with a heart like a rock not to love hearin' words like that. Know what I mean?

To the church, Ricky's just "Preacher," and that covers it for most people till a special need comes up. But the "pastor" role's a lot more, and none of it really fits what you'd think of as friendship. The clean-cut face in that morning mirror is a friend's countenance for just a handful. I'm glad I'm one.

Rick's always been realistic. Challenges? He eats 'em for breakfast! Gets along with people real well, but Beulah, South Carolina, means *buddies* to him. When he accepted the call from Union Street, he didn't expect the jolt. When he looked, it was his definition of friendship that took the hit. His call cuts to a minimum any list of friends.

You have to spend time with friends and time he doesn't have. He makes his way with care and prayer, and he ministers the love of God, which is what he wants to do. Loves the folks and they love him—man, woman and child. He's their pastor—friendly, but not really their friend, not like a buddy. Baptist pastors are an informal lot, but they're busy, always busy like him. He talks to me and he's happy most days. Moish and Shirley—yes, but two really aren't enough. Quentin's far away, and the standoff between him and Moish complicates everything. By the time Rev. Palmer arrived, the lack of friends was becomin' a thing though Ricky didn't know it. On this cold mornin' as he studied the face of th' visitor, he got it: the Lord had sent 'im a friend.

"Where did you go to seminary, Pastor Palmer?"

"Pat, please. I went to Caldwell College . . . over in East Wood," he said, smiling. "Dr. Ian Primrose was president—a real, tried and true ARP he was. We used to lay bets he had the entire psalter memorized. No bet against him ever stood. Never looked at that ARP hymnal and he sang every verse! Nice baritone." Palmer delivered this obscure bit of Presbyterianalia with a deep-throated chuckle. "Caldwell is small, too small for a seminary. But it's respected—even in Presbyterian circles." The chuckle was rocking his belly now.

Right off the *Miracle on 34th Street* lot, Rick told himself, then said to Palmer, "I know several Caldwell grads. We've sent some of our youth, as well. East Wood's close enough. They come home a few weekends, but after a while, not much. Makes a statement. It's a pretty campus."

"Yes, and the general tone is *pretty straight-laced*, you can be sure!" Palmer shook out another chuckle, straight from the belly.

He's like most pastors, Ricky was thinkin'. Prefers to have the floor. That was all right. The sore throat made it easier to listen than talk.

"Nowadays, Caldwell's a marvel." Here the visitor paused like he was figurin' somethin' out. "Well, what shall I call it? Not a relic, not just old-fashioned." He smiled, opened his eyes like making a discovery. "It's a marvel of upright living. Young people thriving on it: rosy cheeks, sweethearts, all-out sports, studying to make the Dean's List, friends on the faculty. Quite amazing. It was like that when I was there, as well.

"However, I also have it on good authority—the word of a female seminarian who had a room in a women's dorm. After one especially dark, spring night, an orange bra appeared, hanging from a windowsill in the other wing!" He made a right angle with his hands and broke into a rumble of laughter so heartfelt Ricky had to join him. The exertion fired the apple cheeks a hot pink, Ricky told me. Maybe the room was too warm.

We're talkin' straight-laced, and the topic turns to orange bras! Ricky was somewhere between amused and astounded. Couldn't wait to tell me, a straight-laced Presbyterian bra—nice orange lace, I bet—for the Clemson fan.

"I became interested in Caldwell when I learned my grandfather was there," Palmer went on. "I was sixteen. My mother gave me his Greek textbook. I have it—to this day."

"He studied Greek? A pastor?"

"No, in those days a classical education was a gentleman's credential. They had Latin, of course, but also Greek. When I was a boy, I had to finish my Latin before I could go fishing, but by then . . . no more Greek. One of the schools in Virginia still teaches it, I hear—puts on tragedies in the original."

"I've wondered about the differences," Rick put in. "Classical, Koine Greek. Folks like to contrast biblical Hebrew and today's Israeli version."

"Classical Greek, Koine, modern Greek . . . they're like three languages. Hebrew? Some of that talk is politically motivated, but business has its own vocabulary, and much of the day-to-day language has been reconstructed. They're generally the same, Biblical and Modern Hebrew. In the Bible, you have several—the straight forward narratives, early and late poetry in the psalms, pithy super-Hebrew of the proverbs. Then there's that Hebrew cousin, Aramaic, in Daniel and Ezra. You know all this! Why am I telling you!" He chuckled again, barely opening his mouth when he laughed.

How does the sound get out? Ricky's wonderin'. It's bouncin' from those healthy lookin' whiskers over to the bookcase, the chairs, the pictures, floor to ceilin'. Like ventriloquism!

"The proverbs—'super-Hebrew.' An interesting way to put it."

Rick was listenin', storin' up details to lay on Moish.

"Well, Hebrew's nothing if not succinct. It's like the bouillon cube you could use right now for that cold. Probably make you sicker if I gave you one to chew, but in boiling water it's just the thing."

Palmer smiled radiantly, catching Rick off guard. Was the cold that obvious? The Presbyterian continued, clearly not caring that he might get it.

"Proverbs . . . the pithiest of the pithy: the Big Apple serving apple pie à la mode at the Waldorf. Think *minimalist*, not big, juicy, Delicious. There's that 'BDB' the Brown, Driver, and Briggs folks put together when somebody needed another dictionary. It's something else—the 'big dam' book, seminarians call it. I'm sure you remember . . . and don't bother to correct me," he commanded, leaving Rick to wonder what possible thing might be coming next. Correct him? He might as well correct Santa Claus on the location of the North Pole!

"I'll admit, the apparatuses in Hebrew Bibles are big—lines and lines of tiny print! No correction on that either. I say 'apparatuses' because I speak English! *Ap-pa-ra-teye* would be the feminine! I don't say *cac-teye* or *sylla-beye*. Wrong, improper! Show-off talk! They're just flaunting that Latin plural so you know they know it. Then they mispronounce it. Humbug! Show-offs!"

This old fellow is workin' up a passion, Ricky thought, astonished.

This is Santa Claus's twin brother, Professor Claus off duty, sitting down for gruel, no ghosts in sight, or maybe Santa Claus himself—the night's work done, reindeers fed and bedded down. Cousin of Julius Caesar, on top of it. Next thing I know, the old guy will get out his pipe, blow smoke rings like holly wreathes with thorns and berries. No, he won't smoke, not this Caldwell Presbyterian. Santa Claus, a Presbyterian?

Rick was struggling not to laugh, cold miseries forgotten.

This man even sparks the dead languages, he told himself. Hebrew: think minimalist? That's how it is when Shirley Levy talks—no extra words . . . not a one.

"Ever heard of Eleazer Ben-Yehuda?"

"Afraid not, Pas . . . uh, Pat."

"Well, he was a Russian. Made his way to the Land about thirty years before the Balfour Declaration. The Bible said a pure language would be restored to the people—a new nation, Hebrew! He bet his life on it. Ironically, his worst enemies were the Jewish town fathers in Jerusalem. They'd made a life in the City and detested the thought of everyday Hebrew—Hebrew for haggling in the fish market? Impossible! Hebrew was 'the tongue of the prophets'"!

"In a literal sense, Hebrew *was* the 'tongue of the prophets.' Truth was on his side! Fly to Tel Aviv, get there before today turns into tomorrow, Hebrew is what you hear!"

The old guy's eyes were flashin', Rick told me. Ricky was stuffin' down a belly laugh, thinkin', this man prob'ly shakes exclamation points on his breakfast cereal!

"A friend of mine married an Israeli," Rick told 'im, hoping for matter-of-fact. "She speaks in summaries—Hebrew filter, I guess. Right-to-the-point with everything—short, but not rude. Just says it in a few words."

Palmer smiled at the cameo of Shirley Levy. In Rick's imagination, the face was scowlin'. She'll be furious about those tests if Moish doesn't tell her, he was thinkin'.

"I'll bring you a copy of Ben-Yehuda's biography," Palmer was sayin'. "Precious part of my library, called *The Tongue of the Prophets*, of course. I bought it from the man's daughter. She was an old lady when I met her in Jerusalem. Years back. She had copies to sell. Packed four in my suitcase, gave one to an anti-Semite." More chuckles.

The chat ended without fanfare. Palmer was having lunch with his Clerk of Session—to all appearances, lookin' forward to it. This pastor . . . somebody to know better.

Palmer said goodbye, and Rick made progress on the Courage series. A good morning . . . actually a good morning.

Now Ricky's mullin' over that surprise visit and the cold Palmer made him forget. He's smilin' as he drives through springtime fields toward Calhoun. Hebrew, Eliezer Ben-Yehuda! The Courage series went well; that Palmer break actually helped. Minute by minute time management? Isn't always the best thing.

I haven't seen enough of the man, Rick's thinkin'. Can remedy that, but is he a *preacher*? Tape in, button pushed, a big voice. He reaches for the volume control.

"My friends," the voice booms, "we will examine a gem of a letter tucked away toward the end of the Bible—the Book of Jude."

"If I didn't know different," Rick told me, "I would've called this a young man's voice. But Jude?" That big voice was boomin' on, fillin' the cab of Ricky's truck.

"Scholars disagree about who Jude was. That's the business of scholarship, isn't it? Scholars will disagree on various points, won't they? The smaller the better!" A burst of laughter. His listeners are with him. They've heard the poke before.

Presbyterian anti-intellectual? Can't be! Those guys invented it! I've never done a Jude text, Rick was thinkin'. My Ricky doesn't hear sermons much . . . never, from the Presbyterian side. He was shiftin' his legs, tellin' himself that mashin' the foot feed's tirin'. Ears were sproutin' all over his head like mushrooms because Pastor Palmer was talkin' to *him*. A quiet thought drifted in, Ricky said, and to his mind, there was an exclamation point.

Supposed to do that, Apricot

"Cruise control next time for sure," he said to me. "Seats never go back far enough."

The voice had his complete attention.

"Scholars question whether this writer is indeed the brother of James, our Lord's half-brother. If you listen in faith, you hear that voice. The letter speaks strongly to me when I read it this way. Authority! It says: Listen up, son! I lived with him!

"The writer calls himself 'a slave of Jesus Christ and brother of James.' Isn't that wonderful! If this is the Lord's own half-brother—and I am convinced it is— he's one of those folks who didn't believe in Jesus' ministry . . . for a long time, it seems. The Gospel of John records this biographical detail.

"Now here's Jude—'a slave of Jesus Christ, the brother of James.' Jude won't even put himself in the same sentence with the Lord and he's a half-brother. Half-brother of Jesus of Nazareth, another son of Mary! He claims no connection! 'Brother' is not the way Jude sees Jesus! Jesus isn't the carpenter of Nazareth, adopted son of Joseph. He's the Messiah, the Son of Man! Somewhere in his deepest heart, the deepest part of his spirit, Jude also knows that this is God the Son. It will take the church another few hundred years to make this a point of unshakable, unalterable doctrine!

"Jude's humility here holds an ocean of significance for me. Jude has instructed me in the middle of the night, in the middle of conflicts, in the middle of successes when it would have been easy to pat myself on my own back and say, like Pat Horner (little Jack's brother, you know)—patting myself on the back and saying to myself: 'What a good boy am I!' And all I had done was put in my thumb and pulled out a plum!"

Ricky said he had to laugh. "This man moved from biblical scholarship to nursery rhymes in a breath, and he was reaching his congregation. Smile in his voice . . . chuckles here and there, folks echoing his enjoyment.

"It's clear Palmer likes preaching," Rick told me. "Talking about Jesus, making a bridge from the text. Scholarship putting on shoe leather—walking around, scuffing up the toes. Jesus has to love this Presbyterian!"

The discovery hit Rick as a surprise. Presbyterians twanging the Lord's heartstrings? They sure don't understand baptism! Not the time for that, he said, stoppin' himself. The voice boomed on.

"Jude cautions us against two things: diluting and corrupting the faith. Irreverence is the root cause. Notice: he links the arrogance of angels and humans who corrupt the church. Students from New Life Academy, you have an advantage over your parents! *Paradise Lost!* You know what Jude is talking about!"

More laughter here. Younger voices. One or two untamed guffaws.

"You resonate with this! Jude mentions 'angels who didn't keep their own position, but left their proper dwelling.' The 'dreamers' are humans who corrupt the church. They 'defile the flesh,' he says. They 'reject authority and slander the glorious ones.' The false Christians? Arrogant as the angels! Jude laces into these people. He calls 'em 'autumn trees without fruit, twice dead, uprooted; wild waves of the sea, casting up the foam of their own shame; wandering stars, for whom the deepest darkness has been reserved forever.' What a picture!

"Jude calls out sin. He expects accountability, promises judgment—not popular topics today! Our psychology-soaked culture isn't comfortable with sin and judgment talk. Jude is direct. He falls just short of naming names. God will judge, he declares!

"These false Christians are 'grumblers and malcontents; they indulge their own lusts. They're bombastic in speech. They use flattery for their own advantage.' What an array of sins! He speaks of these people as 'scoffers, indulging their own ungodly lusts,' as 'worldly people, devoid of the Spirit,' trouble-makers 'causing divisions.'

"Jude is a short book. Learn it by heart! Memorize it! You'll be better equipped to shun the sins Jude wants us to hate.

"Yes, hate! We hate things when we suffer from them! No one wants to be on the receiving end of wicked effects. Do we hate these things in ourselves? We must if we're to be the true saints of God! We must hate flattery, mockery, rebellion, arrogance, pride. We must loathe godlessness, worldliness and lust, divisiveness, grumbling! Purge these things from your lives! I have to too."

The words fell like dropping boulders, Ricky said. He was scannin' the roadsides, recallin' the name somebody back there gave this part of the county. "Moore's Mountain," we call it. He was imaginin' a sign: FALLING ROCK, but that was just a distraction.

"For each vicious sin Jude names, there's an opposing virtue—a trait we must cultivate for our own sake, for the sake of others, and to honor the holy God: for arrogance, humility; instead of rebellion, respect. No cynical critiques of excellence (isn't this what it is to 'slander the glorious ones'?) but instead, an eagerness to give the credit due—even when jealousy knocks on the door! No flattery, mockery, discontent, divisiveness! We must speak the plain truth and speak it *in love*!

"These virtues help us exchange the true for the false: for fruitlessness, fruit in God's service; for rootlessness, strong roots in the good soil of faith; for wild and wandering doubts, certainty in God the Almighty; for shame and darkness, hope and peace and the light of eternal life!

"Jude brings a message! This little book—short enough to memorize, I promise—will change your life! Memorize it! You'll be changed. Remember, the Word of God is a sharp sword, sharp enough to divide between the bone and the marrow. Discerns the very thoughts of the heart!

"Yes, my friends—memorize the Book of Jude. You'll be glad you did!

"Notice this: Jude speaks to the *people of God*. He speaks to us! His message is brief, wonderful!

"Do you use the word *wonderful* loosely? We mustn't do that! The word *wonderful* belongs to the Lord of Glory! Isaiah said, 'He shall be called Wonderful, the Counselor, the Everlasting Father, the Prince of Peace!' The rest of the Book of Jude *is wonderful* because it shows what a truly Christ-like person is, a Christian filled with the very Spirit of Christ, that wonderful Spirit—a Christian who listens to the wonderful counsel of the wonderful Counselor! The first part of Jude's letter shows us the false Christian, the last part—the true Christian!

"A true Christian is 'beloved'! Bask in that word! The Lord loves you! You are beloved of the Lord! Rest in that love; He rests in His love for you! You are beloved! And there's more wonderful stuff here!

"A true Christian is 'built up in the most holy faith'! This is intentional. The true Christian man builds himself up; the true Christian woman builds herself up! And notice the material used for the construction: the 'most holy faith!' You may say to me that faith is a gift, and I will say, 'Preach it, Brother! Preach it, Sister!'"

The congregation's laughing again. Sister? Yep, Presbyterians have women preachers, Ricky's thinkin,' shakin' his head, tellin' himself, I should ask him about it, but do I really want to? He was movin' his hands to another part of the wheel and shiftin' in his seat. The voice resonated, but the boom was a bit less intense. Pat must've moved away from the pulpit, he told me. Walks around too, not using notes. Rick reached to turn up the volume.

"Yes, faith is a precious gift of God. But remember, faith is a seed! A seed grows or dies. Let your seed of faith grow strong as you build it up in the Word, in prayer, in lovely fellowship with the King of Kings, with his people! The light of God . . . let it shine into your life! Seeds need sunlight . . . Son light, that's with an "o"!

"Notice, too, that the true Christian 'prays in the Holy Spirit.' This we must do! We must pray in the Spirit. Do you wonder what it is to pray in the Spirit?

"Look at what Paul tells the Ephesians, 'full armor of God' passage: 'Pray in the Spirit at all times in every prayer and supplication.' Some translators put it this way: 'Pray in the Spirit at all times with every sort of prayer and supplication.' Makes sense to me. I encourage you to set up camp in this verse!

"Pray every way you can think of! Pray for others; pray for yourself; pray for the work of the Gospel; pray for leaders, for missionaries; pray for those in prison for the Gospel, prisoners for any reason; pray for the sick and dying; pray with joy and gratitude; pray when you're weary and over-burdened; pray when you're worried; pray in tongues…yes, that's what I said! PRAY IN TONGUES if you want to. If the Lord tells you to, go ahead! You go ahead and pray! If somebody fusses, tell 'em I said so."

Lots of laughter.

What?

Praying in tongues? Shaky ground here, but the voice boomed in his head and Ricky hit the button again. "Pat's an engaging preacher," he told me.

I mean! Hope my Ricky's rememberin' all this.

"Pray the prayers of praise and adoration. Pray without ceasing. Pray at all times with thanksgiving. You will never lose a moment of sleep. I'm convinced the Lord of Glory gives to his beloved even in their sleep and he gives *sleep* to his beloved, both translations! If you find yourself awake and tossing, PRAY."

My goodness, Rick's tellin' himself, this Presbyterian is shouting . . . and he's talking about sleep! Bet his congregation doesn't drop off much.

"Yes, dearly beloved of the Father—yes, true Christian: Pray. The Lord will listen with delight. Then He, our gracious God, will rock you to sleep in his mighty and holy arms.

"You'll reach the heart of the God who loves you, the heart of Jesus, the heart of the great King! And you'll wake refreshed.

"Yes, loves you . . . loves you with an everlasting love, the love of eternity, of Calvary, the spiced and empty tomb!

". . . never, never, never forget the love of God. This is another thing Jude tells us. He says, 'Keep yourselves in the love of God, looking for the mercy of our Lord Jesus Christ to eternal life.'

"Do you fear the end of the world? Do you fear judgment? You should *fear*! We all should fear! The Lord Jesus said not to 'fear those who can kill the body, but to fear the One who can kill the body and afterward cast it into hell!' Then he repeats it: 'Yes,' he says, 'fear Him!'

"What good child doesn't fear the wrath of his father—yes, fears that good man who is his father! That little boy fears him, and that's partly why he loves him! That is partly why the little girl loves her daddy. She fears him because she knows he's bigger than she is and wiser and knows the world and how to get around in it better than she does! Maybe even better than her mama . . .."

Chuckles, more laughter . . . female laughter.

"The love of those children is all mixed in with the fear they rightfully feel for that good man who is their good father! We are to be good children, good mothers, good fathers because the good God who loves us wants us to be like him. It isn't hard to respect true goodness! We love and honor true goodness! It is lovable! We love God because God is truly good. God *is love*!

"In Leviticus the word is HOLY. We're to be whole and good and righteous, clean in thought, word and deed. We're to be like our good God. God expects it because the way for that to happen has been made! God has given us Calvary and the blood of atonement, the obedience of His precious, precious and dearly beloved Son; we've received the Spirit so we can be good, good with God's goodness!

"We can be true Christians! This is the blessed promise so sweet it tugs at my heart and causes earthquakes in my spirit!"

Earthquakes in his spirit, Rick's thinkin', feeling more ears sproutin' up to catch each syllable. This man's good!

"Here it is," the voice booms. "This the wonderful promise. Jude ends his letter with it. The promise is for the good Christian, the true Christian! I'll read it to you. Carry it away with you. It's a precious gem in a precious, perfectly made—*richly* made—jewel box . . .."

Here the preacher paused for a minute, Ricky told me. When he spoke again, his voice was different—quiet. It was soft like he was moved, barely gettin' himself onto the tape. Rick leaned closer and turned up the volume.

"No, I won't be able to," the voice was sayin'. "Douglass, will you come up here? Come up here and read with me. This is a magnificent promise for God's people. It's too much for me. I can't read by myself. It's too true, too rich and too fine. My voice won't hold. Yours will carry us along.

"While he's coming, get your pew Bibles and find the last two verses in the Book of Jude. You'll find it right before the Book of the Revelation of Jesus Christ. It's right there, nearly the end of the Bible."

Some rustling around, coughing, shuffling of feet then another pause before a second voice starts speakin'.

"Jude verses twenty-three through twenty-five."

Now, two voices—the quieter voice of the preacher and a sure, rich voice of somebody named Douglass.

Ricky told me the two voices read with a swelling resonance that filled up the spaces—the sanctuary of the church Rick was imaginin' and the cab of his truck.

"Now unto Him who is able to keep you from falling and to present you faultless before the presence of His glory with exceeding joy! To the only wise God our Savior be glory and majesty both now and forever, Amen."

Another pause. Then the pastor went on. He quietly thanked the reader and offered the benediction. The worship service was over. My Ricky turned down Meadowlark Road toward the new folks' house.

What was that name? He was turnin' onto a smaller road, this one dirt, and glancin' at notes on the seat beside him. He's bad about that. One of these days, he's gonna drive off the road, I keep tellin' 'im.

"Yes, Patsy and Steve Whipple. Whipple, Whipple. Patsy and Steve, Patsy and Steve . . . Steve and Patsy Whipple." He had it now.

They'll be home, he's thinkin'. Joe's recoverin' from surgery. Shouldn't stay long.

The white house ahead seemed to have sprung up like a crop in the open field, a square in a huge garden. A small truck farm?

How does Steve manage all this if something's bad enough for surgery? Does Patsy work this field? Maybe so. Unusual lady probably. Canning and freezing too, I bet.

Have lunch with Pat Palmer . . . soon as possible. Call him tomorrow for a time. I can drive over there, Ricky's thinkin', but I better call first. Might not be there if it's Monday.

Rick parks the truck and looks around. Palmer's voice is still resonatin' in his head. He can preach, no question about it, Ricky thinks. Typical Presbyterian—open mind, but not so open-minded he can't talk about sin. How many "frozen chosen" tell their folks to pray in tongues? My goodness! Open heart, open mind. Too open maybe. An open heart's more important. It's not just the Methodists that think that. And he's old . . . a true elder. That's what Presbyterians call their Board, isn't it?

Honeybabe, I am amazed, let me tell you. My Ricky's not too old to learn something.

Presbyterian church polity, one more thing to freshen up on. I'm getting older myself, he's thinkin'. Well, not that old. Nice to meet an old fellow like Palmer. So energetic.

Yes, Whipple . . . Patsy and Steve.

Pore Betty. That's all I can say about this moment in her church-secretary life. She was doin' the best she could. Enjoyed tellin' me about it later though.

"This is Union Street Baptist Church, Betty Berttison speaking. How may I help you?"

"Felix Feinemann. Good morning, Betty. I have some sad news for your pastor. If you'll be so kind, I would like to speak with him."

"Oh, g' mornin', Mr. Feinemann. No, he just left. He's headed out toward Calhoun . . . visitin' this morning. Would you like me to take a message?"

"Yes, please tell him that our fine neighbor, Alice Faber, passed away this morning about five-thirty. The nursing home called. They were not able to reach the rabbi, they said, so they called us. We are her closest neighbors—next to the Levys, of course. When do you expect your pastor to return?"

"He should be back by noon, Mr. Feinemann. Do you want him to call you?"

"Please convey my message to him. I will try to speak with him just after lunch. Thank you very much, Miss Berttison. Today is a sad day. I'm sure the pastor will know what to do. I will continue to try and reach Rabbi Levy."

"I'm sure he will, Mr. Feinemann."

"Goodbye now."

"Goodbye, Mr. Feinemann. I'll give Pastor Rick the message."

Betty scribbles a note on a sticky then pats it on the door of the study, the only way to be sure he gets it. She came up with the method after some real mix-ups. Who forgot? Well, whoever . . . this way nobody misses a message.

The phone's ringing again.

"Good mornin'. Union Street Baptist Church, Betty Berttison speakin'. Can I help you?"

"Good morning, Betty. This is Saul Finkelstein. I've just received word that Mrs. Faber passed away this morning. Can you tell me the funeral arrangements?"

"Oh, hello, Mr. Finkelstein. No. I just heard about it myself. I didn't get funeral arrangements yet. If you call back later, I may be able to tell you somethin'."

"Yes, thank you, Betty. I will call back. Goodbye."

"G'bye, Mr. Finkelstein."

The church secretary looks at her fingernails. Hard to keep 'em lookin' nice with so much typin' to do. It's fingernails or a hundred words a minute . . . one or the other, she thinks. They really don't mix. Another style of nails maybe? Have to ask Madeleine's daughter. She's always up on the latest.

As she writes "Finkelstein too" on another sticky, the phone rings again, several times. Reaching over her coffee cup, she grabs it before the call can drop.

"Good mornin'. Union Street Baptist Church. Betty Berttison speakin'."

"Yes, how are you, Betty? Joel Rubenstein here."

"Oh, hello, Mr. Rubenstein. I'm fine. How are you?"

"Well, I just heard from the Feinemanns that Mrs. Faber died early this morning. Can you tell me anything about her funeral?"

"Actually, I can't. No arrangements yet. But if you call back . . . maybe by tomorrow, I can pro'bly tell you somethin'."

"Thank you very much, Betty. I'll do that. Have a nice day."

"Thanks—you, too, Mr. Rubenstein. Goodbye."

Betty takes a sip of coffee and makes a face. Cold. She gets up from her desk to head to the workroom where the coffee pot lives, but the phone is ringing again.

"Good mornin'. UnionStreetBaptistChurch, BettyBerttison. CanIhelp you?"

"Yes, good morning. Goldberg here. When is the Faber funeral?"

"Good mornin', Mr. Goldberg. We haven't heard anything yet. If you call back tomorrow, maybe—"

"Thank you." The phone goes dead.

This coffee's black as death. Deciding in favor of some non-dairy lightener to cut the bitterness, Betty frowns then dumps it all and pours herself another cup. The phone is ringing. Hurrying and balancing a full cup of coffee, she just makes it to the desk. The voice beats her to a greeting.

"Oh, Betty dear... I'm so sad to hear about Alice Faber. She died this morning, Miriam says, so sad . . . so sad. Do you know about . . . well, when will she be buried?"

Mrs. Goldberg this time! Is the whole of that synagogue callin'? How interested can they *be* in the death of a Baptist? They really have a heart!

Betty flashes the questions around in her head, answering Mrs. Goldberg as if by voice-over.

"Yes, it is sad, isn't it? We haven't heard anything yet though, Miz Goldberg . . .. Maybe by tomorrow. If you call back then, we'll know something pro'bly. Can you do that, ma'am?"

"Yes, I will, dear. I will call back tomorrow . . . thank you so very much . . . so sad, so sad. We will miss her so much. She was such a star, known the world over. Well, goodbye for now."

"Yes, that's true . . . we will. G'bye, Miz Goldberg."

Betty stirs the dangerous-looking liquid with a little stick from the Styrofoam cup and finds the stack of mail to go through. The phone is ringing. She puts down the cup, noticing that it isn't so hot.

I feel like a robot, she says to herself, telephone robot or somethin', maybe a human-robot answerin' machine cyber-girl—

"GoodmorninUnionStreetBaptistChurchBettyBerttisonspeakin.C'nIh'lp you?"

"Yes, I'm calling to ask about the funeral arrangements—the Faber funeral?"

The slightly accented voice of Jonathan Stein, the new owner of Beulah's first Jewish deli. Mr. Stein, too? He's barely been here a year!

What's going on, she thinks, rubbing one eye. Feels like it has a speck in it. "We haven't heard about arrangements yet. I think we might know somethin' by tomorrow afternoon . . . late afternoon. If you'll give me a number and the best time to reach you, I'll have the pastor call back."

"Sure—this is Jonathan Stein, over at the deli. Thank you. No need to call . . . get the details tomorrow. Shalom."

"All right. Goodbye . . . uh, shalom too, Mr. Stein."

He actually sounded grieved! How does he know Miz Faber? Betty thinks. Hasn't been in town long enough, has he? She can't go to the deli! Maybe Augusta goes for her.

Like most folks in small Southern towns, the secretary defines "new people" by decades. There are some guidelines. The ones who've been in Beulah less than twenty years are still "not from around here." If a scandal comes along, people can say, "No, I don't believe I know them . . ." though they really do. If you talk funny, you stay "new." The Steins are different. Everybody knows Jonathan Stein because of the food. Who would've thought? Nobody really knew what Yankees ate. Mr. Stein's friendly too, but Miz Stein doesn't hear real well. Maybe having to shout is a help. People have grandmas they have to shout at. You can't shout and be too formal . . . or too far away. I guess that explains it. It's part of livin' near your kinfolks. Everybody does that around here. The Steins fit right in.

Remembering that somebody mentioned they have two new sandwiches this week, she looks at the clock. How close to lunch?

Why do we need that ol' clock, she thinks. My computer has a clock.

The phone's ringing.

"Good mornin'. Union Street Baptist this is Betty. How may I help you?"

"Oh . . . Betty dear. I am so . . . so grieved. Can you . . . tell us when . . . the funeral will be?"

"Oh, hello, Mrs. Feinemann," she says, catching a quaver in the familiar voice. Weepin'?

"Actually, we don't know anything yet, Miz Feinemann. The pastor just left. He's out visitin', but he's supposed t' be back by noon. We may know somethin' by tomorrow. Do you want me to have 'im call you?"

"Yes, dear. I would appreciate that so much . . . so much. So sad . . . such a tragedy this is. How we will miss dear Alice, so . . . so tragic—"

The voice trails off like a sigh.

"I will have Pastor Rick call you, for sure, Miz Feinemann. Does he have your number?"

"Yes, he has it, I am sure. He may call Felix at the store. Thank you, my dear. We will be waiting . . . for the call." She hangs up without saying goodbye.

Is she slippin', Betty asks herself. The whole town knows about that depression! A few months ago she . . .. Well, she didn't do it, and everybody says she's better. But she doesn't sound good. Better tell the pastor to call 'em right away. When he gets here.

Betty checks some envelopes and dumps in the trash a catalog advertising purple pulpit robes "designed for today's pastor." Pastor Rick? No way. The phone is ringing again. How many more?

Should I call the pastor's cell? No. Off limits. With all the interruptions, he'd never make it through the day if I broke that rule. Besides, he doesn't use his phone and drive. Nothing short of Gabriel's trumpet if he's doin' a sermon, even if the phone's right here.

Betty hates decisions like this. Phones aren't usually a problem. But today Betty's thinkin,' they have to let 'im do what they're payin' 'im to do. I'm the one who's supposed to be answering the phone. Still, when it's all on one subject like this, I'm not sure what to do.

She's lookin' at the clock. Pastor should be back in an hour or less. What can he say anyway?

Still thinking about the Whipples, Rick pulls his truck into the spot marked PASTOR and looks at the church. Unusual, back in 1896. Controversial. Pillars of the congregation resisted, even families of charter members. "Peculiar," they said. "No columns to hold up the roof. Different. Not the way a church should look."

Rick studies the small tower and dome. Amazing. Baptist church and no steeple?

Stepping inside from the heat, he marvels at some other differences. One part of the sanctuary angles off to the side, big doors that slide into the walls. Mechanism still works. The doors can separate off this part of the sanctuary, make an assembly room.

If we still did assemblies before Sunday school, he's thinkin'. No one fusses about the stain glass windows. Who wouldn't like that rich brown? Ruby red dots too, like big round jewels. All that colored light on the south and west. Some of our great-grandparents still remember the complaints about the architecture. Too much of a departure, folks said.

Ricky's mullin' over an odd fact.

I like it, he's thinkin,' even better than St. Michael's. Wonder why Union Street looks like St. Michael's? Some Baptist over there started out as an Episcopalian maybe. Early on, old Richard Furman made South Carolina Baptist. Baptist himself from sixteen when he started preaching, and Cornwallis put a thousand pound bounty on his head! Said he feared his prayers "more than Marion's men."

In the office, Betty's on the phone. Ricky takes the mail from her outstretched hand. Listenin' to her, he's thinkin,' funeral arrangements? No funeral this week, I'm sure of it. Who died? If they did, it's too soon for arrangements.

"Thank goodness it's you, Pastor!" Betty slams the phone down.

Lucky for the phone bill, he told me eyebrows arched, she doesn't do that too often.

"The phone's ringin' off the hook! Miss Alice Faber died this morning, and the whole Beth Shalom has been callin' and wantin' information about the funeral! It's sure broken up my morning! I didn't tell 'em you'd call back—just too many. But Miz Feinemann did ask you to. Like I said, the phone's been ringin' and ringin'. Maybe you'll know what to say to all these people!"

"I guess you said we don't know yet."

"Yes, sir. That's what I said. But I had to say it to ten or eleven people this morning and then repeat it a couple of more times to two or three of 'em!"

"Well . . . the rabbi and the Feinemanns are neighbors, you know. The closest friends she has . . . uh, had in town . . . . But it's a bit surprising that everybody else—"

"Surprisin'! It's unheard of! Exactly what it is: unheard of!"

The phone's ringin' again. Betty turns to answer it, poutin' her lips and shruggin' 'er shoulders as the pastor escapes into his study.

"hrd faberge dyd in bUla sc."

"tll bcrelli."

I got this from Bacarelli himself. Just had to tell that redhead at the next pump . . . so hilarious. He heard the original from Tony. Tony was puttin' gas in the limousine, not payin' attention. What a stitch. That Bacarelli's really somethin'. He can make you think you're hearin' the real thing, but he has wanderin' eyes, that man. Famous or not.

Something . . . ringing, ringing. Tony Mascatori groaned and slammed his fist down in the general direction of what oughta be a semblance of the alarm button. He didn't find it. He shut his eyes, turned over, and smashed the pillow over his head to block out the miserable racket. He was drifting into a dream about cream puffs and Chianti and the new pizza topping his brother came up with last week when the ringing found him out again. A bit softer now but just as insistent.

This woke him up enough to fix the sound at some place beyond the clock and he turned over again.

Throw somethin' at that noise, he thought.

He propped on one elbow, scratched an ear, grabbed a handful of hair and yanked, pulling out a few curly strands—a gesture he's known for. Seemed to help him think.

The only light came from a blinking red sign above the cleaner's at the corner—on and off, on and off, on and off. The ringing didn't do that. It was just on . . . ringringringringringringring.

He staggered to his feet, stumbled over some stray shoes, and located the pants he threw over the chair last night. Last night? Maybe it was tonight . . . tonight, tonight, and there ain't no girl named Maria.

Maria, M'riaaMriangaMringaringaringaringringringring . . .. The ringing mocked at him as he swung the pants around in the dark trying to find the pocket.

Belt loops! Tony thrust three big fingers into what should be a front pocket. Empty space was all he found.

"Law of the Opposite Pocket," he growled. "Whatdaya know about that . . .."

Feeling in the other pocket, he pulled out the phone, pawed it for the button marked TALK, jammed the thing to his ear, and scowled into the dark, intending the look to freeze whatever idiot was calling at this hour, whatever hour it was.

"Yeh, I'm goin' back to sleep now."

"No you aren't, you annoying stuffedcreamedcabbage head, you goat's toenail, you green overripe, semi-melted Sicilian cheese log, you miserable, moldy hunk of fermented squid brains . . .. I could scream!"

A second's pause, a breath . . . the river of invective flowed on.

"You . . . you paint-peeling, fungus-inflamed, dankandsmelly old cheese barn! Your head's full of nothing but forty-five bats, toads, and field mice, and . . . and cheese reek! You don't even know the difference between anchovies and black olives smashed into a pulp and spun into cotton candy, let alone how to compose a sentence in decent English. What is it? You just got off the boat?"

"Gina! What're ya doing? You crazy or somethin'? Why're you calling me in the middle-a-th' night, baby? Didn't I tell you not to do that? Whatsa mattah widyou?"

"This is *what'sa mattah . . ..*"

Mascatori caught the mock. The impression was startlingly close to the real thing. Gina works at a radio station, and everything coming out of her mouth is perfect. He likes to say, "Miss Plastic Mouth," to get her goat. Does it every time. The queen of "well-modulated" never slips into some type of brogue—even when she is angry. Always that plastic. Sounds like it had some kind of girly color. Pink. Yeh, pink plastic mouth—shiny, pink plastic voice too. Tonight she forgot herself.

Man, is she good at pickin' up on how people talk, Tony was thinking. Do an impression of anybody. Makes me laugh. But she crossed th' line this time.

This raging Mascatori nearly missed the next blast from the phone side.

"One more of those and you won't ever see me again—*ever* . . . get it? You spell that *E-V-E-R* dumhead! You know how I hate all that nonsense junk you've been sending. I told you not to send me any more of it . . . stupidwhateveritis, didn't I tell you? If you want to talk to me, you have to use your *voice*, get it? You fill up my phone with that stuff then you get mad when I mess up what you told me to do! Enough! You think you're some kind of techno-wizard or something. Well, let me tell you, you big baluski! I've stayed up this late, missing my much-needed rest, just to call you when you got good and sound asl—"

"What? Gina!" Tony's yelling, trying to halt the flow.

Getta a grip, he told himself. Can't let fly and smash th' cell on the wall over there.

Just in time, he thought of the cost of replacing his favorite toy and managed to slam the brakes on the only good way he could think of to end this insanity-prodoocin' conversation. Smashin' the phone would make problems, not fix 'em. Had to figure out something else . . . think quick.

Calling me in the middle of th' night, he told himself, muddily working on ways to morph rage into a weapon. I said it clear enough! She ain't that stoopid! Blasted night person! She's gotta stop this callin' stuff . . . always startin' chatty conversations two hours after I turn out th' lights. Anyway, Gina oughta be here in my bed, lettin' me rock her to sleep! What kinda girl is she, anyway? Didn't she hear? *Verchoo* is old school! How come Miss Plastic thinks she has to go to bed alla way across town?

Before he could breathe, another burst of angry female volubility assaulted his ear, effectively shutting down his rant, spoken and unspoken.

"Yes, this is your little Gina, and I am at this very startled and upstanding minute respectfully complaining to St. Peter himself about every inch of your over-stretched and tattooed hide, especially your big fat fingers—they've gotta stay off that phone, Tony! St. Peter is duly informed of your horrible, aggravating case—and all your scarlet red and purple sins, you warmed-over from yesterday's stale pile of th'ashes of a burnt-up toasted garlic bun stillsmokingtheheightsofGo d'sblessedheaven!

"No, two! Both of your . . . a box, I mean a pox on both . . . both of your horrid, blasted, pudgy-and-dimpled tuckus buns! Didn't I tell you not to send anymore of those written-in-some-language-that-for-sure-isn't-mine-whatever-they-are's? And then you get mad at me if I don't do whatever the stupid thing was you were telling me!"

Pudgy . . . dimpled? What—?

Struggling to formulate a plan, Mascatori was momentarily frozen by the awful thought of one steamy afternoon when he mistakenly convinced himself that the sight of his stark naked body might, just might, turn Gina on. Forcing the very different consequences of that bright idea from his mind, he slammed the ATTENTION button in his head, hoping to blow off the last of the fog.

Yeh, he told himself a few seconds later, I've got it.

Taking a deep breath and sighing audibly into the telephone, he turned his face a little to the side and enunciated a perfectly contrived message in a quiet but clear stage whisper—syllables just loud enough to make it through the airspace, through the wires, through that mop of black hair curling around the other ear.

"It's Gina. Go back to sleep . . . yeh, it's just Gina."

A pause. Tony could see the wheels turning in the head stuck to the other phone. His wait was rewarded. The sound he expected struck his ear in three and a half seconds, right on time, in decibels not yet known to man. The length of the pause was so predictable he had time to back the phone off. No sense losin' an eardrum.

"YEEEEEEEEEEEEOOOOOU . . .."

Silence. The scorched air shook, then settled. He could hear Gina's breathing.

"So. Some girl's at your place! I should have known . . . and, and that's just fine. *You* deliver to my brother your own mixed up message in some unknown tongue of your own creation. See how he likes it, especially when I get through with him on your behalf. He'll forget he ever knew your name, buddy budinski! You go right back to sleep. I hope you dream about leg irons on every one of your thirty-seven feet, you slimy salamander, you tadpole, you three-toed swamp mold! You . . . you, you spotted-slug-meat-floating-in-its-own-extra-non-virgin-olive-oil-till . . . well, never mind till when. I don't want to ever see you again and don't you forget it! You remember that . . . youremerberthat! Besides, you dumbnut creep, you think my brother never reads a newspaper?!"

The phone went dead, for sure slammed to smithereens on her bedside table.

That's just fine, Tony said to himself in a line borrowed from Gina. He was thinking, 'I still have my phone and hers is smashed. I can still text, and she can't call me when I'm sound asleep!'

He was too worked up to check the logic of texting a phone now reduced to bits.

Gina . . . he knew her like the back of his hand. But who would guess she'd get worked up over a text message? Time she got up to date, in more ways than one!

Mascatori found the light and checked the clock. 12:53 a.m. He'd been sleep one hour . . . deep into it. Blasted women! Gina was mad at a text message? Her grandpa was Greek. Must be it, he thought, no other explanation. But I'm not breakin' it off, and I ain't spendin' hard-earned cash to get that tattoo off. Orthodox. Shoulda thought twice.

"But I can let Bacarelli know Fabergé died," he said to himself, arranging things in a new format. "And Gina can't tell 'im anything that'll do me damage. She's just mad. She'll forget everything by morning. It'll be no sweat to tell Bacarelli. Easy enough . . . probably more persuasive first hand. She'd be sure to mess up the message. 'My little Gina' was right about that . . . .."

I'll get the job drivin' him to Byoolah, South Carolina, wherever that is. Better yet, a plane ticket to some airport and drive the rental for him the rest of the way. South Carolina . . . probably no airport. Fly into Florida or somewhere—long drive, more money. Might work out nice. I'll have to get Gina a present though. Need some sweetenin' up.

The thought of finding a gift for city-girl Gina in some place that couldn't make it onto a map was too much for him. Tony fell across the king-size and was asleep in seconds. The light he forgot to turn off was no bother. Three days before, he also hadn't bothered with a newsflash—*Skybox* obit in papers around the world: **Diva Fabergé Dies**. But three days before, Bacarelli, renowned tenor (retired), sloshed orange juice all over the *New York Times* he was reading at breakfast and in minutes was on the phone with his travel agent.

"Where, on God's green earth, is it . . . this, this 'Beulah, South Carolina'?"

That's what he told me, babe. And you're right, he's high on himself as a ski lift ridin' the Dali Lama up Mount Everest. At least he tried to be a little modest with that third person! Bowed when he said "renowned tenor (retired)." Try to picture it, hon. He was about to kiss my hand!

CHAPTER EIGHT
Good News, Bad News

HONEYBABE, I GOT THE GIST OF THIS FROM MR. Batterman's paralegal. She doesn't like stayin' late, but sometimes even she has to. Not this night. I've added some color here and there.

Nine hundred and fifty miles south of Mascatori's loft apartment and a state away from Quentin's littered Decatur study, Jonas Batterman is lockin' up his office in the Dunstan Building across from the Beulah, South Carolina, Courthouse. The daylight hours aren't his preference, and as he often does in the throes of some thorny procedural headache, he's pushed on well into the night. A dozen files from the Warren Case. As a rule, the law office gets no phone calls after ten, even from attorneys, and nobody is rushin' in to remind him of the appointment he's nearly forgotten. Even the street traffic quiets down after eight-thirty. Now, it's two in the mornin'. Time to quit.

He goes downstairs and opens the street door, its frosted glass window advisin' the world in plain letters that the law offices of Rubenstein and Batterman can be reached within. The attorney is thinkin' about his life in this small South Carolina town, relivin' things.

Unlikely, he thinks. As a boy, bringing tools and rags and stuff when needed, he watched his father work on Judge Solomon's old Austin-Healey. One day the judge engaged him in conversation, just passing the time of day. Somehow he'd amazed the big white man, wasn't sure how. To him a photographic memory was just the way you thought. Didn't everybody think like that?

His daddy used his brain the way other folks used a fix-it manual. Only they didn't talk. Daddy would say, "What's on page forty, son? You know the place. It's where that'ar discussion of the carbuerator starts. No, you can skip the part about the bonnet. That's British. Jus' means all that stuff's under the hood."

The judge stood there listening, just taking it all in. Then he said something that had the swish of an opening door.

"Come around and visit me at my office, Joe. I'll have something for you."

That's what he said and that's what I did, Jonas says to himself.

What the judge had for him was a nice fountain pen. No, it wasn't just nice. It was beautiful. The judge had to show him how to use it. He had one too. Then Judge Solomon gave him a bottle of ink.

He also gave me a job, Jonas tells himself, smiling. After five years of running errands for the judge, I never got used to the way the judge stared at me. Seemed to be looking into my soul. Something was on the judge's mind.

The year Rick Apricot, Quentin, and I won the state championship for Beulah, the judge—he never missed a football game—yeh, that day the judge shook my hand and asked me to bring my daddy up to the law offices. They were a home away from home for me by then, and I was proud to bring my daddy to the place I worked. He was proud, so proud.

My daddy scrubbed on his hands, changed his shirt and shoes and followed me downtown. At the Courthouse, they showed us into the judge's chambers like folks. I'm remembering the day like it wasn't even yesterday . . . like it was happening right now.

"Come in, Mr. Batterman. Please sit down. Can I ask JaneAnne to bring you some coffee?"

"Nossuh, I's just fine, thank y'," daddy said, smiling at the consideration, wondering what in the world this was all about. What it was all about was Harvard. It was Harvard.

"Ev'lyn . . . how you doin' this mornin'?"

"Oh hey, Lucy. Good to hear your voice. How is everything over in Calhoun?"

Evelyn Martelote smiles, knowing what her friend will say. Always says the same thing. No one is quite sure what it means.

"Fine as rain, M., fine as rain. We need some though. My garden's sufferin'."

"What do you have this year?"

"Well, Joe Paul talked me into planting some of those hot peppers, and they're coming on like it was Mexico! That's partly why I called. What do you do with 'em anyway? I'm gettin' so many I can't figure it out. Joe Paul likes hot salsa, but you can only eat so much . . . I mean, he can. I don't touch it myself."

"How about hot pepper jelly?

"No, I'm tired of that. Besides, I have a bunch of it already. June Hill gave me some last winter. Do you put hot peppers in spaghetti or what?"

"I don't make spaghetti. Madeleine doesn't either. I buy it . . . the marinara, I mean. How about chili?"

"Well, I guess that's obvious, but I don't make chili. I just get it in a package when I get it. Joe Paul's into stuff like that, but I'm not so much. Still, I'm gettin' used to hot things. Supposed to be good for you."

"Give me a minute . . .. Quentin gave me a cookbook with spicy recipes last Christmas. I'll go and get it."

"Okay . . . there's somethin' else, too. Don't let me forget when you get back."

The phone goes silent while her friend walks to the kitchen. The pause gives Lucy a minute to think about the something else she wants to take up with her friend.

"Here's one that might do," Evelyn says, returning. "It's called 'Open Your Eyes Corn Bread,' and it has something called habañera peppers. Have a pencil?"

"Yes, but it sounds horrible. Joe Paul says habañera peppers are the hottest . . . the hottest there are! If I made it, he'd be the one to eat it. Besides, I'm not growin' any habañabas . . . whatever-you-call-'em peppers."

"Well, how about this? 'Double Hot Pancakes.' You mix in the minced peppers—in the batter, I mean—and also some crumbled up 'scalding hot sausages.' No maple syrup or anything . . . nothing sweet, just those two kinds of hot. The recipe says that—'scalding hot sausages' and specifically advises leaving off the syrup. It says those words exactly. The menu section mentions something called *Huevos Rancheros* too. I don't know what that is. Maybe it's some sort of

Mexican crepe. You eat the eggs on the pancakes . . . that's what the illustration looks like, anyway. Wait a minute. The cookbook adds a warning, mentions how hot this is. It says you can hurt your mouth if you aren't used to it. Water doesn't help, it says. Here's another one. Mexican-hot Hot Chocolate. It's guaranteed to open your sinuses, the book says. Do you want that one?"

"Okay, never mind. I'll ask around. Somebody's sure to have a recipe that's not too hot. I have to do something with these peppers though. Maybe I'll just pass 'em out at church on Sunday. Joe Paul says he doesn't know anybody he can give 'em to."

"Hot time in th' old town tonight! What will you Methodists be doing next?"

"For shame, Evelyn! We're back down to earth and you know it! No more of that charismatic stuff goin' on now."

"Settle down, Lucy. I wasn't faulting you. What's the matter with charismatic, anyway?"

"Well, you may think nothin'. I guess charismatic's somethin' like hot peppers. Better in little doses. We've had ours."

Her friend is beginning to chuckle. If Lucy only knew . . ..

"What was the other thing you wanted to tell me?"

"Well, I wanted to ask you. Is Betty Berttison . . . she's your neighbor's granddaughter, isn't she? Is she still engaged to that fella over in Miller?"

"No. She gave him back his ring. They had some sort of disagreement; it became a problem. Couldn't come to an understanding. She told Emmaline it was better to end it now than—"

"She's probably right . . . so many break-ups these days, the kind that shouldn't be happenin'. After you're married, it shouldn't happen."

"Well, she's not marrying him. I guess it's for the best."

"Prob'ly . . .. Okay, I'd better be goin'. I still have to get things together for Sunday . . . new hymns to practice an' all. Do Episcopalians ever do new hymns?"

"Come on, Lucy. Who do you think we are, anyway?"

"Well, you did have that father that played the guitar. I guess he got your bunch into new hymns or somethin'."

"Or something."

"Okay, I'll see ya later. Come 'n see me when you're in Calhoun next."

"I will. Oh, by the way. Quentin is coming again next week, and Lucy, think of some reason to come over to Beulah . . . be sure to come while he's here. I know you're not wasting gas money, but you must have some reason to come over. We can have tea or lunch or something. A real visit. He hasn't been coming much recently. It's been so hard, but his vision has returned, as you know, and I'm so grateful. We still don't understand it, but when he comes he'll be glad to see you. He's at Agnes Scott now, you know."

Yes, I do know 'cause you've told me often enough, Lucy Jenkins thinks. My, my, my . . . she is still so proud of that boy. This is the fith or sixth time she's told me he's at Agnes Scott! Well, she deserves to be, I guess. And that blindness was prob'ly breakin' her heart. I'm proud of Joe Paul, too . . . can't stand in judgment.

"I'll try to come over. Tell 'im I said hello."

"I surely will. He asks about you every time he comes home. He still plays the piano, you know. Always said you were a grand teacher. Funny how he could play the piano, even without vision."

"Always did well. I'm glad to know he's still playin' . . .. Well, bye. I'll see y'soon. No no, wait. I thought of somethin' else. I heard down town that the rabbi has become a Christian!"

"You told me that. He was baptized?"

"No no, Evelyn . . . he believes! He believes in Jesus."

"Well, I haven't heard anything about that! Are you sure?"

"The odd thing is that he isn't talkin' to anybody about it . . . because of his health issues, I hear. I know you've heard about his health issues . . .. I'm surprised he's still hangin' on in such bad shape."

"Do you think he'll take part in Alice Faber's memorial service?"

"What memorial service? I thought her funeral was yesterday."

"Yes, it was—pretty simple, but well attended. That daughter didn't come. But the whole opera world wants to pay respects, it seems. A memorial has to happen some way. I hear from Emmaline that Betty was flooded with telephone calls at the Baptist church. Like telephone Grand Central Station to hear her talk about it. They have to do something. The motels are already booked up for next week . . .."

"They must be doin' something then."

"Well, Susan says it's a toss-up between Jewish, Baptist, and Pentecostal. I guess you knew she grew up in the Assembly of God here in town."

"No . . . you don't say."

"I just did. Anyway, a memorial service is scheduled for Thursday. I'm not sure what kind it will be, but they're having one. And the entire United Nations of Opera will have it's May meeting right here in Beulah. In honor of Alice." Chuckles here.

"Hmmm," said Lucy.

Sometimes Lucy Jenkins just gets carried away, Evelyn thinks. Her own gossipy chats in town are still fresh, but the details don't need to be repeated.

Too bad Quentin doesn't see as much of the rabbi as he did when they were boys, she tells herself. I'm sure he'd know if the rabbi's come to believe. Just have to wait and see. Something is going on, but I don't know what. If the rabbi believes, the service will be smoother. But maybe he won't participate, not if he's terminally ill. Sometimes people do soldier on. He seems the type.

"Well, let me know if you hear anything about his condition," Evelyn says to her friend. "If he's on the point, you know . . . .."

"Okay . . . if I hear anything. Bye now."

"All right. See you soon."

The call ends—two old ladies shakin' their heads, wonderin' what the world's comin' to. Too much hot food, too much change in the church, too little change in the church, folks we love too far away, folks we love fallin' in love with sharp-tongued young ladies, young people breakin' their engagements. What next? The rabbi dyin'? A Christian? Wouldn't somebody know a thing like that?

One old lady goes off to pray, the other (just as faithful) goes to practice the organ.

With Shirley, there aren't any questions. She doesn't see this about herself, but I notice it. In her universe, life's stated, not queried. You deal with the givens, no fatal delays. Givens? They rise up when you least expect 'em—knives, pistols, pipe bombs, explosive belts, all at the ready. Our bug wasn't on for this conversation. Shirley told me about it. Moish forgot that appointment card.

"We are Jews forged in two furnaces," Shirley's said.

Yeah, I can see the difference. This is how Moish describes it. "The danger is betrayal and assimilation—the threat of being a half-gentile, half-Jewish somebody the other Moses wouldn't recognize. My name's a reminder! Have to be on guard. Assimilation's a hazard for everybody, and my congregation expects me to lead."

"On my side?" Shirley says, "the heritage? Unquestioned. My Hebrew school was how to survive. Life is defended--more than being a Jew."

This is pretty wound up for Shirley, I have to say. She notices my puzzled look and goes on.

"Me?" she says. "I am more cautious than Moshe. He says I am 'more wary, more daring, more shrewd about risks.'" Here, she laughs. "More daring? Maybe . . . when the situation requires it."

I'm thinkin', for sure you say less, babylamb, but come to think of it, you may be more discernin' too.

Right now, she's discerned plenty. Moish can hear it in her voice. "I'm in trouble" is what he's hearin'.

"Going to the doctor in Columbia, *motek*?

"I was going to tell you . . . uh, just waiting for you to come in and well . . . for supper to be finished."

"So. Tell me."

"Well . . . it's just something Harry wants me to do. You know . . . extension of my physical. I listened to you and had that physical . . . the Feinemanns were pushing it too. Harry just wants me to get looked at in Columbia—just the end of the physical, Shirley. Nothing more than that."

It's taken Moish an effort to muster up that assured tone. Fake assurance is what it is and Shirley knows it's fake. He knows that too.

"Oncology Associates."

Shirley taps the appointment card on the dining room table. She's skewered him with those two dusky, hazel eyes now the greenish color of the cloudbank that closed down on Beulah the year of the tornado. There's this ominous quiet in his wife's voice that forecasts with more accuracy than some TV meteorologist the storm brewin' right here under Moish's own roof. Already upon him, it is. He's bracin' himself, and when he catches her look, the tension starts tightenin' his neck muscles like a tug of war. He's stiffenin' to meet whatever storms will burst upon 'im . . . any minute now.

Shirley can do emotion. He doesn't need a forecast by any weatherman actual or metaphorical. He knows the signs and so does Shirley. She reads him like a book.

Maybe I'll just have a stroke or a heart attack and get it over with, he's thinkin', tryin' a stand-up routine he's pretty sure won't work. No, not with Shirley.

"I was just about to tell you if you'll let me. Tomorrow, in Columbia . . . you'd better be at home to take calls. You can visit later."

How lame can you get, baby? Nobody needs to take calls for him. He'll have his cell phone! This is the end. In a minute she'll know everything!

"I will go with you."

If it was me, I'd say panic's stokin' everything. Though he's havin' trouble with several kinds of emotion, Moish knows there's no point in objectin'. Shirley will go to Columbia tomorrow, no argument. Her flat statement paints an awesome picture: Moses coming down with the Tablets, inscribed by the very finger of G-d. That's how it is. The word's not spelled out. No human hand carved out the Law, and that alone says ABSOLUTE in great big letters you do spell out. What Moish is thinkin' is that Shirley can do absolute pretty well too.

But people don't obey absolutely, not perfectly . . . and I don't either, he's thinkin', still picturin' the tablets of the Law. He's said all this to Shirley from time to time. She can tell what's goin' through his mind.

Shirley says Moish is pulled into the Internet. *Liposarcoma.* The word draws him like the edge of a cliff. He can't stop gazin'. He knows the details so well he's an expert, and every day its takin' him another surgical centimeter closer to the cracklin' edges of fear. Might as well be a fever from the cold chills shakin' him--inside and out. Like tryin' to make a bed on an iceberg in the Atlantic. What's worse, the cold's spreadin'. Shirley says that famous picture of Socrates about to die and his students gathered round is grippin' her husband's imagination. He hears 'im sayin' "My feet are gettin' numb."

Moish is beginnin' to wonder if God is against him. He can't look at Shirley. His mouth's dry, and he goes into the kitchen for some water. He finally says the thing that's troublin' him. "Can I ask God to do something special? For me?"

Seemed to be sayin' the words half to himself, half to God, to me too, Shirley said. He was in the kitchen, so she didn't think she had to say somethin'.

Comin' back in where Shirley's still standin' with that appointment card in her hand, he says sarcastically: "Ask to be healed, ask that it not be cancer? Do I deserve it? I know, God sees Levy as the one who always has a good sermon, always arrives right on time, does everything absolutely right! But what about the Law? No rabbi will contest it, the Law is absolute. And what about the fine points . . . have to deal with those too. Lucky Christians. They get out of everything . . . 'the Age of Grace,' Rick says. A dodge and a cop out! But who knows?"

Shirley is stunned. Her husband doesn't do much soul-searchin' in her presence. And it's just spilled out, one angry question after another. He prob'ly regrets sayin' it. It's proof the worries are pilin' up, she says. I know she's right.

Moish doesn't wait for her to answer, prob'ly thinkin' there aren't any answers. Seems like he's just thinkin' about wifely companionship in Columbia. But though he won't admit it, he's glad he'll have Shirley with 'im tomorrow. Shirley can tell it easy enough.

He looks out the window. Doesn't want Shirley to see the relief washin' over his face. He knows it's there. Better keep his back to her. If she can't look at him, maybe she won't see the pleasure or the fear he's strugglin' to keep down. He needs her to be . . . *Shir-li*. If he ever needed somethin' like a song, it's now.

Alice Faber comes to mind. They won't be waked in the middle of the night again, not ever. He almost misses the hair-raisin' screeches. A wonder the physical roof has stayed on that house with that mighty, three-foot shofar Frank liked to blow and Alice too. Around here, when they mention that daughter, somebody always says, "Bless her heart, she had a noisy mother." Didn't come to the funeral.

In Atlanta, Rivka and Ben make their way through the Hartsfield-Jackson hubbub, negotiating people-movers, stopping here and there to talk, find a better sense of what to do next.

Seasoned travelers, they travel light. He carries less, but the scene is more familiar to her. When they go through customs and security in Newark, she has a slight advantage. Caught up in the moment, they watch lines, clocks, schedules, arrival and departure boards. Destination—Beulah, South Carolina. Right now, it's the center of the world. Rivka stops to make a call.

"Please let me talk to Felix now, Miryam."

In a long pause, Rivka's found a corner more or less quiet, away from Ben. She wants no distractions while she talks . . . out of Ben's hearing. Her father's ear: she chooses words with care.

"I'm coming with a friend; he'll stay with us. The friend is male . . . yes, Papa, he's a Jew. You'll find him . . . well, you'll see, you both will see. He is a Southern Jew—at least he was," she says. The ambiguity is intentional. He'll miss the message, mix it up, she thinks. Content at minimum, that is the best. His hearing, not so weak as Miryam's, but one must shout a bit, even with him.

The presence of Ben Steingaard, what to say? If they can only know him as a Jew, they can support her plot to bring him back into the central swim of all he's lost. He has some strange opinions, but she thinks that with the help of Levy—Felix, too—they will at last bring him back in. Indeed, it is a matter of both heart and head.

These professors. What can you say about 'em, babe. They live in a world of words, and if you try to get it down to brass tacks, you miss most of it. It's like they're livin' a script somebody wrote, know what I mean? Anyway, I just have to let 'em have it. Ask your patience, in addition. I do have an advantage over you, hon. I know these two brainy fellas. They both talk to me now and then and I do like 'em. It is what it is.

Quentin's lookin' across the academic jumble of his study, glad the plans have worked. Ben's here, he's thinkin'. He'll weigh these quandaries, catch me up on what's going on in his life. Israel's the other side of the world and the mail, e or otherwise, is no substitute for conversation.

"What did you tell Rivka?"

"The truth."

"Well, sure. But how did you back out of those plans—like getting her to Beulah?"

"Nobody has to get Rivka anywhere. How well do you know her?"

"No better than you do, or maybe than you used to . . .."

"Your two friends?" Ben says.

"Not sure about Rick, but Moshe knows her quite well. The Feinemanns are in his congregation. Rick's been at Union Street even longer than Levy's been back, so he knows Rivka and her family—distant kind of way, Baptist pastor to Jewish family. As you know, Moshe and Rick and I grew up together, but I've been away a lot of years—in and out. Everybody knows who Rebekah is, I mean Rivka—competent, succeeding in Israel." Quentin pauses as if to check a dozier. "On her way to a world-class journalist's bio. I don't know her personally. Weren't in school together; she's younger.

"Something else . . . when you and I ran into each other at Hartsfield," Quentin says, "and I saw we were all headed for Beulah, it occurred to me that Beulah's a lot nearer USC than it is to Atlanta. Once you're in South Carolina, why come back to Georgia . . . to Decatur, just to see me?"

"I guess you saw it too. But I'm wondering how the two of you worked out the logistics of the trip home. She'd be getting home by herself. Her parents were expecting you, weren't they?"

The question could be heard as criticism, Quentin thinks. In addition, Ben's travel arrangements are none of my business. But Rivkah and Ben? Ben's a little younger than I am, but he's older than she . . . quite a bit.

"She needs no escort," Ben says, "not to get anywhere. When we ran into you in the airport, it was pretty obvious we're friends from a long time back. She and I went for the bags, and I said I had something to talk over with you. Might take a little while. You could get me to Beulah the next day. As a journalist, she understands fortuitous encounters. Then I got her a place on the shuttle—a risk, I'll admit. I may have offended her," Ben adds, laughing.

"Truth touched up with a bit of . . . smooth gallantry? Blunt the chauvinism?"

The quip is wrong. Ben does not flatter, doesn't do "smooth."

The man's a phenomenon, Quentin says to himself. The consistently truthful human being. The salient quality, just sharpened by life in Israel. Ben is Ben—that rock-solid consistency, veined with candor . . . as if he were dyed all one color.

Quentin indulges a surreal moment with a true blue Benjamin Steingaard—blue blood, blue hair, blue fingernails, every scrap of clothing blue, blue, blue . . . everything about him blue except his mood. That's always a shining gold or silver, light reflecting from every surface.

The back and forth has flagged and Quentin feels like apologizing. No, apologies have little place in Ben's universe. If he sees a wrong in himself, it's deep repentance; the facile apologies of others just puzzle him.

"Only curious . . . I'm the one who needs to talk to you. You covered for me. Thanks for doing that."

"Not covering . . . just discretion," Ben says. "Your email mentioned some personal stuff. You know Beulah better than I, but I'm guessing it's like any small town—energized by gossip. I was going to rent a car. If you came with us and we talked on the way over . . . well, that wouldn't have worked. Had to be a better solution. You don't need a leak even before you get there. The Feinemanns may not indulge in loose talk, but everyone has a best friend. Rivka doesn't talk much. Writes but doesn't talk . . . maybe to settlers or jihadis. Protects her sources as if she were in some intelligence organization. You know, 'Don't curse the king in your bedroom . . . a bird of the sky may report it.'"

Quentin laughs. Solomon's counsel is still good.

"Besides," Ben says, "what's Rivka's need-to-know?"

Clasping his hands behind a bald head, Ben smiles and stretches his legs, knocking to the floor a stack of books. He sits up, rearranges the stack, and finds an uncluttered space for his feet. Once again, Quentin is struck by Ben's impressive ability to relax. Nothing tilts him. Cool, a kid would say.

An odd comment comes to mind: "The city of the great King," Ben said that day, thumping his chest with clasped hands. "*Here*—nothing else matters." The aside has stuck. Unaccountably, some lines of a camp song he picked out on the piano the summer he was seventeen drift through Quentin's thoughts. "Joy is the flag flown high . . . on the castle of my heart. The King is in residence here." No stress in Ben's life now, he tells himself. It wasn't stress then either, back before his new life began. No, it was war! Now Ben's sitting across from me, relaxed as if he's just beat me at poker.

The angles and planes of the study seem to expand, changing the volume of a stuffy room. Like air from an open window. Quentin feels it like a breeze ruffling his hair. A wave of contentment washes over him. This unlikely friend has made a place for himself. Great to have him here, he thinks. He's good counsel, lot of common sense.

He'll have perspective on that Coffee Shoppe encounter. Quentin remembers how that lunch marked a change—sandwiches, coffee and tea, conversation, not much more than that, but things took a turn toward different. Rick's pushed and shoved, he tells himself. Always hopes for improvement. I guess he gave up after a while. It's what we have to do—pray and give up. But sitting down again with Levy—alone, this time—will be different. Won't be a superficial chat, no curtain of blindness. I will see my adversary and he'll see me.

The word stops him cold. No, he's not my enemy. I will not see Moish that way; no hope at all unless I climb out of that trench.

The thought of open, seeing eyes, both pairs seeing, unnerves him. But there are other problems.

I love them both, Quentin thinks, trying to veil Davita's lovely face in the place where he lives. It takes effort. Reminders of Davita are like tsunami warnings—any time, any place.

It's not that I see . . . as if with an inner eye, he thinks. Not that way . . . no, she's the eyes I see with! The KJV translator had it right, "the apple of his eye." I see the world as if through an image—of Davita Levy.

Come back…come back.

If he only could, if she only could . . ..

Through a surge of emotions, Quentin hears Ben's voice from across the room. Turning toward the voice, he makes a promise—I will.

"Funny, isn't it . . ." Ben says, not guessing the lifeline his casual talk throws to Quentin. "Rivka's like other journalists. They're all in the gossip business. Professional interest in gossip, but they've gotta protect the confidences. They hear the stuff and guard it, but then they publish it . . . both at the same time. They publish their take on what they've heard, but in a way that doesn't ruin everything.

Gain trust then use it. Have to keep the contacts, the ones who opened up. The whole thing's a function of professional conduct! Still, even knowing that Rivka's trustworthy and professional, you'd have to explain a lot for her to see the need for discretion."

Quentin nods, shrinking from the thought of Quentin-and-Davita as dinner table chat at the Feinemanns. Never mind that years have passed. As usual, Ben has it right and Quentin feels a new indebtedness. He owes him, but what can he do for Benjamin Steingaard?

A point of light, a shining full stop hangs in the air, silencing his questions.

Yes, the truth. I've spoken the truth to him. Ben would call it *everything*.

"Your topic . . . not what you'd want for dinner conversation at the Feinemanns' this evening—veiled or discreetly handled or whatever," Ben says, as if reading his thoughts. "By the way, how much does Rivka, or her parents, know about your son?"

"Everyone knows Aunt Ev and me. We're related to half of Beulah. I grew up there. Then I went to school then started teaching . . . haven't gone back to live, not like Moish and Rick. But people in town know the important things about me. How much the Feinemanns, Rivka included—how much they know about my relationship with Moshe, I can't say. He's the key, the only person in Beulah who knows everything. He's not a gossip, but the rift between us has been talked about, I'm sure. I've been away for years, in every sense of the word.

"He was away a long time too. Rick knows about Aaron. The Levys have died . . . not many others who'll remember. The distance . . . Moish and me, it bothers Rick, always has. The Feinemanns are Beth Shalom. Rivka's younger than . . . .."

Quentin stops to consider a point that can only bother an English teacher, a grammar question blocking for the moment the wash of grief, old sorrows cresting in waves from the familiar blackness. Even to puzzle the syntax is painful. What verb here? Moish and I are still alive, not Davita. I can't say, "Rivka is younger than we are." Also can't say, "than we were." We're still . . . .

Tonight, I need two things, Quentin tells himself desperately. I want Ben's counsel, but first, in order to get it, I have to tell him what happened. Odd how it's never come up. We've talked about other things—theology, Lit., or teaching, sometimes the Bible.

Quentin, well-schooled in the reserve that marks his Southern heritage, rarely disburdens himself. Tonight, I will, he tells himself. Ben can be trusted—the brother I've lacked. Rick is a given, Quentin thinks, part of myself almost and Ben's not a replacement. But having one brother's never meant you can't have two . . . or more than two. The thought is startling. Moshe?

Quentin glances at his friend and thinks, he's leaned on me.

When truth engaged the cynic and won, Ben leaped into spiritual life with a ravenous hunger. He devours the Bible; he eats different food. His clothes are different. Puts up with the sartorial protocols of academia, but even here, a new preference. To his bizarre collection of ties, he's added a different Jesus T-shirt for whatever hour he can find outside the classroom!

Quentin remembers seeing them all in Jerusalem—several on Ben. He was as pleased as if swathed in a banner. What a sight: a man walking around Jerusalem, Old City and New, wearing shirts with things like "Jesus is My Final Answer" and "King of Kings and Lord of Lords." His favorites are "Jesus Made Me Kosher" and "Jesus Made Me Jewish." People complain, but they can't stop him. Confronted on the street one day, Ben blithely cited the famous doctrine of religious liberty underwriting all freedoms of the modern Jewish state. Ben, a fully vested citizen, pulls out all the Right of Return privileges and a big smile rests his case. Incredible.

"Besides," said Ben that day, bringing out the T-shirts for inspection, "can you tell the Chasidim not to wear their black or observant Jews in every sort of blue and black stripes they can't put on a prayer shawl or wear a kippah? And what about the women? Can you forbid them to lay the tfilin or force them go around with bare arms and no head coverings? Dress codes are set in stone, and no laws about T-shirts are on the books. Israel's a free country!"

Ben's Jesus T-shirts prove Isaiah's point: "No weapon formed against you will prevail; you will refute every tongue that accuses you." Quentin imagines the powers that be in Jerusalem scratching their heads, searching the laws, religious and secular, looking for strategies to halt, one sweet day, the unbearable offense. Jesus T-shirts! Where is the statute? Consult the Chief Rabbi . . . both of them! So far, nothing, not a single point of law that will hold. Implications for women are the worst. Who wants to go there? Enough to turn a man gray! Indeed, a horribly gray area! *Oy v'voy!*

The day a bearded academic from the university confronted him on the street, Ben prevailed again. The professor listened, scowling, but could only laugh. In his briefcase was one of the Orthodox dailies with a front-page piece on clothing.

"There is a witness in what we wear! Recall to mind what Moshe Rabbenu said about the *tzittzit*! Criticize our tassels? Let them have their say. The righteous will affirm our obedient hearts with our clothing!"

"No MK will tangle with the Orthodox on that point," Ben said, "whatever their shade, and Conservatives—they're firmly secure in their head coverings. Heavens! In the Knesset, there's every flavor of practicing and non-practicing Judaism, and the major parties have to keep the peace. Success means coalition. They have to achieve some sort of stitched together, semi-agreeable compromise or the other side wins the day! And it isn't just Labor that needs the votes."

The silence of Quentin's study stretches itself out as questions of all sorts drift through their minds. The keen edge of sorrow bites into Quentin's pleasure at seeing Ben. Easier to blunt the painful thoughts with reflections on his life in Israel. An easy escape. Why hurry?

Life in Israel?

Judging by his mood and what he says, Ben seems to love it. The constant hubbub of controversy is like the breath of life for him. If he's flattened—an eye blackened, his back stretched out against the stones of some little street—the more pleased he is. In one encounter he described, Ben leaped up and offered his other cheek. The rage his T-shirts spark in some delights him. One day he was bloodied. He got up, smiled, and quietly asked his assailant, "Brother, do you have a handkerchief?" The one who bashed his nose fled, unable to withstand a man in a Jesus T-shirt who called him "Brother."

A car passes. On Ben's side of the room, the sound breaks in, brings up a question. Why did Quentin stop in the middle of that sentence? Almost five minutes ago.

To Ben, who spends every hour of his professional day with the fine points of English usage, the glitch correctly suggests a gnarly syntactical puzzle. But with Quentin, politeness is always first. A wrong, disrespectful word? Callous lack of consideration? A sentence problem or something painful? Tonight Quen wants to dig into the deep memories—personal archeology almost. Candor will be a struggle. Embellishing, excuses, hedging? Probably none of that. Quentin won't obfuscate or deny. For a polite, private man like Quen, a man of good will, it won't be easy.

Quentin's unfinished sentence hangs in the air. Ben rethinks the words: *Rivka was quite a bit younger—*

Patience. What a private person needs. Whatever it is won't come out with badgering. Wait . . . just wait.

To Ben, Quentin's study feels like home—books and papers strewn everywhere—on shelves, desk, stools, chairs. Cave dwellers in the cave. The comfortable ambience is a promising context; Quentin is readying himself, Ben thinks. Let him be. Nothing to do for five or six hours, even longer. I'm here to listen. We'll get to Beulah tomorrow, share the driving. Talk all night if we have to . . . like the Russians.

"You know . . . the things on my mind."

Ben waits.

"We should pray first."

Steingaard gets up and walks to a window. The urban scene is peaceful: streetlights of a quiet neighborhood, lights in windows, the college for women where his friend teaches less than a block away. Peaceful enough. Few cars, a traffic light cycling red and green. Most of the houses, dark.

I'm prayed up, Ben thinks. But Quentin was right when he said that time, "Who's ever prayed up?"

Packing in Jerusalem, Ben pictured the visit. The encounter at Hartsfield made things easier. Quentin's heaviness seems overwhelming, he thinks, but he will find strength for the troubling questions . . . Lord willing. No, the Lord is willing.

Ben lifts his arms, reaching for the Presence, the locus of life. The impulse to pray comes from the throne and Ben says yes. A sense of beckoning draws him to private praise, to worship. The room fades toward another familiar place.

Quentin stands, but standing isn't his chosen attitude of prayer. He pauses, rubs one hand across his forehead. Then he kneels, as he often does in this study, head in his hands, his heart opening, waiting to be received.

No, I receive, he says to himself. I'm already a resident in the King's heart.

CHAPTER NINE
Jewish, Baptist, and Pentecostal

I RAN INTO AUNT LUCY AT THE GROCERY STORE—THAT
new one they built between Beulah and Calhoun. She said, "Evelyn Martelote
doesn't have the story straight. Neither does Miz Feinemann." Miss Evelyn told
Aunt Lucy, "Miriam makes it darker by the minute. What a muddle . . . the
more we talked the more muddled it got! So odd and illogical. Impossible to
unscramble," she said. She's exasperated, let me tell you. I know some stuff, but
I'm not sayin'.

The two old ladies found each other in the history room, Longstreet Memorial
Library. It's empty and the bright blues and reds of the Longstreet window are
makin' the table red and blue. Messed up rows of magazines indicate other folks
around. Miss Evelyn's whisperin' because Miz Feinemann is.

"Diabetes?"

"So . . . so sad. Sarah says they will . . . remove the toes."

"What? Impossible!" Miss Evelyn blurts out, for the moment forgettin' to
be polite she's so surprised. The rabbi, seriously ill? She thought it was the judge.
Changes will occur if he should—

"I guess you're sure?" she whispers, stoppin' the horrid thought and theorizin'
about the future. She's wonderin' why's she whisperin'. Shirley, return to Israel?

"He declined David's dinner invitation . . . missed a meeting . . . the broker.
If the rabbi is ill . . . what will happen?"

"What does Shirley say?"

"Nothing, but . . . a terminal—

"Terminal?"

"And a new telephone system is going in at the Levys', some new kind of system . . . connected with a . . .a computer."

Impossible, this thing! Miss Ev's tellin' herself.

"Why wouldn't she say something? Ask for prayer or something? What is it?" she says, forgettin' to whisper. "He would tell his wife about amputated toes, wouldn't he? He couldn't walk!"

"When he . . . was at our house, he was faint . . . white, Evelyn! I had Rebekah . . . bring the car and drive him . . . to his home. He was ill . . . quite ill."

"Does that mean he has diabetes?"

"He is seeing a medical person . . . in Columbia. Tests, as well. Susan whispered . . . in the deepest, deepest confidence, Evelyn. Susan told me the judge—Judge Solomon has observed his gait, says it hurts him to walk . . . very painful to see. An infection that will not heal? No doubt this is correct . . . the true report. So sad. He must not be taken."

"But that doesn't mean Shirley doesn't know, does it?"

"You know how men . . . how they are. Do not talk, do not consult a doctor . . . then, much too late. Or listen to their wives."

"But what makes you certain about the diabetes?"

"He was ill . . . in our home, Evelyn!"

"But what is it?"

"I have explained this to you, Evelyn. Your hearing must be checked."

"But he has spoken to—?"

"Have Harry look at your ears, Evelyn. The rabbi has . . . not . . . talked . . . to anyone. Harry ordered the tests. He would not discuss . . . not even consider a consultation. I do not know what he has said . . . to Shirley.

"Columbia? The tests?"

"YES. HE. HAD. AN. APPOINTMENT. But now it's TOO. LATE. Except for SURGERY."

Some librarian walks past, smiles and nods. A scoldin' for talkin' in the library? Miz Feinemann quiets down to a whisper that's nearly nothin' and Miss Evelyn has to lean in to watch her lips.

Miriam will tell the story, Miss Ev's thinkin,' librarian or no librarian! Details all over the place! With that voice so low, I cannot get things straight!

"What has Shirley said?"

"NOTHING. SHE WANTS THE *APPROPRIATE MOMENT*, WHICH HAS *NOT COME*. NOW, IF HE'S DYING, SHE HAS TO BE . . . PARTICULARLY CAREFUL WITH . . . E-VER-Y WORD. HE MAY HAVE ONLY A LITTLE TIME . . . A FEW MONTHS. It could happen that . . . she never tells him—ever, poor dear man." Here, she starts whisperin' again. "The poor dear . . .. But she should."

"Dying? I thought you said diabetes. Surgery on his foot."

"Now I am . . . wondering. Sarah Stein does not hear well. She could have heard *dying*. Or *diabetes* or . . . *diet*. I will call. She told Hazel 'dying.'"

"Well, let me know. Quentin will want to hear."

"Yes, I will. We need a clearer . . . picture. Felix is asking. He is the one . . . he should . . . make the call. WHEN HE CALLS . . . I WILL CALL YOU."

They nod like conspirators. Miz Feinemann's positive—believes the judge, saw that white face, knows what she's seen! Like the rabbi says, what in the world?

A shadow crosses between the window and the table.

Rebekah. Here for the memorial service, Miss Evelyn sees. So sad about Alice, and now the whole opera world will descend on us. A circus! Have to pay their respects. Rebekah's still so thin, poor thing. Bless her heart, like a stick, but who is this odd man with her—bald, glasses like the Chinese. Shorter than she is. What *is* that he's wearing?

"How are you, Mrs. Martelote, I hope . . ." Miss Evelyn said she stopped like she wasn't certain what she hoped.

How can you answer a greeting like that, Miss Ev's thinkin,' puttin' out a hand to steady Miz Feinemann, who's tryin' to get up from that big soft chair. The young man notices and moves over in her direction.

Should take the straight-backed chair, Miss Evelyn thinks. Better for everybody.

"I hope that you are very well today," Rebekah says in that voice. It's doin' pirouettes with the blues and reds, and the music makes Miss Evelyn smile. She notices a pothos on the window ledge—tendrils curlin' with delight. Yep, that's what she told Aunt Lucy, swore it was true. That girl should do somethin' with her voice. Printed words on a newspaper page? It's a waste.

"Yes, my dear. I'm very well. Last visit, Harry said, 'Wellwell, picture of health. You are well, as fit as the judge.' Then he added a few more wellwellwell's. You know Harry, how he says that and looks over his paperwork. No one makes charts, graphs, and forms the way he does . . . piece of paper for everything. Prescriptions beyond that. Quentin thinks he should computerize—more up-to-date, you know. No. He should just say something besides 'well, well, well.'"

The two laugh, and Rebekah looks at the bald man. Odd glasses, just big enough to see through. Puttin' an arm under Miss Miriam's, he eases-pulls-lifts her to a standin' position. She's freshly coiffed and smiles at him.

How does Gretchen get her into the shampoo chair, Miss Evelyn's wonderin'. Maybe Rebekah helps. Or Madeleine's little teenaged granddaughter. Someone has to. Miss Evelyn's congratulatin' herself on her own convenient hairstyle—that thick braid wrapped around her head. But hairpins? Hard to find—no white ones, just silver, She's smilin', watching their exit—Rebekah on one side, the bald man on the other.

I didn't know Ben at this time, hon. All that would happen later.

Miriam should lose weight, Miss Evelyn's tellin' herself. They should not walk together. More obvious. Why does she whisper one minute, shout at me the next? Of the three, the man's the oddest! Bald head, old-fashioned glasses like a jade merchant. And that Jesus sign in big black letters. Orange!

Unnatural orange! Miss Ev's sayin' to herself. See-in-the-dark, doubtless. Clemson man? Rebekah is her father's daughter. Miriam should lose weight though. Extra pounds can bring on depression!

That young librarian was crossin' the room, lookin' in Miss Ev's direction. Aunt Lucy said she was prob'ly thinkin,' what is it about getting old. Just get fat! Taste buds die. Have to have sweets all the time, bless their hearts.

Aunt Lucy's vain about her figure.

"Shirley, I caught you! Your husband just left. We need to talk."

"Talk, Mishmish."

"Miss Alice died a peaceful woman."

"*Ken*, Annabelle and Augusta went. I was in Columbia."

"Rick did too. He told me he had to get out of her room she was singin' so loud—Hallelujah Chorus or somethin'. Before he could escape, she started callin' 'im. I don't know who she thought she was seein', but what she told Rick—when he got up enough nerve to go back in—was that it wasn't Col. Mitchell in her garden. It wasn't him a bit, it was the Lord!"

"Mishmish!"

"She first thought it was Col. Mitchell in his dressin' gown! Then she said the Lord told her he had her rose garden all ready. 'We'll walk there, together,' he told 'er. After that, she never mentioned 'Col. Mitchell' again. Just—"

"Yeshua?"

"Yes! She was pos'tive. So it was okay for the roses to get sniffed!"

I'm laughin' and wipin' my eyes. Silence on the other end says Shirley's listenin'.

We understand the silences. Long silences are not a bother. We were feelin' sad, but sadness was all tangled together with wantin' to laugh. The situation had some funny parts if it *was* sad. The mixed-up emotions felt strange.

Did Miss Alice get it? A happy endin' to that story? If so, laughter was prob'ly okay. I wasn't too sure right then how I should feel.

Shirley broke into my thinkin' about now.

"I am laughing too, Mishmish . . . roses, ghosts, but it's the Lord? All okay. We can laugh."

That American expression's as universal as hallelujah.

"And somethin' else, Shirley. Miss Alice said she was ready to go home . . . somethin' about an angel, an angel and her mama. I don't think she thought her mama was an angel. Maybe there was one. But mainly, she was ready. Wasn't afraid."

"A blessing, Mishmish!"

"Yes. Another thing . . . she was askin' for you. Will you speak at the memorial?"

"I will speak."

"Moish and Ricky are workin' on the service . . . talkin' to Pastor Atlee. He's AG."

"Yeshua will lead, Mishmish."

"Yes. We better pray. They don't know what to expect. It's such a mix of . . . different things. The Lord will have to take over. Ken, buhsedd'r."

Shirley laughs. "Yes, *b'seder*. But Moshe is coming now. We will talk. *Lahitraot*."

My Ricky's beside himself. Could teach Moish a few lessons in worryin'. Not like him at all! Prob'ly did 'im some good to talk about it. Confession's good for the soul and all that, if you know what I mean.

"What a mess," Ricky's growlin', "Headaches and problems. Just waiting to jump on me. That study clock ticks! Time's passing . . . pushing me. Clock sticks on eternity then it lets go and leaps ahead a few centuries! Maybe the hands on a clock just move when you're not looking. No! A pastor's clock does donuts, looking or not. Before those hands get too far, I have to organize this thing . . . exercise caution—not just make decisions. Pentecostals, Baptists, Jews? Opera singers? Who knows what they expect in a memorial service! Unbelievable! Maybe in novels, really bad ones.

"I'm telling myself, 'Pray, Apricot!'" Right away, I heard my own voice . . . defensive. I was telling myself to pray like it was a law or something and then—"

"Valentine? A valentine just . . ."

Listening

"Prayer's like that, isn't it, babyluv?"

"I guess so. Better if it comes on like breathing," he says, "and you barely know it. Desperation and down-to-business searching help. Hot-button happiness too. I guess you know."

'Course I know.

Ricky finally got the message and settled down. A holy . . . *place?* Like a room with windows? In a crunch, he gets it, but he needs remindin'.

Today, the facts are marchin' through Ricky's brain like a parade of monsters: Miss Alice dead. Funeral happened. Now, I AM COMING, says eighty-somethin' telegrams from senior citizens of the opera world (nobody's heard of email). Three times that many calls from uppity assistants. In view: Ancient opera stars and a parade of 76 trombones inchin' down the street, Siegfried Funeral March backed up by two dozen kettle drums and out front, a drum major with feathers. All that's in my Ricky's head.

The facts have outed dozens of problems and my comments yesterday at breakfast didn't help, pore ole baby.

"Sugaryplum, didn't you know she was a Pentecostal?" I said it casually . . . like didn't y' know it's tomato sandwiches for supper? In this worried condition, my Ricky's actually facin' up to a besetting sin.

"Assumptions . . . ugh," he said and quoted some smart aleck. 'If you assume, it makes an ass of you and me.' Yeah, and I know it will take more than chidin,' by me or that smart aleck, for Ricky to change much.

"You didn't know it?" I said, pushin' the point, and sweepin' his space with my radar eyes. (I can do that, baby. Come over sometime and I'll show you.) No, he didn't know it.

"Wasn't that before Alice was discovered? Ancient history . . . shouldn't matter now. Just the facts, ma'am," said Ricky, tryin' to bring in some humor.

Yep, Assembly of God was her old church. Miz Faber's first voice coach was a Miz Lottie Morgan, family still on the AG roles. Other side of town. Ricky hates the sound of that, but there it is . . . *the other side of town.* That I-am-Miz-Morgan's-great-niece phone voice is still tappin' on his eardrums: "Has t'be *here*, Miss Alice's church! She was discovered at *our church*!"

"Young musician . . . wants a contact in the music world," he said then dismissed the thought in favor of a glance at his watch. AG pastor coming in a few. Just the facts.

I knew about Miss Lottie. She taught our world-class singer when she was little Alice Jones. The day little Alice's voice took over the house the whole town heard about it.

"If the Morgan girls feel like they own somebody who turned into a shinin' star of the opera stage, can you fault 'em?" I said to Ricky. "She was discovered by their grandmama!"

"Great aunt," he said.

Ricky doesn't want this battle, and the whole Deacon Board of Union Street Baptist agrees: "Do what they want. Let 'em have that service," they told 'im.

"The Board's just relieved," Ricky said. "The AGs may be doing us a favor. But Pentecostal? What will that be? Whatever, I'm up to organize it. Levy can't duck out—Pentecostal or whatever! The Beth Shalom folks are all in, and the whole thing's for a gentile Pentecostal! Pentecostal Baptist?"

Almost wringin' his hands here, pore ole baby.

"Atlee will have some thoughts—whether I like 'em or not," Ricky said. "Even if he does—and even if I do—anything can happen!"

My husband looks at the clock. Twenty minutes gone!

"World-class reputation and Beulah AG? Not just incredible, it's nerve wracking. But time's passing. Gotta get busy."

At the church, Ricky checks the phone messages, mail—a pile, two piles. All opera. Time? Place? Five star hotels? Where *is* this town? No one's ever heard of it.

Ricky's worryin', decides to call Moish (me listenin'). Worry like misery loves company. Rick means to see how Moishe's doin', but his own worries take over.

"How did we miss the Pentecostal connection? I knew Mrs.Faber got her milk and eggs, the laundry picked up and returned, but I wasn't too clear who—"

"Half the tradesmen in Beulah look after that house, Rick. A banker drops in, talks to Augusta then comes over here. We give neighborly support, Feinemanns too, but many are helping."

Rick was oblivious, but not me. I noticed—just business as usual. We look after our own, shuggababe.

"Who thinks about Pentecostals," Ricky says to Moish. "They're . . .. How to say it? Yeah—*unrestrained*, that's it. Emotional! You just don't think about 'em. Wrong to call 'em 'holy rollers,' but when somebody slips up, who fusses? Fired by ecstasy! Emotion-driven. Can't gloss over the facts."

What's that about? Moish asks himself. Christians aren't all Catholics, but beyond Rome and all that, the mind fuzzes over.

My pastor husband moves uncomfortably in his big desk chair. I can hear it creakin'. If he doesn't do somethin', the stress'll just get worse. He tries to dodge, but somethin' like a sign with big letters sayin' *Repent* is out there in his line of sight.

Of what exactly?

Not ready for anything like that. He's too busy.

"Anyway, I could have it wrong," he mutters. "Might be just a feeling. You can't trust feelings. But still—" He starts to pray then stops. Isn't workin'.

"This chair's supposed to be comfortable!" he's mutterin', stretchin' his legs. "At least no foot feed to mash." Movin' his shoulders, tryin' to untighten 'um, mutterin', "Worse than a two-hour road trip in traffic!"

The searchlight's pokin' around in the dark corners, can't be dodged. Feels like somebody's dentist chair—bright light, pick checkin' the soft spots. It pokes and hurts.

"Lord, show me . . .."

Ricky doesn't really want to see. Another thought eases in, and he's all for it—better than thinkin' about the sins of Richard Parker Apricot III. It's that last encounter with Miz Faber. Panic calls came in, me even. He dropped everything, drove to the nursin' home. The staff was holdin' back (they're professionals), but desperation started leakin' from every pore.

"Some improvement," they said. "But there's a new problem. No more screams from 53 (Yes, Room 53, here and at the hospital, Pastor. Coincidence). Like I said, no more screams. Now she's singin'. Two or three in the mornin'! And it's unpredictable! The whole wing's roused!" Interruptin' one another, spillin' out the story.

"One night *The Messiah*, one night Mendelssohn then Puccini then Mozart. Chorales in German or the Brahms Lullaby—sweet, but top volume." Grim chuckles. "Those were the good nights," somebody says. Beatrice, the social worker, finally lets loose.

"My music degree gives me an edge," she says. "I know the numbers, but the noise is botherin' me even. Folks tryin' to sleep! Have to think about *her* health too." Bea's voice tightens. "Strains her heart! Please, *talk* to her!"

"If anybody can get through," the administrator cuts in, "it's Pastor Apricot! She mentions you a lot—the Levys too."

The business-like Debra Quarles and Jessica Lynch, the charge nurse, join in, sputterin' out problems. When cracks form in the unshakable, rock-solid calm of a professional, complaints get heard.

Sittin' in his study, my Ricky cleans his glasses, puts 'em back on. He's teeterin', on a cliff edge about to cave at his very feet. Another encounter moves in. He'd like to escape this horror flick, but he's strapped to his seat and can't.

Characters: Miss Alice, international diva in decline; the Rev. Richard Parker Apricot, Union Street Baptist Church of Beulah, SC, SBC. Setting: Beulah Nursing Home, Room 53. Time: 5:33 in the evenin,' Act Three, ready to roll. ACTION.

He's walking down the hall with a mix of feelin's. Other side of that door . . . what?

He knocks softly and waits.

Go in? What's happening? Wouldn't a nurse say if Mrs. Faber's having a bath, getting helped with her clothes?

Opens the door . . . a crack.

Like settin' off an alarm, the motion triggers a blast. The shock forces him out into the hall again.

"Hallelujah! Hallelujah! Hal-leh-eh-eh-lu-jah!"

He eases from the door, tries to catch his breath. More Handel, volume increasin'. I'm a wimp, he tells himself then takes a breath, smiles his best smile and reenters.

The old lady sits up in bed, head thrown back, mouth wide. Her chest swells to draw in support for what's comin' next. She's not watchin' the door.

Ricky can't bear to think about what happens. This is it: He just leaves! Half-hearted salute puts him back into the hall. Out he goes.

Can't do anything here, he tells himself, avoidin' the nurses' station. The selection's changin' down there, but not the decibels.

"And he shall lead his flock like a sheh-eh-eh-eh-perd, and he-e-e sha-all ga-a-ther the la-ammbs in his ah-ahrms, i-i-i-i-n his arms . . . .."

She's gatherin' strength for a big breath and he walks faster. Through the window, his gray Ford 250 offers escape.

Now Ricky's back to worryin' about the service. His study's a better haven than the truck, but the familiar surroundin's don't help. Another scene got into last night's nightmare, and it's playin' in his memory like a low-budget movie, another one he doesn't want to see!

Now, like strapped into a seat with an ejection button to get 'im outta there and he 's lookin' but can't find it—*Breakfast with Ruth*. It's stuck on REPLAY, but he could start it anywhere and be blown into the Van Allen Belt. This is a mixed-up business—part memory, part nightmare. You know how that is. The stressin' stuff gets into dreams like a wacky remembered somethin'. Then you try to tell it, it really gets mixed up because you're rememberin' again!

"You're pouring orange juice, and it's like that orange tinges the whole scene." Ricky tells me. "That hair rings your face like a permanent orange juice-colored cloud somebody steamed, curled and bam!—there it is."

No, my hair's brighter than OJ, and it's got more body than a cloud, a lot more body!

This was how Ricky's nightmare started. He just had to tell me. Scared 'im—made him downright poetic.

"In the morning light, that orange hair was like a light bulb. Incandescent! You were seriously vexed. Vexation was powering right on down to the split ends—passion, flaming the entire room. Have to admit, you owned the floor. You're talking . . . the words were little flames flickering in the air—orange letters weaving in and out with tongues of fire swaying all around.

"Might as well be seated with the apostles and elders," Ricky said, forgettin' for a minute that he was strengthenin' my argument. But more about that in a minute.

"The women too—mighty rush of wind filling the house . . . my house!"

I'm the star of this scene. In my own defense, I hafta say I always try for restraint, but this time I guess I outdid myself, try as I might. The movie—it's more like a documentary and it's wound and folded into the furrows of his brain and can't be coaxed out. The thing makes 'im wince, rememberin'.'

"Sugary-plum-puddin'," I'm tellin' him in this dream, "you know as well as I do that St. Paul said, 'I wish you *all* spoke in tongues.' This too: 'I speak in tongues more than all ya'll'." As you know, this is St. Paul entirely, and in the dream I'm settin' the room on fire, shakin' my flamin' hair around (that's how Ricky put it).

Ricky's rubbin' his forehead. A headache's comin' on. He knows I won't let it go. And he knew what he was gettin' into when he said he wanted to marry me, told my daddy, the president of Emmanuel College, Mt. Zion of Pentecostalism! He just thought, all Pentecostals need is some good Baptist influence to help 'em get things right. Bad assumption . . . again! He's still a pretty delighted husband, but what's a man to do with a Pentecostal wife? That's what he thinks, all the time.

One more time to circle this nightmare burning bush. I wasn't done.

"You just look up those verses in First Corinthians, ThornyRickyrosebud," I said. "There they are even if nobody even gives 'em a tip of the hat—nobody but Pentecostals and 'specially not Baptists or the rest of the Fundamentalists you Baptists make up a part of—never mind the fact that y'all say you believe every word . . . *every word*. All this stuff about the inerrancy of the Bible is hooey! Y'all are just like the liberals, Lammybabe. You're dodgin' what you don't want to see!"

The mornin' I said all that in the kitchen—raw material for the nightmare, y'know—I smiled in his direction to show I love him anyway, whatever theological error he's currently mixin' himself up in.

"You believe what you want to," I said. "You and all those good folks skid to a full stop when you get to First Corinthians, chapter twelve through fourteen— even chapter thirteen! Well, maybe not thirteen. Nobody wants to talk about twelve and fourteen, so they preach hundreds of sermons all on First Corinthians thirteen! I've counted 'em, babe.

"And they mess that up too! All anybody knows to talk about is that the perfect thing has already come and that's the Bible. Never mind the fact that the rest of the time they're arguin' about which translation!"

About now, I'm holdin' out the wooden spoon like a bazooka and it's pointed in his direction.

"And what about that Baptist church—a Baptist church, PastorRicky! You remember the one. It had a Bible burnin' because it wasn't the pure King James Version! What's perfect about that? And everybody thinks that, since we can read the Bible in King James English, God doesn't do anything anymore! Why didn't the Holy Spirit just leave out all those instructions about usin' the gifts? You really think they aren't for anything now? You can't think that! It doesn't make sense!"

In the kitchen, he could look in another direction, not point himself in line with my bazooka, but he couldn't dodge that nightmare. I know how he switches the films—first Miss Alice singin', then me talkin' about St. Paul then that horror movie he's put together when he thinks about the service. He prefers the horrors. I guess he was lucky I didn't start start preachin' to 'im in tongues.

He's always the director, as well as the audience. And he's good at duckin' in or out to escape the effect of my flamin' hair, as well as the unpleasant case I'm makin' way too persuasively.

He said to Moish that in the dream the scorn flamin' my voice "was filling the kitchen. Overpowering, like some sort of inflammatory gas. Made me dizzy. Ecstatic language, for sure, just what they call it. Ruth . . . on her high horse."

The director's chair says APRICOT, like I said, and there's plenty of vivid color. The cameras are rollin'.

"There she is," Ricky told Moish in that phone call, "royal robes white as snow on fire, a golden crown on her head. Ruth and that thoroughbred, a real high horse. Palomino . . . lifting its elegant neck, shaking that beautiful mane, waving that white tail. Well-trained feet precisely placed, one in front of the other, and Ruth, tall in the saddle, eyes raised like Joan of Arc. Holding a banner . . . orange, of course."

"What's on the banner," Moish asked 'im.

"This was it," Ricky said.

'BLESSED BE THE LORD GOD OF ISRAEL, WHO ONLY DOETH WONDROUS THINGS!'

I have to laugh, let me tell you what, darlin'.

"I won't argue with that," he said to Moish. "We just interpret things differently."

"Just psychology and salemanship, RichardtheLionhearted," I told 'im later when the subject came up again. Had to see to it. Not finished with that conversation, you can be sure, babe.

"What does that mean," Ricky shot back. But he didn't want to hear.

In his study, it's time to hit PAUSE and turn off the problems. His head hurts, and I'm winnin' all those remembered battles, hands down. Or up.

Ricky knows the Pentecostal speech by heart and he can usually ignore it. But right now, with a Jewish-Baptist-Pentecostal memorial service to organize, he can't think of anything but what I've said and that congregation-to-be: the whole town of Beulah, delegations of the whole opera world—New York, Washington, D.C., maybe London, Paris, Milan, maybe even Moscow and Israel—half the African American community, and that neglectful daughter-turned-jazz-singer from New Orleans, even the amazin' Rivka flyin' in from Jerusalem. Probably here already. Somebody's drivin' her from Atlanta, we heard. Congregation? More like a circus. A disaster in the makin'!

Somehow, he has to figure it out. His hopes are comin' down to roost on an AG pastor. Can't depend on Moish . . . worries of his own, tons of 'em. Anyway, what does he know about how Pentecostals do things?

Don't know myself, Rick's thinkin'. "All thy waves have come over my head," drifts in from the psalms. Yes indeed.

Now all we need is a reporter from *The State* paper. Who cares about the *New York Times, Washington Post*, even the *Atlanta JC*. Go ahead, have a field day. Just another story about those rednecks down in some South Carolina hick cotton field. The reporter will try not to say what will they do next, but he'll work in a 'possum. The joke is, who cares? Sure, some folks read the *NYT*, but they take it with a grain of salt. (He's hopin' I do, haha.) Isn't it just another Yankee paper? But *The State*? That's different. Lord have mercy! What am I going to do?

It's a prayer, actually, served up from a reverent heart, double the desperation. Nothing like this . . . *ever before*, he's thinkin'. And Moish, home from Columbia, worrying about the tests. Enough on *his* plate.

My poor friend, Ricky's thinkin'. Is there something behind that knee? He's gotta take part in the service, and all the time his mind's full of funeral details—his own!

Strange how Levy's congregation called the church—every soul. Did Alice mean that much to 'em? Played bridge in the neighborhood, close to Shirley, friends with the Feinemanns. That doesn't explain the Goldbergs, the Steins, the

Rubinsteins, the Greens, the Finkelsteins and all the rest! Everybody's asking about arrangements . . . and the rabbi's right in the middle, fighting off cancer fears.

Rick's heart goes out, searchin' for the friend drivin' home minutes before he called him, all caught up with the tests when the phone call Rick was makin' started ringin' at the Levys'. Does Shirley know? If not, things will just get worse, my Ricky's thinkin'.

Shirley? For sure, Ricky dislikes broachin' this stuff with me though I know Shirley's thoughts. Easier for Moish if she takes part. Pentecostals? American Christians may seem odd to her, he's tellin' himself. She blends in, but what does she really think? AG's? Baptists? Christians in small Southern towns? Believers in Israel will be different.

The Ruth-Shirley bond amazes him. Shirley's a fixture in my world, the woman part. We can't do without each other. Cryin,' lost babies wake us in the night as if to be fed. We've shared some tears, a lot of tears.

Ricky frowns at the phone he's just put down. All the things he doesn't know about women could fill an Olympic swimmin' pool! Moish . . .better informed? Ricky sits there, rubbin' his eyes, lookin' at that clock. The AG pastor in twenty minutes . . . .. Time sure does fly.

The AG pastor turns out to be taller than Ricky, has a better tailor. Not too many trump my Ricky's height and it gives him a start. Tilting his chin a centimeter or two to meet his visitor's smile, he shoves out a hand as the man ducks comin' in the door.

Familiar face.

Ricky knew the AGs had a new pastor and that he was black. He'd seen him from a distance in town. Baptists don't do much with Pentecostals in South Carolina towns likes Beulah. Joint services, public prayer gatherin's maybe. Not many chance encounters.

Do I know him? Ricky's wonderin'.

"Gerald Atlee." Low bass register—genial but noncommittal. The offered hand is huge, grip polite.

"Good to see you, Pastor. Please come in, have a seat. Lot to talk about."

It was all my Ricky could think of as an opener. Certainly was the truth. Two big men facing one big challenge . . . better get to it. Who'd guess Miss Alice would create such a stir? Worse than the 2 a.m. shrieks. She's still giving Beulah, South Carolina, a wake-up call, no doubt about it, and it could get worse.

"The service . . . three days." The enunciation is crisp, direct approach. Just a statement of fact—nothing extra, no fussin' around with the obvious.

Transgression's inevitable with too many words, Rick thinks unexpectedly. Every vain word will have an accounting . . . odd thing to remember. The Bible treats words like precious coinage. Atlee's not squanderin' any of those riches!

Have to be on my toes, Ricky's thinkin'. Where have I seen this impressive clergyman? Phony familiarity won't do, he cautions himself. The man's self-possessed, confident. He'll notice condescension. Friendliness? Not excessive.

"The Morgan family is fine with arrangements so far."

"We're looking at Thursday, two in the afternoon," Rick said, matching the business-like tone and looking over his desk calendar.

Now he's kickin' himself for sayin' all this to the pastor of the church where this staggerin' event will occur . . . as if he, not Atlee, were the host. What am I thinking, Ricky's askin' himself. I'm not the one to set day or time, certainly not the one to pass it on like new information!

His face is pricklin'. He wishes his skin had a thermostat to regulate at will. Can't be blushin'! The thought makes his shoulders tense. His hands are sweatin'.

Black people don't blush, something inside him says. Where did that come from, he asks himself.

Another prejudice?

Two ears. One for the world, one for instruction.

Yes, I need both kinds of hearin', Ricky tells himself. He moves from his desk, grabs a chair, and sets it at a comfortable distance from his guest, measuring with his eye a space wide enough to accommodate two pairs of very long legs. Somebody might want to stretch.

No, too casual, he tells himself . . . not a casual meeting. But I won't address a fellow pastor from behind a desk! Still, don't want to crowd him. Lesson here, but what is it?

Just listen. Berating yourself is vain.

My Ricky sits down, cocks one knee over the other, and turns to his visitor. Time for business.

"I will not think about *liposarcoma*," Moish is mutterin' to himself. "Quite enough challenges in this memorial service."

He puts his keys in the basalt bowl on his desk and looks around. Orderin' himself not to think about cancer is easier than doin' it. The room's a worry place, as well as a work place. Right now, worry's the trump.

"The trip to Columbia . . . too smooth. 'When the lab work's in, you'll be notified—results, in a week or so.' That's what the harpy at the desk told me . . . then smiled. Crooked leer of a horror movie! What's 'a week or so'? Seven days, ten with weekends? Month with a holiday!

"Miss Crisp Voice," he's tellin' that face, "what do you know about hell?"

Even if Moish is darin' the bookshelf he's railin' at to fall down on him, Shirley's takin' things in stride. "Pretty good front on my side, too" Moish mutters. "Does she know how much this bothers me? No indication. And now, the memorial service . . .."

"Alice Faber had to die with me out of town. Beth Shalom's obsessed! Writ in stone that we wring our hands . . . and our hearts. More to come with that service the whole opera world wants. Have to take part. Beth Shalom will be there in force. Rick Apricot's working with that Atlee fellow at the Assembly of God. Those people aren't Roman Catholics . . or Protestants. What in the world? Rick has an advantage. At least he's a Christian. Knows the scene. All of it in neat, churchy pigeonholes. Bet he has a church-shaped birdhouse in his back yard!"

Shirley calls from the kitchen. Tea.

"*Motek*, tell me again . . . that concert." On the table milk, lemons, spoons from their favorite Jerusalem silversmith. Alice seems to have the other chair and Shirley's sad.

I know what Moish's thinkin,' Understandable, the loss Shirley's feelin.' She was the link. She ran over for this and that—baked goods, advice when things got bad. Had a way with both old ladies—black one, white one. Could make Miss Alice see when nobody else could, even Augusta. Augusta's at her wits' end? Call Shirley.

One time the two were discussin' music. It came out that Israel's national anthem was Alice's favorite encore. She launched right into *HaTikvah*, sang with such a passion, Shirley was in tears.

"Part of the world culture," Moish told Ricky once. "Citizens of the world like us, only we're exiles. Opera stars? Property of the world, homies everywhere. That's what "world-class" means, isn't it?

François Fabergé was world class too . . . if "Frank" to most people.

Moish launches theories about Shirley's bond with Mrs. Faber. She loved Shirley's visits. When Shirley didn't come, she wanted to know. Took Shirley's counsel when she ignored everybody else. As dementia worsened, Shirley went more often. Probably a stand-in for that lost daughter, he thinks. But she'd appeal to Miz Faber all on her own. "Amazing," Moish told Ricky one time. "Shirley's amazing." Everybody knows that.

Today Moish reaches for the teapot and tries to shove Columbia from his mind. There is no *liposarcoma*. Shirley can see it in his eyes.

"The concert . . .?" Shirley asks again.

"Okay. When the proposed concert series didn't go over, somebody suggested that we do our own. Not many small towns have a retired diva. The ball got rolling when Alice took over. She did the auditions—knew talent!

"It was a winning idea. She sang *HaTikva*, probably as a gesture to Beth Shalom. Our folks were the most enthusiastic supporters." He reaches for the sugar bowl, stirs demerara into his cup, and squeezes a lemon.

"Everybody went. Our young people were involved. Rebekah—uh, Rivka— wore black, recited from *Hamlet*. You could hear a pin drop." The rabbi smiles, shakes his head. "Made a realistic Renaissance bow and received huge applause— several minutes of it. A few yelled, 'Brava, brava!' I guess some World War II vet recovered from wounds in Italy and got a crash course in opera hall ettiquette."

Moish bites off half a scone and wipes his fingers—more to tell.

"One or two sang their special numbers. David played 'Blue Moon' on his tenor sax. One kid attempted 'The Flight of the Bumblebee' on a piccolo trumpet—did a creditable job. A ferocious marimba player broke one of his sticks that night. I've forgotten the details."

Shirley smiles sadly and gets up to open a window. She's facin' the light, but turned kind of sideways. Light spikes her eyes with green sometimes, like now. They're hazel.

"And Alice?"

"Alice Faber was the climax. She 'broke up the meetin', as they say around here.

"Nobody in Beulah knows when a voice has passed its prime. She sounded just fine to this crowd, and the volume? Well, everybody expected that. Beth Shalom folks . . . we were all on our feet. Everybody got up. Then cheering and clapping—for minutes on end. Somebody thought about timing it, but I think they only caught about half.

"We went wild. *HaTikvah* meant something to us. Everybody else just knew they'd heard a phenomenal performance. Made you feel like picking up an uzi and a shovel, or whatever, to turn over your square meter of Israeli dirt, plant something then arm yourself to defend it against all comers."

Shirley's silent, just smoothin' the napkin in her lap. "Ahleece is gone, Moshe. I shall miss her."

"Yeah. What'll we do with all the peace and quiet around here?"

"He meant no harm," she told me later. "Just to avoid . . . .."

"Sappy?" I said.

"Yes . . . sappy. Moshe is not liking sentimentality. No intended sharp edge. Not best just then. And he knew. Got up, cleared the table, said, 'Time to get to work. Going to Rick's to talk about the memorial service.'"

'Ken,' I said and he left.

I've wondered about the origin of the Hebrew word for *yes*. All you can do is guess. Even Moish says that. Some people think Hebrew's the language of heaven—Adam and Eve's, for sure. When he came over, Moish said some music was runnin' through his brain. His front license plate says, SOUTH CAROLINA

NATIVE, and he knows the tune: "heav'n, heav'n, ev'rybody talkin' 'bout heaven ain't goin' there, heav'n . . .."

"Pastor Apricot, Gerald Atlee here. Good time to talk?"

"Sure is," Ricky says, thinking that 9:00 a.m. is just about perfect, but why's Atlee saying, "Pastor"?

"Glad you called. I have some stuff to discuss, as well. What's on your mind?"

My Ricky's feelin' more comfortable with Atlee since he placed the face. Two nights ago, awake and mullin' over the service, it came to him. Yes! The USC basketball player. Bet his youth group loves him. He could turn 'em into a winning team any day he wanted. Probably no youth associate though.

Nice to get it finally, but the AG team Rick was picturin' flashed black and white faces in about equal numbers as they dominated the court. He shut down the scene to worry about the service. Problems there, no question about it.

Now the voice in the phone rumbles into a chuckle.

"Our sanctuary isn't big enough for everybody with all the crowds from out of town. We need a bigger space . . . extend our tent cords, so to speak."

Rick gets the Isaiah reference and laughs too. The service is loomin' larger hour by hour, and a cloud of anxiety shadows his mood. This thing has the makings of a permanent highpoint—or low point—in the history of Beulah. Each new development breakin' over the horizon brings him up short, but the comfortable chuckle helps a bit. My Ricky doesn't see it, but reassurance is what he needs—buckets of it.

"Why not move the service over here?"

The AG sanctuary *is* too small, have to change the venue. The suggestion feels gracious and accommodatin'. Too late, he catches his condescendin' tone: We'll bail you out, brother, if you're in over your head; we're the bigger church, we can accommodate the crowds since you can't. He didn't say it, but the implications came out loud and clear.

My Ricky's kickin' himself black and blue these days. A bit unnervin' to make plans with an at-ease AG pastor, taller too, Rick told me. Doesn't faze him that his little church is on the wrong side of town . . . budget a fraction of ours. And he doesn't seem to care that we don't share every point of his odd theology. Add to all that, he's a . . .

Just in time, my Ricky caught himself, squelched the word mid-sentence. He won't say it . . . not even in his head. This man leads the one and only diverse congregation in Beulah, and his portrait's flickerin' like a silent bomb blast from a black-and-white news clip. I feel for 'im, but my Ricky's a bit of a church snob sometimes.

Ricky's runnin' his hands through his hair, cleanin off his glasses, rubbin' his eyes. Time to pay attention to what the man's telling him.

"No, like I said, it's too late to change the location," Atlee says, repeating himself for a conversation partner who's gone silent. "There's this, too. Alice Faber's daughter called. She wants a graveside service. Never heard of a graveside memorial service, but she's the nearest relative. Should honor the request."

May complicate this thing, Ricky's thinkin,' but with nothing to add, he says nothing as Atlee rumbles on.

"Brother Samuel over at the Church of God says he has a revival tent. We're not looking for rain this week, so a tent should work fine. Bealls Funeral Home has some registers to put out. Their folks can escort everybody to the cemetery when they've signed. The tent can be near the Faber grave—edge of the graveyard. Jewel Marie, uh . . . I mean Jane Marie Fabergé says, 'Near the grave. That's where it should be.'"

"It's close, isn't it . . . your church and the cemetery?"

Rick's rerunnin' the zoning fights. One outcome was to allow the cemetery crowd first option on the old county fair grounds. They got the bid, and now there's a new memorial garden next to the AG. Not the best part of town. Atlee's plan's workable, Ricky's thinkin', but no rain will mean hot, very hot.

"Yes, close enough," Atlee says. "A morning service won't be bad. Our parking lot joins the cemetery. Folks can walk over. But we need more chairs. The Church of God just got rid of their old ones . . . no new ones yet. Revival's in August. Twenty or thirty good chairs is all they have. Bealls has a ground cover and maybe a hundred folding chairs. We need a lot more than that."

"I can help there."

A promise I'll deliver, Rick's thinkin'. Quick purchase if necessary. We don't have tent revivals, but we have chairs . . . just not sure how many. We'll stir around and get some. And what about this daughter? Nobody's heard from her in years. Can't refuse a request by the nearest kin. If it's reasonable.

"What I hoped," Atlee says. "I'll let you know how many we need when we have a better fix on the out-of-town numbers. Jasper McClintock down at the Inn is calling the other desks. He'll compile the reservation figures and come up with a number. That'll give him braggin' rights; his place is already full."

More basso chuckles. "I'll be in touch. Thanks for helping with the chairs."

Ricky's shakin' his head, wonderin' how this will end. Heaven never looked so good. Lucky Miss Alice . . . all she has to do is be remembered! That tent . . . and two Pentecostal pastors with a better idea?

"Couldn't have cooked up a plan like that if I tried for a month," he told me. "No church budget I know has a line item for revival tents! Perfect solution."

Wonderin' why I put you through all this, honeybabe? Be patient, there's more to come. Actually, this is just half. As for the why, it's good for you. That's what I think.

Glossaries

HEBREW TERM	ENGLISH TRANSLATION
Avraham	The patriarch, Abraham
Ashkenazic	Jewish communities of Eastern Europe
Baali	"My husband" in Modern Hebrew
Balagan	Thoroughly fouled up situation
Bat Mitzvah	Religious coming-of-age ceremony for a young girl, corresponds to a bar mitzvah
Batter bees	pancakes
Bevakesha	Excuse me, pardon me
B'seder	"In order," lit.; something like "fine" or "okay"
Chasid	An Orthodox Jew
Chaverah	"A female friend," Heb.
Ebenezer/Evenezer	Heb. "stone of help"
Egged	Public bus transportation used by Israeli Jews
Hamoodi	"Darling"
HaShem	"The Name." Used in reverence as a substitute for references to God
Hummus	Spicy paste of chick peas, sesame seeds
Jeremiahu	The prophet Jeremiah. Heb. transliteration
Kvod m'od	"Excellent" or "very nice"
Ken	"Yes"
Kippah	Yarmulke
Kotel	The Western Wall
Lahitraot	Heb. "See you later"
Lo	"No"
Meeshtarah	Police
Melech haOlam	A title of God, King of the world or King of the Universe or Eternal King
Minyan	The ten men required to start a synagogue

HEBREW TERM	ENGLISH TRANSLATION
Mishmish	Apricot, the fruit
Motek	"Sweet"
Pesach	Passover
Sabra	Prickly pear. Native of Israel, "Sharp on the outside, sweet inside"
Sephardic	Jewish communities of Southern Europe and the Mediterranean
Shabbat	The Sabbath
Shule	Religious school
Siddur	Prayer book
Stuttgartensia, Biblia Hebraica Stuttgartensia	The Hebrew Bible published in Stuttgart
Tallit	Prayer shawl
The Torah	Pentateuch; lit., "law, teaching, doctrine"
Tov m'od	Heb. "very good"
Tzitzit	Tassels of the tallit
Ulpan	Hebrew language school
Yaacob	The patriarch, Jacob
Yerushalaim shel zhav vshel nehoshet vshel	"Jerusalem of gold, of bronze, and of light"—line from the popular song "Jerusalem of Gold" by Naomi Shemer
Yeshua	Jesus. The name is equivalent to "Joshua," in Hebrew "the LORD saves." The name, "Jesus," comes into English through Hebrew, Greek, and Latin.
Yod	Hebrew letter corresponding to i or y in English
Ytzak	The patriarch, Isaac

CHARACTER NAME	DESCRIPTION
Alice Faber	Mrs. Faber, Miz Faber, Miss Alice, Alice Fabergé, Little Alice Jones, little Alice, and the diva.

CHARACTER NAME	DESCRIPTION
Benjamine Steingaard	Joel Schiffman in Quentin's piece, "The Jewel." Also the T-shirt fella to the Apricots. Moshe Levy refers to him as Steinman and Stein-something on one occasion.
Evelyn Martelote	Quentin's Aunt Ev, Miz Martelote to Ruth, also Miss Evelyn. Evelyn to her friends, Miriam Feinemann and Lucy Jenkins.
Harold Wellhem, MD	Harold or Harry to patients of long standing; Dr. Well to Ruth, maybe others.
Lucy Jenkins	Joe Paul's Nana, Ruth's Aunt Lucy. Lucy or Miz Jenkins to others.
Miriam Feinemann	Miriam to the rabbi, Miryam to Rebekah, who calls her parents by their first names and thinks her mother's name in Hebrew. To Ruth, she's Miz Feinemann or Miss Miriam.
Moshe Levy, the rabbi	Moish to Ruth and Rick, Moshe to Shirley, his wife. Other variations are Moishe or Moishie. The name means Moses, sometimes used by Rick. Shirley calls him *baali*, my husband in Hebrew. He objects because the word literally means, "my master."
Pat Palmer	The Rev. G. Patrick Palmer, Presbyterian minister from Miller. Pat to his friends.
Rebekah	The Feinemanns' very successful journalist daughter. She uses the Hebrew equivalent, Rivka, now.
Richard Parker Apricot III	Rick. The rabbi twits his friend, calling him Father, Rev, and Richard, also friend. To Ruth, he's Ricky, but other variants are too numerous to list, and she's already thought of a dozen more.
Ruth	RuthAnne Marigold Wilkerson Apricot. Mishmish to Shirley, Ruthie to herself, Miz Apricot to Betty Berttison and others.
Shirley	Shirli, "my song," in Hebrew. Shirley is the Americanized version.

About the Author

SIGRID FOWLER IS A JOURNALIST AND graduate of Agnes Scott College, Emory University, and Erskine Theological Seminary. Most recently, she studied spoken Hebrew at Hebrew University in Jerusalem. Her articles on literary and other topics have appeared in professional journals, and she currently writes a weekly column for *The Edgefield Advertiser*, Edgefield, SC, where she lives. Fowler has enjoyed teaching English literature to college freshmen, but her passion is to point readers to the all-time best seller, the Bible. Her pleasures include creating party cakes, reading the Bible in languages other than English, playing the piano, drawing, and making road trips in her Miata. *Soli Deo gloria!*

Made in the USA
Middletown, DE
01 April 2018